"A comprehensively imagined alternate world with surprises at both global and personal levels. Alternate history with rigor, inventiveness, mystery, suspense, and flair—What more could you ask for?"

—David Alexander Smith

"An amusing alternate history... *Of Tangible Ghosts* succeeds in original fashion on many fronts."

—*The Denver Post*

OF TANGIBLE GHOSTS

"offers a genuinely interesting variation on the usual alternate history approach while delivering a competent mystery and a nicely-worked-out one-man campaign of pseudo-terrorism.... This is an appealing world, both in its geopolitics and solidity with which the everyday life of New Bruges is imagined."

—*Locus* (R. Letson)

Tor Books by L. E. Modesitt, Jr.

The Saga of Recluce
The Magic of Recluce
The Towers of the Sunset
The Magic Engineer
The Order War
The Death of Chaos
Fall of Angels
The Chaos Balance

The Ecolitan Matter
The Ecologic Envoy
The Ecolitan Operation
The Ecologic Secession
The Ecolitan Enigma

The Forever Hero
Dawn for a Distant Earth
The Silent Warrior
In Endless Twilight

The Timegod
Timediver's Dawn

Of Tangible Ghosts
*The Ghost of the Revelator**

The Soprano Sorceress
The Spellsong War
Adiamante
The Green Progression
The Parafaith War

*forthcoming

OF TANGIBLE GHOSTS

L.E. MODESITT, JR.

A TOM DOHERTY ASSOCIATES BOOK
NEW YORK

This is a work of fiction. All the characters and events portrayed in this book are fictitious, and any resemblance to real people or events is purely coincidental.

OF TANGIBLE GHOSTS

Cover art by Nicholas Jainschigg

A Tor Book
Published by Tom Doherty Associates, Inc.
175 Fifth Avenue
New York, NY 10010

Tor Books on the World-Wide Web:
http://www.tor.com

Tor® is a registered trademark of Tom Doherty Associates, Inc.

ISBN: 0-812-54822-1
Library of Congress Card Catalog Number: 94-21748

First edition: October 1994
First mass market edition: November 1995

Printed in the United States of America

0 9 8 7 6 5 4 3 2

For Kevin,

his mother,

and Toffee and Triscuit

OF TANGIBLE GHOSTS

I

ONE GHOST IN my life was bad enough, but when you have two, an inconvenience can become a disaster. That Saturday night in October, I wasn't really thinking about Carolynne—the family ghost—disasters, or any other ghost. All I wanted to do was lock the office door and get back to the recital hall for Llysette's concert because I'd lost track of time.

My mind was on Llysette when I left my office and walked down the stairs and through the Natural Resources Department offices. I stepped out onto the covered porch and the almost subsonic shivering that tells you there's a ghost around hit me. I thrust the key in the lock, feeling uncomfortable and hurried, without knowing why at first.

Then I pulled out my key, and the shivering went up two notches before the sobbing began.

"No . . . no . . . I wouldn't tell . . . wouldn't listen . . . no . . . no . . ."

The light on the porch of the old Dutch Republican that had been converted to the offices of the Natural Resources Department came from a low-powered permanent glow square. The glow square made seeing the ghost a lot easier because she didn't wash out under the light. Ghosts, even fresh ones, aren't that substantial, and this one was a mess, with white streaks and gashes and droplets of white ectoplasm dripping away from her figure.

I swallowed, hard, because the ghost was Miranda—Miranda Miller, the piano professor—and you don't usually see ghosts like that unless someone's been murdered. Murders aren't that common in the Republic, especially at universities located out in the hinterlands. Miranda was an easy grader, so it couldn't have been a disgruntled student, although that has happened, I understand, but not at Vanderbraak State University. Llysette was more likely to be a target of some burgher's pampered daughter than Miranda.

"No . . . no . . ." The ghost's hands were up, as if trying to push someone away.

"Miranda . . ." I tried to keep my voice soft. The books all say that you have to be gentle with ghosts, but since I come from a pretty normal family, I'd never seen a ghost right after it had been created by violent death. Grandpa's ghost had been pretty ornery, but he'd been ornery enough in life, and he'd faded before long. Most ghosts did, sooner or later.

"Miranda, what happened?"

"No . . . no . . . no . . ." She didn't seem to recognize me. She just projected that aura of terror that felt like subsonics. Then she was gone, drifting across the faculty green toward the administration building—a stone and mortar horror, what the first Dutch settlers had called native-stone colonial. Campus Security had offices there, but I doubted that they were really set for ghost handling, nor were the county watch, even though Vanderbraak Centre was the county seat.

Almost as an afterthought, I closed the door and pulled the key out. I started walking, then running downhill toward the watch building—not even taking those long wide stone steps that led past the car park and down to the lower part of the campus. Halfway down the hill, I skidded to a stop on the browning leaves that the university zombies hadn't been able to sweep up as fast as they fell and looked down at the town square. I was across from the new post centre. The old one had burned down forty years ago, but in Vanderbraak Centre, a forty-year-old building is practically new.

But that wasn't why I stopped. I was going to claim that someone had stabbed Miranda because her ghost had drifted by me, sobbing and incoherent? That might have gone over all right in New Amsterdam, or some other big city like Columbia City, where the feds understood ghost theory, but not in Vanderbraak Centre. The watch were mostly old Dutch stock, stolid, and you seldom saw Dutch ghosts. Don't ask me why, but that was the way it was. The odds were I'd end up in one of those cold iron-barred cells, not because I'd seen a ghost, but because they'd more likely believe I'd committed the murder and claimed I'd seen a ghost.

So I gritted my teeth and turned around to walk back up the hill to the old Physical Training Center that had become the Music and Theatre Department when old Marinus Voorster donated a million guilders to build the new field house—all out of spite with Katrinka Er Recchus, now the acting dean. Then she'd been running the strings program, even before she became department chair. Rumor had it that she'd been more than friendly with old Marinus, hoping for a new performing arts center she could run.

I glanced farther uphill at the Physical Sciences building that held the Babbage centre, but only the outside lights were on. My eyes flicked back to the Music and Theatre building. All the old gym doors were open, since it was a warm night for mid-October. I stopped, straightened my damp collar and my cravat, took some deep breaths, and wiped my forehead on my sleeve before I walked up the stone steps into the building.

As usual, even though it was less than ten minutes before the recital started, only a handful of people walked across the foyer and down the side corridor in front of me.

"Good evening, Doktor Eschbach."

"Good evening." I took the one-sheet program and nodded at the usher, a student whose name momentarily escaped me.

The recital hall had actually been a lecture hall, the only one in the old PT building, so that the "renovation" that had turned it into a recital hall had consisted of adding a full stage, taking out several rows of seats, and removing the lift-tilt desktops attached to the sides of the seats. The seats were still the traditional Dutch colonial hardwood that made long recitals—even Llysette's—tests of endurance.

Miranda Miller—dead? Why Miranda? Certainly, according to Llysette, she whined a lot in her mid-south English dialect. I could have seen it had it been Dean Er Recchus or Gregor, the theatre head who bellowed at everyone, or even Llysette and her perfectionist ways.

The program looked all right:

Llysette duBoise
Soprano
In Recital
Featuring the Mozart *Anti-Mass*

She was doing mostly standard stuff, for her, except for the Britten and Exten. She'd protested doing the Mozart Anti-Mass, but the dean had pointed out that the stipend from the Austro-Hungarian Cultural Foundation had come because they were pushing their traditional musicians, even Mozart, even the later ultraromantic stuff composed after his bout with renal failure, even the weird pieces no one sings much anymore, if they ever did. She'd wanted to do Lady Macbeth's aria from Beethoven's *Macbeth* or Anne's aria from his *Heinrich Verrückt,* but the Austro-Hungarians were pushing Mozart's less popular pieces, and the Foundation had suggested either the Anti-Mass or the love song from *Elisabet.*

You don't turn down a two-hundred-dollar stipend, nor the dean's suggestion, not if you're an academic in up-county

New Bruges. Not if you're a refugee from the fall of France trying to get tenure. And not, I supposed, if you were linked to the suspicious Herr Doktor Eschbach, that notorious subversive who'd been forced out of the government when Speaker Hartpence's Reformed Tories had won the elections on a call for a clean sweep of the ministries. So Llysette had opted for the Anti-Mass as the least of the evils.

I settled into a seat halfway back on the left side, right off the aisle, and wiped my forehead again. I was definitely not in the shape I had once been. Yet it hadn't seemed that long since I'd been a flying officer in Republic Air Corps, and my assignments in the Sedition Prevention and Security Service had certainly required conditioning. So what had happened? I shook my head and resolved to step up my running and exercises, and I wiped my forehead once again.

By the time the lights went down, Llysette had a decent crowd, maybe a hundred fifty, certainly not bad for a vocal performance. The Dutch have never been that supportive of vocalists. Strings, strings, and more strings, with a touch of brass—that's how you reach their hearts, but, as Katrinka Er Recchus found out, not their pocketbooks.

Llysette swept onto the stage, all luminous and beautiful, dark hair upswept and braided back, bowed, and nodded at Johanna Vonderhaus, her accompanist, seated at the big Steinbach.

Llysette was in good voice, and everyone thought she was wonderful, so wonderful that they gave her a brief second ovation. I hadn't heard that in New Bruges in the three years I'd been there, except for her concert the previous spring when she had proved that a singer could actually master oratorio and survive.

I should have brought her chocolates, but I only brought myself backstage, and came to a sudden stop as I reached the open wing—the dressing rooms were down a side hall toward the practice rooms and studios—where she stood, pale and composed.

Two watch officers were there in their black and silver, and one was talking to her, one to Johanna. I listened.

"When did you see Doktor Miller last?"

Llysette shrugged in her Gallic way. "Perhaps it was midafternoon yesterday. I went home early to prepare for the recital. Preparing for a recital, that is always hard."

"You went home alone?"

"Ah, *non,* monsieur. Doktor Eschbach there drove me in his steamer. Then we ate, and he drove home. This afternoon he drove to my home, and brought me to his house for an early dinner. Then we came to the hall together, and I prepared for the recital."

"Did you see Doktor Miller tonight?"

"Mais non. I even sent Johan away while I was dressing and warming up."

"Was anyone else here?"

"Johanna." Llysette inclined her head toward the slender accompanist. "Before the hall was opened, we practiced the Exten."

"Did you see anyone go down the halls toward the studios?"

"Non. You must concentrate very hard before the recital."

"Were you alone here at any time after Doktor Eschbach left?"

"I could not say." Llysette shrugged wearily. "Worried I was about the Exten and the Mozart, and people, they could have come and gone. That is what happens before a recital."

There were more questions, but what else could she add? We'd left early on Friday, and on Saturday afternoon we had been together until she started to warm up and dress. That was when I went up to my office.

The tall and chunky watch officer, of course, had to question me then.

"Doktor Eschbach, what did you do when you came back to the university tonight?"

"When we came back, I dropped Doktor duBoise off in front of the theatre building. I parked the steamer in the car park between the theatre building and the library. I walked into the building to make sure Doktor duBoise had everything she needed. When she said she needed to warm up, I went to my office to check my box for any messages, and then I did some paperwork for a new course for next semester. After that I came back and listened to the recital."

"Did you see or hear anything unusual?"

I frowned, on purpose, not wanting to lie exactly, but not wanting to tell the whole truth. "I *felt* a low sound, almost a sobbing, when I left the department office. I looked around, but it faded away."

"Ghost formation," said the other watch officer, the young and fresh-faced officer I hadn't seen around Vanderbraak Centre before. He reminded me of someone, but I knew I hadn't met him before.

"Ghost formation?" I said almost involuntarily, surprised that the locals were that up-to-date on the mechanics of ghosting and equally surprised that the younger officer would upstage the older.

"There was an article in the latest *Watch Quarterly*. Subsonics apparently often occur during and immediately after ghosting occurs." The younger officer blushed as the tall chunky man who had questioned me turned toward him.

"What time did you feel these vibrations?" asked the older watch officer.

"Mmmm . . . it was about fifteen minutes before the concert. Quarter before eight, I would say."

"How well did you know Doktor Miller?"

"Scarcely at all. I knew who she was. Perhaps I'd spoken to her a dozen times, briefly." I wouldn't have known her at all if I hadn't been seeing Llysette.

The questions they posed to me went on even longer than those they had posed to Llysette, but they were all routine, trying to establish who was doing what and where and if I had noticed anything unusual. Finally both officers exchanged glances and nodded.

"We may need to talk to you both later, Doktors," added

the taller officer—Herlingen was his name. When I'd first come back to Vanderbraak Centre the year before, he had suggested that I replace my Columbian national plates on the steamer with New Bruges plates as soon as practical.

They bowed and departed, leaving the three of us—me, Llysette, and Johanna—standing in the wing off the recital hall stage. I wiped my forehead.

"Are you up to walking up to the steamer?" I asked Llysette, then looked at Johanna. "Do you need a lift?"

"No, thank you, Johan. Pietr is waiting outside." The tall accompanist smiled briefly, then shook her head. "Poor Miranda."

"*Moi,* I am more than happy to depart." Llysette lifted her bag with her makeup and other necessities, and I took it from her.

Outside, a half moon shone across the campus, and between the moon and the soft illumination of the glow lamps, there was more than enough light to make our way along the brick wall to the car park and the glimmering sleek lines of the Stanley, a far cry from the early steam-carts or even the open-topped racing steamers of early in the century.

Llysette fidgeted for the minute or so that it took for the steam pressure to build. "Why you Columbians love your steamers—that I do not understand. The petrol engines are so much more convenient."

"Columbia is a bigger country than France." I climbed into the driver's seat and eased the throttle open. Only two other steamers were left in the car park, and one belonged to the watch. "Internal petrol engines burn four times as much fuel for the mileage. We can't afford to waste oil, not when Ferdinand controls most of the world's supply, and Maximilian the rest."

"I have heard this lecture before, Johan," Llysette reminded me. At least she smiled.

"That's what you get from a former subminister of Natural Resources." I turned left at the bottom of the hill and steered around the square and toward the bridge that would take us to my house. The breeze through the steamer windows was welcome after the heat of the concert hall.

"More than merely a former subminister. Other worthwhile attributes you have, as well." She paused. "With this event, tonight, is it wise that I should stay with you?"

"Wise? A woman has been murdered, and you want to stay alone?"

"Ah, yes, there is that. Truthfully, I had not thought of that."

I shook my head. Sometimes Llysette never considered the obvious, but I supposed that was because, no matter what they say, sometimes singers are just unrealistic. "Why would anyone want to kill Miranda? She whined too much, but . . . murder?"

"Miranda, she seemed so, so helpless." Llysette cleared her throat, and her voice firmed. "Still, there are always reasons, Johan."

"I suppose so. I wonder if we'll ever know."

"That I could certainly not say."

The breeze held that autumn evening smell of fall in New Bruges, the scent I had missed so much during my years in Columbia City, the smell that reminded me of Elspeth still. I swallowed, and for a moment my eyes burned. I kept my eyes on the narrow line of pavement for a time. Sometimes, at odd times, the old agonies reemerged.

Once across the river and up the hill, I turned the Stanley left onto the narrow lane—everyone called it Deacon's Lane, but that name had never appeared on any sign or map that I knew of—that wound up the hill through the mortared stone walls dating back to the first Dutch settlers. The driveway was dark under the maples that still held most of their leaves, but I had left a light on between the car barn and the house.

I let Llysette out under the light, opened the barn, and parked the steamer. It was warm enough that I didn't worry about plugging in the water tank heater.

She was waiting under the light as I walked up with her bag. I kissed her cheek and took her chin in my hand, gently, but she turned away. "You are most insistent tonight, Johan."

"Only because you are a beautiful lady."

A flicker of white appeared in the darkness behind her, and I tried not to stiffen as I unlocked the side door and opened it for Llysette. She touched the plate inside the side foyer, what some called the mud entrance, and the soft overhead glows went on.

"Do you want a bite to eat? There's some steak pie in the cooler, and I think there's still some Bajan red down in the cellar."

"The wine, I would like that."

I closed the side door and made my way down into the stone-walled cellar and to the racks my grandfather had built. There was still almost half a case of the red. I picked out a 1980 Sebastopol. It's not really Bajan, but Californian, and a lot better than the New French stuff from northern Baja, but I wasn't about to get into that argument with Llysette, and certainly not after her recital.

"No Bajan, but a Sebastopol."

"If one must."

"It's not bad, especially now that Ferdinand has cut off real French wines."

"The Austro-Hungarians, they have already ruined the vineyards. Steel vats and scientists in white coats . . . bah!"

I shrugged, then peeled back the foil and twisted the corkscrew. The first glass went to her and the second to me. I lifted the crystal. "To a superb performance, Doktor duBoise."

Our glasses touched, and she drank.

"The wine is not bad."

That was as much of a concession to a Columbian wine as I'd get from my Francophilic soprano, and I nodded and took another sip. The Sebastopol was far better than "not bad"; it was damned good.

We made our way to the sitting room off the terrace. Llysette took the padded armchair—Louis XX style, and the only mismatched piece in the room, but my mother had liked it, and my father had thrown up his hands and shrugged his wide Dutch shoulders. The rest of the room was far more practical. I sat in the burgundy leather captain's chair, the only piece in the room that I'd brought back from Columbia City.

"Still I do not like the later Mozart."

"You did it well, very well."

"That is true, but . . ." Llysette took another long sip from her wine glass. "The later Mozart is too, too ornate, too romantic. Even Beethoven is more restrained."

"Money has always had a voice in music."

"Alas, yes." She lifted her left eyebrow. "It still talks most persuasively. Two hundred dollars—a hundred crowns—for a single song and a line on the program. I, even I, listen to such talk. It is almost what little I now make for half a month of hard work."

"Don't we all listen to that kind of money talk?" I laughed and got up to refill her glass. I leaned down and kissed her neck on the way back to my chair.

"It is sad, though. Gold, gold and patience, that is how the Hapsburgs have conquered Europe. My people, the good ones, left for New France, and the others . . ." She shrugged. "I suppose they are happy. There are no wars in Europe now."

"Of course, a third of France is ghost-ridden and uninhabitable."

"That will pass." She laughed harshly. "Ferdinand always creates the ghosts to remind his enemies of his power." Abruptly she tilted her head back and swallowed nearly all the red in one gulp. Then she looked at me. "If you please . . ."

I stood and refilled her glass. "Are you sure?"

"To relax after a performance, some time it takes. The wine helps. Even if it is not true French."

Not knowing what else to say, I answered, "You sang well."

"I did sing well. And where am I? I am singing in a cold small Dutch town in Columbia, where no one even understands what I offer, where no one can appreciate the restraint of a Fauré or the words of a Villon—"

"I do."

"You, my dear Doktor Eschbach, are as much of a refugee as I am."

She was right about that, but my refuge was at least the summer home of my youth.

I had one complete glass of the Sebastopol, and she drank the rest of the bottle. It was close to midnight before she could relax and eat some of the sweet rolls I had warmed up. I left the dishes in the sink. Most days, Marie would get them when she came, but she didn't come on weekends. I decided I would worry about dirty dishes later.

At the foot of the stairs, I kissed Llysette, and her lips were warm under mine, then suddenly cold. She stepped back. I turned around in time to see another flicker of white slip toward the terrace and then vanish.

"Someone was watching. Your ghost. That . . . I cannot take." Llysette straightened the low shawl collar of her recital dress. I tried not to leer, at least not too much. "Perhaps I will go home."

"No. Not until we know more about what happened to Miranda. We've been over that already."

"Then, tonight, I will sleep in the . . ."

"Just sleep with me. I'd feel you were safer." I glanced toward the staircase up to my bedroom.

"Just sleep?" She arched her eyebrows, as if to imply I couldn't just sleep with her.

"Just sleep," I reaffirmed with a sigh. At least, I wouldn't have to fire the steamer up and drive across to the other side of the river with the local watch running all over the township.

At the same time, I was scarcely enthused about Carolynne's appearance, but what could I say? Carolynne never spoke to me, hadn't since I was a boy, not since that mysterious conversation she had had with my mother . . . and neither would talk about it. Since I couldn't force answers from either a ghost or my mother, I still didn't know why.

2

SINCE, FOR A nonbeliever in a believing society, the worth of any church depends on the minister, I attended the Vanderbraak Dutch Reformed Church. Father Esterhoos at least understood the need to make theology both practical and entertaining. Besides, I'd gone there when the house had been my parents' summer retreat from the heat of New Amsterdam. Now my mother lived with her younger sister Anna in Schenectady, when they weren't visiting some relative or another.

When we'd spent the night together, Llysette and I usually went to church together, perhaps because Klaus Esterhoos, unlike Philippe Hague, the college chaplain, treated us more as old members or potential converts than scarlet sinners. Who knows? He could have told the deacons that saving us was worthwhile, not that I really believed that either of us could be saved.

On Sundays, we took my steamer. Although I still kept the Stanley's thermal-electric paint polished, after more than a year the flaxen-haired children walking up the mum-lined gray stone steps to the church no longer pointed at the car as my normally bright red Stanley glided around the square toward the church. It didn't have to be red, but that was the color when I left the thermal switch off. Without the red paint, the steamer would have appeared almost boring, a staid dowager of vehicles. That didn't include the actual engine or the suspension or the extras, of course, just the smooth-lined and sedanlike appearance. Columbia City had taught me the value of misdirection, although what I'd learned had barely been enough to engineer my escape from my past and the intrigues of the Federal District with a whole skin.

That Sunday was different. I guided the Stanley across the one-lane stone bridge over the River Wijk and around the square toward the church. On the west side of the square, adjacent to the campus, was parked a single dull-gray, six-wheeled steamer, all too familiar—the kind you normally saw in Columbia or the big cities like Asten or New Amsterdam, the kind the Spazis used.

"Mother of God!"

"God had no mother, not for you, Johan, you virtuous unbeliever." Llysette's voice was dry as she straightened the dark blue cloak around her shoulders and against the chill breeze that crossed the sunlit square, ruffling leaves on the grass by the bandstand.

"That is a Spazi steamer."

"Spazis?" She shivered. "Are they—do you think they are at the church?"

"With the Spazis, who knows?" My own thoughts were scattered. The steamer had to have come from Schenectady or Asten. The Spazis had a regional headquarters on the naval base outside of Asten. The last time I'd been there was when I'd been the Subminister for Environment, to see if the ruins of a house from the failed English colony at Plymouth should have been saved under the new Historic Preservation Act. That poor colony had been doomed from the start, with the Dutch bribing the *Mayflower's* captain to land in New Bruges, rather than Virginia, and with the plague among the Indians that had left the shore scattered with bones and the forests littered with ghosts. One of the women had jumped into the ocean and drowned, and her ghost supposedly still haunted the ruins.

I'd never understood why the Congress gave Natural Resources the historic preservation program or why the minister had decided it came under environmental protection, but you don't argue with either Congress or your minister if you want to hold your position in Columbia. I hadn't argued, not that it had helped me keep my job once newly elected Speaker Hartpence set the Congress after Minister Wattson. My background certainly hadn't helped, not with the Speaker's distrust of the intelligence community and not my not-hidden-enough background in it.

"You must know, Johan. You were in government. Aren't the Spazi government?"

"Former subministers are the last to know the plans of the Sedition Prevention and Security Service."

"Government ministers, they do not know what their own security service plans?"

"Good government ministers have to use all their contacts to discover that when they're in office. You may recall that I haven't exactly been in office anytime recently, and the Spazi aren't about to go out of their way to tell an ex-minister." And they hadn't. Since they hadn't, and since the only strange thing that had happened was Miranda's death, more than a little was rotten in the Dutch woodpile, so to speak. Simple homicides didn't trigger Spazi investigations, and that meant Miranda's death wasn't simple.

The bells ringing from the church tower forced my thoughts back to the mundane business of parking the Stanley.

Even before we reached the steps to the side entrance of the gray stone church, another couple joined us. Alois Er Recchus was more than rotund; he wore a long gray topcoat, a cravat of darker gray, and a square goatee, nearly pure white, and dwarfed the still ample figure of his wife. His suit was a rich dark brown, typically somber Dutch.

"Ah, Llysette. I heard that you sang so beautifully last night." The dean of the university, Katrinka Er Recchus, smiled broadly at us above an ornate lace collar. "I did so wish to be there, but . . . you understand. One can only be in so many places."

"The demands of higher office," I murmured politely, tipping my hat to her. Out of deference to tradition I did wear a hat to church, weddings, ceremonial occasions, and when my head was cold.

"But you would so understand, Doktor Eschbach, from your past experiences in government."

I almost missed the slight stress on the word "past." Almost, but not quite. "I find those in Vanderbraak Centre are generally far less caught up in artificiality than people in Columbia City." I accented the word "generally," and received a polite smile as she turned back to Llysette.

"I do so hope you will be able to favor us with another recital before long."

"I also, honored dean, although one must take care in ensuring the composition of a vocal program, that it is, how would you say, appropriate to the audience. I would be most pleased to know if you will be attending such a recital."

"One would hope so, with such a distinguished visiting performer." Dean Er Recchus glanced toward the growing clouds overhead. "I do hope the rain will hold off until this afternoon."

The slight emphasis on "visiting" was almost lost—almost.

We nodded and continued our progress into the church. The pews were filled with the local burghers and their spouses, all in rich browns, blacks, or an occasional deep gold that verged on brown. There were more than a few wide white collars among the women.

"That woman," murmured Llysette. "She believes herself so clever."

"All politicians do, until we learn better."

"A politician I am not."

Except she was better at it than I was. While I could recognize the interplay between the two women, one quick comment was all I had managed. Sometimes I couldn't manage that much. Perhaps that was why I had not been totally averse to the forced early retirement from the government. Still, the pension was welcome, and with the investment income from the family holdings, the scattered consulting, and the income from teaching, I was comfortable financially.

We sat down near the rear, the third pew from the back, waiting for the old organ to begin the prelude, still the recipients of covert glances from a few of the older Dutch families near the middle of the church.

I grinned at a little blonde girl who grinned back above a white-collared dress. She waved, and I returned the gesture.

"You are corrupting the young, Johan," whispered Llysette as the organ prelude began.

"I certainly hope so. You can't corrupt the old, not in New Bruges."

The prelude was a variation on Beethoven's *Ode to Joy;* at least that was what it sounded like.

I waved back to the little girl. She reminded me of Walter, although they didn't look the slightest bit alike, except for the mischief in their eyes.

"Johan." Llysette whispered again. "Are you enjoying yourself?"

"Immensely."

All good things must come to an end, unfortunately. The young matron smiled pleasantly at us and turned her daughter in the pew.

"Beloved of God, we are gathered together . . ."

I straightened and prepared to listen to Father Esterhoos.

3

AFTER MY ELEVEN o'clock class on Monday, Environmental Economics 2A, I crossed the upper green from Smythe Hall to stop by my office before lunch.

Gertrude, a blonde zombie who worked for the university's grounds staff, was carefully clipping the dried marigolds at ground level and putting them in her basket. Snip and place, snip and place, snip and place—I stopped and watched, almost mesmerized by the dreadful and precise rhythm.

"Do you enjoy your work, Gertrude?"

"I like to work, sir." As she spoke, the continual smile remained on her clean and clear face, young looking, for all that she was probably well over thirty. Snip and place, snip and place . . .

I repressed a shiver, offered her a smile in return. "Have a good day, Gertrude."

"Every day is a good day, sir," she answered unfailingly.

Another zombie—a gray-haired man with the same cheerful smile as Gertrude's—was digging small weeds from the cracks between the walkway bricks. I smiled, but did not address him, since he was new and I did not know his name.

I stopped by my office, ignored the university mail—all circulars and announcements—dropped my leather case on my desk, and walked out into the coolness and down to Delft's, the café a half block below the eastern end of the university. The café smells like a cross between a *pâtisserie* and a coffeehouse, more French than Dutch, despite the name, and that might have been why I liked it. Dutch food is like everything else Dutch, heavy as lead bricks, if tastier.

As always, I got there before Llysette and found a table on the covered porch that overlooked the square. I was seated not all that long after the clock in the post centre rang out the noon hour. The single Spazi steamer remained in the lower car park, looming over the smaller steamers used by the locals and the few students well-off enough to afford private transportation.

The breeze swirled more leaves from the trees in the square. Several women leaving McArdles' Produce fastened their broad-brimmed hats with scarves, and Constable Gerhardt retrieved one young woman's hat with a flourish and a broad smile under his sweeping mustaches. I'd never be a good burgher. I like my hair short and my face clean, and that will always mark me as an outsider in Vanderbraak Centre, even if the house has been in the family almost a century.

While I waited for Llysette, I sipped my iced tea, something I enjoy all year round. After a year back in Vanderbraak Centre, Victor, the owner of Delft's, had condescended to make it for me, even in October. We'd see about December.

As usual, Llysette was late, and her wine waited as I started on a second iced tea. Delivering lectures is a thirsty business. I rose to seat her just as the post centre clock struck half past twelve. Monday was the only day we both had free for luncheon.

"So nice to see you this afternoon, Doktor duBoise."

"You are kind, Johan." She settled herself in the oak chair, its light finish glistening. "That Jaccardy girl stopped me. Complaining she was about her recital preview. Why do they not understand that singing is true labor? To sing, it does not just happen." Llysette carefully pushed back a strand of hair that had escaped from the tight bun she wore when she taught, piled up on top of her head to make her that much taller. She paused, took a sip of the red wine, and made a slight face.

"It's just a New Ostend wine," I reassured her. In Vanderbraak Centre, you did not have to worry—I hoped—about knowing the exact bouquet of whatever you drank. East Coast wines, even I have to admit, aren't that wonderful. But I applaud their spirit, especially given the cost of Californian or smuggled French vintages.

"That I can discern." She set the glass down for a moment, and I half wondered whether she had a lithograph strip to test for poison, but it wasn't twenty years earlier when I had had to worry about such matters.

"What have they found out about Miranda?" I asked.

"They have found little. The piano studio is closed off, and the technicians come and the technicians go." She shrugged. "The ghost, it is sometimes there, and sometimes not, but it says little. At times, when it is quiet, and when I leave the studio and it is in the hall, I can hear the screams. So I must stay in my studio or depart. It is most disturbing. Some of my students will not come." She took a sip of the wine. "Doktor Geoffries, he says that the studio may not be used for some time. It is a pity."

"How did she die?"

"She was stabbed, many times. The person who murdered her wore a large overcoat from the prop department. They found it with blood on it."

"Did they find a knife?"

"I do not know. Doktor Geoffries thinks it was a prop knife, but no one has said."

"That makes it sound like someone familiar with the building."

"One would think so."

"Still . . . there must have been two hundred people in the building. Why didn't anyone hear anything?"

"In the studio, Johan?"

"Oh." I understood. The reason they insulate all the studios is so that no one can hear students and performers practicing. So poor Miranda could have been screaming her lungs out, and no one would have heard. "It had to be someone who knew that."

"Most certainly." Her lips quirked after she sipped her wine.

I understood her expression. Although the music faculty was not large, there were still a good dozen full- and part-time professors and lecturers, and that didn't include nearly a hundred music and theatre students. It also didn't include another few hundred people around the university and Vanderbraak Centre who also knew the Music and Theatre building. Besides, anyone with a motive could have scouted the building during the week when classes were ongoing. Just wear a dark coat and cravat and walk around looking preoccupied.

"You would like?" asked Victor, appearing at Llysette's elbow and winking.

"La même, comme ça," she answered, offering him a smile but not a wink in return.

"Oui, mademoiselle," he answered, except he pronounced it "mam'selle." He turned to me. "And you, Doktor Eschbach?"

"The soup and cheese, with the shepherd's bread."

Victor bowed.

"You like Victor?" I asked after the owner had departed.

"His French is not that good, but it is a help, Johan. The others, except you, for them France is an embarrassment."

"People don't like to admit their weaknesses."

"Not for us poor French. Your government did not wish to lose a single ship to Ferdinand's submersibles. Nor one of your few precious aircraft carriers. Not in 1921. Not in 1985."

"That was after my time in service."

"You do not talk much of it." Llysette downed the rest of her glass, and Victor appeared to refill it. He also set a small salad in front of Llysette and a side plate with the shepherd's bread in front of me. Behind her back, he shook his head sadly at me, as if to say that it was a pity she did not savor the wine.

"What is there to talk about? I flew reconnaissance for several years during the time Ferdinand did nothing." My throat was dry, somehow, and I swallowed the rest of the iced tea and signaled for a third, hoping Llysette would drop the subject, but she continued as if I had never spoken.

"And the English and the Irish? What could they do? Now they must wait for the inevitable. You Columbians will wring your hands. You will talk in the League of Nations. You will not act." She took a forkful of greens and glanced toward the square, where Constable Gerhardt was admonishing a hauler for bringing his twelve-wheeler into the square, either that or for the plume of unhealthy black smoke from the steamer's burners. "His panzerwagens, they rolled down the Marne road and through Troyes, and you did nothing. Even at the gates to Versailles, nothing." Llysette sniffed.

"Speaker Colmer was not known for his love of overseas adventure, and Europe is still far away, even with the new turbojets. As for Speaker Michel . . ." I had to shrug.

"Did not the pictures—" Llysette broke off. We'd had the discussion before, and nothing we said would change the past. Finally she said, "I prefer the comfort of the dirigibles. They are less stressful on the voice."

"And far less crowded, but expensive."

"Once I would not have had to worry," she pointed out.

Victor's son set my soup in front of me and a cup of chilled consommé before Llysette. I nodded, and he departed.

"Still . . . Johan, when will you Columbians act?"

"When it is too late." I laughed, not without a bitter undertone. "We believe in letting each man go to the devil in a coffin of his own making. Or each nation."

"And women also?"

"That is becoming more popular, although some still

suggest that women's coffins be made by their fathers and husbands."

"My own coffin I must make. For alas, I have no husband, and Ferdinand's regiments killed my father, old and ancient as he was."

There was little I could say to that, not at the moment. So I took a small spoonful of the soup, a properly flavorful Dutch broth. The cheese was a white New Ostend cheddar, extraordinarily sharp, the way Victor knew I liked it. I nodded at the tang, then broke off a piece of the crusty bread. Llysette took the consommé in precise spoonfuls, interspersed with the red wine.

"Johan, why is it that you showed no interest in Professor Miller? She always wished to talk with you."

I finished chewing the bread before answering. "I could not say, not exactly. But she seemed to show a certain lack of discipline. In any case, she appeared far more interested in Gerald Branston-Hay." The first part was certainly true—I couldn't say exactly why I hadn't been attracted. The second part was a polite way of saying that she was a lazy and round-bottomed widow who was required to support herself in any way she could, but who was really looking for a husband. My background and hers certainly would not have fit.

"Considering that the good Doktor Branston-Hay is thoroughly married," Llysette laughed, "you retain the manners of a public servant."

"At your service, my lady." I gave her a head bow. Like Llysette, I had wondered about Miranda's more than passing interest in Gerald Branston-Hay, as conveyed by Llysette. The man must have had some charm, although I had seen more manners than charm in my assorted conversations with him. I refrained from mentioning that I knew Llysette had spent more than a luncheon or two with him. "Professor Branston-Hay is indeed a gentleman of the old English stock." I finished my soup.

"Ah, yes. He is very polite." Llysette's voice was measurably cooler.

"And far more reserved than Professor Miller, I presume."

"She is, she was, not reserved, I think."

I glanced at my watch, my father's old Ansonia that still kept perfect time, and rose.

Llysette glanced at the clock on the post centre. "Do you not have a half hour before your two o'clock?"

"Ah, yes, dear lady, but duty calls. I must stop by the post centre before class because I must attend a meeting of the curriculum review committee after class."

"This is the committee which nothing does?"

"The very same."

"Yet you attend when nothing will be done; is this not so?"

"Absolutely. Then we can claim that we have met, and that the best course of action was to do nothing."

"Like your government."

"Exactly. Except it appears that people get killed at universities, while I cannot recall the last time a public servant was murdered, not when it was apparent. Will I see you for dinner?"

"Not this evening, Johan. I must complete previews for student juries."

"I had hoped . . ."

"You always hope, Johan. One of your best traits." She smiled.

"Thank you." I bowed and turned.

Although I had hoped that the monthly pension cheque had arrived, the only item in my postbox was a long, narrow brown envelope, the type I had seen too many of in Columbia. Of course, it had no return address. I took a deep breath and locked the box.

"Ye find anything interesting?" asked Maurice from behind the counter.

"You know better than I would. You saw it first." I grinned at the post handler. He grinned back.

I hurried back to my office, grateful for the cool breeze.

I smiled toward Gilda as I passed the front office, but she was engaged in a conversation about nouveau-Dutch painting with Andrei Salakin, and with his accent, listening alone was a full-time occupation. Once back in my office, I closed the door firmly.

Except for the clipping from the *Columbia Post-Dispatch,* the brown envelope was empty. I laid the short clipping on the desk.

COLUMBIA (RPI)—Representative Patrice Alexander (L–MI) announced a shadow investigation into charges that the Austro-Hungarian Empire has infiltrated Columbian universities. "Through such blatantly transparent ruses as the Austro-Hungarian Cultural Foundation and the Global Research Fund, Ferdinand VI is encouraging the dissemination of pro-Hapsburg values." Congresslady Alexander also disparaged "so-called scientific research aimed at undermining traditional Columbian values." She claimed the investigation will bring to light a de facto collusion between Speaker Hartpence's "trained liberals" and Ferdinand's "pandered plunderers." Neither the Speaker nor President Armstrong was available for comment, although the president is known to have received a visit from Ambassador Schikelgruber shortly after Congresslady Alexander's announcement.

Schikelgruber, one of the few political ambassadors from the empire, was always sent to smooth things over. He was supposedly captivating and charming, and cultured. His mother had been a fair actress and his father a landscape painter.

I didn't need a detailed explanation. Schikelgruber was there to put pressure on the president to put pressure on the Congresslady, since they were of the same party, and Ralston had sent me the clipping to highlight his concerns about such "infiltration."

Ralston McGuiness was the president's special assistant for budgeting—no one special to anyone outside the Presidential Palace, just the one man who not only recognized the growing, almost tyrannical, power of the Speaker but also knew how to use the few powers of the presidency to check that power. Now he finally had a president willing to try and good old idealistic Johan, willing to offer a little observation, a little assistance.

I was beginning to wonder if my idealism were going to be my undoing. Ralston's clippings were showing an increasingly effective campaign against the Speaker, a power struggle that had so far gone unnoticed in the press but, clearly, not by the Speaker nor by the Spazi who worked for the Speaker. I folded the clipping back into the envelope and placed it in the left breast pocket of my coat, then picked up the leather folder which held the notes for my two o'clock class. Gilda was still listening patiently to Andrei when I left, but I made a point to wave and flash her a smile. She probably deserved it.

My two o'clock class, Environmental Politics 2A, was in Smythe 204, a hot room on the southwest corner of the second floor. I always had to open the windows. Peyton Farquharson taught Ecology 1-B immediately before me, and his Louisiana heritage was always clear enough by the temperature of the room. He was leaving as I entered.

"Good afternoon, Johan. Terrible business about Miranda Miller."

"Absolutely awful."

"Did you know her? Was she close to your 'friend'?"

I smiled politely, ignoring the reproof implied by his choice of words, knowing that, with his Anglican-Baptist background, he really was being as tolerant as he was able. "Llysette and Miranda were colleagues, but not what one would call close."

"And at her recital, too, I understand."

"It was upsetting. At least Llysette didn't find out until after she finished singing."

"Yes, it would be difficult to sing right after a murder. Do you have any idea how it happened?"

One of my students, Peter Paulus, nodded to me, and stepped back. I was sure he wanted to ask the reason for the low grade on his first paper. None of them were used to my requirement for short papers throughout the term. Most academics simply lectured all term, then required a single massive research project or logical proof and a final exam that was more regurgitation than thought.

"The rumor is that she was stabbed, but the watch officers did not tell me." I inclined my head. "I have a student with a problem, I can see."

"Good luck with young Paulus," concluded Farquharson. "He is inclined to inflate the magnitude of his difficulties."

"I have noticed."

I waited for Paulus, but he was scarcely bashful.

"Professor Eschbach, could I trouble you to explain this comment?" He pointed to the brief phrase I had written in the margin of his greenbook—*"Mere assertion."*

I held a sigh. "Mister Paulus." They hated my use of English formality, but it worked, at least for me. "As I have explained a number of times in the course of the past few weeks, when you make a broad assertion, you must prove it with either example, fact, or logic. You have left this statement dangling in the breeze, so to speak."

"But, Professor, it is true that Speaker Taft's failure to adequately capitalize the Environmental Subministry—"

"I know, Mister Paulus. I spent considerable time in Columbia City, and a fair amount of it supervising the Environmental Subministry. You never explain how much funding would have been adequate and why, or the actual results of such underfunding. Did you mention any programs that were reduced? Or initiatives that were canceled? You just wrote that it contributed to the rise of Speaker Hartpence's

Reformed Tories. How? What demographic trends did the new Speaker tap? Did the president play a role as titular head of state? Was the environmental funding issue merely a political ploy between the two? What changes in funding have happened under the new government?"

"I see, Doktor Eschbach. Thank you." He nodded and walked to his desk in the rear of the classroom. His tone indicated that he hadn't really the faintest idea of what I meant. Someone had told him, or he had read, that the environmental funding issue had led to the fall of the Taft government, and that was that. Black or white. It was in the book, so it must be true. Never mind about why it happened, or even, heaven forbid, if it might not be true. Thank God I only had him for Environmental Politics.

But I supposed people in every country are like that. So long as the trains run on time and the lights go on when they press the switch plates, how many really understand the power base of their system? After all, who really cared that the presidency was the only remaining check on the power of the Speaker? Or that the only real tool the president had was his budget examiners and their ability to uncover blatant favoritism? Who cared that the Spazi obtained more and more real power every decade? After all, they didn't really bother most people, just those involved in treasonous acts. But when the Speaker controlled both the Congress and the Spazi, and one defined treasonous acts and the other had the right to detain and punish such acts, that power could become very disturbing, as Elspeth and I had found out when I had applied for permission for her treatment in Vienna.

By the time I had opened the windows, I was perspiring. I wiped my forehead on the soft linen handkerchief I carried mainly for that purpose and surveyed the room. About a dozen of my twenty-three students had arrived. All the men, except mister Jones, wore cravats, but not all wore jackets, and the women wore knee-length skirts or trousers. Most wore scarves.

I opened the case and took out my notes, waiting for the

rest of the class or the chimes of the post centre clock. I tried not to think of the president's special assistant or the Spazi steamers, but I couldn't escape the conviction that they were both waiting for me to make some sort of mistake.

4

LYSETTE HAD INDICATED rather clearly that she was tied up for the evening, although student previews would not last *that* late, but I certainly had no claim on her, not unless I wanted to formalize our relationship, and I did not feel all that comfortable about that at present. So I reclaimed the Stanley from the faculty car park as the post centre clock struck five and headed down Highland toward the square and home.

After deciding against stopping for a case of ale from McArdles', I turned past Samaha's and pulled up at the west side of the bridge to wait for another steamer, a bulky Reo, to finish crossing. For some reason I recalled the time in London when I'd driven a steam lorry. I suppose it was the waiting. You always wait in those assignments. People think intelligence and undercover work is glamorous, but it takes a lot of patience.

Marie had left before I arrived home, as usual, but the table was set, and there was a veal pie in the oven, with a small loaf of bread and some sliced cheese. I fumbled together some lettuce, peppers, and carrots with some oil and vinegar for a salad. The table gleamed, as did the white-enameled windowsills.

I forced myself to eat slowly and not to wolf down my food. After I washed the dishes and set them in the rack, I walked into the main parlor and glanced at the videolink, then shook my head. None of the three channels available in Vanderbraak Centre offered much. In fact, none of the eight in the capital offered much. I walked on into the study, wondering if I should get to work on the article I had promised the *Journal of Columbian Politics* on the reality of implementing environmental politics. After the editorial controversies over my recycling article, I was faintly surprised that they wanted another one.

In the dim light I glanced toward the difference engine. Mine was one of the newest electric-fluidic types, not the mechanical monsters that hadn't changed that much after Babbage invented them, but one of those based on Bajan designs. I never have had much of a problem with using a New French concept, not so long as the manufacturer was a solid Columbian firm, and Spykstra Information Industries, SII, is about as old-line Columbian as you can get. Of course, Bruce had added more than a few frills, both for the extra fees he got and because we went back to the old days, when he was a techie and I a mere expendable. He was smart and got out early, but for some reason he has a warm spot in his Jewish heart for me.

SII makes its machines about twice as heavy and twice as tough as they probably need to be, and that means twice as much power, and an equivalent monthly bill from NBEI, not to mention the cost of having the house rewired and breakers installed in place of the old Flemish fuses. I even had a no-flicker screen and a nonimpact printer, again on recommendation from Bruce.

Under the desk, tucked right into a bracket behind the front leg, was a standard watch truncheon, a lot more effective against intruders, most of the time, than firearms. Also, you don't have to go through the license business. I still retain some occupational paranoia.

The whole system sat on a low table beside the antique

Kunigser desk my father had obtained from somewhere, but from either the desk or the Babbage engine table I could see out the double eight-pane doors across the veranda and down the lawn to the sculpted hedge maze.

I still hadn't quite restored the maze, but another year might see it back close to its original condition. Gardening does help heal the past, I had found, at least sometimes.

Because I was restless and did not feel like writing, I finally opened one of the double doors and slipped out onto the veranda, so welcomingly cool in the autumn. When I had been with the government, when I had been free from assignment for several weeks, my family had enjoyed taking holidays, infrequent as such occasions had been, not only in the summer, but even in the fall. I had liked winter, but Elspeth had been a southern girl and spent her days before the fire or the big woodstove, while Waltar and I skied on the long grassy slope down toward the river. Hiking back up, to me, had even been pleasurable. Waltar would have been ready to enter college by now.

For a time I stood and watched the purple twilight drop toward black velvet above the hills across the river, watched the lights of Vanderbraak Centre blink on, some reflecting in a patch of the River Wijk. As the chill built, I realized that I did not stand on the veranda alone, that a white figure stood in the shadows closer to the house.

Slowly I sat down on the white-painted wrought-iron chair, but the floral patterns felt like they were cutting right through my trousers. So I sat on the stone wall, but Carolynne had not moved.

"Carolynne . . ."

She drifted across the stones until she stood almost by my shoulders. Her hair was in a bun, as always, and she wore what Llysette would have called a recital gown, an old-fashioned one that covered her shoulders and upper arms, the kind they still wear out in Deseret.

"You used to talk to me."

An indistinct nod was her sole response.

"I am an adult. Elspeth is dead, and so is Waltar. Whatever—however—my mother bound you, that should not hold you now."

Only the whisper of the breeze through the ancient oaks and the pines planted by the builder of the house, the English deacon, greeted my request. My father had said there was more to the story than her murder by the deacon's wife, and more to Carolynne, and that someday he would tell me. But he died in a steamer accident while I was in Columbia, at my time of troubles, and he never did. He never left a note, not that I found, but Mother had sorted through his papers.

"Please, gentle singer, why are you here? Why do you linger? Why do I dream of you?"

Just a sense of tears, perhaps three notes sung so softly that even the breeze was louder, and she vanished, leaving me alone in the twilight on the old stones of the porch. For a time longer I watched the lights of the town, and some winked out, and some winked on, just like life.

Finally, when the breeze turned even colder, I walked inside, closed the door, and went upstairs to go to bed alone.

5

Good morning, Doktor Eschbach." Marie Rijn swept into the house with her usual smile and bustle of gray working skirts.

"Good morning, Marie. This time I do believe most of the dishes are clean, and—"

"You leave me little enough to do, Doktor Eschbach. Be on your way, and leave my work to me."

"Things are fairly clean."

"Fairly clean is not clean, Doktor." Marie insisted on recleaning everything until the house shone, and then, I think, she went home and did the same there. Good, clean Dutch stock.

I shrugged. Being alone for the past three years, I'd had enough time to clean up and do laundry—especially at first, in the Federal District. Even if my efforts weren't quite to Marie's standards, my houses had been clean, probably because without sisters I had learned enough growing up. Besides, after the accident and Elspeth's death, it had helped to keep busy. Yes, anything to keep busy.

"As you wish, Marie."

"And for dinner, Doktor?"

"Tonight for one. Perhaps two tomorrow night."

"Someday, will you marry the French woman?"

"I have not thought that far ahead."

"But perhaps she has." Marie gave me a sidelong look, one that warned me about scheming women preying on lonely men, as if I needed more warning. Still, Llysette had not pressed me, and she had shared my bed, offering warmth in a chill world.

Although my breath steamed in the morning air as I opened the car barn, it was measurably warmer than when I had awakened and run to the top of Deacon's Lane and along the ridge and back. The chill had been especially welcome after the run, when I had stepped up my exercises.

I tossed my leather case into the Stanley and clicked the lighter plug, then sat and waited until the warning light flicked off before backing out of the car barn onto the hard bluestone of the drive. I put on the brake, closed the car barn door, climbed back into the steamer, and turned it around before heading down the long driveway to Deacon's Lane.

In the field across the lane from the house, Benjamin's sons were harvesting the pumpkins that had grown between the last rows of corn. The squash had already come in. I waved, and Saul waved back, but Abraham didn't see me.

Most of the thin layer of frost had melted in the morning light by the time I drove across the River Wijk and stopped outside Samaha's to pick up my copy of the *Asten Post-Courier*. The sign outside the cluttered display window says that the store has been there for over a century. So had some of the inventory, but Louie—he refused to be called Louis—was the only shopkeeper left in town who had special narrow paper boxes for his customers. I do have a fondness for some traditions.

Samaha's Factorium and Emporium is dark, with wooden counters and rough-paneled walls that contain fine cracks older than any current living souls in Vanderbraak Centre. Even the modern glow panels in the ceiling do not seem to penetrate the store's history.

I walked past the bakery counter that always featured breads and rolls heavy enough to sink a dreadnought or serve as ballast for a dirigible and pulled my paper from its slot, fifth down in the first row, right below the empty slot labeled "Derkin." In the year and a half since I returned to Vanderbraak Centre, I'd never seen mister Derkin.

"Here you go, Louie." I left my dime on the counter. The *Post-Courier* was only seven cents, but the other three I had pressed on Louie on principle as a fee for saving back issues for me when I was away.

"Thanks be ye, Doktor. Have a pleasant day."

"The same to you."

The front-page story below the fold caught my eye, and I read it even before I left the store.

San Francisco (RPI)—A fire of undetermined origin destroyed the entire Babbage center of the California Polytechnic Institution late last night, killing one professor and a night watchman. Arson is suspected, but the destruction was so thorough that it may be weeks before federal investigators can determine even where in the massive complex the fire began. The dead professor is believed to be the Babbage research coordinator, Elston Janes.

CPI has been the site of recent protests against psychic phenomena duplication studies. Webster VanBujirk, speaking for the Roman Catholic Diocese of the Pacific, denied any church involvement. "Although we have expressed grave concerns about the direction of Babbage research [at CPI], such widespread destruction is reprehensible."

Selkirk Means, Anglican-Baptist bishop of California, released a statement which claimed in part that "all devout Anglican-Baptists deplore such wanton destruction." Even so, Bishop Means added that he hoped that after rebuilding the facility the Institution would reconsider its policy of accepting federal research contracts on psychic phenomena.

The Alliance for World Peace asked Speaker Hartpence to begin an investigation into charges that the CPI research was in fact disguised Defense Ministry research. This allegation was denied immediately by the Defense Subminister for Procurement and Research. Speaking on behalf of Minister Gore, Subminister Allard Reynard stated, "The federal research conducted at CPI was exactly as contracted. It was research of purely psychic phenomena. . . ."

I folded the paper into my case and climbed back into the Stanley for the short drive to the faculty car park. As I turned up Highland Street, the clock on the post centre struck half past eight.

Only a handful of spaces remained, but then, the car park only contained four dozen places, and twice that number of faculty lived outside of easy walking distance. The rest parked where they could, but not, of course, around the square. The parking issue almost had had Dean Er Recchus and the town elders before the magistrates, and might yet again.

I vented the Stanley before locking the doors and walked to the Natural Resources Department's offices. Gilda had not arrived, and there were only two messages in my box. One was from my esteemed chairman, the most honorable Doktor David Doniger—a reminder of the faculty meeting, on the special memo paper he used as chairman. The other was a note from the Student Affairs office that Corinne Blasefeldt would be absent because of her father's funeral. I wanted to send a note back that I would have been surprised if she had been in class, but the dean's office would not have appreciated the humor.

Once in my office, I read the *Post-Courier* from front to back, but there were no other stories related to the California Babbage center fire. The Asten Braves had finally decided to move to Atlanta as a result of falling attendance and the failure of the city fathers to allow hard liquor in the old stadium. Then again, soccer has always been a participatory sport for the Dutch, unlike the English, and Atlanta was far more English.

I read the CPI story again. Finally I dug out the student file I needed and looked up Gerald Branston-Hay's wire number in the faculty directory. I should have remembered it, but I never did. Then I picked up the handset and dialed the numbers.

"To whom do you wish to speak?"

"Gerald, this is Johan Eschbach—"

"Ah, Johan. How might I help you? Or should I ask, what might be the problem this time?"

"You know, you Babbage types always create problems." I laughed.

"So you insist." His voice was dry.

"I have a rather delicate problem with one of my advisees, a Peter Paulus. I'd rather not discuss it on the wire. Is there some time you might be free for a few moments?"

I waited.

"Ah . . . I was checking my schedule. How about eleven o'clock?"

"I am sorry, but I have a class then."

"Well . . . it's a bit short, but I could do it now. I have an appointment at ten."

"It shouldn't take that long. In ten minutes, then?"

"That would be fine."

While I did have a problem with Peter Paulus, I really wanted to talk to the good Doktor Branston-Hay again before there were any more fires of suspicious origin, particularly in the vicinity of Vanderbraak State University.

Gilda had claimed her desk by the time I headed out. Bulking over the corner of the desk in his black suit and maroon cravat was the junior member of the department, Wilhelm Mondriaan, some shirttail relative of the painter. The young Doktor Mondriaan had received his doctorate from The University—Virginia—and had yet to realize that most of us had ceased to worship unquestioningly at that altar of higher education, Thomas Jefferson notwithstanding.

"Please do not let any of the students see the exam when you duplicate them." Mondriaan attempted to cultivate a rumbling bass, but a mild baritone was all he could manage. He turned to me. "Good day, Johan. What is the festive occasion?"

I looked down. My jacket was light gray, but the cravat was a maroon brighter than normal by Dutch standards. "No special reason. I suppose I felt cheerful." I looked at Gilda. "I am headed over to the Babbage offices to see Professor Branston-Hay about a student whose problems we share. I won't likely be too long."

"Dare I guess?" she asked.

"I'd rather you did not. You might be correct."

Mondriaan frowned at my levity. He'd learn, unfortunately, that levity was often the only escape from academic insanity.

The brick-paved walkway to the additional steps up to the hillside building containing the lords of the difference engine was nearly untraveled, since it was between classes. I passed only Gregor Martin, and he scowled indifferently.

Gerald Branston-Hay was not even the department chairman, but his office was twice the size of Doktor Geoffries's—Llysette's chairman, who had a Steinbach upright in his spaces—and easily three times the size of Doktor Doniger's, although David had neither difference engines nor pianos to worry about.

More interestingly, every Babbage man or woman I knew was surrounded by stacks of paper, piles of disk cases, or pieces of hardware, or, more usually, some combination of all three. Every surface in Branston-Hay's office was always clean and had been every time I had come to see Gerald. Even my office isn't that empty, and with my government experience, I knew the danger of loose information.

He did have a modern electro-fluidic difference engine—although mine was probably close to his in capability. Both our machines probably made most recent machines look as obsolete as Babbage's original mechanical model, the one that sat unrecognized for its capabilities for nearly fifteen years after his death, until it fell into the hands of John Ericson.

"Please have a seat."

I took the chair across the desk from him and opened the file I had brought. Best to begin with the ostensible reason for my visit. It might even offer an opening. "I noticed that young Paulus received a warning in your introductory class. From what I recall, this is not a difficult course, assuming one does the work."

Gerald offered a quick smile. "While I would not characterize the course as particularly easy, virtually any student who matriculates here should be able to master enough of the material to turn in acceptable work. The reason Mister Paulus received a warning is relatively simple. He seems to be one of those few students with an inability to understand a series of logical commands. To use a difference engine requires using Babbage language or one of the newer programming systems. All are based on logic. While Mister Paulus has demonstrated the ability to memorize the structure and commands, he seems unable to fathom anything which requires either logical analysis or construction." He shrugged. "There it is, I'm afraid."

"Hmmmm," I temporized. "That would seem a serious flaw. I am surprised that it's not more widespread, in some ways."

"There are always a few students like that, but most seem able to grasp the use of logic."

"Do you suppose that . . . doctrinal background has anything to do with it?"

"Doctrinal? Oh, I suppose you're referring to the religious fundamentalists."

"They do seem to oppose logic. Did you see the *Post-Courier* this morning?"

"I haven't read it."

"Apparently some fundamentalist group burned the entire Babbage center at the California Polytechnic Institution. Didn't you do some graduate work there?"

"No. I did work with Immanuel Jobs, who now runs their program. Burned the entire Babbage center, you say? So," he mused, "I thought I heard something about that on the videolink this morning, but I really didn't pay much attention."

"One group claimed that CPI was actually doing Defense Ministry work on psychic phenomena." I shrugged. "Why is it that people want to link Babbage research with ghosting?"

"They have since before I got my doctorate." Gerald shifted his weight in his chair and looked toward the door.

I ignored his hint and went on. "We've talked about this before, but aren't most university Babbage people doing some work on the psychic side?" I waved off his objection. "I know you can't tell me exactly what you're doing because of the government contracting rules and all that. That's not what I'm talking about. But you Babbage people have both the expertise in correlating data and the most expertise in electrical fields, particularly those of a transitory or almost nontangible nature. That makes it pretty hard to avoid this sort of speculation, doesn't it?" I smiled broadly and, I hoped, in my friendliest manner.

"Johan, as you well know from your own past experience in government, people will always speculate."

"It looks like those speculations are growing, not to mention some strong objections, particularly from the Anglican-Baptists or from Deseret, to researching ghosts as transitory electrical phenomena."

"They're certainly transitory, although there seems to be some evidence that magnetic fields enhance their duration. Sellig-Ailes actually plotted ghost duration phenomena along the strongest lines of the earth's magnetic fields. The data were rather convincing." Branston-Hay shifted his weight in the chair again.

I continued to appear oblivious. "It would take a large difference engine to do that, I can see. Has anyone tried to replicate the effect with a magnetic field in a laboratory?" I watched the tightening of his face before I added, "Do you suppose they were doing something like that in California? That would certainly have upset a great number of souls." The pun was intentional, although I suspected it would be lost on Gerald.

"Unless we attempted murder in the laboratory, which no one in his right mind would do, Johan, it would be rather difficult to study a ghost here or in any Babbage center. Ghosts don't just appear at will in our laboratories. That's one of the reasons studying them is so difficult and why so many projects work on simulations—I mean simulations of ghost behavior, not simulations of ghosts," he added hastily.

"Of course." I laughed. "I didn't mean that." I stood. "I really didn't mean to go off like that, but when you mentioned logic I thought of the religious types and the mess in California." I shrugged, then bowed. "I appreciate your clarifying Mister Paulus's problem. I must confess that I had a similar experience with the young man, but I had thought it was more related to stubbornness than to logic."

"I have also found Mister Paulus stubborn." Branston-Hay stood up. "Lack of logic and stubbornness often go together, often, as we have discussed, even within the government of the Republic."

"So right. So right." I nodded. "Perhaps at some point we should have lunch."

"I would like that."

"So would I. Thank you again for the explanation about Mister Paulus." I nodded again and left, offering yet another nod to the clerk in the outer office, a square-faced older woman in the somber hues of brown that declared her Dutch origins more surely than a sign painted on her forehead could have. She reminded me of the government clerks in Columbia City. Her nod was barely more than perfunctory, but I bestowed a broad smile on her before I headed back toward my office.

The smile I bestowed on Gertrude, cheerfully sweeping the steps down to the middle of the campus, was more genuine. I even smiled at Hector, who is one of the few somber zombies I've seen. Surprisingly, he smiled back.

I was still wondering about the smile when I entered the department offices and Gilda gestured at me. "Doktor Eschbach?"

"Yes?"

"Someone called from a Deputy Minister vanBecton's office." After a glance at David's closed door, Gilda grinned at me from her desk. "They asked for Subminister Eschbach. I told them that we had a very distinguished Herr Doktor Professor Eschbach."

"You can't really add all those honorifics together."

"I know, but I hate government, and the clerk who placed the call was snooty." Gilda extended a piece of paper.

"Most federals are, even down to the clerks." The name on the paper was Gillaume vanBecton, and the number on the paper was a federal exchange. I didn't recognize the name, not that I would. When Speaker Hartpence had been elected, he'd removed all the old ministerial appointees, and I had recognized very few of the new names then. Two years later, especially after Waltar's and Elspeth's deaths, I recognized even fewer. Unfortunately, I did recognize the number, and I tried not to sigh. "I'll return the call."

"I'll place it for you." Gilda grinned again, and I returned the grin, since we both knew it was returning snobbery with snobbery. Still, I'm petty enough to be able to enjoy that and was grateful to Gilda for offering, since I never would have asked. And it was better that she place the call, rather than have me retreat to my office, if the message were what I thought it might be.

She picked up the headset and dialed. I waited.

"This is Doktor Eschbach's office, returning a call from a Herr vanBecton." Gilda raised both eyebrows. "Just a moment." She looked at me. "They're connecting him."

"I'll get it in my office. That way I won't tie up your wire."

By the time I lifted my handset, Gilda was saying, "Just a moment, Minister vanBecton."

"I have it, Gilda. Johan Eschbach here. I understand you had called."

"Bill vanBecton here. I do appreciate your prompt return of my call, Doktor Eschbach." At that point, there was a click as Gilda left the wire. "I regret the necessity of the call, but I was hoping you could pay me a visit here within the next few days. The return of the prodigal son is a mixed blessing."

I stiffened at the deadly words recalling me to service, but only said, "Mixed indeed. I could be there on Friday afternoon."

"That would be more than adequate. Call it a consulting assignment based on past services. Of course, as in the past, we will pay your daily fee and expenses, and a bonus upon completion of your work."

"I thought I recognized the number."

"If so, you'll know my office. I look forward to seeing you on Friday."

"And I you. Good day, Minister vanBecton."

"To you also, Doktor Eschbach."

I set down the handset slowly and looked out into the graying skies and swirling leaves. Being recalled to service in the Spazi was scarcely what I had expected. While it was technically possible, I'd never heard of it happening before. And why now? Were Congresslady Alexander's charges of Austro-Hungarian infiltration correct? Or did vanBecton know of my work for Ralston?

I took a deep breath as the leaves swirled beneath me on the green. Nothing was ever simple, and nothing ever ended. I took another deep breath.

6

WEDNESDAY STARTED LIKE Tuesday, with a smiling Marie Rijn.

"Today I intend to wash and press the curtains, Doktor. They're dusty, and the windowsills are a disgrace. You may be neat, but . . ."

The implication was that I wasn't clean enough, and that the white lace curtains—did any truly Dutch residence have anything besides shimmering white lace curtains?—weren't either.

"I do appreciate it, Marie."

"I know, Doktor. Long hours you work and there being no family to be as clean as it should be . . ."

I nodded and searched out my overcoat, leaving the house to her.

The day was gray and windy. I didn't see mister Derkin at Samaha's, not that I probably ever would, and I did get to my office early.

After reading and discarding David's rewriting of the minutes of the last faculty meeting, I picked up the wireset and tried to reach Llysette. She answered neither her home number nor her office extension. Perhaps she was in class, although she usually managed to avoid teaching before nine-thirty.

I rummaged through my case and laid out a draft of the test for Environmental Economics. Was the question on infrastructures too broad? Would they really understand— There was a rap on the door.

"Johan?" Young Grimaldi stood in the door of my office. In his European-cut suits he was always chipper, and I suppose I would be too with that much money, even if his family had been forced to flee from Ferdinand. "Do you have a moment?"

"Almost an hour, if you need it." I grinned. "What's on your mind?"

He slipped into the hard chair across the desk from me with that aristocratic elegance. "They reopened Monte Carlo—the casino."

"Ferdinand did? When?"

"Sometime last week. There's always some delay in the news coming out of the Empire."

"At times I have thought it would be nice if our reporters had some delays imposed. Then a lot of trash wouldn't make it to print."

He looked appalled. So I added, "I don't mean Ferdinand's kind of censorship—just delays. Does it really matter whether an aging movie star like Ann Frances Davis could never forget her one great love, an obscure football announcer named Dutch? Or whether Emelia vanDusen is going to wed Hans van Rijssen Broekhuysen and unite the two largest fortunes in New Amsterdam?" I took a deep breath. "The reopening bothers you?"

"It shouldn't. I've lived almost half my life in Columbia." He glanced toward the window and the gray clouds before continuing. "Sometimes, Johan . . ." He offered a self-deprecating grin. "It would be easier to forget the past."

I understood, although I didn't know that he knew that. "Sometimes . . . but without the past we wouldn't be who we are."

"I suppose. And I suppose that things could be worse."

"There is always the issue of progress," I offered.

He frowned. "Do you really think the world is a better place now? That progress in technology has meant anything more than better ways to kill?"

"Medicine is better. Women don't die in childbirth, and that makes for happier homes with fewer tormented ghosts."

"It also makes for bigger battles with fewer ghosts to remind us of the horrors of war."

"That's true enough. On the other hand, we don't see civil wars in the Balkans. There aren't any pogroms in the Polish and German parts of the Empire. The Greeks stopped killing the Turks generations ago—"

"That's probably because Ferdinand's father killed most of the Greeks, like his grandfather killed off most of the Serbs." Grimaldi snorted. "And that left the Croats with all the land."

I shrugged. "Some rivalries only end when one group is exterminated."

"You approve of genocide?"

"I didn't say that." I forced a laugh. "I have noticed, however, that peace among human beings tends to exist only as a condition of some sort of force, and some groups seem destined to fight forever—like the Irish and the Brits, or the Copts and the Muslims."

"Or Japan and Chung Kuo? That could get nasty—maybe nastier than Ferdinand's March to the Sea—although I don't see how."

"Don't say that. From what Llysette has told me, it was pretty horrible." I paused. "Still, things can be horrible anywhere. DeGaulle's efforts to push New France's boundaries right up to the Panama Canal haven't been exactly bloodless, and the Panamanian Protectorate is effectively a Spazi police state."

At the mention of the Spazi, Grimaldi glanced toward the open door.

"I've said far worse." Still, I changed the subject. "You said that the story about the casino upset you."

"I don't know," Grimaldi mused. "The story about the casino—I can recall running for the dirigible, and hearing the roar of the panzerwagens. My father never opposed Ferdinand. He even offered to accept an Austro-Hungarian protectorate. Ferdinand didn't even bother to respond. The armored divisions just poured out of San Remo. What could President Bourbon-Philippe do? The Spanish had already caved in, and Columbia . . ." Grimaldi shook his head.

"I'm sorry."

He laughed harshly. "There's not much you can do, Johan. Not more than fifteen years later. At least they had to wait almost twenty years for my father's ghost to fade."

There wasn't too much I could say about that. So I nodded.

"Everything's so quiet—here or in what remains of France. So clean, so efficient. Even Ferdinand's gas ovens are environmentally safe—except to the Gypsies and the outspoken Jews. Everyone just goes to sleep and doesn't wake up. It's a hell of a quietly efficient and environmentally sound world, Johan." He looked at me. "Why did you leave the government?"

"It got harder and harder to do my job. Let's leave it at that."

"I think I understand." He shook his head and stood up. "Time to face the well-groomed and empty-minded masses."

"All young in any culture tend to be empty-minded," I pointed out. "I suspect we were."

"We were probably happier then." He gestured from the door and was gone.

I looked at the test for a while, made some corrections, and packed up my leather folder for my first class.

As I walked across the green, absently waving to Hector, bagging leaves in a dun-gray canvas bag, I wondered how many people like Grimaldi and Llysette were tucked away in the back corners of Columbia, unable to protest for fear of losing their last sanctuary. Even I had looked to the door at the mention of the Spazi.

The wind, almost warm, blew through my hair, but I shivered anyway.

7

MIRANDA'S MEMORIAL SERVICE was on Thursday afternoon at four o'clock. When I had talked to Llysette on the wire in the morning, after trying to reach her for nearly two days, she had indicated she would not be free until close to dinnertime. She had been almost curt, with a student waiting. So I had called Marie on the wire and told her not to prepare anything for dinner. I had also refrained from telling Llysette about the trip to Columbia and decided to go to Miranda's service alone. The watch had released no information on Miranda's murder besides a perfunctory statement on continuing the investigation, but after vanBecton's call, it was clear I was going to be involved through more than mere curiosity.

Following my two o'clock class, I put on a black armband I had dug out of my armoire that morning. From the office I headed to the Bank of New Bruges to deposit the errant pension cheque that had arrived on Wednesday, and then I walked down to the small Anglican-Baptist chapel two blocks off the main square. No one saw the mourning band because it continued to drizzle and I wore my camel waterproof. I've never liked umbrellas, perhaps because they tied up one hand, and in the past that could have been a real problem.

After slipping in the side door at a quarter before the hour, I sat near the rear of the church on the right-hand side. I eased out of the waterproof as soon as I sat down because, despite the drizzle, the day was warm for mid-October. Watching as people drifted slowly into the small church, I was not entirely surprised to see Llysette. She wore dark blue flared silk trousers and a white blouse with a loose blue vest that matched her trousers. She carried an umbrella, but had not worn a coat. She entered through the main door, carefully closed the umbrella, and sat halfway back. I bent down to check my boots before she looked in my direction.

The pipe organ began with something suitably somber, and a young and clean-shaven man and a woman walked down the aisle and sat in the front pew on the right. Presumably he was one of Miranda's sons, and she was his wife. They both wore black, and she had a heavy veil.

Behind them, on both sides of the aisle, were a number of people from the university, including Doktor Dierk Geoffries and his wife Annette; Samuel Dortmund, the brass instructor; Wilhelm Mondriaan; and Johanna Vonderhaus. I didn't quite understand why Mondriaan was there, except as a matter of courtesy, and he did have the Dutch penchant for courtesy—not to mention the somber clothes that fit in so well in mourning situations.

The crowd was small, less than a hundred souls, not even half filling the small chapel, and the faint scent of perfume was overwhelmed by the pervading odor of damp stone.

Philippe Hague, the college chaplain, stood up to conduct the service, although he was of the Dutch Reformed persuasion.

"In God is our salvation and our glory; the rock of our strength, and our refuge, is in God. Praise be to the Lord, for our world, our souls, and our salvation. Let us pray. . . ."

Although the liturgy was not exactly familiar, I opened the book, found the words, and bowed my head with the rest.

The service was standard, commending the soul of the dear departed to the care of a merciful God, praying that

God would cause her murderer to repent of his sins, and saying what a wonderful person Miranda Miller had been. No one mentioned that she had been somewhat tight, even by old Dutch standards, but I did find out that she had been widowed young. Her husband had died in the confusing mess that had marked the abortive Columbian intervention in the rape of Singapore by the Chinese.

Good Chaplain Hague did not call the incident by any of the commonly accepted terms, instead characterizing it as "that sadly unfortunate involvement" in Asian affairs. Maybe that was symptomatic of the reasons I casually detested him. We might be too weak to get involved on the far side of the Pacific, especially with the limited range of our electric submersibles and the lack of fuel depots for our handful of aircraft carriers, but the only thing unfortunate about our attempt to forestall Chung Kuo's annexation of Malaysia was our inability to stop the Chinese. Of course, we hadn't been able to stop the Japanese from taking over half the islands in Southeast Asia, either, and the Philippines seemed likely to fall any day. Since we'd left them to the Aussies as a protectorate after taking over Cuba in the Spanish-American War—no one had wanted American ghosts in faraway Asia back then—it wasn't a Columbian problem.

Philippe seemed to think that pacifism was a workable philosophy. Ghosting may have reduced conquest, but it has never stopped it. In fact, I suspect ghosts gave a slight but significant advantage to nations with policies of accretion, or small conquests.

The eulogy was all too long. When the time came I hoped mine would be shorter, or nonexistent. That Miranda deserved better than being murdered didn't excuse gross beatification of what had seemed to me a small personality.

I slipped from the pew just before the final blessing and out into the heavier rain. I got wet, of course, because I didn't try to put on my waterproof before I went outside.

After waving to the fresh-faced watch officer who had known all about ghosting and shouldn't have, I sloshed back up to the department offices to check my box for messages. Even the main door was locked, and everyone had left. So I used my key. There weren't any messages, except for a note from David Doniger, as chairman, requesting that we keep photoduplication to an absolute minimum in view of the energy costs to the department and to ensure the department set a good example. Why hadn't he just brought it up in the departmental meeting?

I left David's pedantic sermon in my box and locked the main door behind me. Then I trudged back across the south green to the steps to the Music and Theatre Department and along the corridor. Unlike the Department of Natural Resources, the building was filled with people. Sometimes I wondered how the music professors ever got the reputation of laziness. They worked longer than almost anyone else, except maybe the poor library staff, and they got paid less.

Martha Philips was still at her desk in the main departmental office. I stepped inside.

"Martha."

"Doktor Eschbach, Llysette is in her studio." Martha was stolid, square, open, and seemed honest.

"I think I'm early." I glanced at the wall clock. "I saw Doktor Geoffries at the memorial service. How is he taking this?"

"We are all in shock, I think. You read about murders in Asten or New Amsterdam, but they are cities. You don't think it could happen here."

"I know. It must make things hard for Dierk."

"You don't know how hard. Between Doktor Branston-Hay and the watch, and Miranda's ghost—sometimes it—she—drifts by here, but she never stays, and all she says is something about not listening and screaming no. It must be hard on Llysette, because her office is one of the closer ones, but at least it never enters her studio. One of her students ran off screaming yesterday."

"That must have upset Dierk."

"It upset everyone."

"I can see. Has the watch said anything about coming close to a suspect?"

"Not to any of us. The way they keep asking questions, I don't think they know."

I shrugged and glanced at the clock. Martha smiled, and I headed out of the main office and down the hall. Before I went to Llysette's office, I turned toward the piano studio. The glow strips outside the studio were off, and the hall was dim there, almost gloomy. I stopped when I saw the video camera mounted and trained on the padlocked door.

I retraced my steps and took the outside doorway, then walked along the wall of the building until I could look in the studio window. Despite the dimness, I could see the covering on the piano—and what looked to be a Babbage console, a small video camera, and a cable running between them. I wasn't sure, but I thought I saw a flicker of white, but I kept walking. A ghost and now Babbage engines connected with the ghost? Just what else was Gerald hiding?

When I reentered the building, I made my way back to Llysette's studio, where, by placing my ear against the door, I could barely hear the piano and her voice. After she came to a break, I opened the door.

Llysette lifted her hands from her studio piano when she saw me inside the door. "Johan . . . I did not expect you here . . . so soon."

"I went to Miranda's memorial service," I said.

"I also. She had few true friends, I think." Llysette frowned. "I did not see you there."

"I was in the back. Philippe was not all that eloquent."

"He did not seem so." She cleared her throat before asking, "And why are you here?"

"Because time is short." I smiled. "An old client called me up and offered me a consulting job. I must go to Columbia tomorrow morning."

"You did not tell me this morning. I had thought . . ."

I tried to smile apologetically. "You sounded so rushed, as if you wanted me off the wire, and you said you would not be free until now. If I had known, we could have gone to the service together."

"Ah, yes. That I would have liked. I knew so few there."

"I thought we might at least have dinner."

"But then, then you must drive back . . ."

"You at least deserve a dinner at Cipoletto's."

"Johan, the food, it is good, but it is not . . ."

"I understand. But I am tired, and so are you, and we do require some form of bodily sustenance, even a little luxury. I could follow you home. That way you could leave your steamer, and we would only take one."

For a moment her green eyes were hard, as if she were looking straight through me. I smiled apologetically once more and waited.

"Ah, well, it is not as though we were children. I will be but a moment."

She began to pick up music and stack it on the old wooden desk in the corner. Her office was really a studio, with the old Steinbach in one corner and bookcases on the inside wall. The glass in the three windows was all graying, except for the two panes that had clearly been replaced recently. The hardwood floors sagged slightly, even after last year's refinishing. A rag rug beside the piano added a touch of warmth, but it should have, since I'd offered it to her when I'd turned the old parlor into my study.

"I am ready." Llysette carried her coat over her arm.

"No music? No umbrella?"

"The umbrella, if I do not keep it here," she lifted her shoulders and dropped them, "then I do not have it when most I need it."

The rain had diminished to a scattering of droplets by the time we emerged through the side door and walked up to the car park. She climbed into the tiny Reo runabout. As usual, she didn't wait long enough for the steam pressure to build fully, and the Reo lurched out onto Highland Street.

I followed Llysette up Highland and out old Hebron Road until we reached the stone-walled and white-windowed cottage she rented. As in almost every other Dutch-owned house, the front windows showed lace curtains. She put the Reo almost right in front of the porch.

I set the brake and stepped out onto the damp packed clay. "Do you need anything?"

"A moment I will just be." She was already unlocking the door.

"I'll just wait here." Somehow Llysette's cottage depressed me. It was neat, although she had a tendency to stack her music in piles. Perhaps it was just that it was so modest, so little, really, for a woman who could have been a great diva in old France, had Ferdinand not annexed it.

The top branches of great oaks behind the cottage waved gently in the wind, barely visible in the growing darkness, and a few more droplets caressed my face as I waited and watched. Llysette left on the porch glows.

"Voilà—I am not long."

"Not long at all."

I held the Stanley's door open for Llysette, then closed it and walked around and climbed in myself. As I turned back onto the old Hebron Road toward Vanderbraak Centre, I asked, "Have any of the watch been back to talk to you?"

"Yesterday, the young one, he stopped by to ask a few questions."

"About you, or about Miranda?"

"First, about where she lived he must know. Then about her working hours he wanted to know. Then he asked why Professor Miller was working late on a Saturday."

"Did you know why she was there? That does seem strange." I edged the steamer to the right edge of the road to avoid a fast-moving Williams that was taking the big turn too fast.

"They should not travel so quickly."

"Not on wet roads. Did you know where she lived?" I prompted after I turned back onto Highland.

"I did not know where she lived. And as I have told most, the hours she worked were . . ." Llysette shrugged. "They were not terribly long. I told the watch officer I did not know why Professor Miller was there that night."

After another silence, I turned right at the edge of the square and continued past the Anglican-Baptist chapel toward the south end of town.

"Perhaps she was waiting for someone?" I eased the throttle down as we neared the edge of Vanderbraak Centre and the bend in the river where Cipoletto's overlooked the weirs. Only a handful of steamers were parked outside the restaurant, but it was early for the college types and late for the burghers.

"How would one know?" Llysette pointed out reasonably. "If one had meant to meet Professor Miller . . ." She shrugged again.

"Then that person either killed Miranda or would be afraid to admit the meeting because of being accused of the murder." I pulled up beside another Williams, this one a racing model that few in New Bruges could afford and fewer still would want.

"This is most kind of you, Johan," she said as I helped her out of the Stanley. "You do not need to pack?"

"It's a one-day trip, perhaps an overnight. Clients never like to pay extra, and I'm certainly not in the mood to pay federal city prices." I offered my arm, which she took, and we crossed the brick-paved courtyard with the light wind flicking the faint odor of woodsmoke around us. I held the door for her.

"You have not a good opinion of your capital city?"

We stopped by the raised table where Angelo waited with his book and list of reservations.

"Not of its prices." I nodded to Angelo. "Two, in the red room." The red room was for nonsmokers.

"Doktor Eschbach, of course. I even have the table where you can see the river." He bowed, and I nodded back.

"You would like some wine? Red or white?" I asked as we walked through the main room toward the small corner red room.

"White, I think."

Angelo gestured to the table set in the bay window. A brass lamp cast a flickering light over the red tablecloth. He pulled out Llysette's chair.

"A bottle of your house white, Angelo, if you would."

"Of course, Doktor Eschbach." He smiled, and gestured to the slate propped on the stand against the wall. "Tonight's fare."

In the flickering lamplight, we studied the slate.

"Fettucini alfredo again?"

Llysette pursed her lips. "I think the pasta primavera."

"Then I will have the fettucini."

Angelo returned with a green-tinted bottle. I did not recognize the label, but it was from California, and most of his wines were good. So I nodded, and waited for him to pour some into the glass. I sniffed, and then tasted. "Good."

He filled both our glasses and set the bottle in the holder by my elbow.

I raised my glass, and Llysette followed. The rims of our glasses touched, and we drank from our glasses without speaking.

A waiter I did not know appeared. "Have you decided, sir and lady?"

"The pasta primavera, with the tomato rice soup," said Llysette.

"I'll have the fettucini alfredo with the barley soup. Two of the small salads with the house dressing."

Llysette nodded in confirmation.

After the waiter left, I took another sip of the white. I liked it. So I looked at the label—San Merino. While I was looking, Llysette finished her glass, and I refilled it.

"I saw Miranda's ghost," I volunteered.

"This ghost you saw recently?"

"No. I meant the night she was killed."

The waiter placed warm cranberry rolls on the butter plates and set our soups before us.

Llysette took another solid sip of the San Merino. "You did not tell the watch." She lifted her soup spoon.

"I walked out of my office, and there she was. She mumbled some meaningless phrases, and then she was gone." I tried the barley soup—hot and tangy with a hint of pepper and basil, an oddly pleasing combination.

"That woman, always was she talking meaningless phrases."

"How is your soup?"

"Comme ci, comme ça. Less of the tomato, I think, would be better. How do you find yours?"

"Quite good. Would you like a taste?"

She inclined her head, and I held the bowl so she could try the barley soup.

"Better than the tomato," she confirmed. "You should see."

I tried hers, and she was right. The barley soup was better, fuller. I broke off a corner of the cranberry roll, still almost steaming, then finished my soup.

"I really never knew Miranda," I said, after the waiter removed the soup bowls. "Was she always talking nonsense?"

"Nonsense, I would not say. She always repeated the small . . . the trivial. One time, she spoke at a meeting four times about the need to revoice the concert Steinbach. And Doktor Geoffries, he had agreed to approach the dean for the necessary funds after she spoke the first time." Llysette finished her second glass of the white. My glass remained about half full, but I refilled hers.

I frowned. "Did she keep confidences?"

"Confidences?"

"Secrets. If you asked her not to repeat something . . ."

"Mais non. A tale she knew, everyone knew."

"Still, it is very sad."

"Very sad," Llysette agreed.

The waiter arrived with our pasta, and another cranberry roll for me. Llysette had scarcely touched her roll.

The fettucini alfredo, especially with the fresh-ground

Parmesan, had that slight tang that subtly lifted it above the mere combination of cheese, cream, garlic, and pasta.

"How is the primavera?"

"It is good. You would like a little?"

"If you could spare it."

"I eat all of this, and into no recital gown will I fit."

I didn't have a witty response. Instead I leaned over and tasted some of her dinner. The primavera was as good as the fettucini, but you expected that when you paid Angelo's prices.

"It is good," I said. "Would you like some of the alfredo?"

"*Non*. I will not finish what I have."

Several minutes passed before Llysette wiped her mouth on the red linen napkin and took a swallow of her wine. Then, glass still in her hand, she asked, "Johan, what was it—did you miss something the most when you left the capital?" Her eyes were thoughtful.

I finished a small sip of my own wine before answering. "Most times, when you leave a place, you do miss things, especially at first. I thought I might miss things like the museums, or that something was always happening. At first, I missed the newspapers. I missed the up-to-date radio and even the stuffy television news. But I noticed something after a while. I started missing items in the news, and nothing changed. I mean, the names change, but the problems continue, and they go on and on." I shrugged. "What do you miss about France?" I grinned. "The food?"

"Ah, yes, the food I miss." Her eyes clouded for a moment, and she swallowed more wine.

"Or the singing, the culture?" I prodded gently.

"Johan, you understand . . . and still . . . you are here." She shook her head. "That I do not understand."

"There is little more culture in the Federal District of Columbia than here in Vanderbraak Centre. The most popular play at Ford's Theatre is the updated revival of *The Importance of Being Earnest*. The most popular classical music is either

Beethoven's Ninth or the *1812 Overture.* Yes, there is more to choose from, but given the choice . . ." I let the words drop off.

She finished her wine, and I poured the last of the San Merino into her glass.

"You sing better work than often appears in Columbia."

"And yet, I am here, forced to teach spoiled Dutch burghers who believe one note is much the same as another."

After looking at the remainder of the fettucini, I nodded to the waiter, who removed both plates.

"Some coffee?"

Llysette shook her head.

"Perhaps a brandy?" I asked.

"Not this evening, Johan. Perhaps we should go. You must rise early."

"The check, please?" I beckoned, and the waiter nodded. He returned as Llysette drained the last of the wine.

I left a twenty and a five, and we walked to the front, past a scattering of couples in the main room.

"How was the dinner?" Angelo stood by the door as we left.

"Very good, as usual. The barley soup—I'd like to see that more often. And," I winked at Llysette, "perhaps a shade less tomato in the tomato rice potage."

"What can I say, Doktor? Your taste in wine, women, and food is impeccable."

"The lady is even more discriminating in wine and food, but more tolerant in men, thankfully." I nodded.

Angelo bowed to Llysette.

Once we were in the courtyard, Llysette glanced back toward the restaurant, and then toward me. "Here, no one believes a woman has taste—except you."

"That's because few men or women have taste."

"Johan, sometimes you are more jaded than I."

"Only sometimes?" I helped her into the steamer.

A light rain began to patter on the roof of the Stanley as I drove back out the old Hebron Road to Llysette's cottage. Her tiny Reo runabout was still parked in front of the porch, and her trousers got damp when we scurried up to the front door, despite my trying to keep the umbrella over her.

"Thank you for the evening, Johan."

"Thank you."

I bent down and kissed her. Her lips were warm, welcoming, but not quite yielding. I did not even suggest I should come in. The next morning, I knew, would come all too early, and I had an hour-and-a-half drive westward to the Blauwasser River to catch the train in Lebanon.

"Good night, dear lady."

"Good night, Johan."

I stepped back into the rain, and to the Stanley, but I waited until she was inside before I pulled out of the graveled drive and onto the road back to Vanderbraak Centre.

8

I CAUGHT THE EARLY-MORNING Quebec Express in Lebanon and took it into New Amsterdam, and then the Columbia Special from there to the capital—the Baltimore and Potomac station just off the new Mall. Even with stops, it took only a bit over six hours, and the sun was still high in the autumn sky when I stepped into the heat and looked toward the marble obelisk on the edge of the Potomac.

I still couldn't believe that they'd finally finished the Washington Monument after more than a century of dithering. Now they were talking about a memorial to Jefferson, but the Negroes were protesting, especially Senator Beltonson, because they said Jefferson had been a slave owner, not that there had really been that many slaves after the horrors of the *Sally Wright* incident. Speaker Calhoun's compromise had effectively led the way to civil rights for the Negroes, and Senator Lincoln's Codification of the Rights of Man had set an amended compromise in solid law. Personally, I still thought Jefferson had been a great man. You have to judge people by the times they lived in, not the times you live in.

The same drizzle that had enveloped New Bruges the day before had reached the Federal District of Columbia, except it was warmer, steamier, unseasonably hot, even in the former swamp that was the Republic's capital.

I wiped my forehead on the cotton handkerchief, sweating more than I would have liked. At least I didn't have to go to the congressional offices. Electric fans were their sole official source of cooling; only the White House was fully air-conditioned. That had been one of Speaker Roosevelt's decisions—that air conditioning would only make the Congress want to spend more time than was wise in Columbia.

As ceremonial head of state, of course, the president was obliged to stay whether he liked it or not. So he got the air conditioning, and so did the rococo monstrosity that housed his budget examiners. His budget reviews and public criticisms were about the only real substantive powers the president had. I had seen a lot done with budget reviews, and members of Congress didn't like to seem ridiculous.

As for the heat, the Congress made do with fans or left Washington, and the civil servants sweated. Of course, ministers did find ways to cool their individual offices, but no one talked much about it, so long as they spent their own money. In the 1930s, Speaker Roosevelt had also insisted that the growth of the various ministries would be restricted by the heat. I hadn't seen that—only a lot of sweating civil servants. Anyway, how could one imagine a government much larger than the half million or so on the federals' dole?

I hailed an electrocab outside the station. "A dollar extra for a single ride."

"The single is yours, sir." The driver opened the door. "Where to?"

"The Ministry of Natural Resources, Sixteenth Street door, north end."

We passed the new Smithsonian Gallery—Dutch Masters—built to contain the collection of Hendrik, the Grand Duke of Holland. At least he had been Grand Duke until Ferdinand VI's armies had swept across the Low Countries.

Columbian Dutch, the oil people, had paid for the building. The Congress had approved it over my objections to the design—heavy-walled marble, stolid and apparently strong enough to withstand the newest Krupp tanks, even the kinds the Congress had shipped to the Brits and the Irish to discourage Ferdinand from attempting some sort of cross-channel adventure. Not that a gross of metal monsters had ever stopped any would-be conqueror.

Besides, Ferdinand was through with conquests. The Austro-Hungarian empire was nothing if not patient. England would not fall until Ferdinand VII took the throne. By then, most of the ghosts in France would have departed, and the remaining French would be dutiful citizens of the Empire, happy with their taxes and the longest period of peace and prosperity in their history—bought only at the cost of thirty percent of their former population.

Ghosting worked both ways—but basically too many ghosts hurt the locale where they were created. That was why ghosts almost stopped William the Unfortunate's conquest of England, but not the Vikings or the early Mongols. They also stopped a lot of murders and slowed early population growth—second wives didn't take too well to a weeping female ghost who had died in childbirth.

I was probably being too cautious, but strange wire messages recalling former agents to duty and promising stranger assignments have a tendency to reintroduce occupational paranoia all too quickly. I could feel my chest tighten even as I thought about it.

"Here you be, sir."

I nodded and handed him two dollars and a silver half-dollar.

"Thank *you,* sir."

After offering my identification card to the guard—I'd never surrendered it—I walked to the corner of the building and took the steps to the basement, and then those to the subbasement. A guard sat at the usual desk around the bend in the tunnel.

"Your business, sir?"

He wasn't a problem, but the armed sentry in the box behind him was.

"Doktor Eschbach. I'm here to see Subminister vanBecton."

He picked up the handset, and I waited.

"You are expected, Doktor."

I nodded again and walked down the tunnel under Sixteenth Street until I came out in the subbasement of the Spazi building. Another set of guards studied me flatly, but I just nodded. They were there to keep people from leaving, not entering. Officially, it was called the Security Service building, but it was still the Spazi building, with the flat gray ceramic tiles and light-blond wood paneling designed to hide the darkness behind each door. The smell of disinfectant was particularly strong in the subbasement.

VanBecton's office was on the fourth floor. I walked up, in keeping with my recent resolve to improve my conditioning, but I was still panting, and stopped a moment on the landing to catch my breath. Even on the fourth floor I could smell disinfectant, common to jails and security services the world over.

The disinfectant odor vanished when I opened the landing door and stepped onto the dark rust carpet on the corridor leading to his office in the middle of the floor. Corner offices, for all their vaunted views, are too exposed.

His clerk, though young, had a narrow pinched face under wire-rimmed glasses, and presided over a large wireline console. "Might I help you?" Her eyes flickered to the bearded man in the loud brown tweeds perched on one end of the leather settee. The bearded man glanced at me impassively.

I extended a card to the clerk. There was no sense in announcing my name unnecessarily. "Minister vanBecton invited me for a meeting."

"Yes, Doktor." She picked up one of the handsets and

dialed. "The doktor has arrived." She listened for a moment, then added, "Yes, sir."

I smiled pleasantly as she turned toward the bearded man. "Your meeting may be delayed slightly, sir."

The other's eyes narrowed slightly, but he nodded. I returned the nod.

"Doktor, it may be a moment. If you would be so kind . . ."

"Thank you." I took the straight-backed chair in front of the dark mahogany bookcases. I picked up the Friday *Columbia Post-Dispatch,* since the fellow in brown English tweeds clearly had either read it or had no interest in doing so. There was another story on religious protests against psychic research, and more speculation about the full extent of Defense Ministry funding of such projects. I also enjoyed the story which speculated that Senator Hartpence's private office in the Capitol had seen some very private uses, and which suggested that, improper as such uses might have been, a politician's private life remained his own. How could it not be? Then again, perhaps even the mention of the incident might be a disturbing trend. Would the masses decide that they would buy more newspapers if such tidbits were more frequent?

"Doktor? Minister vanBecton will see you."

She opened the door in the blond-paneled wall to her left, but did not enter, and closed it behind me.

The office was almost the same, except that vanBecton had added an Escher oil in place of the copy of the *Night Watch.* It looked like an original, not that it surprised me much.

"Good afternoon, Doktor Eschbach." The man standing behind the wide, dark English oak desk gave me a half-bow.

"Good afternoon, Minister vanBecton." I returned the bow, and he gestured to the straight-backed leather chair facing the desk. I slipped into it, and he sat back down in the slightly overpadded burgundy leather swivel chair. The office was still that combination of Dutch and English—dark Dutch furnishings and English lack of spark—that created an impression of bureaucratic inertia. The windowsills were dark wood, not dusted frequently enough, reflecting the less astringent standards of the English-settled south.

Gillaume vanBecton was a particular type of man raised from money and boarding schools. They are the ones who wear tailored gray pinstripes, their cravats accented in red, their graying hair trimmed weekly, their gray goatees shaped with that squarish Dutch cut to imply total integrity, and their guts almost as trim as when they once jumped over those lawn tennis nets they now only reach across in congratulating their always vanquished opponents. As they get older, they take up lawn bowling with the same grace as tennis, and the same results.

I've always distrusted the vanBectons of the world. I hadn't liked Hornsby Rogers, either, when he'd been seated behind vanBecton's desk.

If he had actually done a tenth of what he'd probably ordered, Gillaume vanBecton would have been a bright-eyed, ex-ghosted shadow—a zombie cheerfully pushing a broom for the city or hand-sorting glass for the recycling bins. Instead, he was the honorable Gillaume vanBecton, Deputy Minister for Internal Security of the Sedition Prevention and Security Service, in short, the number-two Spazi, the one responsible for all the dirty work.

"I am at your disposal."

"I am pleased that you recognize that." VanBecton smiled briefly.

"I try to be a realist."

"Good."

"What is this 'consulting' assignment, if I might ask?"

"It has to do with your Fräulein duBoise—"

"Doktor duBoise?"

"We have some concerns about who she really is."

"You don't know? Perhaps I can help you. Her name is Llysette Marie duBoise. After obtaining her degrees, she apprenticed at the Académie Royale, then premiered in

Marseilles, where she eventually sang and bedded her way into the roles she deserved and needed to support her family. Her mother died, and later her father was killed by Ferdinand's troops. Because she had some stature, and because of some intervention by the Japanese ambassador, who had heard her sing, she was allowed to leave France—although not without, shall we say, some detailed interrogation." I inclined my head politely.

"How detailed, Doktor Eschbach?" VanBecton's voice remained smooth, and he leaned back in the heavy swivel chair.

"Enough to leave scars where they are not normally visible."

The subminister leaned forward again, but his eyes did not hold the smile of his mouth. "That would certainly seem to provide some indication that she has no love of Ferdinand. But . . . how do you know she isn't an agent of New France? Maximilian VI—"

"He's a fifteen-year-old boy. We both know Marshal deGaulle runs New France." I shrugged. "These days anyone can be working for anyone else. But, even assuming Doktor duBoise were an agent of New France, why on earth would she be in New Bruges?"

"At first glance, that would seem odd." VanBecton continued to smile. "Although Maurice-Huizenga has been known to recruit other . . . refugees." He covered his mouth and coughed, and his hand brushed the top drawer. That was where Rogers had kept his gun, and probably where vanBecton kept his. Stupid of him, since, if murder had been anyone's objective, including mine, vanBecton would have been dead before he could reach the weapon.

"At first glance?" I decided to oblige him.

"Don't you think this whole business is rather odd, at least from the federals' position? A former New Tory subminister returns to teach at a mere state university in a small town in New Bruges where he once spent summers. All very innocent until we consider that his position as a subminister was essentially to fatten his pension for his previous services to his country and to provide some consolation for the personal trials occasioned by his service. Then a refugee from the fall of France appears, a lovely and highly talented . . . lady, and she immediately becomes close to this widower, a man possibly—shall we say—vulnerable . . . Then another academic with a past better left not too closely inspected is murdered for no apparent reason."

"And might you tell me why Professor Miller's past is better left not too closely inspected? Was she an agent of Ferdinand? Or perhaps of Takaynishu?"

VanBecton smiled politely. "We actually are not sure, only that she was receiving laundered funds and instructions."

"What instructions? I'd rather not get in the way of a murderer trying to find out what you already know."

"She was instructed to find out what you were doing and to try to compromise you in a way to cast discredit upon the government."

"Someone seems to have looked out for me."

"No one that we know of," vanBecton said blandly.

"Perhaps it was fortuitous." I offered another shrug. "Murders occur, but rarely are they openly investigated by the Spazi. That was just obvious enough to show your interest."

VanBecton steepled his fingers together. "A nice touch, I do believe. I trust that it will make Doktor duBoise more reliant upon your protection."

I didn't have to force a frown. "I doubt that you are paying expenses merely to encourage Doktor duBoise to rely upon me. If anything, my traveling here right after the murder would make her somewhat suspicious."

"You will have to work to allay her fears, Doktor." He smiled broadly, fingering the standard-issue pen.

"But of course." I returned his smile with one equally as false.

"You can be quite convincing." VanBecton cleared his throat before continuing. "According to Colonel Nord."

I held my temper. "Considering my patriotism cost me my son and later my wife . . ."

"I am certain that Minister Reilly handled it as well as he could."

". . . and that the Spazi blocked further treatment in Vienna, treatment she wouldn't have even needed . . ."

"You knew the risks. As we know, Doktor Eschbach, the Austro-Hungarians only *claim* to have an effective treatment for degenerative lung fibrosis."

"The Health Office of the League of Nations has verified it."

"The League of Nations also verified that General Buonoparte used no poison gas on the French strikers in Marseilles."

I forced a shrug of reluctant agreement. Nothing I offered would convince vanBecton. He was one of the true believers, and nothing existed beyond his narrow vision of the world. In a way, his attitude reinforced my reluctant support of Ralston, though I suspected Ralston, in his indirect way, was the more deadly of the two.

"Does it really matter, Doktor Eschbach? We're men of the world. Only perceptions count, not reality." He smiled again.

"And what else do you want?"

"If you could trouble yourself to find out why Professor Miller was murdered, and why she wanted to discredit you—certainly in your interest—it would be helpful."

"It's also clearly in your interest not to have me discredited."

"Not so much as you think, Doktor Eschbach. It could be merely embarrassing for us."

"I so appreciate your concern. I presume I will be hearing from you again."

"As necessary." He stood.

I followed his example.

"I assume you know the way out." He gestured to the rear door.

"I have been here once or twice."

"I look forward to seeing you again."

"And I, you."

The narrow corridor had two one-way doors, both steel-cored in steel frames, before it opened onto the main hall. The second door looked more like a closet door than one to an office. Overkill, in a way, given the guards in and around the building.

Just to make matters a shade more difficult for whoever might be following me, I retraced my path back to the Natural Resources building, except I had to show my identification to the guard on the Spazi side of the tunnel. Then I went up to my old offices on the fifth floor.

Estelle was there. She smiled as I walked in. "Minister Eschbach! It is so good to see you." Turning to the black-bearded young man beside her, she added, "Doktor Eschbach was the subminister before Minister Kramer."

"Pleased to meet you, sir." He edged back ever so slightly. Clearly, he had heard of me.

"I should only be a bit, Stephan," Estelle said brightly. "We don't get to see Doktor Eschbach much anymore."

"I'll check back in a few moments." Stephan looked at me once more before he stepped past us and out into the main hallway.

"How do you like being back in New Bruges?"

"It's definitely a change." I laughed. "But not so much as I'd thought. The teaching is interesting. Other things aren't that different. What about here?"

Estelle glanced around, then lowered her voice. "It hasn't been the same since you left. Everyone worries about whether the Hartpencers will go after them."

"Hartpencers?"

"The Speaker put his own people everywhere—" She broke off and forced a smile as the door to the right opened. "Minister Kramer—do you remember Minister Eschbach?"

"It's good to see you, Kenneth. I hope the job is treating you well." I gave a half-bow.

"It has been an education," my successor offered. "And Estelle has been most helpful." He glanced toward her.

"I understand. Perhaps the next time I'm in the Federal District . . ."

They both nodded. I stepped into the corridor, then made my way to the Seventeenth Street exit. From there I took a cab up to the Ghirardelli Chocolatiers right off Dupont Circle. Llysette would enjoy some chocolates, even as a peace offering. The cab waited, for an extra dollar, then eased through the heavy afternoon traffic in a stop-and-go fashion.

Up New Bruges Avenue, I could see the rising-sun flags where the massive Japanese embassy stood on one side of the avenue, less than two blocks above DuPont Circle. While I could not see it from the cab window, the embassy of Chung Kuo stood across from it, just as the two Far Eastern empires squared off across the Sea of Japan. I also could not see the cordoned-off section of the sidewalk where the ghosts of ten Vietnamese monks still wailed fifteen years after they immolated themselves there in protest. Still, I knew they were there, and so did the Chinese—not that it seemed to stop them. They seemed to like the reminder of the futility of protest to their endless expansion.

Although the Chinese Empire was far larger than the Japanese, even the Chinese understood that Japan was unconquerable, especially because the Japanese were fortifying every island and creeping ever closer to isolated Australia. Once the Low Countries had fallen to Ferdinand, the Chinese and the Japanese had intensified their efforts to annex the former Dutch possessions in Southeast Asia. Again, I wondered how long the Philippines would last.

It wouldn't be in our lifetime, but what would happen when the Chinese, the Japanese, and the Austro-Hungarians finally assimilated Asia and what was left of Russia?

The cab jerked forward and around the circle, turning

back onto New Bruges and thence back to the Mall and directly to the B&P station. Although I would have liked to have made some other stops, the stops would not have been fair to those people. So I caught the five o'clock to New Amsterdam.

9

AFTER MY BREAKFAST, exercise, and shower, I dressed and took the Stanley down to the post centre to see what had arrived in my absence.

As always on Saturday, the square was crowded with steamers, the flagstone sidewalks filled with dark-clad shoppers. I had to park over by the church and walk across the square.

"Greetings to you, Doktor Eschbach," offered the young watch officer who had known about ghosts.

"And to you, Officer Warbeck," I said politely enough, finally close enough to read his name plate.

He smiled politely and walked past, up toward the college, while I continued north to the post centre.

"Good day, Professor Eschbach," offered Alois Er Recchus with a broad smile as I went up the steps to the post centre. His dull-gray work jacket was thrown open by the expanse of his abdomen, and he wore bright red braces over his gray work shirt and trousers. I hadn't thought him the type for red, even in braces.

"Good day. I don't see the dean."

"She's off to some conference in Orono. Something

about the need for interlinking among women in academia."

"Interlinking—that must be the latest term."

Alois shrugged, smiled, and waddled down toward the hardware store. I went inside and opened my box. Besides three bills and an announcement from the New Bruges Arts Foundation, there was an invitation. The return address was clear enough: the Presidential Palace.

I closed the box, preferring to wait until I got home before opening anything. After another handful of casual greetings, I retreated to the Stanley and headed back across the river, waiting for several minutes at the bridge for a log steamer to cross.

Of course, once at home and in my study, I dropped the post offerings on the desk and opened the invitation first. It was standard enough—the envelope within the envelope, the inner envelope addressed to the honorable Johan Anders Eschbach, Ph.D. The wording was also standard:

President and Mrs. Armstrong
request the honor of your presence
at a state dinner
honoring his excellency, Yasuo Takayama,
ambassador of
the Imperial Republic of Japan,
Thursday, October 28, 1993,
at seven o'clock.
Répondez s'il vous plaît.

A nice gesture, certainly, and my presence might be listed as one of many in the *Columbia Post-Dispatch*, if that. The timing of the invitation indicated I was a late addition to the guest list, since it was for the coming Thursday. I didn't have much choice about going, since Ralston had clearly had the invitation sent to get me to the Presidential Palace for further instructions. Things were moving. David would not be averse to my going, even if I had to cancel classes on Thursday and Friday. My students would certainly like the break.

I set aside the card announcing the New Bruges String Quartet's performance at the university for Llysette to see; their presence resulted from the dean's infatuation with strings of any sort. After leafing through the bills, I stuffed them into the top drawer to do all at once later.

For a time, I sat behind the Kunigser desk and just looked out over the veranda into the patchy clouds in the deep blue of the fall sky. Finally I picked up the handset and dialed in Llysette's wire number.

"Hello." Her voice was definitely cool.

"Hello. Is this the talented and lovely Professor Doktor Llysette duBoise of the enchanting voice and the charming manner?"

"Johan. Where are you?"

"At home. Where else would I be? I took a late train and got home rather late last night—or, more accurately, early this morning. I slept as long as I could, then got up and did chores. I do have a few, you know. Then I called you."

"Your trip to the capital? How did it go?"

"I got paid, or I will. But I'm afraid it may be a dead end. This client wants a great deal, but he isn't really very specific." I laughed. "I've told you about the type. You know, the ones who want the world, but they only say something like 'find out what you can.' Whatever you find is never enough. In any case, if you want to know the details, I can tell you later . . . assuming that you would be interested in company later."

"Johan, I am not feeling terribly well, but it will pass—as these feminine matters do. I would be more appreciating of your company perhaps tomorrow."

"How early tomorrow? Perhaps right after midnight?"

She did chuckle for a moment, I thought, before she answered. "Dear man . . . you are impossible." She pronounced "impossible" in the French manner.

"That's my specialty—impossibility."

"At three, would that be agreeable?"

"Of course. Have I taken you to the Devil's Cauldron?"

"Mais non. The Devil's Cauldron—what is that?"

"That is a place up the river valley where the river has hollowed out a cauldron. They say—but I will tell you that tomorrow."

"As you wish . . ." Her voice trailed off.

"Then I will see you at three o'clock tomorrow, for a drive to the Devil's Cauldron." I paused. "I have one other problem. Perhaps you could help."

"And so?" The suspicion resurfaced in her voice.

"Miranda. I remember that she loaned me a book, something she thought I should read. I never did, and now I can't remember what it was. I think Marie must have reshelved it."

"Ah, Johan, and never in all those shelves could you find it. So polite you are . . . but no one would know if you kept it."

"Alas, I would—even if I don't remember what it was." I laughed. "I feel rather . . . rather stupid. Did I ever mention it to you? I hoped I might have."

"Non. But outside of the music, I think—I do not know, you understand—but once she asked me to read something by a Doktor Casey, excepting he was not a real doctor."

"An Edgar Cayce? Perhaps that was it."

"That may have been. I do not know."

"I thank you, and I trust you will be much improved by tomorrow afternoon."

"I also. But also see to your own sleep, dear man."

"That I will, even if I must sleep alone in a cold bed."

"You will survive."

"Cruel lady."

"You think the truth is cruel?"

"Sometimes, and sometimes you are a truthful lady."

"Point toujours, I hope. Some secrets I must keep."

"Well, keep them until tomorrow, and take care."

"You also."

I set down the handset and leaned back in the chair for a moment, my eyes flicking across the massive Dutch Victorian mirror set between the windows overlooking the veranda. With its overelaborate gilt floral designs and bosses, it was one of the older items in the house. I kept thinking about replacing it, but since it was literally built into the wall, I had put off undertaking such a chore, and had instead replaced the lace curtains and about half the paintings. I didn't have to have lace in my study, and even Marie hadn't said anything about that—but she had washed and pressed the box-pleated blue curtains.

With a head shake at what I had yet to do, I slowly got up and walked over to the bookcases, starting at the far right. I always go through things backwards. It's faster for me that way. I tried to find a book that would suit my purpose, one that would fit the psychic mold, one that Miranda was unlikely to have had.

When I saw the title after having scanned nearly two hundred books, it didn't exactly leap out at me: *The Other World—Seeing Beyond the Veil.* But I pulled it out and studied it. It was a sturdily bound book, published by Deseret Press, but not an original, written by Joseph Brigham Young, a former elder in the Church of the Latter Day Saints and later the Prophet, Seer, and Revelator of the Church.

After leafing through *The Other World,* I decided it would do. An entire section dealt with the spirituality of music and the role of music in "piercing the veil." While it was a gamble, the only one who was likely to call me on it was dead.

I found some brown paper in the kitchen and wrapped the book in several layers of paper, tying it carefully with twine I had to fetch from the car barn. I debated writing something on the paper, but then demurred. The whole point was not to leave the book, but to talk to young Miller and his wife.

The day was sunny, and I decided to sit on the veranda and catch up on reading. I had several potential texts to review, although I was dubious about the authors, since they had spent little time in the federal city and not that much time dealing with the environment. I didn't want to write a text, and the Carson text I was using was badly outdated.

Comfortably ensconced in the canvas sling chair, I struggled through thirty pages of the Edelson text, but it was too journalistic, sacrificing accuracy to a golly-whiz crusading spirit. After discarding Edelson, I wandered back to the kitchen, made iced tea, and finally walked back out to the veranda, moving my chair into the shade by the dining room windows.

The Davies text wasn't much better. While the environmental science was good, he didn't understand even basic Columbian politics. After forty pages, I set it aside and got more tea. Then I just sat and enjoyed the view and the scent of the fallen leaves, listening to their rustling as the light wind occasionally picked them up and restacked them.

The more I learned about Miranda's murder, the stranger it seemed. Why would anyone murder Miranda? There could be reasons to murder Llysette, me, probably Gregor Martin, certainly Gerald Branston-Hay, and those reasons didn't count normal jealousy, either personal or professional. It was also clear that vanBecton intended to set me up to discredit the president in the undeclared struggle between the Speaker and the president. That meant trouble and more trouble, unless I could come up with a solution fairly soon.

Could vanBecton have had Miranda murdered, just to set me up? It was possible, but who did the actual deed? I shivered. Who was on whose payroll, and why? I knew the dangers of being on Ralston's "payroll," although I'd never received a cent directly, just an early retirement indirectly arranged. I doubted vanBecton had known all the details—until now, when his agents certainly could have found enough to point indirectly at my involvement with the Presidential Palace. There was nothing on paper, but both vanBecton and Ralston were old enough hands to know that by the time you had real evidence, it was too late. That was my problem—if Ralston or vanBecton wanted me framed for something or out of the way, by the time I could prove it, someone would be digging my grave and Father Esterhoos would be saying the eulogy.

After a deep breath, I drank the last of the iced tea as the sun dropped into the branches of the apple tree halfway down the lawn.

After a light supper in the kitchen—cold leftover veal pie—I drove the steamer down Emmen Lane, out to the bungalow owned by Miranda Miller, noting the lights in the window. The curtains were white sheers, not the white lace of New Bruges. I pulled into the paved area beside the house next to the steamer that had been Miranda's. Knocking on the door, the wrapped book in hand, I waited until the young, clean-shaven man I had seen at the memorial service opened the door.

"Doktor Miller? I'm Johan Eschbach. I teach in the Natural Resources Department. I saw you at the service, and I wanted to return this." I held up the package. "I would have just left it, but since you were here, I didn't want to slink away and leave you with something else to worry about."

"Please come in, is it . . . Professor?" He stepped back.

"Technically, Doktor or Professor, but . . ." I slipped into the small foyer, but waited for an invitation to go farther.

"I'm Alfred." He turned to a young woman in slacks and a cardigan sweater over a synthetic silk blouse. "This is my wife, Kristen."

"Pleased to meet you." I bowed. "I wish it were under other circumstances."

"So do we," she answered in a calm but strong voice.

"You are Miranda's younger son?" I asked, again lifting my package as if unclear what to do with it.

"The medical doctor," he acknowledged with a brief grin that faded almost immediately.

"She was proud of you," I said. After a brief pause, I added, "But I am wasting your time, and I had just meant to drop this off."

"What is it?" asked Kristen Miller.

"It is a book she had suggested I read, that I might find interesting. Something called *Seeing Beyond the Veil.*"

"Mother—she was always looking for something beyond." Young Alfred shook his head as he took the wrapped book. "I appreciate your kindness in returning the book." He gestured toward the sofa and chairs. "At least sit down for a bit. You don't have to run off immediately, do you?"

"No. I would have returned the book sooner, but I had to take a short trip yesterday—I do some consulting in addition to teaching. I did not think it would have been appropriate to descend on you Thursday night." I took the couch, since it was lower and left them in the more comfortable superior position.

The couple sat across on a set of wooden Dutch colonial chairs on each side of the copper-bound table.

"Could you tell us anything else about . . . about . . ."

"Perhaps a little," I offered over his hesitation. "I was leaving my office that night when I felt something strange, and I thought I saw a ghost. I heard, I think, the word 'no' whispered, and then her ghost was gone." I shrugged. "I do not know if that is much help. I cannot say I knew your mother well, except that once or twice she and I and others shared a luncheon." I frowned. "Do you not have a brother? Is he not well, or his business . . . ?"

"Frederick." Alfred glanced at Kristen. "I suppose it's no great secret. He is—was—in the electronics import business in San Francisco. He liked to import the latest Bajan designs. The last time he went to Los Angeles . . . he did not come back. He was imprisoned for some form of export violation."

"When did this occur?" Despite my best resolve to appear disinterested, my eyes scanned the room, and I noted absently that the white enamel of the windowsills had begun to chip and appeared soiled. No, Miranda had not been Dutch.

"Almost a year ago. It was September 17. I remember because it was the day after Mother's anniversary."

"That must have been doubly painful for her."

"It was," said Kristen.

"The entire episode does not sound . . ." I shrugged. "Your mother struck me as a careful person. Was not your brother much like her?"

"Rick? Of course. I mean, he did have some wild ideas about electronics, but he knew what sold, and Rick was very careful. It's some sort of excuse, something."

"It doesn't make sense," added Kristen. "Rick reported *everything.*"

"He was almost paranoid about being careful," confirmed Alfred.

"These are strange times. I would never have thought of a murder here." I shook my head. "That makes no sense, either."

"A jealous lover—or would-be lover, do you think?" asked Kristen, looking intently at me.

"Kristen . . ." muttered Alfred.

"One never knows, lady. But in response to the question you never asked, I was widowed several years ago. Currently I am attached to Doktor duBoise, and she is the only one with whom I have been, shall we say, intimate."

Alfred blushed, and Kristen nodded.

"How did Doktor duBoise and Mother Miller get along?"

"They were professional colleagues, but not friends. They seemed friendly."

"Were there . . . other men?" asked Kristen.

I liked the young lady's directness, and I answered directly. "I know Professor Miller had luncheon occasionally with Professor Branston-Hay, but I was led to understand that such was merely friendship. He is a Babbage type and, I think, thoroughly devoted to his wife, or as devoted as any Babbage type might be to mere flesh and blood. There are few unattached men here in Vanderbraak Centre," I added.

"So Mother wrote," commented Alfred.

"But it makes no sense," protested Kristen. "No one had any reason to kill her, not that the watch or anyone we've talked to can discover. She was lonely, but not totally alone. She could be a shade self-pitying—"

"Kristen . . ." murmured Alfred.

She glanced at him. "Mother Miller is dead, and I loved her, but there's not much point in sugarcoating her character. She was raised to be wealthy, and that all came apart when your father died. She worked hard, and she got you and Rick through your educations, and if she had a trace of self-pity, well, I think maybe she deserved it." She took out a plain white handkerchief and blew her nose, then continued as if she had never stopped. "Besides, no one ever murdered someone for feeling sorry for themselves. There has to be a reason. She had friends and men friends, but no lovers that anyone could even hint at. She was not robbed, or attacked in . . . untoward ways."

"Murder is untoward enough, I fear," I said, and added, "but what you say makes sense. Did she have enemies from where she came from?"

"How?" asked Alfred. "She's been here for almost fifteen years. The teaching was her life after I went to Louisiana and Rick to California."

"It does not make sense," I agreed. "I assume the watch has questioned every member of the music faculty."

"They still are." Alfred sighed. "But everyone was miles away or with someone else—usually two others."

"I am afraid I have taxed your hospitality at a trying time." I rose. "I did not mean to intrude so long, only to return what should be returned."

"And perhaps," added Kristen with a faint smile, "to try to make some sense out of something you also find senseless?"

"You are perceptive, young lady. Yes," I admitted, "that also. But there is no point in overstaying my welcome when you are as baffled as I." I extended a card. "If there is anything with which I could help, please do not hesitate to ask."

"Thank you." Alfred belatedly rose and took the card.

"We appreciate your concern." He grinned briefly. "And your forthrightness." He looked at the card, and frowned. "You aren't *the* Johan Eschbach?" He handed the card to his wife.

"I'm afraid you have the better of me."

"The former Subminister of Environment that the Hartpencers went after, I mean. Why are you here?"

"In Vanderbraak Centre?" I smiled—wryly, I hoped. "My family had a home here, and there really was nowhere else to go. I had the doctorate, and I still needed to make a living."

"Even stranger," he murmured.

"How so, Alfred?" asked Kristen, except her words were too matter-of-fact.

He shook his head. "Mother once wrote about you. She said you were the only honest man in a den of thieves, carrying about a lantern looking for another honest man. I'm sorry. I just didn't connect. I guess I am not thinking very well."

"Your mother must have been mistaken." I wouldn't have characterized myself as a Diogenes.

"No." He looked at me. "She also said that you were looking for a ghost in Doktor duBoise, and she—Doktor duBoise—was all too willing to oblige you, as desperate women often are."

I must have staggered, or reacted, for Kristen stood at that point. "Forthrightness is all very well, Alfred."

"No," I demurred. "I would hear more, if there is more."

"There's not much. She just wrote that she felt that all the recent arrivals at the university carried secrets too terrible to reveal and too heavy to bear. She meant the newer faculty, I think."

"Was your mother psychic?"

"Sometimes we thought so. But most of the time she kept her secrets—that's what she called them, her little secrets—to herself."

"It's amazing what you never know about people."

"I can see that." Alfred's tone was friendlier, for some reason. "How many people at the university really know your past?"

"You probably know more than most. I have said little, and most of the older Dutch do not ask. I would not, certainly."

"You would characterize yourself as older Dutch?" asked Kristen.

"By birth, but not by inclination." I frowned. "But how did your mother know? I cannot recall providing so much detail."

"I fear I'm the guilty one." Kristen grinned. "When Mother Miller wrote about you, I was skeptical, afraid that you might not be quite so honest. So I had a Babbage search done on you."

"She's a librarian," Alfred explained.

"The articles on you were interesting," Kristen added.

"You are too kind."

"Not much seems to have happened in your life," she continued inexorably, "after you got your doctorate from the University of Virginia, not until you were appointed deputy subminister of natural resources."

"I was a midrange government employee who did his job, got married, had a child, lost a child, and lost my wife."

"Murder is rare in Columbia," she said. "Yet a number have occurred around you. Why do you attract them?"

I shrugged. Anything I said would only make things worse in dealing with a very bright young woman who was clearly sharper than her husband.

"Do you know what I think, Alfred?" She turned to Alfred. "I think Mother Miller was right. Doktor Eschbach is an honest man, but, since there are so few left in our world, many people are afraid of his honesty. Yet killing him would create an uproar, perhaps bring to light the very things people want to hide. So whenever someone learns too much from the doktor's honesty . . . they die."

I shuddered. Could what she said be partly true? If so, it was even more horrible than the truth I knew.

"You've upset the doktor, I believe," Alfred remarked.

"It shows his honesty." Kristen inclined her head. "I apologize for my directness." She extended a card to me. "If you find out more that you can share with us, please let us know. We have to return to Lake Charles on Wednesday."

"That I will," I promised, taking her card. "I was sorry and have been deeply troubled by your mother's death."

"That is obvious."

"We appreciate your kindness and honesty," added Alfred as he held the door for me.

"And I yours."

By the time I fired up the Stanley and drove back in to town on Emmen Lane, I was almost happy to have escaped Miranda's children without revealing more than I had. Young Kristen Miller would have tied both Gillaume vanBecton and Hornsby Rogers in knots, I suspected, except that she was too direct to have survived in the Spazi organization. I almost hadn't, the Lord knew, especially once I'd left field work.

When I got back to the unlit house, looming like a monument on the hillside, I pulled off my coat and hung it on the knob of the stair railing, intending to take it upstairs when I got ready for bed. Then I went to the study, turned on a single light, and sat down at the old desk, looking into the dark. The more I knew, the worse it got.

How long I sat there before Carolynne appeared beside the desk, I didn't know, and really didn't care. In the dimness relieved only by the single lamp behind the stove, she appeared almost solid, in the recital gown that she always wore. It must be hell for a female ghost to always appear in the same clothes, I mused.

"Is it, Carolynne? Is it difficult to always wear the same gown?" I didn't expect an answer, but I got one. As I watched, she flickered, and appeared in another dress, high-necked and lacy.

"I didn't know ghosts could do that." Then again, there was probably a lot I didn't know about ghosts. "Can a ghost really say who murdered her?" I was thinking about Miranda, not Carolynne.

"Murder most foul . . ."

Her voice sent shivers down my back, but was that because of the fact that I heard her voice in my thoughts as much as in my ears? Or because I had not heard her speak in more than thirty years?

She drifted next to the window, seemingly more solid there. "A little water clears her of this deed . . . what need we fear who knows it . . . Macduff, Macbeth . . . damned be he who first cries . . ."

I considered her words. Who was the woman to whom Carolynne referred? What did the murder have to do with Macbeth? Was murder the deed or the cause of the deed? How did that apply to Miranda Miller?

". . . that death's unnatural that kills for loving."

Death's unnatural that kills for loving? Like Wilde's words about men killing the one they love? Or was it a question of not being strong enough to love? Was that why Llysette and I never got too close? But who wasn't strong enough to love? That brought up another thought.

"Do we always kill the ones we love? I didn't fire the shots that killed Waltar and ruined Elspeth's good lung. I might as well have. Spazi field men shouldn't have hostages to fortune." My eyes flicked to my sleeve, as if I could see through the pale cotton to the white scars beneath that ran from arm to shoulder.

Carolynne said nothing. Neither did she flicker or depart. So we remained for a time, ghost and the ghost of a man.

10

BEFORE I LEFT the house to get Llysette, I walked down the lawn to the remnants of the orchard and picked half a basket of apples and the few pears that actually looked decent. I carted them down to the root cellar, except for a handful of each which I put in the fruit bowl in the kitchen.

With the box of chocolates on the seat, I waited for the steamer to warm up, then headed down Deacon's Lane toward town. Vanderbraak Centre was its usual sleepy Sunday afternoon self, with only students passing through the square.

After passing but a single steamer on the old Hebron Road, I brought the Stanley to a halt beside Llysette's Reo at almost precisely three o'clock, according to the pocket Ansonia that was nearly a century old. Llysette was not waiting breathlessly on the porch for me, but that was always to be expected. I shut down the steamer and stepped up to the door, holding the chocolates behind my back.

After lifting the heavy brass knocker and letting it fall, I waited, and waited. Finally the sound of footsteps neared the door, and the lock clicked.

"Come inside, Johan. Only a moment will I be."

As I watched her figure, shapely even through the robe she had thrown on, retreat to the hallway leading to her bedroom, I doubted her estimate of the time.

Rather than sit, with a drive up the valley ahead, I wandered to the table that served for both filing and food. I put the Ghirardelli chocolates on the corner. On the other corner, the one closest the small kitchen, was the same stack of old-fashioned vinyl discs I had seen the last time. Beside them were piled various music publications—*Musical Heritage, Opera News, Main Line Musical.* A higher stack of letters, notices, circulars, and the like spilled around the dried floral centerpiece and came to rest against the dog-eared news magazines—*Look, Life, Newsweek,* and *Columbian World Report.*

I picked up the latest issue of *World Report,* which I had not seen, since subscribing to two news magazines and a daily still seemed extravagant. In some matters, my Dutch heritage did linger.

Newsweek arrived in my postbox, perhaps because *World Report* had always seemed somewhat more liberal in its speculations on the meaning of the news. Flicking through the pages of *World Report,* I caught a glimpse of red and stopped to read the article.

The ghost of Pope Julius Paul II appeared before the College of Cardinals last week, prompting speculation that his death earlier this month had not been from the natural causes announced by the Vatican. "The Pope clearly wished to convey his blessing upon the college and offered the traditional benediction before his shade vanished," stated Cardinal Guilermo Moro, spokesman for the Vatican.

Julius Paul had been thought to favor easing the absolute Roman Catholic ban on psychic research. Earlier this year, he had remarked in a small audience that the "true mysteries of God are not so easily solved by mere mortals."

After that audience, Pope

Julius Paul had been visited by the ambassadors from both Columbia and Austro-Hungary, and later by Archbishop Konstantin from the Apostolic Eastern Catholic Church . . .

Psychic research seemed to be an increasingly touchy subject. Why now? Ghosts had been around forever.

"Johan?"

Llysette stood there, in stylishly quilted blue trousers and a matching jacket, carrying a heavy quilted down coat and an overnight case.

"You are ready in a moment, indeed. Are we headed for the Arctic?"

"You a polar bear are. I am not. The wind is blowing from the north, is it not?" She arched both eyebrows.

I grinned in submission and set down *World Report*. "You know best for you." Then I glanced toward the table, and her eyes followed mine.

"Oh . . ." She moved to the table and looked at the box. "You are very sweet."

"Those are because I care, and because I never did bring you something at your recital."

"Would you mind if I had one now?"

"Of course not. Instead of lunch?"

She smiled and opened the box, but she offered it to me. I guessed, looking for a caramel, and was lucky. Llysette actually had three before we walked to the door. I waited on the porch while she locked up.

After seating her in the Stanley and setting her case in the back seat, by the time I was behind the wheel and had lit off the steamer, the wind made me glad that I had worn a sweater and the heavy Harris Tweed jacket. I wondered if young Ferdinand would let the Scots continue with Harris Tweeds when he overran the isles in the next century.

The center of town was nearly deserted, even by the students, except for a few steamers gathered around the Reformed Church, when we circled the square and headed north on Route Five.

The winds had ripped away the last of the leaves, and the birches, oaks, and maples were bare, stark, letting the evergreens stand out against the brown and gray of the harvested fields and leaf-stripped woodlots. The white enameled windowsills of the colonial stone houses stood out more, too.

"It is quiet," noted Llysette as we passed the empty car park at Vanderwerk Textiles, the sole remaining mill north of Zuider. The sign read VANDERWERK TEXTILES, A DIVISION OF AZKO FIBERS. The plant had been expanded a decade earlier when Azko bought it and a number of other facilities. That had been when Azko had moved the last of its operations out of the Low Countries before Ferdinand's final push to the English Channel.

Sometimes I bought sweaters and heavy work shirts at the factory store, but not often, since their woolens generally lasted forever.

"It's Sunday, and even the industrious Dutch like time off."

We passed the road that led to the Wiler River covered bridge and beyond to Grolle Mountain and one or two other smaller skiing slopes. The Covered Bridge Restaurant was out that road, as well. Llysette smiled.

"Stop smiling," I commanded sternly.

She smiled more broadly, and I smiled back. What else could I do? Our second dinner, I had actually run out of fuel coming back from the restaurant—and who could I tell that I hadn't even planned it?

North of Vanderbraak Centre, Route Five generally follows the River Wijk, at least until you get near the top of the notch. The wind rose as we climbed northward, and heavy gusts rocked the Stanley when I pulled off the main road.

The parking lot for the state park that holds the Devil's Cauldron was nearly empty, and the wind blew down from the notch, past the craggy Old Dutchman jutting from the mountain, picking up force as it swept southward. Had I worn a hat, it would have blown halfway to Asten or Haartsford.

Llysette tightened her scarf after she stepped out of the Stanley and onto the blacktop.

"The wind, it is energetic today."

That was one way of putting it.

We walked past a battered Ford petrol car—there weren't many around—and then past a Reo and a Williams and a long six-wheeled Packard limousine with registration plates from New Ostend. It even had the dark-tinted windows that made me think of the high-tech trupps of Asten.

The damp clay path, lined with matched and stripped logs, wound through the nearly bare birches and maples and the pines along the high side of the stream. A jay became a flash of blue, and even the stiff and cold breeze couldn't quite dispel the odor of damp leaves.

The river twisted over a flat bed of rock before it turned and shot at an angle into the Devil's Cauldron itself, a circular hollow in the rock that extended nearly twenty feet beneath the surface of the swirling and foaming water. In spring, the Cauldron literally spewed water in all directions.

We stopped at the vacant overlook.

"They say that the Pemigewasset Indians called this the cauldron of the seasons, where the spring waters washed away the ice and dank water of the old season, mixing the old and the new."

"That story, Johan, it sounds as though you just made it up."

"Perhaps I did. Don't we all make up history to suit the present?"

"You are cynical this afternoon." Another gust of cold air blew past us, and she shivered, even in the heavy quilted coat.

"Just this afternoon?" I tried not to shiver. I should have brought the heavy tweed overcoat that would have stopped a midwinter blitzwehr.

"Johan, cynical you are not. That is why the government, it was hard on you."

"You are kinder than you know."

"Mais non, je crois." She smiled crookedly, and added,

"This, it is fascinating, but it is *seulement* a river, and I am cold."

"It is cold," I admitted, taking her arm.

Even just getting out of the wind and into the Stanley warmed me enough, but Llysette kept shivering until the heater really got going and I was sweating. By then we were passing the turnoff for Grolle Mountain.

"Do you want to stop for some fresh cider?"

"If you wish."

I decided against stopping.

Whitecaps actually dotted the surface of the River Wijk when we crossed the bridge and headed up the bluff road toward Deacon's Lane. The trees were bending in the wind when the Stanley rolled to a stop outside the house.

I brought in her case and took it upstairs. The house was cold, despite the closed and double-glazed windows, and a trace damp. Llysette stepped inside, but did not take off her heavy coat.

Since I had laid the fire, with shavings and paper, in the solid Ostwerk Castings stove that dominated one wall of the main parlor, it took only a moment and a single match to start it up.

I offered Llysette the tartan blanket in place of her coat, which she surrendered reluctantly. She immediately huddled under the blanket.

"In a bit, the chill will begin to lift."

"I'm sorry, Johan." Her teeth chattered.

"Don't be sorry. It's damp out there. It's a bit damp in here. Coffee or chocolate?"

"Chocolate, I think." She continued to shiver under the wool blanket when I went into the kitchen and lit off the stove, bottled gas, which is good in the winter, since the new oil furnace doesn't work without electric power.

While the milk and chocolate were heating, I turned on the oven and took the pork loin from the refrigerator. I managed to get it sliced, stuffed, rolled, and in the oven by the time the chocolate was ready.

Llysette took the chocolate, and I set a tray with biscuits on the hearth by her feet.

"Biscuit?"

"Yes, thank you."

I ate two biscuits to her every one and was back in the kitchen for refills before I finished half my chocolate. That might have been because I hadn't bothered to eat since breakfast.

"Another biscuit?"

Llysette took two.

"No lunch, either?"

"No. I was sleeping."

I let that lie, and had another biscuit and took another sip from my mug, finally feeling warm from the chocolate and the growing heat from the woodstove.

"What about tomorrow?"

"A working lunch with Doktor Geoffries I must have, and the afternoon session with the choir, and we begin the opera rehearsals in the evening, until ten. And I must complete the schedules for Herr Wustman. Arranging the students and their accompanists, it is difficult. Most nights this week, except Thursday, I am busy. And you?"

"Thursday, I am going to Columbia once more. I was asked to a presidential dinner." I laughed. "A gesture for old times' sake, I guess."

She lowered the mug from her lips. "Do you want to attend this dinner?"

"I have very mixed feelings, but I think I should."

"Pourquoi?"

"For the consulting—it helps to maintain a profile in high circles within government. And this sort of thing allows me to do it without living anywhere near the Federal District. Besides, I imagine that it will give Dean Er Recchus something else to boast about."

"That woman . . ." Llysette snorted, then bit into a biscuit.

"I take it that you are not enamored of our dean."

"Would I consider developing a new course? A course in singing for instrumentalists and actors," she asked.

"Instrumentalists and actors?"

"Gregor, he wanted a course in singing for actors. That I understand. But she, she felt that the instrumentalists, especially those of the strings, should also be included."

I shook my head.

"That also, I understand. But now, she wants to share my next recital. She had Dr. Geoffries suggest that I ask the dean to play for me. She sounds like . . . like a dance fiddler."

Clank. Her cup almost bounced off the stone hearth, so hard had she set it down.

"She does scheme a lot."

Llysette glared at me. "Like saying the hog is sometimes not so neat, that is."

While I wasn't sure of the comparison—or the metaphor—I got the idea.

"What does Doktor Geoffries think?"

Llysette squared her shoulders, letting the blanket slip away. "He says that if there is any way to make the dean happy, it would be better. Better for him, I think."

I nodded. "I wonder why they all bow and scrape."

"Because they are men."

"You're saying I'm not?" I raised an eyebrow.

"Different you are."

I decided not to pursue that line of inquiry further. "Excuse me. I need to finish working on dinner."

"With you I will come." So she dragged the blanket into the kitchen and sat at the table while I worked.

I sliced some of the fresh apples and set them aside in a pan to make fried apples—better than applesauce any day, and chunky, not pureed baby food. Then I dragged out the butter, some cinnamon and nutmeg, and the raw sugar.

"You cook well."

"Experience helps." So did growing up in a household without sisters and a mother who insisted that no man should be slave to helplessness and his stomach. That had worked fine for food, but not so well in other areas.

Beans from the lower garden, via the root cellar, with almonds from McArdles', were the vegetable, and I'd mixed batter for some drop biscuits.

"Cooking I did little of," she admitted.

"I know."

"Johan!"

I grinned. "I'm not primarily interested in your cooking."

"Men! No better are you than . . . than all the others."

"In some things, I'm better." I tried a leer, but she wasn't looking. So I dug a pale cream linen cloth from the butler's pantry, not that we'd ever had butlers, and spread it on the dining room table. I even used the bayberry candles and silver instead of stainless.

Then I dropped the biscuits into the oven, and fried up the apples. After the biscuits came out, and the apples went into the covered bone china dish, I dashed back down to the cellar for a bottle of Sebastopol. Somehow I got all the food on the table warm, and both wine glasses filled.

"In France, you would have been a chef, a great chef," Llysette said after several bites and half of her wine.

"Mais non, point moi," I protested in bad French.

"If you did not speak, that is."

"We all might be in less trouble if we did not speak, I sometimes think."

"But life, it would be dull."

"Dullness can be a virtue," I reflected. Especially compared to the alternatives.

"At times." She lifted her glass and drained the rest of the Sebastopol. "We have seen such times."

I refilled her glass, and tried the apples, just crunchy enough to give my teeth some resistance, soft enough to eat easily, and cinnamon-tart-tangy enough to offset the richness of the stuffed pork. "Some biscuits? The honey is in the small pitcher there."

"Thank you, Johan. Perhaps it is as well we do not eat together all the time. I could get fat."

"I am."

"Non. Solid you are, with all that running and exercise." She took another healthy swallow.

"I need to get more exercise."

"Of what kind?" She winked slowly at me.

"You are terrible."

"Non—it is the wine. With the wine, I can say what I feel. Without, it is hard. The feelings, they hide."

I decided against another slice of the pork, but did take some of the apples. "Some more apples?"

"Just a few."

There wasn't any dessert, not with the fried apples and the need for both of us to watch waistlines, but we had tea, taken in front of the restoked woodstove, after I had washed and Llysette had dried the dishes.

Outside, the wind continued to whistle.

"Here, one can almost forget the world."

I glanced toward the blank videolink screen. "So long as one ignores the news."

"Cynical you still pretend to be."

"Cynical I will always be, I fear." I sipped from the mug, letting the steam and scent circle my face, breathing the steam.

"Non. You are not cynical. You see the world as it is."

"Perhaps. I try, but what we are colors what we see. Truth is in the eye of the beholder." I laughed, more harshly than I meant. "That's why I'm skeptical of those who say they have found the truth."

Llysette nodded. "They are terrible." She meant the word in its original meaning.

"I think I'd rather not dwell on truth tonight. How about beauty?"

Llysette yawned, but spoiled it with a grin.

I grinned back. "You're ready for some sleep?"

"I did not mention sleep . . ."

"Fine. You head upstairs, and I'll dump these in the kitchen." I picked up the mugs.

She winked again.

By the time I took care of the dishes, damped the woodstove, turned off the lights, and got to my bedroom, her clothes were laid on the settee, and she was under the sheet and quilt.

"The sheets, they are cold."

"I'll see what I can do about that."

She was right. The sheets were cold, even for me, but the contrast between their coolness and the silk of her skin made me want to wrap myself around her. I didn't, instead just held her and enjoyed the moment. There were too many moments in the past I hadn't enjoyed, and there might not be that many in the future. Involuntarily, I shivered.

"What do you think? Are you angry with me?"

"Heavens, no. I was just thinking."

A gust of wind, moaning past the eaves, punctuated my words.

"Sometimes, too much we think."

"It's the kind of world we live in. How can you not think when there are murders, and you have to wonder why the Spazi show up in a university town?"

"You worry about the Spazi?"

"Yes," I admitted.

"Are the Spazi like Ferdinand's NeoCorps, Johan, dragging innocents from their beds?"

"All security police have their problems," I reflected. "Even those with the best intentions."

"Do you think the Spazi have good intentions?" She curled upside my arms and shivered, warm as her bare skin felt against me.

"They did once. Now, I am not so certain."

"All of them are beasts."

"At times," I agreed. "It is a hard job, and it makes hard people."

"Why do you say that?" Her lips turned toward mine, and I kissed them, gently, and for a long time. "Tell me," she prompted.

I shifted my weight so that her body did not cut off all the circulation in my arm, and held her tightly, letting that satin skin warm me, taking in the fragrant scent of Llysette and perfume. Finally I rolled back, letting my head rest on the pillow, my eyes on the white plaster of the ceiling, not wanting to look into her eyes, not then. "The world gets harder every year, and people lie more. Ferdinand claimed he would not invade France, and he did. Now he says he will not turn the Spanish protectorate into part of the Empire, but how good is that promise? Marshall deGaulle claimed that New France would not annex Belize, or Honduras, but they did. Here in our country, take Miranda. All the people who were around claim they were innocent and saw nothing. But she is dead. To find the answer, the watch or the Spazi must distrust everyone. I find that cold and hard . . . and perhaps necessary."

Llysette shivered in my arms, and I pulled the quilt over her bare shoulders. In time, she turned to me.

Later, even after she slept in my arms, I held her tightly, wondering how I could protect her when I doubted I could protect myself.

11

On Monday morning, I made it through my run and exercises, and fixed both of us breakfast by seven—not bad considering that we hadn't gone to sleep all that early. While I ran, Llysette slept, or tried to. She still had the quilt pulled around her ears even after I had breakfast on the small table and the aroma of coffee filling the kitchen.

"Young woman," I called up the stairs. "Your coffee is ready. So are your fruit, toast, and poached eggs."

I thought I heard a muffled groan, and I called again. "Time to rise and shine, young lady."

"Young I am not, not this morning, but coffee will I have."

She clumped down the stairs, in slippers, and slouched into the chair on the other side of the small breakfast table, sipping the coffee and ignoring the food. I had hot chocolate, bad for my waistline, but I felt virtuous after my heavy exercise.

"What are you thinking?"

"Many things. The students, now they are getting sick, and they cough in my face. I tell them to get well and not bring their illnesses to me, but still they do. John Wustman, the pianist-coach, he will be here next week for master classes." She shrugged tiredly. "Many students do not know their music, and now come the midterms, and after that, the opera. Then I must start the rehearsals for the Christmas gala, and that music they have never opened." After sipping more coffee, she speared an orange slice, from probably one of the last oranges we would see for a while.

"They never think ahead."

"Think . . . what is that?" She dipped her toast into the half-runny eggs.

I poured more coffee into her mug, and she smiled. "Thank you, Johan. It is nice not to fix the breakfast."

I didn't comment on the fact that I doubted she had breakfast if I didn't fix it.

After we finished, Llysette took a shower while I scraped and washed the dishes. Then I raced upstairs and hopped into the shower while she struggled with her makeup.

I dropped Llysette by her house just before eight and headed back to town and Samaha's for my paper. There was a space right outside Louie's emporium, and I dashed in.

After nodding to Louie, I pulled out my *Asten Post-Courier* and left a dime, taking a quick glance at the headlines before even leaving Samaha's. The Derkin box was empty; another day had passed without my learning who Mr. Derkin was.

The newspaper headline was bland enough: "NO COMPROMISE BETWEEN DIRIGIBLES AND JETS." Since I could guess the content of the story, I folded the paper under my arm and walked through the blustery wind back to the Stanley.

Llysette's steamer was not yet in the faculty car park, I noted as I parked the Stanley in a vacant space closest to the Music and Theatre building. With my folder in hand, I trudged to my office. Although the main office was open and Gilda's coat was on the rack, I did not see her. There was a message from David, indicating that Tuesday's departmental meeting would start at a quarter to four instead of four o'clock sharp.

I took it and made my way upstairs to my office. There I briefly checked the paper.

There was almost nothing new in the *Asten Post-Courier,* not about Babbage fires or political gambits, except for an editorial warning Speaker Hartpence to beware of sacrificing the long-held Columbian ideal of free trade to short-term political goals. With the usual Dutch diplomacy, it did not actually accuse the Speaker of political idiocy.

Then I looked over the master class schedule. Gregor Martin appeared to be free until ten. I picked up my leather folder and headed back out. Gilda waved, and I waved back.

Gertrude and Hector were mulching the flower beds beside the brick walk. As usual, Gertrude wore the unfailing smile and Hector the somber mien, but their hands were quick, and they worked unhesitatingly, taking care to ensure that the wind did not scatter the bark chips onto the bricks of the walk.

"Good day," I said as I passed.

"Good day, sir," chirped Gertrude, and I wondered what personality disorder had rendered her a de-ghosted zombie.

Gregor Martin's office was in the side of the building away from the music wing, and probably only the same size as my office, for all that he was head of an entire area and I was only a subprofessor. His door was open, and he was pacing beside his desk as I rapped on the door frame.

"Yes."

"Johan Eschbach, Natural Resources. We met after several productions last year. I'm also a friend of Llysette's." I extended my hand.

He ignored it. "What do you need, Johan?"

"Well, Gregor, I need to know whether a student absolutely has to take Introduction to Theatre before taking the Two-B course."

"It's a prerequisite."

"Even for an arts school graduate?"

Surprisingly, Martin shrugged. "You know, I really don't care. Most of them know nothing about theatre, not in the performing sense. You have a student who wants to try, I don't care. I'm tired of protecting them from themselves."

"Is this a bad time?" I took the chair by the desk, and he actually sat down. If Miranda Miller had been right, and all the new faculty had secrets too heavy to bear, what secret weighed down Gregor Martin?

"No worse than any other." He picked up a black pencil and twisted it in his fingers.

"You came here from the Auraria Performing Arts School. I imagine it was a shock."

"You imagine?"

"I came from the capital, good old Columbia itself, and found that most of the students knew very little about politics, and cared less. Why would it be any different in the theatre? Vanderbraak Centre isn't exactly the great white way of New Amsterdam or the musical Valhalla of Philadelphia."

"You're right. But it's worse in theatre. They all have this . . . this Dutch stolidity." He set down the pencil and waved his hands, almost disconnectedly. "They can't even imagine being something other than what they are. Theatre is the art of creating a different reality. How can you create a different reality when you can't even imagine its possibility?"

"What is, is. Is that it?"

"More like what isn't, isn't—but it has to be for good theatre."

"What about a sense of wonder? Take ghosts," I offered. "We see a ghost, and whether we like it or not, it exists. You can't touch it, exactly, and you can't tell exactly when it will appear. Doesn't it make you wonder?" I shrugged. "But you talk about . . . what if there were a world where there were no ghosts? How would that change things? I asked that in a class. No one knew. They hadn't even thought about it."

"That's it. They don't even think about it. How could you envision a *Hamlet* without the impetus of his father's ghost?"

"That could be rather discouraging. What do they do when they see Professor Miller's ghost? Just look and plod on?"

He nodded. "I asked one of them to really look at her ghost before it disappeared. He's cast in *Hamlet* next term. You know what he said?"

"I'm afraid to guess."

" 'It's just a ghost.' " Martin slammed his hand on the desk. "It's just a ghost!"

"Sad about Miranda," I mused. "Now she's just another ghost."

"I don't know that the woman was ever alive—always walking around with that self-pitying air, as though the world were about to crush her."

"Perhaps it was," I said. "She was born to money, widowed young, and forced to raise and educate two children."

"Lots of people do that, and they don't carry the weight of the world around so that everyone can see."

"But was that enough to make someone want to kill her?"

"No. I doubt that." Martin leaned forward across the desk. "What did you do in government, Johan?"

"Before they ran me out, I was in charge of environmental matters. Why?"

"Because you've scarcely said 'good day' to me before now."

"I didn't have a student who had questions, and your reputation is not exactly as the most approachable—"

"Ha! Well, that's true. So why are you worried about who killed Miranda?"

"I'm attached to Llysette, and she's single and attractive, and no one knows who killed Miranda or why. Do you blame me?"

"Do you suspect me?"

"No," I answered truthfully. "But you're probably pretty observant, and you might have seen something."

"You don't trust the watch?"

"It's not a question of trust. They may even have a suspect, but they won't arrest whoever it might be unless there's evidence. The good Dutch character, you know. Without evidence, no arrest." I laughed. "Of course, once there's any evidence at all, it's rather hard to change their minds. For now, though, legalities don't protect Llysette."

"You have a point there. Not a very good one, but a point." He frowned. "You can believe me or not. I was in the lighting booth, and I didn't see anyone, except for the students. Martin Winston was one, and the other was Gisela Bars. They were with me the whole time. And I don't know why anyone would even bother with Miranda. I really don't. She tried to flirt with you, and with Branston-Hay, and with Henry Hite, but you never had eyes for anyone except Llysette, and they love and honor their wives, at least so far as I know. Me? She never looked in my direction, thank heavens. With Amy, that was probably a good thing."

"Amy is your wife?"

He nodded. "She got a job as an electronics technician with the state watch in Borkum."

"Yes." I waited.

"That's it. You know what I know. That's also what I told the watch." He stretched and stood. "Have any ideas about getting acting students to think about creating reality?"

I stood, following his lead. "Could you play-act? Make one of them a ghost, and insist that the others treat him or her like a real ghost? And start knocking points off their grades for every unrealistic action they take?"

"You believe that would work?"

"I don't know, but a lot of them live only for grades. Make it real through the use of grades—sometimes that works."

"Obviously a graduate of the school of practical politics."

"Theory often doesn't work, I've found. And Dutch students do respond to practical numbers."

He actually grinned, if only for a moment, then bowed.

I found my way back to my office, noting that the two zombies had finished mulching the flower beds along the one walkway and were working on those flanking the stairs up to the Physical Sciences building. Gilda waved as I passed her office and climbed the stairs.

When I got back to the Natural Resources building, David

was nowhere around, as was so often the case, and Gilda was juggling calls on the wireset console.

"Greetings, Johan. Why so glum?" asked young Grimaldi from the door of his office. His gray chalk-stripe suit and gray and yellow cravat marked either his European heritage or natural flamboyance. I wasn't sure which.

"I just had a meeting with Gregor Martin. He actually smiled once."

"He does sometimes. He's actually a pretty good director, but I'd be grim if I had to work with our students in theatre, too. It's bad enough in geography and natural resources. One of them wrote that a monsoon was a class of turbojet bomber in the Austro-Hungarian Luftwehr."

"He's probably right."

"But in geography class?" Grimaldi laughed. "See you later. Did you get David's note?"

"Which one?"

He laughed again, and went back into his office, while I unlocked my door and stepped inside, stepping on a paper that had been slipped under the door. I picked it up—Clarice Reynolds was the named typed on the cover sheet—and shook my head. Despite written instructions on the syllabus directing students to leave papers in my box in the department office, some never got the word.

I set the folder on the corner of the small desk and sat down. After looking blankly out the window for a long time, I finally picked up the handset and dialed, listening to the whirs and clicks until a hard feminine voice answered, "Minister vanBecton's office."

"Yes. This is Doktor Johan Eschbach. I have discovered that I will be in Columbia City on Thursday, and I thought I might get together with Minister vanBecton sometime in the late afternoon."

"Just a moment, please, Doktor."

I found the tip of my fountain pen straying toward my mouth, but I managed to stop before I put more tooth marks on the case. Outside, the clouds were thickening, but it was still probably too warm for snow.

"Johan, what took you so long? You got your invitation on Friday." Again, vanBecton's voice was almost boomingly cheerful.

"On Friday, you may recall, I was in Columbia. I did not actually receive the invitation until Saturday, and I didn't think you wanted to be bothered over the weekend."

"I'm in a bit of a rush here, but what do you say to stopping in around four o'clock? That will give you plenty of time to get dressed for the reception. Where are you staying?"

"Probably with friends, but that remains to be seen."

"Many things do, but I look forward to seeing you on Thursday." A click, and he was gone.

I looked up another number in my address book and dialed.

"Elsneher and Fribourg."

"Johan Eschbach for Eric, please."

"Just a moment."

The clouds outside were definitely getting blacker.

"Johan—is it really you?"

"Who else? I called because I'll be in town on Thursday. They invited the old hack to a presidential dinner."

"You're more than welcome to stay with us. Judith would like that. So would I. Even if you have to attend the dinner, at least we can have breakfast together on Friday. Can't we?"

"I'd like that. How is Judith?"

"She's fine." He coughed. "I've got a client on the wire . . ."

"I understand. Can I stop by the house about five, before the dinner?"

"Sure. I'll tell Judith. See you then." And he clicked off.

I watched the clouds for a moment, then, before my eleven o'clock, collected the copies of the short test I planned to spring on my students, leafed through my notes, and skimmed the latest copy of the *Journal of Columbian*

Politics. I tried not to hold my nose at the article entitled "Rethinking the Role of the Politician's Personal Life."

At ten before eleven, squaring my shoulders, I collected the greenbooks and the thirty copies of the test and marched over to Smythe Hall to do battle over environmental economics.

Once the class had filed in, I pulled the greenbooks from under the desk.

"Unnnnghhh . . ." That was a collective sigh.

I smiled brightly and handed out the greenbooks first, followed by the single sheet of the test. "You can answer one question or the other with a short essay. You have twenty minutes. Just answer one question," I repeated with a caution created by past experience.

"But, Doktor, this test was not announced."

"If you check the syllabus, you will note that it states that tests may be given in any class."

"Unnnghhhh . . ."

I had the feeling, from the groans, from the distracted looks on students' faces during the lecture following the test, and from leafing through a few of the greenbooks when I returned to my office, that not a few had neither read nor considered the assignment.

My two o'clock wasn't much better, not when half the class failed to understand the distinction between pathways of contamination and environmental media.

After my two o'clock, rather than immediately deal with either exams or the papers I had collected in my last class, I walked down to the post centre. I could have gone at lunchtime, since Llysette had been invited to a working lunch by Doktor Geoffries to discuss the student production schedule for the spring, but instead I'd spent the time trying to scan through some of the journal articles—not that I would ever catch up. Not if I wanted to remain sane.

Constable Gerhardt was by the empty bandbox in the square, chatting with the same young watch officer who seemed to turn up regularly when I was around, thanks, I suspected, to Minister vanBecton. I nodded to them both, rather than tipping the hat I wasn't wearing, since it still wasn't cold enough to wear one.

The chill wind had been promising snow for more than a week, but we had gotten neither cold rain, sleet, nor snow—just continuing cold wind—although the thick clouds to the northwest looked more than usually threatening. Despite the blustery weather and the few leaves hanging on the trees, the grass in the square was raked nearly spotlessly clean; even the hedges had been picked clean, as usual.

The lobby of the post centre was almost deserted, with only a gray-haired, stocky woman standing at the window. I unlocked and opened the postbox. Besides the monthly electric bill from NBEI and the wireline bill from New Bruges Telewire, there were two legal-size envelopes. The brown one had no return address. The other had the letterhead of International Import Services, PLC. Both were postmarked "Federal District."

I tucked all four into my black leather case, which contained, generally, my lectures and materials for the day.

"Ye find anything interesting?" asked Maurice.

"You always ask, and you always see it first." I grinned at the post handler. He grinned back, as always.

I walked quickly back to my office, my breath steaming in the afternoon air. I waved to Gilda as I passed the front office.

"Doktor Eschbach, Doktor Doniger was looking for you."

"Is he in his office?"

"For a little while, I think." She looked over her shoulder quickly, as if to confirm her statement. Her shoulders were stiff.

I knocked on the frame of the half-open door. "You were looking for me?"

"Yes, Johan. Please come in."

I shut the door behind me and looked around the paper-piled office. David believed in horizontal filing. Although he didn't invite me, I sat down in the single chair anyway.

Before he could get started, I said, "I've been invited to a Presidential Palace dinner on Thursday. So I'll have to make up Thursday's and Friday's classes one way or another."

"You always do, Johan, and I will tell the dean. She will be pleased that our faculty continues to travel in such exalted circles." He smiled.

I smiled and waited. Then I added, "Gilda said you were looking for me."

"Johan, I read your commentary in the last *Journal of Columbian Politics.* Don't you think it was a trifle . . . unfounded?" He leaned back in his creaky swivel and puffed on the long meerschaum, filling the office with intermittent blasts of air pollution, the kind I'd once been charged with reducing when it occurred at industrial sites.

"Commentaries are by nature unfounded. Of course, I could have made it three times as long and proved it with examples."

"Do you honestly believe that disposable glass is better than recycling metals? You even cited a recycling rate of almost eighty percent in major Columbian cities."

"Obviously what I wrote was not so clear as I thought." I coughed before I continued, glad that I had not followed my father's pipe-smoking habits. "My point was not that either was environmentally better. You can make a case for either. I was pointing out that the Reformed Tories used the press and half-facts to build a case against the Liberals that had no factual support. In short, that despite all the environmental rhetoric it was politics as usual. Just like the ghost business is more politics than science."

"The ghost business? That sad affair with Miranda Miller? Surely you weren't mixed up with that, were you?"

"Only to the degree that one gets mixed up when a murder occurs before a friend's recital. That wasn't what I was referring to, however. I meant all these bombings and fires in schools across the country, all in the Babbage centers, and all protesting supposed ghosting research."

David looked totally blank. "What does this have to do with the journal article?"

"They're both political. You can make a case for or against disposable glass; you can make a case for or against ghosting research. Does the voting public really pay any attention to the facts? It's a question of which side most successfully appeals to existing prejudices."

"Johan, I'm still troubled about the glass business."

"Most people don't realize it, David, but glass is structurally a liquid. A very stiff liquid, to be sure, but a liquid. It is also virtually inert, and comprised mainly of silicon and various oxides. Provided lead isn't used, as in crystal, you can bury it or dump it and the only harm it can do you is cut you. Metals aren't nearly as beneficial to the environment, and even with recycling, some are lost to the environment. So, claiming that recycled metals are more beneficial than discarded glass is misleading. Glass could certainly be recycled, and if it weren't so cheap, that could have happened long ago. It may still happen."

"Dean Er Recchus asked me if I thought that the commentary would hurt the fund-raising effort."

"Not if it's handled right. Just pretend you never saw it. Pretend that you have so many people writing in so many publications that you can't keep track, and no one will think a thing. Make an issue of it, and I'm sure you both can find a way to hurt fund-raising."

"Johan, I really wish you were not so . . . cynical."

"Realistic, David. Realistic. Besides, if the dean gives you too much trouble, point out that no one made an issue of her rather close friendship with Marinus Voorster."

"I couldn't do that."

I stood up. "Then why are you bothering me about an obscure commentary in a journal no one outside academia even reads?"

"Johan, I never meant to—"

"Good. I need to get ready for my two o'clock." I left, nodding at Gilda with a polite smile that was probably transparent. While I had some indication of David's lack of involvement with the whole ghost business, his toadying to Dean Er Recchus was inexcusable. He had tenure. Meddling much with his budget would have upset the university system budget committee. Just because he was worried that anything might upset the dean, as if he even understood what real pressures were—I shook my head at the thought as I opened my office door. And neither had even noticed the commentary until more than a month after it had been published. David was looking for an excuse, more than likely, but why? Because I didn't put up with his academic small-mindedness?

Back in my office, after I put down my folder, I opened the International Import Services envelope first. It contained an invoice and a cheque. The cheque was for five hundred dollars; the invoice merely stated, "Consulting Services." I didn't recognize the name on the signature line—Susan something or other—but it was undoubtedly genuine. International Imports was a real firm, trading mainly in woolens, electronics, and information. It had a retinue of consultants worldwide, and probably half of them were actually export consultants. I'd always fallen in the other category. Still, five hundred dollars was equivalent to nearly a month's pay as a professor, and I took a deep breath.

I studied the second envelope before opening it. Although I couldn't be absolutely sure, the slightly more flexible feel of the paper around the flap indicated a high probability that it had been steamed open. If I had looked, I suspected that I would have found that most of the envelopes with clippings had been similarly treated, at least recently. VanBecton's people had been tracking me and knew my comings and goings. Presumably they had read my post, including the clippings, untraceably posted in the Federal District, probably at the main post center. The clipping itself was short.

ST. LOUIS (RPI)—A series of explosions ripped through the Aster Memorial Electronic Sciences Center at the University of Missouri at St. Louis shortly after midnight this morning. The ensuing fire gutted the building. Although no fatalities were reported, more than a dozen firemen were injured in the blaze that turned the skyline of St. Louis into a second dawn.

According to early reports, the explosions began in the Babbage wing of the center. Only last week, the chancellor of the University of Missouri system had defended UMSL's policy of accepting Defense Ministry grants for psychic research.

Governor Danforth denounced the action as that of "ill-informed zealots." Speaking for the Alliance for World Peace, Northrop Winsted added the Alliance's condemnation of violence. Similar statements were also issued by the Midwest Diocese of the Roman Catholic Church and the Missouri Synod of the Anglican-Baptists.

At the slapping of rain droplets on my second-floor windows, I glanced out to the north, but the rain was falling so heavily I could barely see Smythe Hall across the green.

I slipped the clipping and the cheque into my folder, and, with a sigh, pulled out the stack of short papers I had collected from Environmental Economics 2B. Most of the students thought they understood economics and the environment. I did, too, until I'd actually had to deal with both.

I'd graded perhaps ten of the twenty-six papers by quarter to five, and was still chuckling over one line: "Money should be no object nor price no impediment to the continuation of our priceless environment . . ." While I understood the underlying sentiment, the writer—one Melissa Abottson—had inadvertently illustrated the fuzzy thinking of her generation. What she meant was that a pristine environment was worth a great deal, but that wasn't what she had written. Priceless meant without a price, and if the environment were priceless then money was irrelevant—which certainly wasn't what she meant. Likewise, the environment means the external conditions and objects surrounding us, or the world, and in the broadest sense, the environment, in some form or another, will continue, whether we do or not.

The problem with environmental economics is not one of willingness, but one of capability. No society has infinite resources, and certainly not a Columbia faced with an aggressive New France to the south, a blackmailing Quebec to the north, Ferdinand in Europe, and the twin terrors in Asia.

With a last head shake at the naiveté of the young, and at the recollection that I, too, had been equally naive, I left the stack on my desk, pulled on my waterproof, and took the umbrella from the corner. The main office was empty, and all the other doors were closed when I stepped out into the continuing light rain. My breath puffed white, and the cold felt welcome after the stuffiness of the building.

Umbrella in hand, I walked past the brick-stepped top landing of the long stairs down to the lower campus and then around the Music and Theatre building, stepping carefully to avoid the puddles and taking my time as I passed the closed piano studio. Even through the rain I could see that the Babbage console that had been in Miranda's studio was gone.

I stepped into the main office of the Music and Theatre Department. "Martha, have you seen Llysette?"

"No. Oh, wasn't she taking some students to the state auditions in Orono?"

I put a hand to my forehead. "I forgot." I offered a sheepish grin. "She told me, and I forgot."

Martha grinned back at me. "It can happen to anyone."

"How's Dierk taking the ghosting business?"

"It's better now." Martha frowned. "As a matter of fact, no one's seen Miranda's ghost for several days now."

"I saw Dr. Branston-Hay removing his equipment. Was he studying the ghost?"

Martha looked around, then lowered her voice. "He asked us not to mention it. People get very sensitive about those sorts of things, even here."

"I understand." I nodded. "Some of the papers had stories about bombings at other universities' Babbage centers."

"Really?"

"Yes. There was one the other day in St. Louis."

"How terrible."

"You can see why Dr. Branston-Hay wants to be very careful. He probably only wanted a few people to know."

"Just Dierk and me, and the watch, of course. Their video camera is still there."

"I won't say a word—not even to Llysette."

"Thank you, Dr. Eschbach."

Instead of heading home, I went back to my office and locked the door. I pulled down the blinds and took out the thick old hard-sided briefcase, filled with a melange of older publications. The small package of tools and the special wedge came out of the false bottom easily, and I slid the flap shut and pocketed the small, soft-leather case. After replacing the publications, I set the open briefcase on the corner of the desk. I took a Babbage disk in its case from the shelf and slipped it into my pocket. It barely fit. After that I sat down and graded another dozen papers in the time until it began to get dark.

Contrary to popular opinion, nighttime is not the best time for marginally savory work. Early dinnertime is, especially on a university campus where most students are of thrifty Dutch stock and actually eat in the cafeteria.

I dialed Branston-Hay's office number, but there was no response. So I picked up the special wedge and put it in my right pants pocket. Then I picked up my black leather case, half-filled with the day's class notes, and stepped out into the hall. Once outside, I locked the door to the department, the former residence of some obscure poet—Frost, I think was the name—and headed across the green to the west.

The main door to the Physical Sciences building was unlocked, as a number of laboratory courses ran late. There were always several early evening classes, but none, according to the schedule, involving Branston-Hay or the Babbage laboratories.

I walked to the main Babbage room and glanced inside.

Perhaps half the consoles were occupied, mainly for word processing by students worried about various midterm projects, I guessed, although I did see one student struggling with some sort of flow chart.

The smaller laboratory, the one Branston-Hay used for research, was at the end of the corridor. I knocked, for the sake of appearances, and was surprised when a round-faced man with cold blue eyes opened the door.

"Yes?"

"I was looking for Gerald."

"He's not here at the moment. Could you check back later, or better yet, in the morning?"

"I'll catch him in the morning. Thank you," I said as I turned without even hesitating, knowing that I dared not.

Although the man I had never seen before had kept his considerable bulk between me and the laboratory, I caught a glimpse of it, enough to realize that I'd definitely missed more than a bet. The windows were painted black, and at least a dozen technicians were still working. There was some sort of strange apparatus that looked like a silver helmet, the kind they use to dry women's hair. Everyone, even the man at the door, wore what looked like a metal hair net.

The doorkeeper wasn't a Babbage type. The slightly thicker cut of his coat, and what it concealed, the fact that the other technicians wore no coats, and the guard's flat blue eyes told me he was more at home in vanBecton's office than in Gerald's laboratory.

After I bowed and left, I made my way back toward the office section, around two corners. When I arrived at Branston-Hay's office, I knocked sharply on the door, but there was no answer, and the thin line between the tiled floor and the heavy door was dark.

After glancing puzzledly around, as if mystified that my appointment had not been kept, and seeing no one, I slipped the lock picks out of my jacket pocket.

As soon as I had the door open, I stepped inside and locked it. Then I tapped the wedge loosely between the bottom of the door frame and the floor. The adhesive rubber would jam if anyone tried to open the door. Simple, and effective. I also unlocked the window, but did not open it. I did lift it slightly to make sure that I could. I have gone out windows before, although I would rather not.

I tried to remind myself of the old adage that you should never try to find it all out at once. Removals you do once or not at all, but information gathering requires far more patience and repetition. That's one reason good espionage is far more difficult than murder.

The first step was activating the difference engine, not that dissimilar to my own recent model. After I turned on the machine and all the lights came on, and the pointer flipped into place on the screen, I typed in the initializing command, and smiled as the substructure menu appeared. Trying not to hurry, I scanned the directories until I found what I wanted, or, I should say, the absence of what I wanted.

If you attempt to hide something, you have to leave a keyhole, and that was what I needed. Branston-Hay hadn't been that subtle. He'd assumed that any datapick would need to unscramble the keys. I could have cared less. I just wanted to copy them.

Still, it took almost half an hour before the machine began to copy what I needed onto the data disk I had brought.

While it copied, I helped myself to his desk. As I had suspected, everything—or almost everything—was strictly related to his teaching, and the office was as clean as when I had visited earlier.

I did find a folder of clippings, which I began to read.

COLUMBIA (FNS) — After meeting with departing Ambassador Fujihara of Japan, President Armstrong today suggested that the Reformed Tories would find that their yet-to-be announced initiative on reducing the VAT on tobacco exports, while desirable from the perspective of Far Eastern relations, was more of a public relations effort than a real step toward solving the growing Asian trade imbalance. Speaker Hartpence had no comment . . .

CHICAGO (RPI)—In his speech opening the National Machine Tool Exposition in Chicago, President Armstrong gently chided the Reformed Tories for even considering expanding product liability tort claim protection. According to the president, "Speaker Hartpence would strangle Columbian business to remedy a nonexistent problem." Neither the Speaker nor his press aide were available for comment . . .

COLUMBIA (RPI)—Even while the general perception of President Armstrong has been that of a vigorous opponent of the Reformed Tories, slashing publicly at their every weakness, his private meetings with members of the House have been exceedingly different.

"It's almost as though the president were running for election to the House, and attempting to line up votes for Speaker," said former Commerce Minister Hiler.

Since President Armstrong's election last year, virtually every influential member of the House has been invited to an intimate and off-the-record dinner or luncheon at the Presidential Palace. While not all members have been willing to divulge the exact nature of the conversations, all indicate that the president was unusually attentive and nonpartisan, unlike in his public appearances, generally asking questions and listening . . .

MEMPHIS (SNS)—Today, in dedicating the Memphis Barge-Railway Terminus, President Armstrong denounced Speaker Hartpence's policies as shortsighted and bankrupt. The president claimed that the Speaker is secretly considering accepting Asian revisions to the Law of the Oceans Treaty which would effectively close both the Sea of Japan and the South China Sea to Columbian traders and provide Chung Kuo and Japan with effective trade advantages in Asia in return for similar concessions to England and Columbia in the Caribbean and the Mediterranean.

"Such concessions, if true,

would be ruinous," declared Cecil Rhodes, IV, chairman of the Columbian Maritime Association . . .

Speaker Hartpence angrily denied the president's charge, stating that he "has nothing to hide."

SEATTLE (NWNS)—In accepting the frigate *C.S. Ericson* for the Columbian Navy, President Armstrong proclaimed "the continuing need for a strong Columbian presence across the waters of the globe."

In a scarcely veiled criticism of Speaker Hartpence and Foreign Minister Gore, the president added, "Reducing the federal budget for ships such as this, or for the long-range electric submersibles such as the *Fulton,* is truly penny wise and pound foolish." He went on to suggest . . .

"Both Minister Gore and Defense Minister Holmbek later denied that the submersible procurement budget was to be reduced . . ."

I flipped through the rest of the clips, jotting down dates, pages, and newspapers for all twenty-odd stories. By the time I had copied the dates of the stories, the machine, faster than the human hand, had copied a far vaster volume of material. I folded my notes, slipped them into my folder, replaced the disk in its case and the case in my pocket, returned the difference engine to its previous inert state, then removed the wedge and stepped confidently into the empty hall. The only student I saw in the science building did not even bother to look up as he trudged toward the gentlemen's facilities at the corner of the first floor.

I nodded to two students I did not know on my way across the green and back to my office, where I replaced the wedge on the shelf, closed and replaced the old case in the closet, and turned off the lights. I kept the lock picks, uneasy as they made me, in my pocket. They almost looked like a set of hex wrenches or screwdrivers, but any watch officer would know instantly what they were.

Then again, if they stopped me, it would either be a

formality or lock picks would be the least of my problems. I picked up my folder and locked the office, leaving the uncorrected papers on my desk. For once, the students probably wouldn't get them back at the next class.

The wind blew, and more drizzle sleeted around me, almost like ice, as I walked to the steamer. By the time I was inside the Stanley, I wished I had worn a heavier coat.

The roads were beginning to ice up, and visibility was poor at best. I was glad for the four-wheel option when I reached the hill below the house. No matter what they say about four-wheel drive not helping on ice, it does.

After I garaged the Stanley and went into the house, I lit off a fire in the woodstove in the main parlor, even before I checked to see what Marie had fixed. After unloading my pockets onto the antique desk and setting the disk case by the difference engine, I climbed upstairs, where I hung up my jacket and pulled on a heavy Irish fisherman's sweater before descending to the kitchen.

The smell of steak pie told me before I even opened the warming oven, although it was probably drier than she had intended, but it still tasted wonderful. I ate it right from the casserole dish, washing it down with a cold Grolsch, both of which actions would have horrified my mother.

I did wash the dishes, though, before I headed into the study. Some Dutch habits die hard.

After I turned on the difference engine, and as it completed its powering up and systems checks, I pulled out the Babbage disk, wondering exactly what I had.

As I expected, the files were encrypted, but, if you know what you're doing, that's not a problem. Time-consuming, but not an insoluble problem. Why not? Because most nonalgorithmic systems used on a single machine have to have a finite and relatively easy key, and because, in most systems, you can go under the architecture and twiddle it. Of course, I made copies first.

The first interesting section shouldn't have been on Gerald's machine at all—his notes and speculations. Most Babbage types fall into two categories. There are those who know the machine so well that everything is custom Babbage language shorthand. I hate those, because it's all unique. Branston-Hay was the other kind, the kind who play with difference engines, who document everything and link it all together. It's as though they have to tell the Babbage engine how important they are—almost as bad as a politician's diaries.

You can figure out either kind, because the way it's structured gives it away in the first case, and the documentation in the second is certainly elaborate.

Still, it was well past midnight before I could break through, and that was as much luck as anything.

Some of the notes were especially chilling.

> . . . headset design . . . multipoint electrode sensors to enhance the ambient magnetic field . . . A-H design overstresses basal personality . . .
>
> . . . Heisler ignored possibility of disassociated field duplication . . . phased array of field sensors . . . duplication of field perturbations would emulate basal personality . . .
>
> . . . personality implantation . . . greater density perfusion at high field strength and minimal transfer rate . . .
>
> . . . Babbage electro-fluidics emulate field capture parameters . . .

That one made sense, given what I knew about ghosting. Instant death doesn't create ghosts. It's a stress-related, magnetic-field-enhanced personality transfer phenomenon, and Gerald had merely quantified the electronic and magnetic conditions.

The last entry in the notes was worse.

> Empirical proof of capture—MM case. Theoretically, the psychic magneto-net should work in most conditions,

since a new ghost is clearly the strongest . . . Practically the disassociator should also work . . . but the ethical problems preclude construction . . . Suspect it might not work unless the subject is in an agitated condition . . . No way to test at this point.

The rest of the files dealt with specifications. Two were actually schematics, and after reading the descriptions of the "basal field disassociator" and the "perturbation replicator" I realized I might need the lock picks again—if I weren't already too late—or a good Babbage assembly shop. The third file that looked interesting was called a personality storage file, and required what looked like a modified scanner, although it didn't look like any scanner I had ever seen.

There was also what looked to be an elaborate protocol of some sort attached to the personality storage file—again with explanations under such headings as "visual delineation file," "image structure," and "requirements for compression/decompression."

I thanked Minister vanBredakoff for the two years undercover as a Babbage programmer in the Brit's mercantile Babbage net. That and a skeptical nature helped.

Theoretically, neither the disassociator nor the replicator looked that hard to build. I began to sketch what I needed . . . and got colder and colder. Most of the components were almost off the shelf, although I'd have to check the specifications with Bruce as soon as I could. Then, almost as an afterthought, I sketched out the scanner I needed before I stumbled upstairs and into bed, leaving my clothes strewn across the settee under the window.

If Branston-Hay were doing what I thought, Miranda's murder was almost inconsequential—unless she had known.

I lay in the darkness, in my cold bed under crisp cold sheets, listening to the cold sleet. Even the faint remnant of Llysette's perfume somehow smelled cold.

12

Because I scarcely slept well, even as late as I had collapsed on Monday night, getting up early Tuesday was almost welcome. Or it would have been if not for the headache that had come with the morning. I treated that by skipping my exercise routine and having a cup of hot chocolate and a bigger breakfast than normal—toast with raspberry preserves, one of the last fresh pears from the tree, picked on Sunday before the ice storm, and two poached eggs. I knew I'd pay later with tighter trousers or more exercise.

A long hot shower helped, and I felt less like a ghost myself when I headed out to the car barn, carrying the empty box that had contained my difference engine. After gingerly stepping down the stone walk to avoid the icy spots, I crossed the bluestone to the barn, where, after opening the door, I put the box in the Stanley's front trunk and closed it.

I hadn't used firearms in years, and although I had a license, the last thing I wanted to do at the moment was to appear in the watch office to register to purchase one. If I used the ones I wasn't supposed to have, that could raise some rather confining issues. The government looks unkindly upon unregistered guns, especially those originating in government service—directly or indirectly.

Since any weapon would be better than none, particularly if I were considered unarmed, I thought about the professional slingshot I had used to keep the crows from my garden. I almost took it from the bracket in the barn and tucked it under the front seat of the Stanley. Then I had to laugh. A slingshot? If things got as bad as I thought they might, digging out what I wasn't supposed to have would be the least of my problems.

That thought bothered me, because I kept thinking that this minor problem or that illegality would be the least of my problems. That meant I had problems bigger than I really wanted to consider.

With all that, leather folder on the seat beside me, I was on the road south to Zuider before eight. I held my breath going down the hill on Deacon's Lane, but after that the roads were clear of the scattered ice.

Zuider sat on the southwest end of Lochmeer, the biggest lake in New Bruges, at least the biggest one totally inside the state. The Indians had called it Winnie-something-or-other, but the Dutch settlers opted for a variation on the familiar, and Lochmeer the lake became, and remained.

I turned south on Route Five, which followed the Wijk south for almost fifteen miles. Fifteen miles of stone-fenced walls, some enclosing winter-turned fields, some enclosing stands of sugar maples, others enclosing meadows for scattered sheep.

The stone walls reflected their heritage, each stone precisely placed, and replaced almost as soon as the frost heaved it out of position. Some were more than chest high, probably for the dairy herds that fed the New Bruges cheese industry.

It took me about twenty-five minutes to reach the spot where the Wijk winds west and Route Five swings east toward Lochmeer and Zuider. The well-trimmed apple orchards before I reached the three Loon Lakes reproached me. The trees made my hasty trimming look haphazard by comparison, and I felt there was yet another task awaiting me—sometime.

Most of Route Five had been redone, with passing lanes every five miles, but I always seemed to run up behind a hauler just at the end of the passing lanes, and that morning was certainly no exception.

Past the last Loon Lake, where I actually saw a pair of loons beyond the marshes, I slowed behind a spotless white tank-hauler—vanEmsden's Dairy, of course. From there I crawled past the fish hatchery and back southeast on Route Five until the hauler turned off for Gessen just outside of Zuider.

Even on the new road with its passing lanes, it took almost an hour from Vanderbraak Centre. I got the Stanley up to eighty once, about half its red line. I actually had it up close to the red line when I first got it. It was after Elspeth's death, and I took it out on the closed runway at Pautuxent. I had turned the thermals on and the Stanley had almost blended into the runway cement. They never did find out who I was, but I wouldn't recommend doing something that stupid.

Closer to Zuider, going that fast wasn't advisable anyway, but I've always had a tendency to push the red line.

Unlike some places, LBI opened at nine, and what I wanted was definitely special. Bruce had helped me with the specifications of the SII fluidic difference engine and the additional modules. Besides, we went back a long way, not in a fashion that was readily available to Billy vanBecton.

Bruce's place is about two blocks behind Union Street, where all the banks are, and there was plenty of parking in his small lot. The sign above the door was simple enough—LBI DIFFERENCE DESIGNERS. The initials stood for Leveraal Brothers, International. I'd never met his older brother, but Bruce had certainly been helpful.

A slight bleep sounded when I opened the door and carried the box into the store. Unlike most difference engine places, nothing was on display. If you go to LBI, it's either custom-made or custom-ordered. The SII logo was displayed, but not overpoweringly.

"Herr Doktor," offered Bruce, emerging from the back

room, looking very bearded and academic under the silver-rimmed glasses, and very unlike a Babbage technician in his cravat and vest. "Troubles already? SII won't be happy."

"No expletives, please. I know how you feel about excessive and overpriced degrees. And there's no problem. The box is empty. I'll pick it up with my next commission for you."

"Do I really want to know what can I do for you?"

"Probably not, but I have a problem."

"We specialize in problems. Don't guarantee solutions, but problems we can certainly create."

I nodded toward the paper-stacked cubicle he called an office.

"Fine. You're paying."

He sat down, and I opened my folder, laying out the first rough schematic I'd drawn the night before. "Can you build this?"

He studied the drawing for a while. "I may have to improvise in places, but I can get the same effect. This looks like some professor's theory." He pointed. "You use that much amperage there and you'll have fused circuits here. A few other little problems like that. Nothing insurmountable." He cleared his throat. "What in hell is it?"

"It should generate and maybe project a magnetic field. Don't point it at anyone you like. As for what it really is—I don't know exactly. And you don't want to."

"Why do I want to build it, then?"

"Three reasons. First, I'll pay you. Second, I'm a good guy. Third, you want to be able to claim you have built the largest number of strange Babbage-related devices in the world."

"I may pass on the third. How soon do you need this?" Bruce took off the glasses and set them beside the blank screen of his own difference engine.

"Tomorrow."

"I can't. I just can't. Hoosler wants a system complete. It's a hard contract." He picked up the glasses and polished them with a spotless handkerchief pulled from his vest.

I sighed and laid two hundred dollars in bills on the shortest stack of papers. "That's half the bonus."

"Reason number one looks even better. Who's chasing you?"

"No one—yet."

"You think so, but you're not sure, or you wouldn't be carrying empty boxes around as if they were heavy."

I pulled out the second schematic and the sketch of the file storage hardware.

"I can't do two more—even with all the money in the world. I have to be in business next year."

"I won't need the second and third until Saturday."

"That I can do. What's this one? Or can you tell me?"

"This one I know. It's called something like a perturbation replicator."

"It replicates trouble? Why would you want something like that?"

"Not trouble. It's supposed to duplicate ghosts and suck the duplicate into Babbage disks."

"That's trouble." Bruce shook his head. "This is weird. No one would believe me if I told them." He looked at me and added, "But I won't."

"The other is some sort of electronic file conversion system." I pointed to my crude drawing. "I think it converts fields into a storage protocol."

"That looks more standard—as if anything you have is really standard."

"I like you, too." I nodded. "I'll be back tomorrow."

"Mornings like this, it feels just like ten years ago, and you know how I feel about that." Bruce's comments reflected the fact that he had never been that thrilled about being a technician for the Spazi.

"I know. Let's hope it's not."

"It really is that bad, isn't it?"

"If you don't hear anything, don't ask."

"It's that bad. You need some firepower?"

I considered. "No."

"You can ask tomorrow."

"I'll think about it."

"I take it you want this first thing portable? How much power? How long do you want it to operate?"

"A spring trigger switch, I think, and as much power as will fit."

"It's not going to fit under your coat. I can tell you that."

"I suspected." I rose. "Just like old times?"

"God, I hope not. Good luck, Johan."

"I don't know as I can rely on luck now."

"You never had the best."

I straightened up and left the drawings on his piled papers. "Tell me about it, Bruce."

"I'm sorry. That's not what I meant."

"I know. But it still hurts." I forced a smile. "I'll be back in the morning. Eight o'clock all right? I know it's before you open, but . . ."

"It'll be done then or not at all."

"Let me buy some spare disks."

"The highest-density ones, I assume."

"Of course."

He bowed, and I paid and carried the case of disks back to the steamer, not noting anyone strange. That didn't mean much, although Bruce had been a techie, and no one paid attention to the techies in government, and they generally paid less attention to them out of government. After all, what harm could a technician do? Didn't they just do what they were told?

The pair of loons had taken flight—or something—by the time I passed the Loon Lakes, and I got stuck behind another vanEmsden tanker, also spotless but puffing gray smoke, a sign that the boiler burners were out of trim.

I got back to the university by quarter to ten, later than I had hoped because I stopped by the New Bruges Bank to deposit the International Import cheque, which wouldn't compensate for what I was spending on hardware but might help. Then I rushed to the office, picking up my messages in a quick sweep.

"My, you'd think something important was about to happen," Gilda observed acerbically.

"I'm sorry. Good morning, Gilda."

"Good morning, Herr Doktor Eschbach."

"I did say I was sorry."

"Just like all men. You think a few sweet words make up for everything."

I caught the grin, and answered. "Of course. That's what women want, isn't it? Sweet words of deception?"

"You are impossible." She arched an eyebrow.

"No. Merely difficult."

"Better Doktor duBoise than me."

I smiled.

"You may go now, Herr Doktor."

"I can see that I stand dismissed." With a nod, I made my way upstairs and unlocked my office.

"At last, he's actually late," said Grimaldi as he hurried past me for his ten o'clock. "Will wonders never cease?"

"Not these days."

After I unloaded my folder, I picked up the papers I had left and finished grading the last handful, then recorded the generally abysmal marks. I swallowed hard and looked at the tests that needed to be graded.

After a moment, I picked up the handset and dialed Lysette's office/studio.

"Hello. A student I have . . ."

"This is Johan. I had to go to Zuider this morning to get some work done on my difference engine. I just got back."

"I will call you in a few minutes."

"Fine."

Click.

Preoccupied or angry? She had been the one who had been busy the night before.

I started in on the tests, which were, unfortunately, worse than the papers, and I had read perhaps a dozen when the wireset rang.

"Johan Eschbach."

"Johan. I am sorry, but the student . . . oh, I was so angry! My fault, she said it was. My fault that the music she had not learned. My fault that she had not listened."

"I'm sorry."

"Oh, I cannot stand it! It is my fault? They have no . . . no responsibility to learn? I should beat notes into their thick little Dutch heads."

"You do sound angry."

"Johan! I am not a child."

"What can I say? They're lazy. I'm grading a test, and half of them didn't read the assignment."

"Lazy! They should have been in Europe while Ferdinand's armies marched. So lucky they are and do not know it."

"I did call to see about dinner."

"I cannot, not all this week. I must beat notes and more notes. Oh, I cannot stand it!"

"Chocolate at Delft's at half past three?"

"That . . . I do not know. There is so much . . ."

"The university can spare you for a half hour."

"They are fortunate to have me."

"They are. Half past three?"

"That would be good. I must go. Another student, and I must beat notes."

I went back to the tests. More than half the class clearly hadn't read the assignment. In one way, it made things very easy. It doesn't take that long to flunk students who have no idea of the question. What takes time is determining the degree of knowledge exhibited. When there isn't any, it's quick. Half the class flunked, and only one student received an A. There were two B's, and the rest of those who passed got C's.

I gathered up both papers and exams and stuffed them

into my folder, then headed back over to Smythe for my eleven o'clock.

I offered a smile to Gertrude, who was raking leaves across the green under a gray sky. She smiled vacantly back and continued raking, happy with the routine work. Hector did not even look up from his perfectly placed piles of soggy leaves.

Natural Resources 1A was the intro course, and most of us in the department had to teach it some of the time. Although it was basic, very basic, you would have thought none of the students had ever even considered the environment and natural resources.

We were working on the water cycle. Now, the whole basis of the water cycle is pretty simple. There's so much water in the world. The amount doesn't change much, and the question really is how much is usable for plant and animal life, particularly human beings, and how changes in the cycle affect that.

"There's enough water in the world that if the earth's surface were flat, which obviously it's not, we'd all be a mile under water. So why, Miss Haasfeldt, do we have drought conditions in the Saheel?"

"There's not enough water there."

I smiled. It was hard, but I smiled. "A little more detail, please. A drought means that there isn't enough water. With all that water in the oceans, *why* do we have a drought in mid-north Africa?"

"Well, it's the wind patterns . . ."

"What about the wind patterns?"

I tried not to shake my head too much. After all, they would be the ones running society before too long.

After the intro course, I ducked by the snack line in the student activities building and picked up a sandwich and tea. I ate alone, quickly, before I headed down to the post centre.

Besides two advertising circulars and the weekly edition of *Newsweek,* there was a letter from my mother.

"See!" exclaimed Maurice. "We do deliver the good material."

"Sometimes."

"Bother on ye, Doktor."

I grinned and opened the letter.

Dearest Johan,

I appreciated your letter of last week, and was delighted that you had managed to bring back the apple trees and even the old pear. While I do miss the old place, my visits to you in the warmer months are more than enough, and I certainly do not miss the winters!

Anna and I went to New Amsterdam yesterday to see *Miss Singapore.* It was good, but terribly depressing. I am glad you did not enter the Air Corps until after that sad situation was over. Your father always felt that we should have annexed the Sandwich Islands much earlier, and that having a big naval base at Pearl Harbor would have prevented much of the disaster in the Pacific. I don't know, only that the play was most moving.

I know that Llysette makes you happy—she seems very warm—but you come from very different backgrounds, and I hope you will be gentle with her. She needs much kindness, I think. I also wonder if the war in Europe took a little something out of her. I cannot say what it might be, and you can discount this as an old woman's fancy.

Here a few leaves still hang on the trees, but they will be gone before long. You were kind to invite me up again, but that week we are going to visit Aunt Elisabet in Baltimore. She is ninety-three, and I do not know how much longer she will be around. She still does beautiful needlework, though.

I enjoyed your article. The finer points were beyond me, but I did get the message. Anna liked it, too, and she made a copy for Douglas. He posted it in his office.

I hope you can see your way clear to stop by when you get a chance in that busy schedule of yours. . . .

I folded the letter back into the envelope as I finished climbing the stairs up to the lower campus.

My two o'clock was Environmental Politics 2B. Since most of them had taken the previous course from me, they knew what to expect. Most of them actually had read at least some of the assignment.

By the follow-on 2B class, we worked more on a discussion basis.

"Mr. Quellan, what are the basic trade-offs between incentive-based and command-and-control environmental laws?"

"Well, uhhh . . . When you give businesses incentives, it's in their interest to follow the laws."

"Please be more specific. Do you mean it's not in their interest to follow a command-and-control law that will fine them or put them in prison?"

"No, sir. I mean, I meant that with incentives they make money or lose less money by following the law. They will obey a command law, but they don't want to."

"Why not?"

Sometimes it was like pulling teeth. We hashed through that section, finishing up just before half-past three. I rushed down to Delft's and still got there before Llysette, but not by much.

Victor had just set the chocolate and biscuits on the table when she stepped into the greenhouse section of the cafe.

"*Bienvenue,* Doktor duBoise." Victor offered her a sweeping bow.

I did him one better and kissed her hand. *"Enchanté, mademoiselle."*

"Johan, Victor, I have need of the chocolate."

Victor bowed and scraped away, and Llysette slumped into the chair. She sipped the chocolate, then bit into a biscuit.

"They are impossible . . . I stood on the stage of the Académie Royale, and to beat notes I must?"

"I ran a government ministry, and I have to give tests every class to get them to read their assignments?" I bit through a biscuit and sprayed crumbs across the wooden surface of the table.

"Johan . . . I did not come to discuss the students. To avoid them I came."

"Do you think that our hoopsters will win their korfball game tonight?"

"Korfball? Why do you ask such a thing?"

"Why not? Or would you rather I discussed the relative merits of postclassic Mozart as compared to Beethoven?"

"No music, please."

I sipped the hot chocolate before saying more. "David—the doktor Doniger—was worried about an article I wrote, because the dean was concerned it would hurt fund-raising. I made a politically inappropriate statement."

Tears welled in the corner of her eyes. "I hate this."

I squeezed her hand, and she squeezed back.

"Did you know that Michener's new book deals with the Sandwich Islands?"

We discussed literature until the clock struck four, and Llysette looked up. "My time . . . it is gone." She took a last bite of her biscuit and drained the chocolate, then rose and pulled her cape around her.

As I stood and left three dollars on the table for Victor, I suddenly realized that I had missed at least fifteen minutes of the departmental meeting.

"You look disturbed."

"It has been one of those days. I forgot that David moved the departmental meeting up to a quarter to four."

"It is important?"

"David thinks it is."

"Ah, the chairs. They think . . . what is the use?" She bent toward me and pecked my cheek. "Later this week, I will see you?"

"I don't know. When you are free, I'm not, and I'm tied to the dinner in Columbia. How about Saturday?"

"Mais oui." She looked at her watch. "I must go."

She scurried away and up the hill. I followed more sedately. If I were going to be late, late I would be.

David looked up as I slipped into the corner of the seminar room.

"I thought I had made the time change clear to everyone." His voice was mild.

"You did." I smiled. "I couldn't change a previous engagement."

"As we were discussing, we are being required to cut one course from our elective load next term. Since Doktor Dokus will be on sabbatical, we will put a zero cap on registrations on Natural Resources Three-B. That's the Ecology of Wetlands course. There are no seniors who need it to graduate."

"Is that wise?" asked Grimaldi. "Why don't we cap one of the baby eco courses?"

"That's where we get almost fifteen percent of our majors," countered Wilhelm Mondriaan.

"If we cancel the wetlands course—"

"Zero-capping is not a cancellation. That keeps the course options open."

"It's the same thing," snorted Grimaldi.

I sat back and listened.

After the meeting, which dragged on until past four-thirty, I reclaimed my folder from my office, locked up, and headed to the faculty car park.

I stopped by the Stanley, unloaded my folder. Then, with an exasperated shrug, I relocked the Stanley and marched up toward the Physical Sciences building, but instead of going through the front entrance, I took the narrow walkway around the downhill side as if I were headed to the Student Center.

Since I knew what I was looking for as I walked unconcernedly toward the center, I found them—inconspicuous little brown boxlike squares, heat sensors, probably with directional scanners behind the thin cloth shields. They only covered the right rear corner of the building. The other thing I noticed was that the laboratory windows did not look like they had been painted black from the outside. They looked like the silvery gray of heat-reflective glass. Someone had gone to a lot of trouble to keep Branston-Hay's research very low-profile, so much trouble that I felt stupid. I should have seen it, and yet I had been bumbling around, transparently pumping the good doktor. I shook my head and kept walking. Where had my brains been? I circled back to the Stanley the long way, feeling more and more foolish by the moment—and more scared.

Tired as I was, I hoped I could sleep—without nightmares—but at least Marie would have left me the main course of a dinner. It was definitely a luxury having her come every day, but I felt better when the house was spotless, and she liked the fact that I didn't hold her to fixed hours so long as she got the job done.

As I drove out of the car park, I did note that Llysette's Reo was still there.

13

WEDNESDAY MORNING CAME too soon, even for me, and I usually like mornings. But I was dutiful and forced myself through the running and the exercises. My legs still ached, and the leaves by the stone walls smelled half of fall and half of mold.

With a look at my waistline, and a groan as I recalled Tuesday's breakfast, I held myself to plain toast, fruit, and unsweetened tea. Then I took a shower and dressed. My stomach growled, and I said, "Down, boy." It didn't help.

The trip south to Zuider seemed longer than usual, perhaps because I got stuck behind a hay truck until I reached the passing zone near the turnoff for Gairloch. I ended up sneezing for another five miles, and my nose itched until I got to the outskirts of Zuider. Across the town beach I could see whitecaps out on the big lake, but at least the morning was clear and sunny. I even whistled a bit as I parked the Stanley in the lot outside LBI.

Bruce had two long boxes and a small one on the counter. One of the long ones lay open, and the gadget within looked something like a ray gun from the paperbacks, not at all like a rifle, except in general shape.

"Two?" I raised my eyebrows. "Do they both work?"

"I thought about it. You'll need two. One for show, whatever that is, and one for you." Bruce smiled. "They generate a damned funny magnetic field, enough to blow my breakers. The batteries are standard rechargeables."

I had another thought. "No fingerprints?"

"No. All the components are standard, too. This isn't signed artwork."

"And the little one?"

"That's your file gadget. Just hook it into the external port. I assume you have the programware."

"Sort of."

"One of those deals? I don't envy you."

My stomach answered with another growl. Bruce laughed. I shook my head and handed him the rest of the fee in bills.

"You sure this won't break you?"

"Money isn't the issue." The worst of it was that I meant that, and, while I may not be a totally typical Dutchman, I'm certainly not a free spender. It wasn't that I liked spending money; it was the feeling that if I didn't get ahead of the game I wasn't going to be around to do much saving or amassing of capital—the modern variety of "your money or your life."

I loaded all three boxes in the front trunk of the Stanley, and sped back to Vanderbraak Centre, hitting eighty only once. I stopped by Samaha's for my paper and the post centre for whatever awaited me there.

Only two bills—from Wijk River Oil and Sammis Pump Repair—graced my postbox. I peered around the empty post window at Maurice. "It's all junk post."

"Doktor, we just deliver. We can't improve the quality of your enemies."

"Thanks!"

"We do our best."

I got to the office not that long after Gilda, and I even managed to say, "Good day."

"Good day to you, Johan." She shook her head and grinned. "I heard that you suggested to Doktor Doniger that faculty meetings were not sacrosanct."

"I believe I was ill."

"Good. I wish more people were."

"Gilda?" David marched through the door. "Here are my corrections to the minutes of yesterday's meeting."

"Yes, Doktor Doniger." Her voice was cool and formal.

He turned to me. "Good morning, Johan."

"Good morning, David."

"We need to talk, Johan, but I'm off to a meeting with the dean. Will you be around later?"

"I'll be in my office from about noon until just before my two o'clock."

"I don't know. Well, we'll play it by ear." He turned back to Gilda. "If you could have those ready to go by the time I get back?"

"Yes, Doktor Doniger."

David swung his battered brown case off Gilda's desk and marched out the door and off to the administration building. Gilda and I looked at each other, and I shrugged. She took a deep breath and picked up the papers David had left.

Once I got to my office and set down my folder, I opened the *Asten Post-Courier.* When I saw the story below the fold, my stomach churned.

KYOTO (INS)—The Japanese Minister of the Imperial Navy announced on Monday night that Japan had successfully built and tested a new class of submersible. The *Dragon of the Sea* is an electric submersible powered by a self-contained nuclear power plant. The ship has a theoretically unlimited range without surfacing.

The Japanese ship was denounced by a spokesman for Ferdinand VI as a violation of the Treaty of Columbia . . .

Gao TseKung, Warlord for Defense of Chung Kuo, declared that deployment of the *Dragon of the Sea* in the Sea of Japan would be a blatant violation of the Nuclear Limitation Agreement . . .

Speaker Hartpence warned against the development of "naval adventurism" that could restrict international trade to the detriment of all . . .

The story on page two didn't help my growling stomach either.

MUNICH (INS)—A raging fire blazed through the difference engine center of the Imperial Research Service laboratories here last night. "Fortunately, the fire did not destroy any vital research," stated Frideric VonBulow, deputy marshal for imperial research.

Outside observers covertly doubted the deputy marshal's claim. "If that were so, why do they have hundreds of technicians sifting through the ruins?" asked one bystander.

Well-placed sources indicate that the Munich laboratories were the center of highly secret research on psychic phenomena, a claim disputed immediately by deputy marshal VonBulow. "While all research has import for the Empire and the people of Austro-Hungary, certainly the research at Munich was of no greater or lesser import than in other research centers."

The wireline bell rang. "Johan Eschbach."

"Doktor Eschbach, this is Chief Waetjen down at the watch center. I wonder if you would have a moment to come down and chat with me this afternoon."

"I could do it from one to two. Might I ask what you had in mind?"

"Just follow-up inquiries on the Miller murder. It won't take long. Quarter past one?"

"That would be fine."

I set down the handset and then leaned back in the too-stiff wooden chair. The chief had been too friendly. Why was he contacting me?

There wasn't much I could do about that. So I worked on the next set of unannounced tests for my section of the intro course, Natural Resources 1A. That was on Tuesdays and

Thursdays. Then came the time to do battle over environmental economics.

The green was jammed with scurrying students, and one or two actually waved or said hello as I plowed toward Smythe.

Once my own students were seated and relative calm prevailed within the confines of Smythe Hall, I handed out the Environmental Economics papers without a word, then watched their faces. At least half of them failed to understand. That was clear from the mutterings and murmurings.

"But . . ."

"I don't understand . . ."

"Supposed to have all term for the reading . . ."

"Ladies and gentlemen. I cannot call you scholars. Not yet. Perhaps not ever. You cannot learn if you refuse to read. You cannot learn if you will not think. You cannot sing if someone else has to drum the notes into you. You cannot succeed in anything by merely going through the motions. These papers show more interest in form than substance. Almost every one is just over the minimum length." I gave a sardonic bow.

"Mister Gersten, how would you characterize the impact of unrealized external diseconomies upon the environment of New Bruges in the 1920s?"

Gersten turned white. I waited. It was going to be a long class and a longer term.

After terrorizing the students in my eleven o'clock, I announced that they would have no class until the following Monday, but that they had better have caught up on the reading by the time I saw them again.

I skipped lunch and made up another short test for the eleven o'clock—a nice present for them for the next Monday, since most of them still wouldn't believe me. After that, I went over my notes for Environmental Politics 2B, the follow-on course to my two o'clock that ran at two on Tuesdays and Thursdays.

David, of course, never did bother to stop in. Before I

knew it, it was time to head down to the watch station, that gray stone building next to the post centre.

The chief was waiting in the lobby, or whatever they call the open space with a duty officer.

"Doktor Eschbach?"

"The same."

I had never met Hans Waetjen, but he looked like his name. Solid and stocky, with graying hair, gray eyes, and a ruddy skin. He was clean-shaven, unlike most older Dutch-surnamed men.

"Pleased to meet you, Doktor Eschbach. Wish it was under other conditions."

"I would guess these things do happen, not that I've seen one in Vanderbraak Centre." I tried not to wrinkle my nose. The watch station smelled like disinfectant.

"I'd guess you probably saw lots of strange things in government, but you're right. We sure don't see this sort of thing here. Must have been a good three, four years since the Adams case. Happened before you came back. Boy took an axe to his old man. Old man probably deserved it—he'd been beating both children. Still, a terrible thing it was." Waetjen shook his head and gestured toward the small office in the corner. "Coffee? Chocolate?"

"Chocolate would be fine."

A young watch officer carried two cups toward the urns on the table in the main corridor. Waetjen walked through the open door to his office and sank into the scarred gray leather chair behind the desk, not waiting for me to sit, but I did without invitation.

The younger watch officer delivered the cups, setting them both on the desk. He closed the office door on his way out, and it clunked shut with the finality of a cell door.

The chocolate was hot, and sweeter than even I liked it. Waetjen had coffee, so bitter I could smell it across the desk, mingling with the sweet-acrid odor of disinfectant.

"Just had a few questions I wanted to ask you, Doktor." Waetjen's eyes ran over me. "Fine suit you got there."

I smiled. "Just a leftover from my days in the big city."

"Don't see those that much here. You must have been an important man in government, Doktor."

I shook my head. "I was so important that I doubt anyone at the university even knows what I did."

"With all your traveling, I was wondering if you had ever met Professor Miller before you came here."

"I've met a lot of people, Chief, and I could have seen her at a reception or something, but I know I never talked to her before I joined the faculty here."

"I thought so, but I had to ask. What about any of the others that were at the concert? Do you know if any of them knew Professor Miller before they came to the university?"

"Not that I know of. She was here for a long time, according to some of the old-timers."

"What about Doktor duBoise? When did you first meet her?"

"I'd say it was six months after I started teaching."

"You didn't know her before that?"

"No. It was even an accident when I met her. She's in Music and Theatre, and I'm in Natural Resources."

"What do you know about Professor Martin?"

"Not much. I have talked to him once or twice. He seems very straightforward."

"Do you think any student could have been involved?"

"That's always a possibility, but it would probably have to be one of Professor Miller's students, and I wouldn't know one of them if they bumped right into me."

"How did the administrators regard Professor Miller?"

"I don't know. I was led to understand that she and Dean Er Recchus got along fairly well, and they certainly were friendly at the new faculty gatherings where I saw them."

Because he was stalling to keep me around, I finally looked directly at Chief Waetjen and kept staring at him. "I've answered your questions. What can you tell me about what you've found out?"

"I can't really say much."

"I know that. Let's try off the record, Chief."

He took a deep breath. I waited.

"The time of death was right around quarter to eight. We know that because of the subsonics you heard, and because Doktor Geoffries found the body just before eight. Both Frau Vonderhaus and Fräulein Matthews saw Doktor Miller at seven before Frau Vonderhaus went to check the tuning on the Steinbach." Hans Waetjen spread his hands before continuing.

"So where was everyone? You were in your office, and three people saw you on the way to and from there. Doktor duBoise and Frau Vonderhaus were on stage practicing. Doktor Geoffries and the box-office manager were together. Gregor Martin was in the lighting booth replacing the gel in one spotlight, and the backstage crew has insisted that no one went down the corridor to Doktor Miller's studio."

"That almost sounds like someone was hiding there or waiting there," I ventured.

"A prop knife was apparently used, and the knife was wiped clean on the coat. The only blood was Doktor Miller's."

I nodded. Not exactly a locked-room mystery, but close. No obvious reason for Miranda's murder and no obvious suspects. No job problems. No romantic ties. No hard evidence. Strange—you pass pleasantries with someone, and suddenly she is dead, and you realize how much you didn't know.

"So who do you suspect, Doktor Eschbach?"

I had to shrug. "Something isn't quite right, but right now I couldn't tell you what it is." Everything I said was perfectly true, unfortunately, since I don't like to lie. I have been known to resort to untruths, generally in desperation, which is where it gets you in the most trouble.

"And you suspect?" he pressed.

"Right now, I suspect everyone, probably, except for Professor Martin, but even that, I couldn't tell you why. And I could be wrong."

Chief Waetjen nodded again.

"If you haven't any more questions, I do have a two o'clock, and not much time to get there."

"Of course." He stood. "I do appreciate your coming in."

"Any time." I bowed and left.

Why had the chief asked me down? It wasn't to tell me what the watch had discovered. So I watched as I left, and, sure enough, there was a young fellow with a portable videolink waiting outside. His presence confirmed that vanBecton was telling the chief what to do—and that I was bait to bring down Ralston and the president, one way or another. How many other lines had he set? Did it matter?

"Doktor Eschbach, do you have any comment?"

"On what?" I asked, letting a puzzled expression, I hoped, cross my face.

"On the murder."

"I hope the watch is successful in apprehending the guilty party."

"Why were you here?"

"While I would suggest you talk to Chief Waetjen, my understanding was that the chief hoped I could provide some additional information."

"Did you?"

I smiled politely. "That's something for the watch to release. As I said, I am confident that they will find the guilty party."

The journalist backed away, looking puzzled. I tried not to smile more than politely as I walked back up to my office. Score one for Johan in the positioning war. Of course, vanBecton had scored a lot more. I felt like I was stuck trying to mark a seven-foot giant in korfball, and vanBecton was that giant and almost scoring at will.

The two o'clock class on Environmental Politics was almost worse than the meeting with the watch chief, and not because of the short rainstorm I encountered on the way across the green. Even more of my students had failed than in my eleven o'clock, and none of them seemed to understand. I repeated my sermon, and they still looked blank.

"Miss Deventer, what was the political basis behind the first Speaker Roosevelt's efforts at reforestation?"

Miss Deventer paled. Students looked from one to the other.

"Come now. It was in the assigned reading. Surely you have not forgotten so quickly. Mister Vanderwaal?"

"Uhhh, Doktor Eschbach, I didn't get that far."

"It was on the second page. Mister Henstaal?"

I finally dismissed them, early, went back to my office, and drafted another short test for the next Monday.

Because I had yet to pack or handle any of the details for leaving, I closed up the office and stuffed the draft of the test in my folder, along with the post and my mother's letter, and made my way to the car park.

Again, Llysette's Reo was left forlornly by itself, and I shook my head at the hours she and the other music people put in.

Marie must have figured that I was working late, because she had left on the side porch light and one light in the kitchen. The lights made driving up to the house more welcoming, and so did the odor of the stew and the crusty fresh bread she had left. I just hoped her husband got the same sort of food. If he did, he was a lucky man.

After I ate, I reclaimed Bruce's work from the steamer and carted all three boxes into the study. I set the two disassociators aside for the time being. Then I turned on the difference engine and called up the specifications for the filing gadget. Although I didn't yet have the perturbation replicator, I might as well figure out how the storage system worked. If I understood the system right, what the perturbation replicator did was capture a pattern that the field storage system converted into an electronic file. If . . .

If that were the case, Branston-Hay's notes and the president's dinners with individual members of Congress made way too much sense.

I connected Bruce's gadget, the external field/formatting device, to one of the external ports of my difference engine. Then I began to see what I could do to devise the program to make it work. My machine language commands probably weren't suited exactly to use the full capability of the device, even given Branston-Hay's notes and specs as a starting point, but it was worth a try.

A try it might have been worth, but when I stopped and brewed a cup of chocolate at half past ten I was still twiddling with the program and restudying Branston-Hay's cryptic notes, as well as the structure of his own files, looking for some more insights. One file appeared to contain the entire structure, almost a template, but there were enough parameters that trying even to plug in values was extraordinarily time-consuming.

While the chocolate brewed, I went upstairs and packed a hanging bag, basically with evening clothes for the dinner and another suit to wear back, but also some extra shirts, socks, and underwear, since I was thinking of coming back the long way, via Schenectady.

After packing I went down and sipped the chocolate at the kitchen table, munching a biscuit or two, still thinking about the proto-program. The file format I didn't have to worry about. Branston-Hay actually had those specs in his files; and so were the field capture parameters, though I didn't yet have that hardware. All I was working on was the transfer section, almost a translation section.

Finally I went back to the difference engine, and back to the files I had stolen and duplicated. I decided to look at the encryption protocol—after all, it was a translation system of sorts. One thing led to another, and it was past midnight when I installed the completed program.

A flicker of white caught the corner of my eye. Carolynne hovered in the darkest corner of the study, where the full-length bookshelves met. I pursed my lips. Why had she appeared now? Was it just because it was around midnight? Supposedly midnight had no special significance for ghosts.

Shrugging, I turned to the difference engine again, then

looked up as Carolynne seemed to drift from the shelves toward me. She seemed to be resisting a current, almost swimming against an invisible river.

"No more of that, my lord . . . no more!" she protested.

I looked around the study. "No more of what?"

"The Thane of Fife . . ." She tried to pull away from me, but it wasn't me, exactly.

I snapped the switch on the difference engine. Something else might have worked as well, but usually the off switch is safest.

Carolynne curtsied and vanished.

I frowned and sat at the blank screen for a time. True, Carolynne never seemed to be around when I worked on the machine. What was it about the machine? Or had it been the new device? What was it about the device?

Not knowing why, exactly, just following a hunch, I went to the breaker closet off the kitchen and threw the master switch. Then I trundled outside, flash in hand, to the NBEI electric meter.

I had turned off everything, but the current meter wheel still turned. Even after I switched off the breakers, the meter turned—slowly but perceptibly.

Why?

I walked back to the veranda. Carolynne stood there, insofar as any ghost could be determined to stand.

"Will you tell me? Why are you still here? All ghosts fade—except those on magnetic fields. There must be a field here—somehow. I will tear up the house if I have to, but you could help."

Carolynne drifted into the main parlor. She just went through the wall, or maybe she vanished outside and reappeared inside, but I had to go around to the side door into the kitchen, since I'd never unlocked the veranda door when I came home. Then I had to go back when I remembered I had left the flash in the study. Carolynne waited in the main parlor, but she still had not spoken, as if speech were unnecessary.

I watched as she floated behind the heavy love seat and a slender ectoplasmic hand pointed to a circular floral boss on one side of the mirror and then the one above it.

I touched the boss to which Carolynne had pointed, and the mirror—that mirror I had believed mounted in the wall itself, with its back to the veranda—that mirror swung out on heavy hinges. I shone the flash into the darkness. Concealed behind the mirror was an enormous artificial lodestone, with old-fashioned copper wires wound around it in coil after coil.

"Who?" I asked, reclosing the mirror cover on the lodestone.

She seemed to shiver, as if crying, but I hadn't thought about it. Why wouldn't a fully sentient ghost cry?

"Was it the deacon?"

She seemed to pause, then shook her head. Even as I frowned, the story came back to me. After the deacon's wife had stabbed Carolynne, he had taken the knife and killed his wife. The next morning he had walked the entire way to Vanderbraak Centre and confessed. He had never returned to the house.

"But he couldn't have built this."

"Boldness comes . . ." Her voice was faint. "Like Troilus, he gathered what he did. Your father, great king Priam, the lodestone was his and hid."

"My father built this?"

". . . conclude that minds swayed by eyes are full of turpitude . . ."

I sat down on the sofa in the darkness. My father—he had built the artificial lodestone. "You were fading, and he built this?"

I got the impression of a head shake, but she said nothing.

"But why?"

"But with my heart the other eye doth see . . ."

"In a way, he was in love with you?" I asked.

"One cannot speak a word."

I sat in the sofa, looking at Carolynne, shaking my head. "Why?"

"Ah, poor our sex!"

"Did you give him a reason?"

"The error of our eye directs our mind."

"But why?"

"It is no matter . . . but now, you have it, you have me in your sight . . ."

"But," I began again, "how does that have anything to do with the lodestone?"

I only got a shrug, but a number of things began to make a crazy kind of sense. Mother had never been happy about Carolynne, but she had tried to keep her away from me, not from my father.

"Did my mother know about this?"

I got the sense of a head shake in the dark, but Mother had known.

I sat there in the darkness for a long time, accompanied by an equally silent ghost, until I finally got up and switched on the breakers and reset the electric clocks.

Again, I had trouble getting to sleep.

14

WHEN I CARTED my traveling bag off the Columbia Special and out of the old Baltimore and Potomac Station—far classier than the shabbier, if newer, Union Station—I had to wait for a cab. That figured. Congress was in session, working on the trade and finance bills, and all the Dutch bankers from New Amsterdam had descended on Columbia City. Portly as most were, each required an individual cab. So I walked out to Constitution Avenue and down toward the galleries, hailing a beat-up blue steamer bearing the legend "Francois's Cabs—French spoken."

"Ministère des Resources Naturels, rue Sixième." I wondered if the driver actually spoke French.

"Oui, monsieur. Voulez-vous la porte este?"

"Non. Dehors la porte norde."

"Ah . . ."

I also wondered about the knowing "ah," but, French or not, the driver took me the back way, passing the B&P station again before turning north and back west. She muttered under her breath in French. As we waited at Eighth and D, I found myself looking at a small sign.

VLADIMIR NOBOKOV-JONES
SPECIALIST IN PERSONALITY UNIFICATION

What a scam. Only a small number of people ever suffered a personality fracture without physical trauma—and that was usually from extraordinary stress and guilt. They'd said I'd come close after Elspeth's death, but not many people go through years like that. So any quack could hang up a shingle and declare himself a specialist in personality unity, since so few ever suffered the problem—and if they did, how could they complain?

The next block held the big Woodward and Vandervaal, the downtown flagship store. The windows were filled with braided corn shucks and other harvest items, such as a scarecrow decked out in a brand-new New Ostend plaid shirt and leather knickers. I was grinning at the incongruity when a white figure darted in front of the cab.

Screee . . . The cab skidded for a moment. The driver released the brakes as the figure vanished the moment the steel of the bumper touched her white coat.

"Revenante! J'oublie . . ."

The driver went on in French, as well as I could follow, about how the ghost, a woman originally from Spain, had run in front of a full steam-bus the week before.

". . . elle croit qu'elle n'etait point la personne seule qui perdait tous!"

Did each person believe that he was the only one who suffered? Or was that a French ailment? I had seen that in Llysette, but wouldn't I have felt the same way? Didn't Carolynne, disembodied and sometimes disconnected ghost that she was, show that as well? I was still reflecting when the cab stopped at the Sixteenth Street entrance to the Natural Resources Ministry.

"Voilà!" The cab driver's words were flat, despite the French.

I handed her two dollars and a silver half dollar.

"Merci." The "thank you" was equally flat, as if she de-

served a greater tip for speaking French, and she pulled away as quickly as any steamer could, but without the screeching tires possible with an internal combustion engine. Were the screeching tires why so many young Columbians sought out the older petrol-fired cars and restored them?

After proffering the identification card to the guard at the Natural Resources building, I left my bag in the locker behind his desk. Of course, I'd had to show him it contained only clothes, but all guards are much happier when strangers don't carry large objects into federal buildings. Then I headed down through the building to the basement, and then to the subbasement and the tunnel guard.

"This tunel is not open for normal travel."

"Doktor Eschbach for Subminister vanBecton."

I waited for him to pick up the headset. He just looked at me.

I smiled, and the young face looked blank. I could tell it was going to be a long day. "I really do suggest that you pick up that handset and get me cleared into Billy vanBecton's office."

"Billy? I don't know who you are, but you don't belong here."

"I believe I do." I nodded politely. "I'm here to see Minister vanBecton."

"No, you aren't. I know his people."

Because I hate wise-asses, I reached down and picked up the handset, hoping that the sentry wouldn't get too upset. I dialed in the numbers.

"Minister vanBecton's office."

"This is Doktor Eschbach. I'm in the tunnel, and the guard seems to want to keep me from my four o'clock appointment with the minister."

"That's station six, is it not? The one from Natural Resources?"

"Yes."

"Put the handset down. We'll call back."

"Thank you."

I put the handset down and looked into the muzzle of the guard's handgun.

"I could blast you for that," he said.

"Not if you want to keep your job."

The wireset bleeped.

"Station six."

I watched as the sentry turned pale. "But . . . he didn't . . . but . . . yes, sir. Yes, sir. At five, sir. Yes, sir."

He looked at me, and if his eyes had been knives, I would have been hamburger. "You're cleared, sir."

I opened the leather folder for him to see and caught his eyes. "It's a cheap lesson, son. Don't ever make threats. And don't ever stand in front of someone older and wiser unless you intend to kill them and pay for it yourself." Facing him down was a risk I shouldn't have taken, but I was getting tired of the games.

"How many . . ."

"More than you want to know, son. We old goats are more dangerous than we look." I sighed and walked past him into the tunnel that led into the subbasement of the Spazi building. The guard there waved me on into the growing smell of disinfectant.

VanBecton's office was on the fourth floor. I walked up, still holding to my resolve to improve my conditioning. I don't think I panted as much as the time a week earlier, but I still stopped a moment on the last landing to catch my breath. The landings were empty, as always. It's against the English ethic to appear to work, and against the Dutch to engage in unnecessary work when there is so much that is necessary.

The pinch-faced clerk gave me a grin, an actual grin, as I walked into vanBecton's outer office. "Thank you, Doktor."

"Glad to be of service."

"The minister has not been happy with some of the guards, but most reports have been too late for him to act."

In short, Gillaume vanBecton had been taking it out on

his staff, and the clerk was more than pleased that someone else was on the firing line.

"You can go right in."

I smiled at the clerk, then opened the steel-lined wooden door, closing it behind me as I stepped toward the desk and vanBecton.

"Johan. Already you're making your presence felt, just like in the old days, I understand." VanBecton offered his broad and phony smile, stepping around the wide desk.

"I doubt that. Your guard wants to kill me, and that's not exactly the impression I'd rather leave. I am afraid my patience has been eroded by age."

"Do have a seat." He sat in one of the chairs in front of the desk, a gesture clearly designed to imply we were dealing as equals.

"Thank you." I sat. "I thought I should stop by, since I was invited to swell the President's guest list at the last moment. I take it that a number of the regulars decided to decline the invitation after the Japanese announcement?"

"There were a few." VanBecton covered his mouth with a carefully manicured hand and coughed. "Have you had any interesting developments in your area?"

"Not really interesting. You have discovered, I presume, that Professor Miller's older son was arrested on trumped-up charges by the New French."

"We knew of the charges."

"His personality makes it highly unlikely that he would ever even skirt the law. That's what the family feels."

"How would that fit with Professor Miller's death?"

"The only thing I can think of is that someone else knew she was working for Maurice-Huizenga. Perhaps she knew too much."

"Oh?"

I shrugged. "Knowing who I was wouldn't be enough. A retired Spazi employee? Come now."

"That puts a different light on Doktor duBoise."

"Why?" I asked, trying to look puzzled.

"Now, Johan. She must be working for Takaynishu. Who else could it be? You have pointed out how unlikely it is that she would be in the pay of the Austro-Hungarians, and with Professor Miller reporting to Maurice-Huizenga . . . who else could it be?"

"You assume that she works for someone. What about some proof?"

"We have some transcripts of wireline conversations."

"Whose?"

"You are good, aren't you?"

"No. But I've played the game for a long time. Whose conversations?"

"The Miller operation was quite professional. She always received calls. She never made them."

"Sitting duck, and that sounds like the New French."

"The transmissions were always illegal—that is, someone tapped a line not far from the New French border—and the caller always said, 'Rick is all right.' "

"And what did the good professor say?"

"Many things, not all relevant to the point I raised. You understand, I know. She did say that—" he looked back toward his desk "—'Doktor duBoise pursues them all, but spends by far the bulk of her energy and charm on Doktor Eschbach. If he but knew what held her soul, he would be far less interested. Ferdinand is not even that evil.' " VanBecton smiled. "Unfortunately, Professor Miller was rather poetic; so it is hard to prove some things literally. I imagine that it must have given Maurice-Huizenga fits, but he was playing out of his depth."

"Yes, he was." I frowned. "You believe that such vague words mean that Doktor duBoise had to be working for the Japanese?"

"Was it not strange that she was released through the intervention of the Japanese ambassador?"

"Why? They do have a reputation for liking occidental music."

"And occidental singers."

"Bill," I said flatly, "you don't seem to know much more than I do. It's all speculation. You have transcripts of conversations by Professor Miller. You have her son held by the New French, but you haven't got a thing on anyone else—except me."

"I didn't quite say that."

I smiled easily, hard as it was, before I lobbed the next one into his lap. "The only other thing I can add is that Miranda Miller also spent a great deal of time, a very great deal, discussing things with Doktor Branston-Hay, the Babbage man."

His eyes flickered, but so minutely that I wouldn't have seen it if I hadn't been waiting. "That is rather odd."

"Not at all. You certainly have read the papers. Something strange is going on in a lot of university Babbage centers. The New French could well be behind it, couldn't they?"

"It's more likely the religious fundamentalists, Johan. You've been in the business too long. Despite our concerns, we know there's not a conspiracy behind every tree." He laughed. "Every other one, perhaps."

"You know best." I stood. "That's all I know right now." All that I was telling, in any case.

"You mean that's all you're telling," corrected vanBecton.

I grinned. "Unlike some, I can't afford to deal in pure speculation, but I will keep working on it." I backed up, stumbled, caught the back of my knees on the edge of the chair, and knocked it against the low table, while almost sprawling across the desk before hitting the carpet. I lay there for a moment before taking a deep breath. As I pulled myself erect, I looked at a red splotch on my palm, then restacked the papers I had disarranged. "I'm getting too old for this."

"Just leave the papers, Johan. They're all administrative trivia."

"I'm certain they are, Minister vanBecton. Little of

import is reduced to ink. That's one reason I avoid speculation."

"Good. Perhaps we'll see you again before too long."

"That's definitely a possibility."

VanBecton nodded and watched as I took the back exit.

After reclaiming my hanging bag from the guard in the Natural Resources building—the tunnel guard had looked the other way as I passed, although I felt his eyes on my back—I went out into the sunlight and looked for a cab. That took a while, but finally a patched Stanley with mottled gray and blue paint stopped.

"Spring Valley, Forty-seventh and New Bruges."

"That's a minimum of four."

"Don't worry about it."

"Don't worry about it? I got to worry about it. It's my living."

I set a five on the dashboard. "All right?"

"You got the money, I drive."

He didn't talk, and I didn't, either, not with what I had to think about. While he drove, I slipped vanBecton's memos—the ones I had swept onto the floor and into my coat—into my folder. They were definitely administrative drivel, but that wasn't why I wanted them. What I needed them for would come later.

I looked out as the cab passed Ward Circle and into Ward Park beyond the seminary. Within a few blocks we turned off New Bruges and onto Sedgwick, where the houses show why the upper northwest in the Federal District reeks of money, with their trimmed hedges, sculptured gardens, and shadowed stone walks.

Supposedly, in the early days, upper northwest was far enough from the capital itself that it served as an interim retreat for Speaker Calhoun, but now such retreats were much farther from the Capitol building.

Eric and Judith's home was a Tudor set on a large corner plot with walls around the entire back of the property and two Douglas firs rising over the walls and the three-story dwelling. Their car barn had space for three steamers.

I tipped the driver two dollars. "It's a long ride back."

"Thank you, sir."

"Johan!" Judith met me at the Tiffany-paneled front doors wearing a bright blue suit, with her sparkling silver hair swept into a French braid, and only the hint of wrinkles around her gray eyes.

"I did not expect you to be here."

She stepped back and held the door as I carried in the garment bag and my folder. "I left early this afternoon. The gallery and the Dutch masters can do without me. How long has it been?"

"Only a little over a year."

"It seems longer. Eric said you were here for a presidential function."

"A welcoming dinner for the new Japanese ambassador. Sometimes they remember the old warhorses, especially when the occasion is less than popular."

"Johan—I doubt that you've reached your midforties."

"Actually, I'm past that."

"You don't look even forty." She led the way up the carpeted circular staircase, past the large crystal chandelier, to the second floor. "You have the rooms on the end. We redid things a bit last year when Suzanne got married. It's now a guest suite. You're actually the first guest."

"I feel honored."

"We don't see as much of you."

"I know."

Her hand brushed my shoulder, and the scars there twinged—all psychological.

"It wasn't your fault, Johan. You did what you could. Elspeth told me that so many times, and you can't blame yourself for what you had to do. Without the government medical program . . ."

"Thank you, Judith. It's still hard." I hung the bag in the

open closet and began to take out the evening wear. "It's really kind of you to be here."

"You could have called me."

"It was hard to call Eric."

"You and Eric are so alike." She shook her head. "I suppose it follows. Elspeth and I are . . . were alike, people said."

And they were, so much that it still ached when she talked, but the ache had almost faded—almost, but not quite.

"Sisters are often alike." I forced a grin. "I think they're supposed to be."

"In some ways, Eric could have been your brother."

"He's far more sensible."

"Do you have time for chocolate? I know how seldom you drink."

I pulled out the old Ansonia—five-fifteen. "Certainly. I shouldn't have to leave here until around quarter to seven. You can wire a cab, can't you?"

"One way or another, we'll get you to the president's. It wouldn't do to have you late."

I followed her downstairs again and out into the sun room off the parlor. "I should have guessed. You had the chocolate and biscuits already waiting."

"I hoped." She eased into the captain's chair on one side of the glass-topped, cherry-framed table and poured two cups. I took the other captain's chair.

"What do you think of the Japanese submersibles?" she asked as she handed me a cup with the gracefulness that recalled another woman.

"About the way you do about modern art, I suspect. Necessary, but hardly something you really want to support in public." I sipped the chocolate, steaming and with just the right hint of a bite. "Good chocolate."

"Thank you." She nodded. "You think the submersibles are necessary?"

"For the Japanese, they're more than that. The home islands either import almost all their raw materials or get them from their possessions. They have to expand through the islands. And now that Chung Kuo is building a navy to rival ours . . . ?" I shrugged.

"Everyone seems to be building more and more weapons. Where will it end?"

"Where it always has. In war." I tried a butter biscuit, probably too fattening but definitely delicious.

"I think you are even more cynical. Haven't you found someone? Elspeth would have liked that, you know. She wasn't possessive in that way."

I sighed. "I know. I've been seeing a singer."

"Another artistic type?" Judith laughed freely, and I smiled back. "Somehow, that doesn't surprise me. What's her name?"

"Llysette. Llysette duBoise."

"Not *the* Llysette duBoise? I thought she had died in Ferdinand's prisons."

"You know of her?"

"She was starting at the Académie Royale back when I did my fellowship there—one of the last ones before Ferdinand. Dark-haired, often piles her hair on top of her head? She was single then, and I think supporting her father."

"The same one. She had a difficult time, but they did release her. It took some diplomatic work, and she had intimated, although I didn't press, some pressure by the Japanese ambassador. He'd heard her sing."

"She was magnificent then, even that young. Why is she stuck up in the wilds? You're charming, Johan, but she would not have known you were there."

"It's a matter of economics and politics."

"Let me guess." Judith's voice turned hard. "She's a foreigner, and she probably had to have strings pulled to enter the country. No one cares if she sings in out-of-the-way places, but the dear Spazi has put out the word to the larger symphonies that they really don't want to be investigated. Something like that?"

I nodded.

"Can you do anything?"

"I haven't had much luck. Neither has she."

Judith studied me for a time. "Things are not looking good for you, are they?"

"No. That's one reason I came. Whatever happens, stay out of it. I should have spent more time with you earlier, but I didn't realize what would happen. I thought they'd leave me alone."

"They never did. Why would they now?"

I sipped my chocolate. "One hopes. Foolishly. But one hopes."

"Don't we all? Elspeth felt so badly for you, Johan, you know? If you can find happiness again, we would be happy for you."

"Thank you, Judith."

I heard steps come through the kitchen.

"Well, if it isn't the long-lost brother." Eric never called me his brother-in-law. "I hoped I'd get home a little before you left."

"You're in luck."

"Some chocolate?" asked Judith.

"Please." He sat in the middle of the love seat and looked at me. "When you're in town, there's usually trouble."

"Am I so predictable?"

He laughed. "The Japanese announced their atomic submersible. The Congress passed a tax increase, and Chung Kuo decided that Kilchu belongs to their great Manchurian heritage. In the meantime, Maximilian has decided that the export tax on Mexican crude will be upped another two dollars a barrel, and, in order not to upset the New French, the Venezuelans will follow his lead. The President is stepping up detailed budget reviews, and threatening to expose a good dozen congressmen for fraud and lying or both."

"And you're blaming it all on me?" I reached for another butter biscuit.

"Who was talking blame?" Eric took the chocolate cup from his wife with a fond smile. "Things just happen when you're around. That's probably why the Speaker was perfectly happy to let you get pensioned off into the wilds of New Bruges, up there with the bears and the cold winters."

"That's what I thought." I drained the cup.

"A little more?" asked Judith.

"Half a cup. In a while, I need to start getting dressed."

"How's the teaching?" Eric shifted his weight on the love seat.

"The teaching is interesting. Most of the students aren't. They're still in the mold of coasting through the term and then trying to cram a half year's work into three weeks."

"I can recall doing that." Eric chuckled.

"You had the brains to get away with it."

"Not the brains, just laziness."

"Hardly. Do your clients really believe that you're just a former korfball player who somehow bumbles through? Are you still cultivating that image despite the years in the Foreign Ministry?"

"Of course," laughed Judith.

"It's what makes people comfortable," admitted Eric.

"Tell me about the children," I suggested.

They did, and I listened while I finished the half cup of chocolate.

In time, I looked at my watch. "I think I had better get ready. If I could trouble you to call a cab for quarter to seven, I would appreciate it."

"Just get yourself together. We'll take care of it," promised Eric.

I took a quick shower, shaved again, and pulled on the formal wear. It was actually looser than when I'd worn it last. Was the additional exercise helping?

I didn't quite dash downstairs, where Judith met me, wrap in hand.

"You look almost good enough for me to throw over Eric." She winked, and I bowed solemnly.

"Almost, but not quite, thank heavens." He stood in the doorway. "Shall we go?"

"Is the cab here?"

"Cab? Nonsense. The least we could do is give you a lift. Besides, we'd already planned to go out."

"I do appreciate this," I offered again, as I seated Judith next to Eric in the front before climbing into the spacious rear seat.

"We were going out anyway. It's only a few blocks out of the way."

Eric wheeled the big Stanley down New Bruges Avenue, past the embassies and under Dupont Circle to where it became Seventeenth Street. Before I knew it, he pulled up in front of the Presidential Palace, right on Pennsylvania.

"Here you are."

"Thank you. I doubt I'll even be close to being late." I waved as the Stanley pulled away almost silently, then straightened and marched toward the gate. It always surprised me how quiet the federal city was, but that was because of the prohibition on internal combustion engines. Steamers only whisper along, and electrics are even quieter.

At the gate, I handed over my invitation and identification card. The guard checked both, and then put a tick mark by my name on the long list. A couple waited behind me.

"Honestly . . . don't know why we have to attend these. . . . So boring, and they even had to pad the guest list, Marcia said."

"We attend because it goes with the job, dear."

"I know . . . what one suffers in public life . . ."

She didn't know the half of it, fortunately for her.

I smiled politely at them as I walked through the gate and up the drive to the porticoed doorway.

"The honorable Johan Eschbach." The announcement carried through the foyer, but no one looked up as I stepped toward the East Room.

"The honorable David Dominick and Madame Dominick."

I smiled at the faces I did not know and made my way

toward one of the bars, the one in the far corner. People always congregate around the first place to serve.

"Red wine, Sebastopol, if you have it."

"Will a Merino do, sir?"

"Fine." I took the wine and glanced around, finally spotting a halfway familiar face. "Martin?"

"Johan." Martin Sunquist extended his hand. "I thought you had retired to the wilds of New Bruges."

"I did. The president was so desperate that they dragged me all the way down here."

His eyebrows rose. "I did hear something along those lines. Still . . ." He lifted his glass. "Whatever the reason, it's good to see you."

"Are you still over with the Budget Examiners?"

"Same building, but a new job." He lowered his voice. "Now, I examine the geographic distribution of federal programs."

"I suppose that knowledge can be used by the president . . . and Ralston."

"This president, at least." Martin took a small sip of wine and glanced toward the corner of the room. "Ralston's done a lot with the budget shop. It's a lot more confrontational than in the old days . . . even your old days."

"Even from up in the wilds I've gotten that impression."

President Armstrong entered the East Room to the sounds of the *Presidential March,* the Sousa piece commissioned to complement *Hail to the Speaker.* He stepped up before the microphones on the low platform with a Japanese in a well-cut Western suit.

"Enough of that. Welcome, Ambassador Takayama." He bowed, and Takayama bowed. "I don't have a full speech, for which I know you are all grateful. I just have a few remarks."

Sighs greeted his comments, since his remarks were known to be often less than brief.

"Truly, you understand me. But I only have a few remarks this evening . . ."

That did get a gentle laugh.

"Thirty-three years ago almost exactly, in 1960, a great and terrible event occurred with the detonation of the first nuclear device at Birel Aswad by the Austro-Hungarian scientific team following the equations developed by their mentor, Albert Einstein. We, of course, followed in 1965 at White Sands, and Chung Kuo in 1970. To date, no one has used the nuclear bomb, even in 1985. With the theoretically great power of the atom to create mass death and possibly millions of terrorized ghosts, the spectre of nuclear weapons has made them too terrible to use.

"The Imperial Republic of Japan has continued to eschew the development of the atom for weapons, a courageous prohibition. Japan has pioneered the development of atomic power plants for the peaceful use of the nuclear genie.

"We share, of course, with the Japanese, a concern that the oceans of the world remain open and free to trade. Therefore, I am pleased to announce that Emperor Akihito and I have reached a general agreement in principle that Japan and Columbia will pool their expertise in peaceful uses of the atom, including the development of oceangoing power plants . . ."

The president smiled broadly into the silence.

". . . a development which I truly hope Speaker Hartpence and the Congress will follow with the necessary implementing treaty. Now . . . enjoy the evening."

As the humming rose to a near-babble, nearly half a dozen figures scurried from the room. I was surprised there weren't more. The president had clearly outmaneuvered the Speaker again, and the Hartpencers would be looking for blood.

Martin raised his glass to me, nodded, and slipped away toward the corner. His warning bothered me—was Ralston getting as bad as the Spazi?

"What do you suppose he meant by that?" asked a graying man, older and considerably heavier than I, accompanied by a slender and well-endowed younger blond woman who smiled at me as her escort asked the question.

"I believe he has obtained the agreement of the Japanese to provide us with plans and specifications to build a nuclear-powered submersible, in return for our expertise in other areas." I bowed. "That, at least, is what I heard. One must be careful in reading too much into political statements."

"I agree," said the older man.

"Why would the Japanese do that?" asked the young woman.

"Because," I answered, "we need that technology more than either Chung Kuo or Austro-Hungary, and because we can outbid Maximilian."

"You make it sound so . . . sordid."

"It is." I laughed softly. "All politics is sordid."

She made a face, and her escort tugged her in another direction.

The reception part of the dinner concluded with "Columbia," sung by a mezzo-soprano—almost good enough to be in Llysette's class—accompanied by the Marine Corps band.

"Our God, we place our trust in thee
For Columbia, gem of freedom's sea.
As humbled souls we pray to be
Upholding those who make us free . . ."

I still wasn't sure about the humbled souls part. After milling around with the others, I let myself follow the flow into the state dining room, as we were discreetly escorted by a number of dark-clad aides to seats bearing engraved place cards.

I was seated near the end of one of the side tables, about as close to the side door as possible, next to a couple slightly younger than me. Their place cards read Doktor and Madame Velski, but we exchanged pleasantries in perfect Columbian English until the main course was being cleared.

"Excuse me, if you would." I inclined my head to Madame Velski, and eased from the chair and through the doorway, heading toward the gentlemen's facilities.

I paused by the wireset, then picked up the receiver and dialed three digits.

"The Special Assistant's office. May I help you?"

"This is Johan Eschbach."

"Thank you, Doktor."

I nodded to the marine guard by the doorway to the staircase downstairs and proceeded to the men's room. When I came out, a nervous-looking young fellow raised his hand.

"Doktor . . ."

"Yes, I'm Doktor Eschbach."

He led me past the sentry and downstairs. Ralston McGuiness was waiting for me in the anteroom, the one off the oval office used for the president's ceremonial meetings, not the office where he did actual work.

"Greetings, Ralston."

"Read this, Johan. Then we'll talk." He handed me a thin sheaf of papers and walked out, closing the door behind him.

Since I've never believed in futile protests, I began to read. After a while I could skim through it, because the minutiae of the technical details were not all that relevant, and because much of the material was recently familiar to me.

> Dr. Joachim Heisler, head of psychic research at the University of Vienna . . . arrived in Paris to review . . . experiments in targeted psychological stress.
>
> . . . theorized that psychic disassociation is not necessarily unitary, based on investigations of battlefield ghosting and investigations of European homicides . . .
>
> . . . marked attempts to conceal Heisler's research and movements . . . significantly increased workloads occurring at GRI military difference engine centers . . . special helmets assembled in Bavaria . . . increased numbers of zombies processed at Imperial reeducation centers . . .

What was happening in Europe seemed almost as bad as what was happening in Columbia. I shook my head as I completed skimming through the material.

"Finished?" asked Ralston from the door to the Oval Office. He closed it behind him.

"Enough to get the gist of it all."

"What do you think?" He pulled out the chair on the far side of the small, circular conference table.

"We've got trouble."

"Tell me why?"

"You know perfectly well why, Ralston. That's not why you summoned me."

"Johan, it's been a long week. Humor me. The president lost four men getting that information. Canfield went part ghost, and he's babbling about disasters and catastrophe."

"Why not run it by Spazi research? That's more their line than mine."

"Very humorous, Johan. Perhaps we will, if we can't figure it out, and we'll attribute it to you. Or to Doktor duBoise." He smiled a smile I didn't like at all.

I cleared my throat. Just what did he want? A reason to put me in one of the dark cells in the subsubcellar of the budget building? Or was it an intelligence test of some sort, to see how obvious the not-so-obvious was? "It seems as though Ferdinand's tame psychic wizards have figured out how to create exactly the kind of ghosts they want. That part doesn't bother me nearly so much as it would bother the Anglican-Baptists or Speaker Hartpence. The other part does."

"The other part?" prompted Ralston, with only a slight delay to my cue.

"What do they have left when they've created a ghost?"

"A happy zombie, usually."

"Humor me this time. What if you could stick someone under one of Doktor Heisler's helmets and just target a few aspects of their brain? You know, facets dealing with integrity, or fear, or conscience?"

"You pass," answered Ralston.

I kept my mouth shut. Ralston hadn't blinked an eye, had been almost matter-of-fact. Despite the dates on the papers, he had already known. I asked, "Is Ferdinand creating ghost-immune troops?"

"There's at least one battalion, but the process isn't foolproof. It only works about fifty percent of the time."

"So we have the ghost-research war?"

"What do you mean, Johan?"

Did I play dumb, still treading between two payrolls? Did I have any choice? If Ralston knew what I actually knew, I'd likely have a heart attack on the spot, a fatal one. VanBecton was playing to set me up, and so was Ralston. I knew why vanBecton was, but not Ralston, unless he had exactly the same idea as vanBecton, which was certainly possible. And I hadn't liked the reference to turning Llysette over to the Spazi.

"You send me clippings that show destruction of psychic research facilities, but earlier this week I read a few clippings of my own, about the fires and explosions in the Munich Babbage center. I'm supposed to believe that's accidental, especially after what you've just shown me?"

"There is that. What if I said we didn't have anything to do with Munich?"

"We meaning the president, or we meaning Columbia?"

"Either."

"Then it looks like someone else is playing. The Turks can't afford to, and that leaves the Far East or deGaulle."

"We think deGaulle. What did vanBecton tell you?"

"Not much. He says that Llysette duBoise is an agent of Takaynishu, and he wants me to look into Miranda Miller's murder."

"I assume you have. What have you reported?"

"It appears as though Professor Miller was co-opted by New France. Her son was arrested on a trumped-up importing charge last year." I shrugged.

"Then who owns Doktor duBoise?"

"Does anyone?" I asked.

"You do, apparently, or she owns you, but I'm interested in the unsubordinated share."

"I don't know. The Japanese ambassador intervened to have her released from prison, and she was tortured by Ferdinand, but . . . I don't see any signs there, and that bothers me."

"It bothers me, too, Johan, and it bothers the president a lot. Right now, we have the Speaker on the run, but one false step and it could all unravel. VanBecton wants you to take that false step."

"But," I smiled, "if I disappeared at a Presidential Palace function, that would also unravel things."

"Yes, it would." Ralston McGuiness did not smile.

"So what do you need?"

"We need to know who Doktor duBoise works for, and we need to have a scandal involving vanBecton, one without your fingerprints on it. So please just keep to your assignment with Doktor duBoise, and report to vanBecton. If you solve the Miller murder, so much the better. Just keep things quiet, the way we like them."

"And if vanBecton falls flat on his face that would be fine—provided no one is within a hundred miles of him."

"That's too close. So don't do it." Ralston glanced toward the door. "You need to get back upstairs. One last thing. Was there any link between Miller and the Babbage center?"

"She had a lot of conversations with Branston-Hay."

"Does vanBecton know this?"

"Yes."

"I wish he didn't." Ralston stood. "Just keep things quiet."

"I'll do what I can, but it isn't going to be easy. VanBecton wants a mess, preferably with me in it."

"We know. We think you can handle it."

"What's vanBecton's clout?"

"You didn't know?" Ralston grinned. "Besides being the

number two in the Spazi, vanBecton is Defense Minister Holmbek's son-in-law."

I wiped my forehead on the cotton handkerchief, wishing I weren't sweating, but your body can betray you more quickly than your mind. "Holmbek's not the Speaker, and he gave up his seniority to take Defense," I pointed out.

"He and Speaker Hartpence both belong to Smoke Hill and bowl together twice a week." Ralston nodded sagely, as if that explained everything. Lawn bowling certainly gave time for exchanging confidences, but that didn't mean that the Speaker would automatically do what Holmbek or vanBecton wanted. It did mean that what they did was probably what the Speaker wanted. At that I did shiver.

"You see?" asked Ralston.

"Thanks." I left and went back upstairs, just in time to finish a sloppy peach melba and to listen to a whole round of toasts that said even less than normal, as if the toasters had been carefully instructed by the president—or his budget examiners. Even for the ceremonial head of state, money talks, just less directly.

After the evening ended I walked up Sixteenth a bit and hailed a cab.

It was past eleven when Eric opened the door for me.

"Judith's gone to bed. Do you want to talk?"

"Just for a bit."

We walked into his study.

"How bad is it?" He eased into his chair in the graceful way that only a large athletic man can.

"About as bad as it can get before it really gets bad."

"No bodies yet?"

"One. A professor at the university was killed for no apparent reason. The Spazi moved in, with just enough presence to advertise to those who might be looking. There seem to be disproportionate numbers of people whose backgrounds are thin, mine included."

"What's the game?"

"Everyone is out to play Pin the Tail on Johan, but I can't figure out why, at least not for everyone."

"Deep game?"

I nodded. "It might have been a setup from before I left here."

"Oh, shit, Johan. Can't they just leave you alone?"

"It doesn't look that way."

"Is there anything I can do?"

"As I told Judith, after tomorrow morning just stay out of the way. I don't think there's anything you can do, and . . . I just can't have anyone . . . anyone else . . ." I swallowed and sat there.

He actually got up and patted my shoulder, and we looked into the darkness for a time before we went to bed. At least he had Judith. Llysette was six hundred fifty miles away physically, and who knew how much further in her mind?

15

JUDITH, DRESSED IN a maroon suit, and Eric, dressed in dark gray pinstripes, were at the kitchen table by the time I managed to stagger through the shower and dressing.

The broad bay window in which the solid-oak kitchen table sat revealed the kind of gray autumn day that had been all too common when I had lived in the Federal District. In a perverse way, it was gratifying to know that some aspects of life didn't change.

"Good morning, Johan. How was your presidential dinner?" asked Judith, rising gracefully. "Tea?"

"Please." I bumbled into the empty chair, dodging the knife-edged perfection of the table edge and old memories raised by a sister-in-law in a maroon suit.

After Judith poured the tea, I loaded it with raw sugar, then began to open the banana laid beside the heavy, honeyed, nut-covered sweet roll on my plate. The sweet roll would have to wait.

"The dinner?" prompted Eric.

"You saw the paper? The business about the Japanese sharing their nuclear submersible technology? I presume it was in the paper?"

"Oh, that?" Eric nodded. "It was in the paper. I'd seen some speculations about that earlier, though."

"Why would the Japanese give us that technology?" asked Judith.

"I doubt that they exactly gave it to us, dear. The question is how President Armstrong thinks he can persuade the Speaker."

I had to snort at that. "What choice does the Speaker have? With the free-traders after his head, he's going to turn down a technology that will give us the upper hand over Ferdinand's navy? At least for a little while." The tea tasted good, and the sugar definitely helped. I took a small bite of the sweet roll.

"Right," affirmed Eric. "I'm sure the Austro-Hungarians are working on their own nuclear submersibles."

"It's all so pointless." Sitting across from me, Judith nibbled on her roll, then sipped her tea. "I mean, what's the purpose in taxing people to raise more money to build better ways to destroy more people? In the end, we're all either poorer or dead."

"God, you're depressing." Eric finished off the last half of the enormous sweet roll in a single bite.

"The truth sometimes is." Another small bite of the banana was all I could manage, followed by more tea. "Maybe that's why it's hard to live here. You either face the truths and get depressed, or don't face them and let yourself be deluded."

"What does where you live have to do with that?" asked Eric as he poured a second cup of tea. "Everyone in the whole country has the same choice."

"I don't know that it's so obvious elsewhere." I finished the first cup of tea and reached for the pot.

"Then if you're looking for honesty, isn't this a better place to live?" asked Judith, her question followed by a bright smile.

I had to nod. "But are most people really looking for honesty?"

Eric snorted again.

"What are you going to do?" Judith asked quietly.

"Try to survive." I forced a grin. "Anything on a higher ethical plane is beyond me right now."

"You aren't *that* cynical, Johan."

"I wish I weren't, sometimes." I swallowed another half-cup of tea in a single gulp, almost welcoming the burning sensation. "I need to get moving if I want to catch one of the midday trains." I looked toward the wireset.

"I'll drop you off," said Eric.

"A cab might be better."

"Better for what? We're family," Eric insisted. "Anyone who's after you knows you stayed here. I'll run you down when you're ready, and that's that."

"Absolutely," Judith affirmed.

After draining the last of the tea, I went upstairs and grabbed the garment bag and my travel case. Both Eric and Judith were standing in the main foyer when I came down the stairs.

"Ready?" asked Eric.

I nodded.

Judith put her arms around me. "Take care, Johan." Her eyes were wet as she stepped back.

"I'll try, but you know how much good that's done before."

She gave me a last hug and turned away quickly.

Eric and I left and got into the big steamer silently. We were headed down New Bruges Avenue and almost to the Japanese Embassy before he spoke. "This whole business has Judith upset, you know."

"I know."

"Is there any way you can get out of whatever this mess is? I don't want a brother who's a zombie. You were pretty close last time."

"I'm trying." I didn't want to think about that. Was I already sliding off into ghost land? "A big part of the problem is that I don't know the whole picture. It's tied up with psychic research, and you know how touchy that's gotten to be."

Eric whistled softly. "I didn't know, but there have been a number of hints in the press lately, haven't there?"

"Where there's smoke . . ."

"Don't get burned, Johan."

"I'll try not to."

He let me out right in front of the B&P Station, which wasn't too hard, since the morning rush had long since subsided. As soon as I got inside the station, I stopped by the first public wireset and used my account number to call Anna's.

"This is the Durrelts'. To whom do you wish to speak?"

"Anna, this is Johan."

"Johan?"

"Your nephew? The crazy one? The professor?"

"Oh, Johan. I thought you were trying to be Johan de Waart, and you don't sound anything like him. Do you want to speak to your mother?"

"First, will you both be there if I come by this afternoon?"

"That's a long drive. Yes, we can be here."

"I'll be there around three, I think."

"Don't you . . ."

"I have to run, Aunt Anna. I'll see you this afternoon."

The next stop was the ticket window. Instead of the Quebec Special, I had to take the ten o'clock Montreal Express to get to Schenectady, and, after my visit with Mother and Anna, I would have to take a local from Schenectady northeast across New Ostend and into New Bruges and a good eighty miles into the state to Lebanon. That probably meant arriving home late on Friday night or in the very early hours of Saturday morning. I hoped I'd be able to doze on the trains.

After I made sure that I had some time before the Montreal Express left, I used a public wireset in the B&P station to call Bruce.

"LBI."

"Bruce, this is Johan. I need a gadget that does the exact

opposite of the last two you did. One that can take a program file and project it into one of those fields and into the atmosphere, so to speak. Can you do it?"

"Johan . . ." There was a long pause. "I suppose so. Is it . . . wise?" He laughed. "No, of course not. Not if it's you. Yes, I'll do it. Monday?"

"You're a saint."

"Probably not. It's against my religion."

"All right, a prophet."

"You can be both, and have the grief."

"Fine. Monday. I'll still pick up the other gear as we scheduled earlier."

"It will be waiting."

"Thanks."

After replacing the handset, I walked across the green marble floor of the main hall toward the gate for platform six and then down the steps to the platform itself. The cars of the Montreal Express were gleaming silver, freshly washed.

The conductor studied me, his eyes going from the pinstriped suit to the garment bag and leather case. "Your ticket, sir?"

I offered it, breathing in the slight odor of oil and hot metal that persists even with the modern expresses.

"Club car, seats three and four."

I nodded and climbed up the steps. The seats were the reclining type, and because the train was a midday, the almost-new club car was but half filled. The odor of new upholstery and the even fainter hint of the almost-new lacquer on the wood panels bolstered my impressions of newness, despite the traditional darkness of the wood and the green hangings.

I sat on the train for nearly half an hour before it smoothly dropped into the north tunnel. We emerged from the darkness in a cut between long rows of brown stone houses, looking almost gray in the late October rain, and glided northward at an increasing pace. I was still holding the unopened case when the express paused in Baltimore, slowing so gently that the conductor's call came as a surprise.

"Baltimore. All off for Baltimore."

The doors opened, and eventually they closed, and no one sat near me.

Finally, somewhere north of Baltimore, about the time we crossed the Susquehanna on the new high-speed bridge west of Havre de Grace, I opened my travel case. As I took out the memos I had pilfered from vanBecton, rain began to pelt the car windows, hard and cold as liquid hail.

Certainly vanBecton knew I had pocketed something with the pratfall, and he had let me get away with it, thinking I would get nothing. What I hoped he didn't realize was that I wasn't after anything that concrete.

He was setting me up for removal, and he was saying, in effect, that I could do nothing about it. My own experiences had taught me one thing he hadn't learned yet, and I could only hope it would be enough.

I took out the pilfered memos and began to read. As vanBecton had indicated, they were pretty much all administrative trivia. One dealt with the allocation of administrative support funds. The second, signed by vanBecton, was a clarification of Spazi regional office boundaries. Another was on the subject of the United Charities Fund and the need for supervisors to encourage giving. There was a three-page, detailed exposition on the required procedures for claiming reimbursement for travel and lodging expenses.

The formats were virtually identical, but what I had wanted was the one with vanBecton's signature. I read it again and replaced all of them in the case. Then I leaned back and took a nap, trying to ignore the uneven rhythm of the rain.

Three stops and four hours later, I stepped out into the rain in Schenectady station, a cold rain that slashed across my face and left dark splotches on my coat.

I found a cab, a New Ostend special that gleamed

through the mist and rain. The water beaded up on every painted surface, and the round-faced and white-haired driver smiled.

"Where to, sir?"

"Kampen Hills, number forty-three on Hendrik Lane."

"Good enough, sir."

Even the inside of the cab was spotless, and I leaned back into the seat as the driver wound his way away from the Rotterdam side, along the river road, and into the hills dotted with houses centered on gardens, now mulched for winter and surrounded with snow stands to protect the bushes.

In the summer, each gray house and its stonework and white-enameled windowsills would be diminished by the trees and the well-tended gardens, the arbors and the trellises. Now, the houses were stolid gray presences looming through the rain and mist.

There is always a price for everything, and that New Ostend special from the Schenectady station out to Anna's cost more than all the cabs I had taken the day before in the Federal District.

"Ten, that'll be, sir."

I paid him, with a dollar tip, and then I stood in the rain for far too long before my aunt finally came to the door.

"Johan, what are you doing out there in the rain? Don't you know that you come in out of such a downpour before you become a real ghost?"

I refrained from pointing out that entering unannounced was poor manners, and also impossible when the door was locked.

"Can you join us for chocolate?"

"I had hoped to," I answered honestly. "The local for Lebanon leaves at seven."

"Good! That's settled. Now off to the rear parlor with your mother while I get the chocolate and biscuits." Anna, more and more like a white-haired gnome with every passing year, shooed me down the hall and past the warmth welling from the kitchen.

"Your ne'er-do-well son is here, Ria," my aunt announced. "I'll be bringing the chocolate in a bit. Let him sit by the fire. He stood in the rain for far too long, silly man."

Mother stood up from her rocking chair, and I hugged her, not too long, since I was rather damp.

"I didn't expect you."

"I wired Anna when I left Columbia."

"She gets rather forgetful these days."

I took the straight-backed chair and pulled it closer to the woodstove. "Don't we all?"

"What were you doing in Columbia, Johan?"

"I was invited to a presidential dinner. I stayed last night with Eric and Judith."

"They're nice people, unlike so many in the capital. How was your dinner?" She picked up her knitting—red and gold yarn in what seemed to be an afghan. "As I recall, you never enjoyed those functions much. Why did you go?"

"It seemed like a good idea." I shrugged.

"Was it?"

"I suppose so. It appears I did not have much choice, as things turned out."

The heat from the stove was drying my suit—thoughtless of me not to have brought a waterproof, or an umbrella, English as that might have been.

"We always have choices, even if none of them are pleasant." Mother smiled.

"You are so cheerful about it."

"Johan, you survived the Spazi. I'm certain you could survive a presidential dinner. How is your lady friend, the singer?"

"Llysette? She's fine. She gave a concert two weeks ago. Unfortunately, the piano professor was murdered—"

"You wrote me about that. Dreadful thing to happen, especially right before she was going to perform."

"She didn't find out until after the recital."

"You see . . . even terrible occurrences have bright sides."

I shook my head. "The professor's ghost did hang around for a while."

"That happens. Poor soul."

"I suppose so. Aren't all ghosts?" I paused. "Speaking of ghosts, who was Carolynne? Really, I mean. Besides a singer who got murdered?"

Mother sat in the heavy rocker, the wide needles in her time-gnarled hands, the yarn still in response to my question. Finally she lifted the needles again. "You needn't bother with her. She must be gone by now. It was a long time ago."

"She's still there. I can see her on the veranda some nights. She quotes obscure sections of Shakespeare and some of the Shakespearean operas."

Mother kept looking at the red glow behind the mica glass of the stove. I waited, seemingly forever. "I told your father that reading Shakespeare, especially the plays she had performed, was only going to make her linger."

"I thought she was a singer."

"In those days, college teachers had to do more. She was a singer—the first real one at the college, according to your father. Sometimes she talked to him. He said she was stabbed to death, but she never talked about it to me. I don't know as she really said much except those same quotes from Shakespeare, but your father said the quotes made a sort of sense. That's why he read Shakespeare back."

"That means she was stabbed at the house."

"She was supposed to have been the lover of the deacon who built the house. His wife had stayed in Virginia, but she—the wife—finally decided to come to New Bruges. She didn't bother to tell her husband. I think she suspected, but she stabbed Carolynne when she found her asleep beside her husband late one afternoon."

I waited for a time, and the needles clicked faintly against each other and the yarn in the ball dwindled slowly as the afghan grew. Finally I ventured a statement. "That had to have been more than a century ago."

"I thought she would fade."

"I think she's as strong as ever."

"Your father's meddling, I dare say. Told him no good would come of that."

"She seems so sad."

"Most ghosts who linger do, son." Her tone turned wry, and the needles continued to click. "So do most people who linger."

"I suppose so."

"Here's the chocolate!" announced Anna, bustling in with a huge tray heaped with cakes, cookies, biscuits, and an imposing pot of chocolate.

I slipped up one side of the drop-leaf table for her, then poured out the three cups and served them. Anna took the other straight-backed armchair.

"Cake?" I asked Mother.

"Just a plain one."

I turned to Anna.

"I'll have a pair of the oatmeal cookies."

After serving them, I heaped a sampling of all the baked goods on my plate—about the only lunch and supper I was probably going to get, and far better than the lukewarm fare on the trains.

"We don't see you enough," offered Anna after a silence during which we had all eaten and sipped.

"I try, but about half the time when I'm free, you two are off to visit someone else."

"That's better than sitting around and watching each other grow old."

"This is the first time I've seen both of you sitting in months."

"We're resting up. Tonight we're going to the Playhouse performance of *Your Town.*"

I frowned, not having ever cared for the Pound satire on *Our Town.* Then again, Pound was just another of the thirties crazies who'd never discovered what they had rebelled against. *Your Town* was the only play he wrote, if I recalled it right, and it flopped in Philadelphia just before Pound moved to Vienna. He'd finally ended up writing propaganda scripts for Ferdinand—all justifying the unification of Europe under the Hapsburgs.

"I need to arrange for a cab," I finally said.

"So soon?" asked Anna.

"I have to meet with an electronics supplier in the morning."

"What does electronics have to do with your teaching?" asked Mother.

"It's equipment for my difference engine."

"Better spend more time with your singer than the machine. Machines don't exactly love you back," said Anna.

"No. But they make writing articles and books much easier."

Mother shook her head. "Just be careful, Johan. These are dangerous times."

Anna gave her sister a puzzled look, and then glanced at me. "Sometimes you two leave everyone else out of the conversation."

"I have to wire a cab." I made my way back to the front parlor and used the wireset to arrange for Schenectady Electrocab to pick me up at six.

"Is it set?" asked Mother when I returned. She had set aside the piece of knitting she had apparently completed and was beginning another section with the same colors.

"Six o'clock." I poured another cup of chocolate and helped myself to two more oatmeal cookies, promising myself that I'd step up my exercise the next day.

"You never did say much about your singer," suggested Anna. "That murder business must have upset her."

My mother grinned and kept knitting.

"We were all somewhat upset—especially the music department. It's not pleasant to have the ghost of a murdered woman drifting through the halls. Luckily, she didn't linger too long."

"Did the watch ever find the murderer?"

"Not so far. I think they suspect about half the university." I was beginning to feel sleepy, with the fullness in my stomach and the warmth of the second cup of chocolate, and I yawned.

"You're not getting enough sleep."

"Too much traveling."

"Well, I say it's a shame," offered Anna. "Might I have some more chocolate?"

I refilled her cup. "It certainly is."

"Universities are almost as bad as government."

"It's hard to tell the difference." I stifled a yawn, and munched another oatmeal cookie. "Except universities don't have to be petty and are, while almost no one in government means to be petty, but the results almost always are."

"He's still cynical," Anna said after lifting her cup for a refill.

I understood why her chocolate pot was so large.

"He's still alive," added Mother.

What could I add to that? Mother had been the practical one, my father the dreamer, and I probably had gotten the worst of each trait.

After arriving right at six, the cab made it through the rain and back to the station by six-thirty. There I joined a small queue of dampened souls at the ticket window and purchased my twenty-one-dollar fare to Lebanon.

The seven-fifteen local back to Lebanon whined its way out of New Ostend into western New Bruges and into the hills that comprised the southern Grunbergs. As the slow train wound north and east through the continuing rain, I sat on a hard coach bench and tried to think it all through.

I'm not exactly a political genius when it comes to unraveling the intrigues of the Federal District, but one thing seemed clear enough. A lot of defense projects in Babbage centers were ostensibly out to destroy the ghosts and the basis of ghosts in our world. On the surface, it seemed plausible.

Why not destroy ghosts? You know, put them out of their misery. Save them from lingering eternally and poisoning the present with their haunting gloom.

Was that bad? I thought so.

Wasn't it just possible that the slow progress of conquest was due in part to the inability of soldiers to accept ghosts on a massive basis? Supposedly the horrors of Hastings almost undid the armies of William the Unfortunate, so much so that it was three generations before his heir fully grasped even England.

Firearms had helped dispel that ghostly influence, especially for those armies with sharpshooters, like the assassin regiments of Ferdinand VI. But sometimes a good general can use horrors, as the New French general Santa Anna did at the Alamo. He was really a Mexican then, but that's not what the New French histories state. On balance, it seemed as though modern technology and medicine were slowly destroying ghosts, except in warfare, which is barbarous by nature.

But all the ghost-related projects were being fired and/or having difficulty—and that went for projects in Europe as well as in Columbia. Except there was something wrong with my logic, and I couldn't put my finger on it.

I leaned back in the hard seat of the local and tried to fall asleep in the dim light, with the *click, clickedy, click* of the rails in one ear and the snoring of the heavyset woman two seats back in the other.

In the end, I neither slept nor thought, but sat there in a semidaze until I reached Lebanon.

In the station parking lot, the dowager-sleek lines of the Stanley waited for me, half concealed in the mist created by the cold rain that had fallen on warmer pavement.

Even after two days the Stanley lit off easily, and I drove eastward through the darkness, alert for moose. The big animals had been making a comeback, and any collision between one and a steamer would favor the moose.

The rain had been warm enough that it had not formed

ice on the roads, and steady enough that few were out, even on a late Friday evening.

The only real signs of life were at the Dutch Reformed Church in Alexandria, where a handful of hardy souls were leaving a lecture on "The Growth and Heritage of the Leisure Class" by some doktor. At least, that's what I thought the rain-damped poster stated. A leisure class of Dutch heritage? I almost laughed.

Marie, bless her Dutch soul, had not only left on the light, but had left a small beef pie in the refrigerator. I wolfed down all of it cold, even before I carried my garment bag up to the bedroom.

I knew I couldn't sleep until I rechecked Branston-Hay's files, the ones I had pirated, but I did change into dry exercise sweats before I returned to the study to fire up the difference engine.

Carolynne hovered by the desk.

I bowed to her. "Good evening, Carolynne."

"Good evening, sweet prince."

"My mother was surprised that you were still around."

"No more but so?"

"Were you in love with my father?" I asked, hoping her words, twisted as they might be, would prove illuminating.

"Rich gifts wax poor when givers prove unkind."

"My father, unkind?"

"O, help him, sweet heavens!"

I tried not to shake my head. "Why do you disappear so much?"

"To have seen what I have seen, to see what I see. Thy madness be paid by weight 'til our scale turn the beam and 'til our brief candle weighs out."

I pursed my lips. What did she mean, if anything? "Brief candle weighs out?"

"The more seen I, the less to see."

Was that it? The more visible a ghost, the shorter its lingering. "But where do you go?"

"Nature is fine in love, and where 'tis fine it sends some precious instance of itself."

I shook my head. "What do you do? Being a ghost has to be boring."

"There's rue for you, and here's some for me. Fennel and kennel and the old bitch went mad." She gave me a smile, not exactly one of innocence. "Impatience does become a dog that's mad. Yet your father left me some rare and precious effects, such as reading . . ."

Ghosts committing suicide? That was what Ophelia's lines were about, but where had the other lines come from and what did they mean? Reading? Did she read when she was invisible?

"You like company?"

"Wishers were ever fools. All's but naught."

Since she was talking, more than we had since I was a small boy, I asked another question. "Some people talk about ghosts taking over people's bodies. Could that happen?"

"The grave's a fine and crowded place, and none but do there embrace." Carolynne laughed. "Mad thou art to say it, but not without ambition."

I tried not to wince at the mixed language. Was everything she spoke the result of her singing and theatre training, drilled into her being so that her ghost reacted semirationally? Or were the words random?

The translation, if I understood, if the words were more than ghostly random ramblings, was that it was dangerous, but possible. "What if . . ." I paused before continuing. "What if someone were dying, and the ghost left the body, and modern medicine saved the person?"

"First it bended, and then it broke, and pansies are for thought . . ."

She drifted away, like Ophelia on a psychic river, and I watched the faint whiteness shift through the mirror, presumably to the artificial lodestone to rebuild her strength.

Shaking my head, I reached for the switch to turn the difference engine back on. Then I rubbed my forehead. I still wondered if the files I had pilfered from Branston-Hay contained any hints of what was going on, and why vanBecton thought I was so trapped.

A good hour of scanning files in my most skeptical manner passed before I found the first hint. The key lay in one almost innocent-sounding sentence.

"*. . . principal interest was in the economic section of the draft report . . . concerns over the elimination cost per ghost . . . laughable, given the costs of any war . . .*"

I kept reading.

"*. . . without further progress in reducing per-ghost costs . . . termination of third extension set for January 1, 1994 . . .*"

At the end of another file, I found the letter steamer, so to speak.

"*RM pleased with improved replicator . . . budget review to be dropped . . .*"

I leaned back in the chair. Branston-Hay had been padding his budget, and the president's budget examiners had caught him—but they hadn't turned him in. They'd asked for some applied research. It all made sense—except Miranda's murder. Branston-Hay had no reason to murder Miranda. First, he wouldn't have really understood the political ramifications, and I had to question if Miranda would have. Except her daughter-in-law had pointed out Miranda's intuitive or spiritual understandings. So what had Miranda known that was so dangerous that someone had wanted to kill her?

She probably knew that Branston-Hay had been doing secret psychic research, but vanBecton knew that, and so had everyone else—although almost no one knew the extent of that research. Branston-Hay wasn't the type for murder; at least I didn't think so. Could vanBecton's tame Spazi have murdered her to put the finger on me? Or did vanBecton already know that I had chosen to work for the president?

What about Llysette? Where did she fit in? I had a feeling, but I couldn't really prove it.

With more questions than answers, I drifted into a doze in the chair, to be awakened by the clock's chimes. It was two o'clock, so I hadn't slept that long. I turned off the difference engine, pulled myself out of the chair, and headed up to bed.

Carolynne was nowhere to be seen, but that no longer meant much, I realized.

16

SINCE THE HOUSE was spotless—Marie did more than she should have when I was gone and less than she felt necessary, I was sure—all the housekeeping I had to do on Saturday was wash the dishes I had used for breakfast.

After I ate and did the dishes, I did get back to running and exercising. I even went over the top of the hill and along the ridge. Then I raked a huge pile of leaves into the compost pile below the garden and sprinkled lime over them.

A hundred years of work on the thin soil had resulted in soil that wasn't that thin any longer, and the grass was more like a carpet. The garden tomatoes were as good as any, and the time-domesticated raspberries and black raspberries—well, I had frozen pies, freezer jam, and whole frozen berries, more than enough to last until the next summer.

After my groundskeeping, with sweat and leaf fragments sticking together and plastered even under my clothes, I stripped, took a shower, and dressed.

Had I seen a flash of white in the study? I looked around, but didn't see Carolynne. With a sigh, I extricated the strongbox from the wall safe and pulled out another sheaf of bills for Bruce. There were still enough left, but how long they would last if I kept funding unique hardware was another question.

Outside it was sunny, but the wind was even more bitter than it had been earlier in the morning and ripped at the last of the leaves clinging stubbornly to their trees. I passed but a handful of vehicles, mostly haulers, as I drove the steamer back south to Zuider and LBI to pick up the perturbation replicator. With just scattered brown leaves on the oaks and maples, the dark winter green of the pines stood out on the woodlots higher on the low hills.

The narrow streets of Zuider were half filled, mainly with families in well-polished steamers, probably taking children to soccer practice or music lessons or the like, or headed out to shop for bargains in the new mall, the latest facet of Columbian Dutch culture.

There was another steamer in the LBI lot besides Bruce's battered Olds ragtop. He'd gotten it when the Pontiac people folded and he couldn't get decent service on his '52 ragtop.

A long-haired man was discussing musical programware. "I need more instant memory and a direct audio line . . ."

I had heard about the so-called synthesizer revolution and the predictions of Babbage-generated music or the reproduction of master concerts on magnetic disks or thin tapes. I shuddered at the thought of music being reduced to plastic. Somehow, at least a vinyl disc had the feel of semipermanence. Music on plastic tapes—that would be ghost music.

While Bruce talked with the would-be Babbage composer, I wandered around, mostly thinking. Bruce seemed able to create all this hardware from rough specifications; if it worked, why hadn't a lot of other techies done the same? Most weren't as creative as Bruce, and most had no need.

There also was another reason. Gerald's comment dropped into my mind—the point that you really couldn't murder someone in a laboratory to study the ghost. Of course, Ferdinand could—and I suspected our own dear Spazi could.

I shook my head. Then again, with all the fires in Babbage centers, I wondered if, in Branston-Hay's position, I'd even want to try freelancing. Bruce had understood it all too well—he'd stayed a techie. Nobody paid any attention to mere technicians.

Eventually the musical type left, and I wandered up to the counter. "Any specials on unique hardware?"

"No. Only on unique headaches." Bruce hauled out my difference engine box and opened the top. "Figured I might as well use your packaging for the improbable perturbation replicator."

Inside were two black metal boxes linked with cables. The bottom box had two switches on the front and Babbage cables. The top box was smaller and sprouted what appeared to be four trapezoids linked together in the shape of a crude megaphone. The top box also had two matching cable ports.

"What are these for?"

"I added those last night. I thought I could link the other gadget—I beg your pardon, the perturbation projector—to this and save some hardware. Whether it will work, I don't know yet, since I haven't built it, but it ought to. Any problem with that?"

"No."

"If you need to have the scanning antenna farther from the conversion box, you can just add more cable."

"Conversion box? I thought that's what the file protocol did."

"They're almost the same, except this is more complex. It converts an image of the field, while the other one actually removes the field and converts it."

"Oh." More pieces fell into place.

"Now . . . the other one's going to be a bear."

"I didn't think it would be easy," I admitted. "Do you need more time?"

"Do you have it?"

"I don't know." I shrugged. "Maybe."

Bruce gave me a nasty grin. "That means you don't."

"Thanks."

"I always try to be truthful. It upsets people more than lying."

"You are always so cheerful." I peeled off the bills and laid them on the counter.

"I try."

"You're very trying." I hefted the box, and Bruce held the door for me.

"The other will be ready on Monday—first thing."

"I don't know if I will be, but I'll be here."

"That's what I liked about you from the first, Johan. You're always ready—even if you haven't got the faintest idea what to do."

Since that was a pretty accurate description, I really couldn't say too much except, "Thanks."

He stood and watched while I backed out and headed back north to Vanderbraak Centre, and to the watch, and all my problems, including a ghost who had started to talk but spouted dialogue and song lyrics or librettos. Was it bad that she was spouting, or worse that I thought it made sense?

The clouds were beginning to build to the north, but they didn't seem to be moving that quickly. Neither was the traffic, once I got behind a logging steamer on the way to the biomass plant outside Alexandria. I speeded up when he took the turnoff for the Ragged Mountain Highway and Lastfound Lake.

Once I got to the house and got the box and its equipment inside, I just tucked it in a corner in the study. With the sun and the breeze I didn't feel like playing with electronics inside, especially since the approaching clouds meant snow or freezing rain later.

First I tried Llysette's wire, but she either wasn't home or didn't choose to answer. So I changed and went back outside and raked up a huge pile of leaves and began to drag and rake them down to the compost pile. The lawn was still partly green, and under the sun I sweated a lot, even with the cold wind.

Three horn toots sounded up the drive, followed by a small green Reo. Llysette parked outside the car barn and waved.

I carried the rake back up the hill and tucked it inside the car barn.

Llysette wore denim trousers and a black Irish cable-knit pullover loose enough for comfort, but with just enough hint of the curves that lay beneath. I saw her overnight case in the front seat, and a gown hung in the back.

"I wired you, but you weren't home. So I went back to working up a sweat."

"Something you must always be doing, *n'est-ce pas?*"

"Pretty much." Sweaty or not, I gave her an enthusiastic hug and a kiss, and got a reasonable facsimile in response.

"Would you like to stay for dinner?"

"Only for dinner?" She leered, which I enjoyed.

"If you insist, dear lady."

We laughed. Then a blast of much cooler air swept across the hillside, swirling some of my hard-raked leaves. Llysette shivered, and we turned to the dark clouds over the hills to the northwest.

"It looks like it might snow."

"I should hope not."

"Perhaps you'll be stuck here."

"I have to sing for the Anglican-Baptist chapel tomorrow."

"Why?"

"Because they will pay me."

"That's as good a reason as any." I laughed and pulled her case from the Reo and headed inside. She carried the gown and hung it in the closet in the master bedroom.

I hugged her again, but reluctantly released her when I heard her stomach growl. "No breakfast or lunch?"

She shrugged.

"I did have some breakfast, but no lunch. Let's see what there is."

I found a block of extra-sharp cheddar, a loaf of almost

fresh bread, and mined some good apples and a bottle of Sebastopol from the cellar.

"Good . . ." the lady murmured after three slices of cheese and a thick slab of lightly toasted oatmeal bread.

"Of course it's good. I prepared it."

"You should have been a chef, Johan."

"I'm not nearly that good. You just need a man who can cook or who can afford a chef."

"I cannot cook, not well; that is true. But choosing a man by whether he can cook . . . that I do not know."

"You already have."

At least she smiled at that.

"Your dinner at the Presidential Palace, how was it?"

I had to shrug. "I guess it was history-making. I heard the president announce the agreement with Japan for us to get their nuclear submersible technology."

"Of this you do not sound too positive."

"It may be necessary, but I'm not terribly fond of ways to improve military technology. You might have noticed that not very many generals or emperors die in wars."

"So? They are the leaders." Her tone was matter-of-fact, as if we were discussing the weather.

"So? I have this mental problem with people who are so willing to send others off to do the killing, but who take none of the risks themselves."

Llysette gave me a sad smile. "In some things you are predictably Columbian. Always there have been rulers, and always there are soldiers. The soldiers die, and the rulers rule. Yet you think it should be otherwise. Would the soldier make a good ruler?"

"Not necessarily. That wasn't my point. I do think many rulers would not be so eager to start wars if they stood to die with their soldiers."

"You are right, but who could make a ruler face such risks? The world, it does not work that way."

"No, it doesn't." I sliced some more cheese and offered it to Llysette. "Here."

"Thank you." She pursed her lips. "You are angry with me."

"No . . . not exactly angry. But sometimes I don't understand. You've suffered a lot, and it's almost like you're defending the system that tortured you."

Llysette took a long sip of the Sebastopol before answering. "I see things as they are, Johan. Not one thing that Ferdinand or your Speaker does, not one thing I can change. You, you still dream that you can make the world better. I lost that dream." She took a deep breath. "That, it makes a big difference between us. You have lost much. I know. But you will die thinking you can change the world. Perhaps you will." She shivered.

It was my turn to sip wine and think. Much of what Llysette said made sense. Even after Minister Dolan denied Elspeth's and my request for her treatment in Vienna, even after Elspeth's death, I kept believing one person could make a difference. I guess I still did. "I suppose I will."

"I know. That is why I care for you. Yet that is also what separates us."

I shrugged. *"Vive la différence."*

"Vive la différence." Her shrug was sadder, almost resigned.

"Do you want any more cheese?"

"Non."

I packed up the bread and cheese, but did refill her wine glass before I recorked it, and we repaired to the main parlor, adjoining the study, where I opened the shades fully. The sun had begun to fade with the approaching clouds, but the day was still bright.

Llysette sat on the couch with her wine glass in her right hand. I sat on her left and nibbled her ear. She didn't protest. So I kissed her cheek, and stroked her neck.

"Feels good . . ." she murmured.

"I certainly hope so." I kissed her again, and let my fingers caress her neck, then knead out the stiffness in both her neck and shoulders.

"So easy to feel good . . . with you . . ."

I kissed her on the lips, very gently, very slowly, and returned to loosening the muscles in her neck and back. Under the sweater and blouse, her skin was like velvet.

After a while she put down the wine glass, and a while after that she didn't need the sweater—or much of anything else—to keep warm.

Later, much later, as I held Llysette, the quilt wrapped around us, and we watched the flicker of the flames in the mica glass of the woodstove, I wondered if Carolynne watched, unseen, and what she thought. Did she see us and wish to be flesh and blood again?

How could she not? I knew I would, were I locked into some place where I was bodiless and could only talk to a handful of souls across a century. But could she talk, or was I imagining it?

I shivered.

"You are cold, Johan?"

"A little chill."

"You who are always so hot?"

"It happens." My eyes flicked to the window. "It's beginning to snow."

"That is what the videolink forecast."

"You actually watch the video?"

"Sometimes. It is . . . amusing."

"Terrifying is more like it."

"Johan, sometimes . . . there is very little difference between terror and amusement." Her lips reached mine again, and they were warm, which was good because I was chilled all the way through to my soul.

17

I CANNOT BELIEVE you are going to sing for the Anglican-Baptists. Especially for just ten dollars." I swallowed the last of my chocolate. Since she was not singing at the Dutch Reformed Church, I wasn't going to be particularly godly. In fact, I was going to work on the definitely ungodly business of psychic phenomena, and trust that Klaus Esterhoos didn't find out. But then I doubted that he would have cared that much.

"It is a comedown, no? But what am I supposed to do? Starve?" Llysette shrugged before picking up her coffee cup.

I tried not to shudder. Either chocolate or tea—those I could take for breakfast. But coffee? I ground it fresh for Llysette, and fresh-ground coffee smells wonderful. I love the smell; it's the taste I abhor.

"You're not exactly about to starve, even on your salary."

"Johan, my recital gowns, once they cost more than I make in a month here."

I nodded, because Llysette does have exquisite taste, and fulfilling good taste never comes cheaply. I'd also priced recital gowns, and while university administrations expect performers to make a good impression, their pay scale always falls short of their expectations of performing artists.

Cost accounting, again—a business professor can teach eighty students in a class and ten in an intensive seminar. A singer or instrumentalist can teach only one pupil at a time effectively. So a three-credit business lecture course generates over ten thousand dollars and takes less than three hours of lecture time for the professor. He generates three thousand dollars per credit. Poor Llysette or poor dead Miranda spent three hours a week with a student, got two teaching credits, and generated only a hundred dollars.

It's no wonder the performing arts have little administration or state funding support. Yet how can you develop the arts without education? I shook my head, but Llysette didn't notice my distraction.

"New recital gowns I cannot buy, and I will not count every penny which crosses my palm."

"How about silvers?"

"One does not have to count silvers."

I refilled her empty coffee cup, and then poured the last from the chocolate pot into my cup.

Outside, the wind whispered past the kitchen window, blowing a few flakes of the light snow off the Reo.

"It's still cold, but I suppose winter had to come sometime."

"Winter? It is October until tomorrow, Johan. Christmas—it is two months away. Winter I am not prepared for. Your winters are too long, far too long."

"Will you come back after you sing this morning?"

"*Non.* I cannot. Yesterday was ours. This afternoon and tonight I must prepare for the advanced diction class—my notes. It is another new class. And when I try to prepare here"—she smiled at me—"I do not prepare."

"You know the material."

"Knowing the material, that is one thing. Teaching it to these dunderheads is something else."

I sighed. "I understand, but I don't exactly like it, and I'm not rich enough to rescue you from such drudgery."

"I did not ask you to rescue me, Johan." Llysette stood. "I

must get ready to perform my single solo for the Anglican-Baptists. And all for ten dollars." She sniffed.

After I washed the dishes, I followed her upstairs.

By then she was applying makeup, not that I thought she really needed very much.

"Lunch tomorrow?"

"But of course. That is one of my joys."

"What? Escaping the students?"

She raised her eyebrows. "How do you know I wish to escape all the students?"

"I forgot. You have some special baritones. Be careful, though. I'm a dangerous man . . . and a possessive one."

"I know, and that is amusing." She slipped out of the robe she left at the house and into the dark green dress, studying her reflection in the full-length mirror. "I look old."

"No, you don't."

"If I know old I look, then old I look." She straightened and lifted her cloak from where she had flung it on the bed. I'd have to make the bed after she left, but she got upset if I continually tidied up the place.

"But these . . . Anglican-Baptists, they will not see, and the money I need."

"You look good enough to . . ." I kissed her cheek.

"That you have already." She smiled, and we walked downstairs.

I took the broom and swept a path to the Reo and brushed the snow off. Then, after I watched her turn onto Deacon Lane, I wandered back into the kitchen and made another pot of chocolate. It was going to be a long day. Llysette had said it was amusing that I was possessive. Why? I shook my head, took a last look at the dark dual tracks in the snow on the drive, and closed the door. If I had thought the snow would stay, I would have gotten out the tractor and plowed the drive, but the six inches were already melting into slush.

When I went back into the study, I set my mug on the

coaster on the corner of the Kunigser desk. Then I dragged out the two boxes with the LBI logo. I shook my head. Why I kept the toolbox in the car barn I still didn't know, but that meant another trip through the whitecapped slush that wasn't really snow.

Because Bruce built things that actually made sense, it almost took more time to get and return the toolbox than to physically install the perturbation replicator. Once again, the hardware was the easy part.

Trying to figure out the necessary programware was a mess, even cribbing liberally from Branston-Hay's files and notes. All I really wanted was what I thought would be about a twenty-line program. It took me almost a hundred and fifty, and it looked more like one of the Brit programs I'd developed years ago.

The sun was setting behind Vanderbraak Centre before I finished the program. Whether it would work or not was another question, but I was very glad of the Brit assignment. I'd grumbled about learning Babbage code—Elspeth teased me about that to the end—but after investing the time, I'd kept up as well as I could with the latest developments. Not only had it kept me busy through some dark times, but it had proved useful—especially now.

After installing the program, I took a break and wandered into the kitchen, where I put on the kettle for tea. I needed some very strong tea. The odds were that I'd fouled up somewhere, and I wasn't up to facing the repair job until I was refreshed.

While the kettle heated, I rummaged through the refrigerator and dug out some white cheddar. Then I cut two large slabs of oatmeal bread, just about finishing the loaf, and toasted them. Just to experiment, I used the Imperial Russian tea that Llysette had given me for my birthday, but didn't let it steep too long as I saw how quickly the boiling water darkened around the tea caddy.

One sip of the tea told me why it was an imperial blend—it was strong enough even to knock over a czar, not that the fading remnants of the Romanovs would be that hard to unseat. I dosed my mug with raw sugar, lots of it, but even before I got through half a cup at the kitchen table my heart was racing. I slapped blackberry preserves on the bread, and both slabs helped calm me down. I was jittery still by the time I walked back into the study, lit only by the glow from the difference engine screen. I turned on the lamp on the desk.

I was right. The first time I tried to execute the program, the engine locked. It took an hour to track down that glitch, one symbol on line twelve. All in all, it was nearly ten o'clock before the system *seemed* to work.

I turned off the difference engine and went back into the kitchen to fix a late supper, not that there was that much left in the refrigerator. Outside, the wind was howling, and it seemed like it was cold enough to freeze the remaining slush and water on the drive. I turned on the light and peered out, nodding at the reflections on the patches of black ice.

Finally I made an omelet with cheese and some mushrooms and apple slices, and slathered it with sour cream mixed with curry powder. Sounds barbaric, like a relic from the days before the British got pounded out of India by the Muslim resurgence, but it was tasty.

Once refreshed, I returned to the fray, except I couldn't do much without a ghost. So I turned down the lights and left the difference engine off.

"Carolynne? Carolynne?"

There wasn't any answer, or response, and not much that I could do. So I looked through the shelves for something halfway interesting to read and pulled out something I hadn't seen before—*The Green Secession,* one of those alternate-worlds fantasies. In this one there weren't any ghosts, apparently, and Columbia was called something like the United States of America.

I turned on the reading light by the leather chair in front of the shelves. From what I could tell after the first twenty pages, the United States had a president, but he had almost as much power as the Speaker. They had a two-house Congress, with lords, except they were called senators, and a lot of representatives who didn't seem much concerned with anything but reelection. Still . . . it was fascinating.

After perhaps forty pages I called, "Carolynne." But she was nowhere to be seen.

I called her name at irregular intervals several more times. By half-past midnight, I had almost finished my improbable novel about a Columbia, or United States, I guess, where status and power almost seemed to be separate.

At almost one o'clock, on the last page of the book, Carolynne appeared at my shoulder, still in her antique recital gown.

"More to know did never meddle with my thoughts."

"Didn't you hear me calling?" I turned off the reading light to see her more clearly.

She smiled coyly. "Your tale, sir, would cure deafness."

I sighed.

"Nor can imagination form a shape, yet once was I a shape."

I thought about that. For all her scrambled quotes, Carolynne was definitely a person, but had Miranda's ghost been one? What had Branston-Hay's trapping done to her? I shivered.

"Dead, what is there I shall die to want, nor desire to give?" She stopped speaking abruptly and drifted a few feet back from my shoulder and into the center of the study. "It would become me as well as it does you."

"I wanted to know if you would help me."

"I am a fool to weep at what I am glad of." She eased toward me.

Although I could sense something like fear as she neared the silent difference engine, I added, "You wouldn't have to get close. If you stay by the doorway, can you avoid being drawn to the difference engine here?"

"But this is trifling." She paused. "And all the more it seeks to hide itself."

"No, I'm not trying to hide anything," I answered truthfully. "I want to test something. It is supposed to make a difference engine . . . picture, I guess would be the closest term. If you feel yourself being trapped or pulled, let me know, and I'll turn it off like I did before."

"You may deny me, but I'll be your servant."

"I'll be more quick." I set up the device so that it was focused on her, then turned on the difference engine. As it came up to speed, Carolynne seemed to flutter, but she hovered by the doorway.

As quickly as I could, I trained the replicator on her, and entered the command lines, one after the other. "Define" was the first, and the machine typed back, "Definition commencing," then "Definition complete." "Replicate" was followed by the response "replication commencing" and then by "replicated file complete." "Structure file" came next, followed by the condensation and storage commands. When the screen indicated that the replicated file was stored, I exited the program and flipped the switch to turn off the difference engine.

Carolynne drifted closer. "Another, yet I do not know one of my sex, save from my glass."

"The other one of you, Carolynne, is more like a painting, or a picture. It is a copy of how you are now, but you will change, and it won't."

"Rather like a dream than an assurance that my remembrance warrants."

"Is all life a dream?" And I had to wonder. Were the words Carolynne spoke meaningful, or phrases for which I was inventing meanings? Was my mind threatened as well as my life?

"It is a hint that wrings mine eyes to it."

"Do you ever rest?" Why was I asking questions to an incoherent ghost?

The ghost seemed to frown. "What should I do, I do not. Rest do I not tossed upon stones."

Stones? Lodestones? Was modern technology actually perpetuating ghosts because of the electrical and magnetic fields it generated? In a strange way, it made sense. Modern technology allowed more people to live in better condition. Why not ghosts? Of course, the religious nuts would have hung me out to dry on that one, since they all believed that ghosts were some sort of divine creation and not natural phenomena.

"My other self, death's second self?" asked Carolynne.

That was a good question, and one I couldn't answer. "I don't know. Somehow, it would be wrong to destroy the file, but it would also be wrong to release her here with you."

"O, 'tis treason!"

Maybe I shouldn't have, but, like a lot of things, what was done was done. Did Ralston and the president feel any guilt? Somehow, I doubted it, although the comparison certainly didn't make things right.

"Hast thou affections?" asked Carolynne.

"You asked a good question. It's just that I don't have a good answer."

"I wouldst thou didst."

So did I.

"And with my heart in it; and now farewell." She was gone. At least, she disappeared from view.

I shook my head. I was troubled, and I was tired. Mornings were coming too quickly, and while I couldn't do much about the troubled feelings, I could get some sleep. So I turned out the lights and headed up to bed.

18

ONCE AGAIN, ON Monday morning, I was off and running—not literally, since I skipped my dash to the hilltop—but I did force myself through a half hour of exercise before eating, cleaning up, and driving back down south to LBI through an intermittent sleet that turned into cold rain as I neared Zuider. Early in the winter, Lochmeer did moderate the weather, until the vast expanse froze over.

The Stanley was actually good on slick roads, despite its relatively light weight, because of the four-wheel-traction option.

I flicked the radio to KCNB, the classical station out of Zuider, and a program of postmodern music. Some of the younger composers, such as Exten and Perkins, actually developed harmonies that consisted of more than four-note tone rows. The only bad part was an Exten aria from *Nothing Ventured* sung by a tenor named Austin Hill. He just didn't have it, strained the whole way through. Maybe he should have been a conductor—or a critic.

When the "Oratorio Hour" began, I flicked the radio to KPOP, just before I entered Zuider. Outside of the *Messiah* and a few other demonstrably endurable works, my tastes for oratorio, Llysette's efforts notwithstanding, are clearly limited. Instead, I enjoyed Dennis Jackson's version of *Louisiana*, even if he weren't an operatic baritone.

After wading through the water and slush in the LBI parking lot, I pushed through the door, with its faint bleep, and up to the counter.

Without a word, Bruce emerged from the workroom and set the equipment boxes on the counter. Also without a word, I peeled off more bills.

Then I looked into the two boxes. The third gadget was simpler than the second, and looked somehow incomplete. Then I realized why. "These attach into the other gadget?"

"I believe you were the one who called it a perturbation replicator. This is the perturbation projector which attaches to the replicator. Now, if you want, we can just call them gadgets, but I defer to your nomenclature."

"You really are ornery."

"I do perfectly well on no sleep, impossible specifications for improbable hardware, and the concern that all sorts of people I haven't seen in years and never wish to see again will suddenly appear."

"But I like seeing you."

"That's true. I haven't seen this much of you in years."

"What was it that guy said in that cult second-rate movie—the beginning of a beautiful friendship?"

"Friendship is based on deception, and you destroyed any illusion of that long ago, Johan."

"So . . . I am impossibly direct?"

"No. Merely improbably less indirect than the average Columbian. You'll be all right so long as no one really figures out that you're about as direct as a sharp knife."

"Some already have. I'm supposed to stab the other guy, though, or take the fall for a stabbing that's already taken place."

"For a nice boy born of cultured parents, you've always played in rough company."

"Tell me." I closed the boxes.

"I have." Bruce picked up the second and followed me out to the Stanley, where we placed them both in the front trunk. "I was more than gratified to be a mere technician."

"Now you're a distinguished man of commerce."

"Times like this, I wish I were still an anonymous technician."

"You're better paid, and people like me don't show up as often." I shut the trunk.

"That's also true, and your presence is always welcome. It's the baggage with the clocklike sounds that bothers me."

"I'll try to leave it behind."

Bruce just shook his head as I climbed into the steamer.

The roads were merely damp on the way back to the university. I stopped by Samaha's and picked up my newspapers, which I didn't bother to read before heading up to my office. As usual, I was one of the first into the department offices, except, of course, for Gilda.

"Good morning, Gilda."

"You're polite this morning."

"Am I not always?"

"Not always, but on average. Doktor Doniger will not be in until late. He wired in that the ice on the lane was too dangerous."

I snorted. "I live on Deacon's Lane, and I got here."

"Doktor Doniger is somewhat more cautious."

I nodded, picked up a stack of administrative paperwork and circulars attempting to entice me into prescribing new texts for all my classes, and tromped upstairs.

"Good morning, Johan," called Grimaldi from his desk. "I see you were one of the hardy few."

"There was only a trace of slush on the roads." I paused by his door.

"Any excuse in a storm, I suppose. What do you think—you were in government—about this Japanese nuclear submersible business?"

"Politicians who don't have to face the weaponry they have built have always worried me."

"Politicians don't have to worry about facing weaponry of any sort. That's the definition of a politician—someone who gets someone else to pay the bill and take the bullets."

"You're even more cynical than I am." I forced a laugh.

"Amen." He stood. "I suppose I will see you later. Or at tomorrow's departmental meeting. I'm off to the library."

"Cheers."

He waved, and I opened my office. Then I sorted through the memos, ignoring David's agenda for the departmental meeting, seeing as the top item was still the business of deciding which electives to cut. Most of the papers I tossed, including the questionnaire asking for an item-by-item evaluation on the cross-cultural applicability of my courses.

All four days of the *Asten Post-Courier* were full of stories about the Japanese development, but there was little I hadn't seen already in the *Columbia Post-Dispatch*—except for one paragraph in Saturday's paper.

Among the attendees at the presidential dinner announcing the Japanese initiative was Johan A. Eschbach, a former Minister of Environment. Eschbach is currently a professor at Vanderbraak State University, recently rocked by a murder scandal and allegations involving clandestine psychic research funded by the Ministry of Defense.

I swallowed. Who had said anything about psychic research? VanBecton? His tame pseudo-watch officer? And tying the murder and the research to me was definitely unkind. After rummaging through the papers and my paperwork, I picked up the handset and dialed.

"Hello."

"Gerald, I need a few minutes with you. How about three-thirty?" I was glad to hear his voice.

"I'm really rather tied up . . ."

"This isn't about philosophy. I think you'll be interested. I'll see you at three-thirty." I owed him something, even if he didn't know he needed it. VanBecton wasn't going to let him know, and Ralston certainly wasn't. I took his "ulp" as concurrence and concluded with, "Have a good day, Gerald."

As eleven o'clock approached, I gathered my folder, my notes, and the next quiz for Environmental Economics, half dreading the still-blank faces that I would see.

Gertrude and Hector were sweeping the remnants of water and frozen slush off the bricked walk leading to Smythe as I passed. Their breathing, and mine, left a white fog in the air.

"Good day, Gertrude. You too, Hector."

"Every day's a good day, sir," she answered.

"Take care, sir," added Hector.

I almost stopped. Hector had never said a word to me before. Instead, I just answered, "Thank you, Hector."

Who was more real—the zombie or the ghost? Or did it depend on the situation? Or were they both real? Certainly, the government recognized zombies as pretty much full citizens, except for voting, but a zombie could even petition for that right, not that many had the initiative. But Carolynne seemed about as real as the zombies I knew, if eccentric; Miranda's ghost, or my grandfather's, hadn't. I pushed away the speculations as I climbed the stairs to the second floor.

Nearly a dozen students were still missing by the time the clock chimed. The missing were the ones who hadn't done the reading. So I smiled my pleasantly nasty smile and cleared my throat.

"As some of you have surmised, I have an unannounced quiz here. For those of you present, the lowest grade possible will be a D. Anyone who is not here who is not in the hospital or the infirmary will fail."

Three or four of the students exchanged glances, at least one with an "I told you so" look. While I wasn't exactly thrilled, what Machiavelli said about the ruler applies also to teachers. It is best to be loved and feared, but far better to be feared and not loved than to be loved and not feared.

I handed out the greenbooks first, then the test. "Write a

short essay in response to *one* of the questions." That was also what the test said, but multimedia repetition is often useful for the selectively illiterate or deaf.

After I collected the tests, we spent the remainder of the period discussing the readings. Most of those in class actually had read the material on the economics of environmental infrastructures. Some even understood it, and I didn't feel as though I were pulling teeth. It continued to bother me that so many of them would only respond to force, even when learning was in their own self-interest.

Because I carried the tests with me, rather than stopping by the office, I made it to Delft's, predictably, a good quarter hour before Llysette, and this time got a table close to the woodstove. With the chill outside, I knew she would choose warmth over a view of bare limbs and gray and brown stone walls.

Victor had just offered the wine when the lady arrived. I nodded to him to pour two glasses and stood to seat her.

"Good afternoon, Doktor duBoise."

"Afternoon it is, Herr Doktor Eschbach. Good, that is another question."

"Perchance some wine? This time it is at least Californian."

Victor faded away.

"This is better." She took a long swallow of the Sonoma burgundy. "Not so good as—"

"Good French wine, I know." I grinned, and got a half-smile, anyway. "What happened?"

"Forms! The Citizenship Bureau—they cannot find my residence report, and so I must complete another. They know I sent one, but . . ." She shrugged. "Perhaps someday they will let me become a citizen—when I am old and gray." Llysette swallowed the last of her wine in a second gulp.

"What would you like to eat?" I refilled her glass.

"You would like?" asked Victor, appearing at Llysette's elbow and winking, as he always did.

"La même, comme ça," she answered, her voice almost flat.

"Oui, mademoiselle," he answered. "And you, Doktor Eschbach?"

"I'll try the tomato brandy mushroom soup with shepherd's bread and cheese."

He nodded and slipped back toward the kitchen.

Llysette sipped her second glass of wine, looking emptily at the table.

"Bad morning?"

"Two of them—two lessons—they did not show up. No courtesy they had, and they did not even leave a message. Doktor Geoffries, he says he wants to observe my advanced diction class—and I have not taught this part before." She glared at me.

I held up a hand. "I'm not your department chair."

"I am sorry. All of this, it is so . . . so . . ."

"Frustrating?"

"Maddening it is." She took another healthy swallow of wine.

Victor brought Llysette consommé, except it was warm, and my soup and bread. "Would you like your salad now, mam'selle?"

"If you please."

Victor nodded.

"Have you seen Miranda's ghost lately?" I asked Llysette.

She gave me a half-frown, half-pout, charming nonetheless, before answering. *"Mais non.* But never did the ghost enter my office, only the hallway." She shrugged. "The ghosts, they avoid me, I think."

Victor eased her salad onto the table and deftly slipped out of sight.

The tomato brandy soup had big succulent mushrooms and was richer than a chocolate dessert. I spooned in every last morsel, interspersed with the cheese and bread.

"A good Frenchman you would have made, Johan. For the way you enjoy good food. The wine, you even appreciate."

"I trust that is a compliment, dear lady."

"One of the highest."

"Then I thank you." I lifted my wine glass. "Would you like dinner tonight?"

"Dinner, I would like that, but for the next two weeks I am doing rehearsals—except for the weekends."

"Then we must make do with the weekends." I sipped the last of my wine. "Some more?"

"Alas, I must go." She stood. "With Doctor Geoffries watching my class . . ."

I stood, nodding sympathetically. Evaluations were never fun to prepare for. "Good luck."

"The luck I do not need. I need more time." She flashed a quick smile, and left me, as usual, to pay the check, which Victor presented quickly.

Then, wondering if I would find any surprises, I walked down to the post centre, my overcoat half open because it was too cold not to wear a coat and too warm to bundle up. I was resisting wearing a hat, except to church—when I went, which hadn't been that often lately.

"No bills for ye, Doktor," called Maurice from behind the window.

"And you'll take all the credit?"

"You give me all the blame."

Two advertising circulars, a reminder card from the dentist, and a single brown envelope posted in the Federal District which I did not open but thrust into my folder—those were the contents of my box.

When I got back to my office, I did open the envelope, which contained one clipping. It was the same story I had already seen in the *Asten Post-Courier* that morning, except that it had come from the *New Amsterdam Post,* and that almost certainly meant that vanBecton had planted the first story.

After gathering up yet another short test and the greenbooks for my two o'clock, I trudged through the cold wind to Smythe Hall. I had to grin as I stepped into the room just a minute before the clock chimed the hour. Every seat was filled. Clearly, the word had gotten out about my policy on missing tests, unannounced or otherwise.

"Miss Deventer, are you ready today to discuss the political basis behind the first Speaker Roosevelt's efforts at reforestation?"

Miss Deventer swallowed. So did several others.

"I meant it, you know." I grinned. That was one of the questions on the test, not that she had to choose that one, but the others were equally specific.

Once again I handed out greenbooks and tests, and repeated the litany about only responding to *one* of the essay questions. After collecting the tests fifteen minutes later, we launched into a discussion—except it was more of a lurch.

"Why did it take the federal government nearly two decades to begin enforcement of the Rivers and Harbors Act?" I pointed to Mister Reshauer.

"Uhhh . . ."

That brilliant answer was equaled only by Miss Desileta's "I don't know."

Eventually we did have a discussion on the relationship of external diseconomies and regional political alliances to the delay in the development of the Columbian environmental ethic.

Still, by the time class was over, I had the definite feeling that an even higher percentage of the environmental politics class than the economics class was going to receive D's.

After gathering my notes, the tests, and the greenbooks into my folder, I pulled on my overcoat and trudged back through the freezing mist to my office, nodding at Gilda while I pulled another of David's memos from my box. This one dealt with something called graduate-level in-loading, and seemed to be an excuse for paying some faculty more for doing less. I carried everything upstairs and set out the two stacks of tests, starting to grade the morning's environmental economics quizzes. The first five were D's; then I finally got an honest C.

At three-twenty, I left the tests on my desk and took myself and my folder back outside and up the hill to the Physical Sciences building and Gerald's office.

He opened the door within instants of my rapping. "I don't like this, Johan."

"Neither do I, but I felt you deserved to know the size of the sharks you're fishing for." After setting my unzipped leather folder on the corner of his desk, I leaned forward, scanning the few memos on it before pointing to a picture. "That your daughter? She's an attractive young lady."

As his eyes moved to the picture, I slipped a memo with Branston-Hay's signature on it under my folder—it was only something about allocation of time on the super-speed difference engine, but the signature would do. Then I settled into the chair closest to his difference engine.

"Exactly what do you mean by all these veiled threats, Johan?" He sat in the big swivel, but only on the front edge, as if I were some form of dangerous animal. His hand brushed over his long, thin, blond and white hair, as if he were trying to recover his bald patch.

"I don't make threats, Gerald. I'm just offering some observations."

"Your 'observations' sound like threats to me."

I leaned forward in the chair. "You know, Gerald, I wonder what your next project will be. This one is going to end rather shortly, you know?"

Branston-Hay frowned at me, as I knew he would. The one thing that defense contractors—even covert ones—never understand is that all projects end.

I stood and ambled over to his difference engine. "You keep your notes on this, don't you, the ones no one else is supposed to read or know you keep?"

Even as he watched, his mouth dropping open, I sat down at the console and flipped the switches, watching as it powered up.

"Johan . . ." His voice was low and meant to be threatening. "No one would ever see you again if I said so."

"Permit me a word, Gerald. First, I would assume that this

office is thoroughly desnooped, and that you ensured that?"

"Of course. That technology I do know."

"Good. Now what makes you think I would say what I just said without a reason?" I entered the sequence I needed, and tried not to grin. It just possibly might work.

"Reformulation beginning" scripted after the pointer.

I stood and walked from the console toward his desk, keeping my body between him and the screen. "I hope your desnooping was thorough. You know, your research is already being implemented."

"They said—"

"Bother what they said. Have you noticed all the Babbage centers going up in flames? I wonder how many professors just had heart attacks, or highway accidents, or drowned in swimming or boating accidents? I'll bet there are more than a few. And with all the religious fervor over psychic research, it's going to be a dead end all of a sudden."

"But Ferdinand would like to see it a dead end. He already has what he needs. So does Speaker Hartpence, and now it will be convenient for that research to stop." Branston-Hay looked smugly at me. "And then we'll get a new contract."

"That brings up something else. You never told the president's people about the disassociator, did you? You were even too timid to build it, weren't you?"

At that point the gun came out, a very small-bore Colt, wobbling enough that I knew he'd never even practiced with it.

I stepped aside so he could see the console screen. The gun wavered, and I moved and slashed it out of his hand, but he let it fall and lunged past me. "You . . . you bastard! But you don't know . . ."

I had the gun, and it didn't waver in my hand. "Sit down, Gerald. We're going to talk."

He looked at the gun, then at the dead screen of the difference engine, and wilted.

"Don't look so depressed. You have backup disks

somewhere, I'm sure, and most of what was on there you could probably replicate anyway. I'm just keeping you out of bigger trouble."

"You're getting in well over both our heads, Johan." His voice was dull.

"We already are." I cleared my throat, even though I wanted to be out of his office. "Now, let's get the players straight. You had a research contract with the Defense Ministry, a fairly straight job to investigate some aspect of deghosting, probably using the magnetic basis of the electro-fluidic difference engine. That was the origin of your so-called filing protocol."

His mouth opened, and he gulped like a carp.

"That contract is really over, but you didn't want to close it out, because who else would pay you that much? Then the president's crew came in with a special request, right?"

"You seem to have it figured, Johan. Why ask me?"

"I don't have it all figured. What I can't figure is why you killed Miranda Miller."

"I didn't! I had nothing to do with it."

"Right." I made my voice as sardonic as I could. "She's an agent of New France pumping you for all you've got, and she finds out that you double-dealt the Defense Ministry—that the contract's really done. You know, sooner or later, because she's not very good, that the Spazi will find out. So you put her away."

"With a knife? I could have—"

"Built your disassociator and turned her into a zombie? Or just put her under one of those helmets in the lab late some night and then carted her back to her cottage and left her?"

"Yes. So why are you baiting me? You know the answers."

"You couldn't leave Pandora's box closed, could you, Gerald?"

"What do you mean?"

"You know what I mean. All the military types wanted was a way to suck ghosts out of an area. You did it, all right, and you're brilliant, Gerald. You saw what else was possible. So did the president's people. Now, I don't know how they got your reports, but I'll bet a check would show you knew someone in the budget review shop—and Armstrong's boys were on you in a flash. They threatened to show that you padded the contract, right?"

Branston-Hay looked blank

"You padded it, didn't you? I can get the answer from the examiners, you know?"

He finally nodded.

"And then they asked what else you could do. You didn't want to let the disassociator out. Even you could see the problems there. So you came up with the replicator and rejiggered your psychic scoop into a filing mechanism. And that's how the president keeps outguessing the Speaker. He has a data bank of tame ghosts."

"Who are you working for, Johan? Ralston will kill you if he finds out what you're doing."

I ignored the question and the threat. Any answer would be wrong. "If I were you, Gerald, I'd stick very close to your family and take a vacation, a sabbatical, anything."

Walking over to his desk, even as he stood there, I opened the top left drawer and pulled out sheets of Babbage Center, Vanderbraak State University letterhead. "You won't need these, and I do."

"But . . . why . . . what are you doing?"

"Trying to keep us both from getting killed." I put the sheets of letterhead and the memo I had slipped under my folder into the folder. Then I took out my handkerchief and wiped off the Colt, setting it on the chair farthest from where he paced behind his desk. I dampened the handkerchief in his water glass, then wiped off the Babbage console keys and the arm of the chair, fairly certain I hadn't touched anything else.

After picking up my folder and walking to the door, I used the handkerchief to turn the knob. He didn't stop me, just looked, almost dazed.

I forced myself to walk slowly out of the building and straight down the steps to the green, and then to my office. The wind had picked up so much that it blew the white steam of my breath away.

I skidded slightly on the bottom steps leading into the Natural Resources building, where a patch of ice remained, looking like someone had spilled something. Certainly the methodical Gertrude and Hector wouldn't have left anything on the bricks. Overhead, the glow strips were glowing as the day faded.

I unlocked the door and stopped by the main office to check my box, but nothing had been added. I looked out the window uphill and watched as Gerald hurried down to his old black Ford steamer, carting two data cases.

Poor bastard. Then I straightened. If I didn't keep moving, I knew who would be the next poor bastard. So I went upstairs to my office and looked at my desk and the mostly ungraded tests lying there.

I left them on the desk. Maybe I'd get back to them, and maybe I wouldn't, but I had more than a few things to do first. I slipped some blank second pages of university letterhead into my folder and headed back out to the Stanley, relieved in a way that Llysette was tied up with rehearsals for most of the week.

When I got home, I unloaded Bruce's latest creations from the Stanley before driving it into the car barn.

Marie—I blessed her industrious Dutch heart once more and added ten dollars to the check I set out for her—had left a chicken pot pie in the oven, and it was still warm. That and the crusty bread were almost enough to make me forget what I was going to attempt that night.

I also tried to forget the tests I hadn't graded. But a little part of me nagged about them. I usually didn't put off grading and returning things. After all, I was the one who believed in the efficacy of immediate feedback.

It seemed like I hadn't eaten in days, although that was probably the result of nerves. Still, I ate almost all of the chicken pot pie and a good third of the loaf of bread. I had a bottle of Grolsch instead of wine, and I promised that I'd run harder and longer in the morning.

Then I went into the study and took Bruce's latest gadgets from their boxes and assembled them. After that, I started in on the programming.

Some of it was relatively easy because I could use the first program I had already developed for ghost replications as a basis. I'd already decided to split the application into a basic system and a separate "personality creation" configuration.

The basic system didn't take that long, a mere five hours. Testing it took longer, and I hoped Carolynne wasn't watching, because I duplicated the replicate of her structure, then recoded it back to simple lines, and tried to project it.

Of course, it didn't work. Nothing I ever try to program works the first time. Or the second. Or the third. On the fourth try, well after one in the morning, the system worked. That is, the antennas indeed projected an image, and it promptly collapsed.

So did I. The system part seemed to work, and I'd have to develop a better file/support structure if I really wanted to create the equivalent of ghosts. Why I'd want to do that was a question I didn't have an answer for, except that my guts said it was going to be necessary, and I hadn't made it as far as I had by ignoring gut feelings. Most people in dangerous occupations don't. You figure out the reasons later, if you have the time.

Since I didn't think very well with headaches and bright rainbows surrounding every light I looked at, I turned them all off and lifted one foot after the other until I reached my bed.

I looked up. A white figure hovered by the end of the bed.

"What are you doing here?"

"Was that a face to be opposed against the warring winds?"

"The ghost I created? I was just trying to see if the system worked."

"Be governed by your knowledge . . . repair those violent harms . . . be aidant and remediate . . ."

"How?" I shook my head. "For most people, remediation in politics is revenge. The best seek justice, even when most, me included, would prefer mercy to such justice."

"Then dissolve the life that wants the means to lead it." With that she vanished.

Carolynne was definitely getting too familiar. It was a good thing Llysette wasn't around. But then Carolynne probably wouldn't have appeared with Llysette around. I wasn't sure they would like each other. Respect each other, probably, but "like" was definitely another question. Forget about communicating. Was I communicating, or were Carolynne's words only in my own mind? Was it her wish for me to create a ghost of remediation—or mine?

My head ached so much that I got back up and took three bayers. Carolynne did not say good night again.

19

"DIFFICULT" WASN'T THE word for the trouble I had struggling out of bed on Tuesday. I pried my eyes open and climbed into my exercise clothes—uphill all the way.

Who would have thought that creating a ghost image for projection was so difficult? Everyone. I was just the one who thought it was possible. As for Carolynne's idea of a ghost of remediation, that was clearly impossible. Even a ghost of justice and mercy—how would I ever do that? Yes, I understood that establishing and maintaining any image was difficult, if not impossible. But the image of justice and mercy, or even of integrity? Politicians did it all the time, but they didn't have to have a logical structure to support it. And I certainly wasn't about to touch remediation, except . . . didn't I have to try?

Llysette had said I was always trying to change the world. Was that it, or was I merely trying to do the impossible until it killed me?

I sighed as I laced up the leather running boots. Some people run in lightweight, rubber-soled shoes, but that's stupid. At least in my profession it is. You don't run that much, but when you do it's under lousy conditions with the world after you, and your feet need protection and support.

Obviously, I'd have to go back to the basics—just create a totally ethical personality. Probably it would have to be a take-off on some combination of mine and Carolynne's, because I had something to start with her image and at least I could fix in the program what went wrong with me. My mother and father didn't get that choice, and at times I suspect they would have liked the option.

I still didn't understand why my father had built the artificial lodestone. Had he been the one who read all the Shakespeare to Carolynne? Or were the lines from her theatrical background? Sometimes they made sense, and sometimes . . . I took another deep breath and stepped out into the cold.

All the way through my run and exercise, through breakfast, and through my shower, I kept thinking about how to layer the codes for a ghost personality.

Finally I shook my head. I needed to take a break, and besides, the disembodied spectre of all those ungraded tests on my desk was also beginning to haunt me. Should I have even worried about the tests? Probably not, but about some things we're not exactly rational.

So, after dressing, I hurried into the study, flipped on the difference engine and roughed out the code lines I thought might work, and then printed them out and stuffed them into my folder.

Then I pulled on my coat and went out under the cold gray sky to get the steamer started. The air smelled like frozen leaves, and there was almost no breeze, a leaden sort of cold calm.

The Stanley started smoothly, as always, and I passed Marie in her old Ford on my way down Deacon's Lane. We exchanged waves, and her smile cheered me momentarily.

After a quick stop at Samaha's for the *Post-Courier,* I parked the Stanley in the faculty car park. Llysette's Reo wasn't there, but, thankfully, Gerald Branston-Hay's black Ford was.

On my way to my office, I nodded at Gregor Martin, but he only growled something about winter starting too soon and lasting too long.

Even Gilda looked dour.

"Why so cheerless?" I asked her.

"It's like winter out, and it's too early for winter."

"That's what Gregor Martin said."

"For once I agree with him. For once." Gilda picked up the wireset. "Natural Resources Department . . . No, Doktor Doniger is not available at the moment."

Rik Paterken, one of the adjuncts, motioned as I pulled two memos and a letter from my box in the department office.

"Yes, Rik?"

"You have Peter Paulus in one of your classes, don't you?"

"Yes."

"What sort of student is he?"

I frowned, not wanting to answer as truthfully as I should have. Instead, I temporized. "Mister Paulus is able to retain virtually everything he reads. He does have a tendency to apply that knowledge blindly even when it may not be applicable to the situation at hand."

"In short, he can regurgitate anything, and he avoids thinking." Paterken pulled at his chin. "He seems like a nice young man."

"I am sure he is, Rik." I smiled politely.

"He was asking permission to take the Central American Ecology course. He never took basic ecology."

I shrugged. "He's probably bright enough to pick that up, but I'd guess he wouldn't get the kind of grade he wants."

"That was my impression."

"Then tell him that," I suggested.

"You're the one with the reputation for bluntness, Johan, not us poor adjuncts."

I shook my head and went upstairs, wanting to see what, if

anything, was in the newspaper. I knew the memos couldn't contain much of value, and they didn't. The letter was a more sophisticated pitch for a new ecology text. I tossed it along with the memos.

The *Post-Courier* headlines were a rehash of the airspace battle between the dirigibles and the turbojets, and the spacing requirements at the main Asten airport. Governor vanHasten wanted to build a jetport and leave Haguen for dirigibles, but the legislature was balking at the funds, and the federal Ministry of Transportation had indicated no federal funds were likely.

I leafed through the paper, still standing next to my desk, when my eyes glanced over the political gossip column. I froze.

. . . One of the more interesting developments, almost unnoticed in the commotion of the ceremonial dinner where President Armstrong announced his Japanese initiative, which, incidentally, the Speaker will probably have to swallow, involved a little-known former politico—one Johan A. Eschbach. Ostensibly, Eschbach is a professor at Vanderbraak State University, but who was at the big dinner, and who disappeared somewhere in the Presidential Palace between dinner and dessert? Watch this space . . .

That was another one of those surprises you really don't like to find. Was it Ralston's doing? Why? To offer me up to vanBecton? I put the paper down and looked at my desk. I had less than two hours to grade the quizzes, and I wasn't giving any more this term. Period. As if I would be around to give any, at the rate I was going.

I plowed through both sets. Eighty percent of the grades were D's. Too bad, but I really didn't feel charitable. No one was providing *me* much charity these days.

At ten to eleven, I finished entering the marks in my grade book and set the greenbooks in separate piles to return the next day. Then I locked my door and went downstairs. Gilda was off somewhere, and I went back out into the leaden gray day. The day seemed even colder than it had at dawn. But then everything was seeming colder.

Despite the cold and the ice, Gertrude and Hector were out on the green, carefully laying a sand and fertilizer mix on the icy bricks of the walk to Smythe. While it was more expensive than salt, the mix resulted in a lush lawn the rest of the year.

I just waved, not really wanting to hear Gertrude's predictable statement about every day being a good day. They both waved back.

I smiled brightly as I walked into Natural Resources 1A. At least we'd finished the water cycle and were working on air, with an emphasis on deposition mechanisms and transport characteristics. I started right in.

"Miss Francisco, could you tell me what air deposition had to do with the Austro-Hungarian decision to require converters on internal combustion engines?"

Miss Francisco looked suitably blank.

"How about you, mister Vraalander? Any ideas?"

"Well, uh, sir . . . didn't it have to do with the Ruhr Valley and the Black Forest?"

"That's a start. Can you take it further, Miss Zenobia?"

"Doesn't acid deposition combine with ozone from internal combustion engines?"

"It does. What does it do?"

"Oh . . . tree damage," blurted out mister Vraalander. "Now I remember."

I tried not to sigh. The rest of the class period was marginally better, just marginally, but perhaps that was because my mind was half on the column in the *Post-Courier.*

Lunch was a quick bowl of soup at Jared's Kitchen, followed by another quick look at the tests I'd already graded to make sure I hadn't been too hurried. I hated the damned tests, and even more the fact that I had to give them to get the students to read the material. After that I scrawled out more

Babbage code lines, amending my hastily printed beginning of the morning.

Then there was my two o'clock, Environmental Politics 2B. I had to collect papers—unfortunately, because it probably meant that very few of those stalwart souls had bothered to do the reading assignment. In turn, that meant I either had to talk a lot or badger them or surrender and let them out too early, which I generally refused to do because it might give them even more inflated ideas about the value of ignorance.

So I talked a bit about relative political values and their links to economic bases, and led them into speculation about why the Brits politically felt they couldn't afford too much environmental protection while the Irish were busy reforesting—yet both faced virtually the same threat from Ferdinand. What made the difference? Was it another hundred miles of ocean?

I was still tired and hoarse when I walked back to my office. I grabbed a double-loaded cola from the machine and went back to work on codes until it was time for David's weekly finest hour—the departmental meeting.

The less said about the departmental meeting, the better. I did not lose my temper. I only said one or two sentences, and I didn't leave. Instead, I sat in the corner and jotted Babbage codes on my notepad, trying to work out the parameters of an ethical ghost while ignoring David's long and roundabout evasions of the basic problem. I sat back and listened, half aware that the arguments hadn't changed in a week. Finally David did what he should have done two weeks earlier.

"I've heard everyone's comments and objections, but no one has a better idea. I will inform the dean that Natural Resources Three-B will be capped at zero next semester and that we will rotate between courses to be capped, but none will be struck."

Unfortunately he didn't quit while he was merely behind. "The next item on the agenda is EWE."

Mondriaan groaned. He hated the Educational Writing

for Excellence program. I just thought it was useless. Most university graduates can't really write, and most never have been able to. It's a delusion to think the skill can actually be taught at the collegiate level. Polished, perhaps, but not taught. Of course, I didn't say that. Why make any more enemies? I had enough already.

After EWE, David proceeded to the department's recommendations for library acquisitions because—what else was new—our recommendations exceeded our share of the acquisitions budget.

I continued to work on Babbage codes until the end of the meeting. No one seemed to notice.

After the meeting, I packed up my folders, decided to leave the Environmental Politics 2B papers behind on my desk, and walked to the car park. My resolve about tests hadn't considered the papers I'd already assigned.

A watch steamer, sirens blaring, wailed out Emmen Lane toward Lastfound Lake. I wondered if someone had had an accident or if the locals were just testing their sirens.

At the bridge I had to wait as two heavy Reo steamers, gunmetal-gray paint and chrome trim shimmering, rolled westward across the Wijk and past me into the square. While they were from Azko, they somehow reminded me of Spazi steamers.

Marie hadn't left me dinner, just a note explaining that she hadn't been able to fix anything because I had no meat, no flour, no butter, and precious little of anything else.

I had apples and cheese, and opened a sealed box of biscuits from the basement. It filled my stomach, and my head stopped swimming, but I definitely missed that hot meal, especially after no real lunch and the way the day had gone.

Then I washed the dishes and began trying to assemble all the code fragments I had developed for a justice/mercy/integrity ghost. When I put them all together and completed the file profile, nothing happened. Nothing at all.

Then I discovered that I didn't have the handshake between the profile and the system set up right, and that meant a minor rewrite of the system program I'd only finished the night before. Why had it worked the night before and not with the new ghost profile? Because I had created a more complex profile—that was what I figured.

I tried again. The system worked, but all I got was a spiral that collapsed in on itself.

Probably I needed some sort of image. Carolynne's profile had the image tied up with the rest, but I didn't know how to do that. But . . . adding an image on top of everything else?

I turned off the difference engine and went to the kitchen for a bottle of Grolsch, probably bad for me, but things weren't going right.

Halfway through the Grolsch, I tried again. Around eleven o'clock I got an image that looked like a one-eyed demon of some sort, even though I'd inputted, I thought, the graphic image of a man with a set of scales in his hand.

So I took a break and decided to finish something I'd started over a week earlier—a transitional identity.

It's amazing what you can do with the right Babbage programs and a decent printer. A laminator helps, too, but you can get the same effect with an iron and certain plastics.

I created Vic Nuustrom—lift operator at the mills down in Waarstrom, in season. The real Nuustrom, of course, had moved out to Deseret, but he looked roughly like me, except he had been heavier. When you've been in the business, you always keep a bolthole open. I already had a complete alternate identity as one Peter Hloddn, a ledgerman who was only marginally successful at the wholesale purveying of office supplies. He had a bank account and a few bills, a credit history, and a driver's permit issued in New Ostend—all real. The depth wasn't that great, but since it predated vanBecton, and I'd never let Minister Wattson know about it either, it was relatively safe, as such things went.

Nuustrom was a transitional identity—you never go straight from one to another. There's a way to phase into a new identity.

After trimming the heavy stock, the seal printed on a transparent overlay, and setting the picture in place, I studied it, then used the tweezers for fine adjustments before setting the plastic down and lifting the iron.

I held my breath, but the lamination worked, as did the pictures taken more than a year earlier in a red plaid lumberjack shirt. They were just overexposed enough to be convincing as a vehicle operator's license. Nuustrom, of course, had a hauler's endorsement, which was no problem since I'd done that for a year in London. You drive a lorry on those roads, and you can drive anywhere.

I reburied the files in the difference engine and totally erased the actual identity section. They'd expect me to have some way of creating an alternate identity. I just didn't want them to know what it was. I also didn't know when I'd need the card, but it looked like it was going to be soon, and when I did, I probably wouldn't have time to create it.

The whole process took less than an hour, and I had something besides lines of code that didn't work. That's a trick I learned a long time ago. When you get stuck on a big project, do something smaller and concrete. It helps your sense of accomplishment and a lot more.

Then I went back to the kitchen, looked longingly at the remaining bottles of Grolsch, and fixed a pot of that excessively strong Russian Imperial blend tea. If anything would keep me going, that would.

Sometime in the early hours of the morning, I got an image, the man with the scales in his hand, who immediately rumbled out, "Justice must be done. Justice must be done."

Those were the words I associated with old Goodman Hunsler—that stern and righteous dourness that makes you feel like your whole life has been one unending sin. For a moment, I shivered. The image was definitely far too strong. But it was worse than that, because it wasn't a ghost, just a hollow projection. So why was I so upset? Because I didn't want to deal with the issue of justice?

I really didn't feel up to thinking about that, so I sucked

him into storage with the ghost-collecting hardware and turned off the machines and the lights.

"Such weeds are memories of those worser hours; put them off." Carolynne perched on the banister halfway up the stairs. She was wearing a high-necked dress of some sort. I guess the aura of righteousness had gotten to her as well.

"No. I suppose not. But it's hard to take all that righteousness."

"O you kind gods, cure this great breach . . ."

"I know. I know. I've created a lot of mistakes."

"Alack, alack! 'Tis wonder that thy life and wits at once had not concluded all." She was gone, and I looked stupidly into the darkness before walking back into the study and through the kitchen.

"Carolynne?" I called several times, but she didn't reappear. "Carolynne?"

Finally I went up to a cold bed and collapsed, still dreaming about how to make my justice ghost more merciful. Pure justice, I just couldn't take. Who could?

"Cure this great breach?" Who could do that, either?

20

WEDNESDAY DIDN'T START much better than Tuesday, and even the feeling of partial success I'd felt four hours before dissolved under the barrage of the alarm's chimes. I finally dug myself out of sleep and pulled on exercise clothes. I even managed to run over the top of the hill and to the end of the ridge, despite the cold mist that pricked my face like fine needles. Each foot hit the ground like an anvil on the way back.

Breakfast wasn't much, not with the state of my larder, but I managed with Russian Imperial tea, the rest of the biscuits, and a pear I reclaimed from the cellar. After leaving the dishes in the sink, I showered and dressed, deciding that I was going to be late. The hell with office hours. I needed to add mercy to justice.

I was standing in the foyer when Marie rapped on the door.

"Good morning, Doctor Eschbach. Have you had the chance to—" Marie had her coat off before I had closed the door.

"Good morning, Marie. No, but I will shop this afternoon. Unhappily, the dishes are merely rinsed."

"A few dishes, that's not much. You leave me too little to earn my pay. But you had best lay in a goodly supply of staples, Doktor. Do you think that you could run down to town for food in a snowstorm anytime?" Her expression was somewhere between a sniff and a snort.

"I will lay in significant supplies. I promise. But this morning I'll be working in the study for an hour or two. I hope that doesn't disturb you."

"Since I cannot bake or prepare food, there being nothing to prepare, I will finish the kitchen and then, if you do not mind, I will reorder the fruit cellar. It has needed cleaning—a good cleaning—for a long time." She looked at me and added, "A very long time." She rolled up the cuffs of her gray long-sleeved blouse. I went into the study and turned on the difference engine.

Adding justice to mercy was far easier said than done, especially with Babbage codes, but when I left at ten-thirty, I had a projected ghost image that felt somewhat softer, with a sense of justice. That had to do, even though it still gave me a chill, knowing that I scarcely measured up to the ideal I'd created. I also wondered if what I felt was merely my imagination or something another person could feel, but I wasn't about to call Marie in for an opinion.

I almost felt guilty when I disassociated the ghost construct, but how could I fill my study with ghosts of justice in various stages of sensibility? And the ethical issues? I just shook my head, imagining that Carolynne was probably doing worse than that, were she even watching. Or *did* she think, or merely quote half-remembered dialogue at me?

When I left for the university, Marie was still in the cellar, mumbling about my various failures. I guess I wasn't quite Dutch enough for her, or perhaps the cleanliness was the feminine aspect of Dutch culture.

Gray and cold—that was still the weather as I drove down Deacon's Lane and into Vanderbraak Centre to pick up the paper at Samaha's. It was more like December than early November, and I hoped that didn't mean a really long winter.

David—Herr Professor Doktor Doniger—was on me as soon as I reached my box. "Johan, I know you've been working hard, but do you suppose you could let Gilda know if you won't make office hours?"

"No. I haven't missed a damned office hour all term."

David swallowed. "It is the policy."

"Bother the policy." I left him standing there even as I realized he would probably be scheming to get me back under control. David liked everything under control, and the results would probably be nasty. At that point I didn't care, but half realized that I would later.

I went up to my office to collect the tests I'd graded so that I could return them.

The wind was blowing again as I walked over to Smythe, although the sky was clearing and showing a coldly cheerful blue. I didn't feel cheerful.

At eleven o'clock I practically threw the greenbooks at the Environmental Economics class. "Someday, ladies and gentlemen, and I use those terms merely as a courtesy, you will come to understand that there are too many unanticipated crises in life for you to postpone what you can do now until the last possible moment. Life often does not give you those moments. Call this a dress rehearsal for life."

Of course, they didn't understand a word of what I meant.

"Sir, how much will this count on our final grade?"

"Is there any way to obtain some additional credit?"

"Life doesn't provide extra credit," I snapped, "and neither do I." I shouldn't have snapped, but they didn't have the Spazi hanging over their heads. Probably half of them didn't even know who or what the Spazi was.

Somehow I managed to get through the lecture and discussion without snapping or yelling again. That was fine, except Gilda and Constable Gerhardt were both waiting for me back at the department office.

"Constable Gerhardt, this is Doktor Eschbach."

"Thank you." He tipped his hat to her and turned to me. "If I could speak with you . . ."

"Let's go up to my office," I suggested.

He nodded, and up we went. I set aside the still-ungraded Environmental Politics papers.

"This business about professor Branston-Hay . . ."

"What business?"

"His accident, of course."

"I'm sorry, Constable, but I didn't know he'd been in an accident. When did it happen?"

The worthy watch functionary gave me one of those looks that tends to signify disbelief before explaining. "His steamer piled into a tree on Hoecht's Hill late yesterday afternoon. He died before they could get him to the hospital."

"I didn't know."

"The throttle valve jammed open." Constable Gerhardt spread the fingers of his right hand about a half-centimeter apart. "A bolt about this big jammed in the assembly."

"Why didn't he turn the bypass valve?"

"He hit the brakes first, and they failed, corroded lines. By then it was too late. He was probably going too fast and bouncing around too much to reach it. He was driving a Ford, not a Stanley, and on the older models, you have quite a reach."

My father had always said to buy quality, and Branston-Hay's example certainly confirmed that wisdom.

Poor Branston-Hay. He'd had to throttle the old black steamer all the way up to climb Hoecht's Hill, and then the throttle had jammed on the downside. Except it hadn't been an accident.

"Who was chasing him?" I asked, since it was clear the constable was there to deliver a message from Chief Waetjen.

"Chasing him?"

"Professor Branston-Hay was a careful and methodical man. He was headed home, or at least in the direction of home. Why would he be going so fast?"

"I don't know, sir. I only know that Chief Waetjen told me to tell you what happened."

I'd done it for sure. Good stolid Constable Gerhardt would tell Waetjen of my question and, sure as the sun rose, Officer Warbeck would know, and so would vanBecton.

"Thank you." I rose. "I appreciate the courtesy and the information."

"I was just letting you know, sir. The chief said you should be told." The constable rose as he spoke, having done his duty and his inadvertent best to roast my gander.

After that, I wasn't hungry. So I graded papers for almost two hours, not the smartest thing to do, especially on an empty stomach. And I probably shouldn't have bothered with my two o'clock, but . . . you take on obligations, and you become reluctant not to carry them out.

When I dispersed the corrected greenbooks and a sermon similar to the one I had delivered at eleven o'clock, there was just silence, the appalled silence of an entire class that has just realized that Kris Kringle is a myth and that Mother and Father filled the wooden shoes with coal, and they meant it for real.

After class I left the pile of Environmental Politics 2B papers and went shopping at McArdles', since, as Marie had pointed out, there was nothing to fix, not even for the most industrious and resourceful of Dutch ladies.

Two women in white-trimmed bonnets looked blankly at me as I left the meat counter, but I heard the whispers after I turned toward the flour and corn and oatmeal.

"Doktor Eschbach . . . say he was once a spy . . ."

"Once a spy, always a spy—that's what I say."

"You know, the foreign woman and him . . ."

I didn't like the term "spy," but "intelligence agent" was even worse, and as for the other terms . . . I took a deep breath and put the flour in the cart.

Once I got home, it took five trips to unload. Marie had actually been so resourceful that, when I walked into the kitchen, there was some type of tart-strudel and a pot of barley soup waiting. I didn't know how she had done it. After the chill of unloading all those packages—they'd filled the trunk and the back seat of the steamer, since I'm sometimes an extremist—I ladled out a bowlful and sat at the kitchen table, letting the spicy steam wreathe my face before each spoonful, trying not to think about vanBecton, Miranda, and poor Gerald. The soup was so good that I almost managed it.

After supper, I sat for a while in the dimness before I had company.

"At some hours in the night spirits resort . . . alack, is it not like that I . . . Oh, look, methinks I saw my cousin's ghost . . ." Carolynne made an effort to sit on the corner stool, even if she had a tendency to drift around and through it.

"Your cousin's ghost. Probably not. Or did you mean the one I created this morning? I felt badly about disassociating him, though."

"Thou couldst give no help?"

"How can one help something that was not quite alive?"

"And bid me go and hide me with a dead man in his shroud . . ."

"Wonderful. If I make a better ghost, I'll then qualify for murder."

". . . that did spit his body upon a rapier's point . . . is it not like the horrible conceit of death and night?"

That was another good question—one I really didn't have a good answer for. Was sleep a form of death? Was Babbage storage of a synthetic ghost sleep or death? "I don't know. I feel it's more like sleep, but I couldn't say why."

Unlike most people, who, when you say that you "feel" something, pester you to give rational and logical reasons, Carolynne did not. She just gave a faint nod before speaking. "So tedious is this day . . ."

"Tedious? In a way. On Monday, I warned a man to be careful that he did not suffer an accidental death. On Tuesday, he died in a steamer accident that I do not believe was an accident. I have this feeling that some others are going to try to prove that I created the accident."

"What storm is this that blows so contrary?"

"Contrary indeed. But that doesn't really count." I forced a smile. "From what I hear, you should know about that."

". . . that murdered me. I would forget it fain, but, oh, it presses to my memory like damned guilty deeds to sinners' minds . . . . How shall that faith return again to earth?"

Faith? Did I even have faith, or was I believing what I wanted? Hearing what I wanted from a demented ghost who at least seemed to listen when no one else did? When I stopped asking questions, Carolynne was gone.

What could I do, even as the noose was tightening? Listen to a half-sentient ghost as if she were alive?

I had enough of Branston-Hay's letterhead to compose a couple of letters, since I could use blank second sheets from our own department's stock; all the second sheets were the same. Sometimes paper helped.

The first letter was to Minister Holmbek, protesting the perversion of the VSU Babbage Center research toward developing "psychic phenomena erasure technologies." The second one was also to Holmbek, protesting the failure to extend the research contract as blackmail. I wrote it more politely than that, suggesting that "the Center's disinclination to pursue psychically destructive technologies has resulted in withdrawal of federal funding contrary to the original letter of agreement."

Branston-Hay hadn't been that courageous, but his family would rather have him a dead hero than a dead coward, and, besides, it just might keep me alive.

I was running out of time, and at least one of the questions was how Waetjen and Warbeck intended to pin Branston-Hay's death on me. Maybe I had nuts or something in my car barn the same size as the one that had seized poor Branston-Hay's throttle.

And then again, maybe I hadn't, but did now. I set down the memos and rummaged in the desk for one of the flashes that I kept putting in safe places and never finding again. There was one behind the Babbage disk case.

I walked out to the car barn through the freezing drizzle and studied the workbench and bolt bins under the dim overhead light and my flash. Was the bin cover at the end less dusty? I opened it. There were two different sizes of nuts in the last bin, and I never mixed sizes. The larger ones were clearly newer.

I pulled them out and pocketed them, then dusted off all the bin covers and the top of the workbench. That way, there would be nothing to indicate that only one bin had been used. I closed the car barn and walked down the lawn in the darkness toward the tangles of black raspberry thickets. There I pocketed two of the nuts and scattered the rest, well back into the thickets where no one would find them unless they were to uproot the entire yard. If they did that . . . I shrugged. Nothing would save me then.

I walked slowly back to the house. My gut reaction was to run, but that was clearly what Warbeck or Waetjen or vanBecton had in mind. Somehow I had to put the light back on them—get suspicions raised about the watch.

I smiled grimly. Perhaps I could plant a rumor or two, get their pot boiling and force them to act hastily. In the meantime, I had a lot to wind up—one hell of a lot.

The first thing I did was polish my prints off the two nuts and put them into the false drawer in the bedroom, the one containing miscellaneous "evidence."

I needed to get my geese in order, so to speak, because I doubted there was much time left before the rotten grain hit the mill wheel. Part of dealing with a problem lies in how you set things up before everything starts flying, and some of that is hard evidence, and some is how you handle the paperwork—and the truth. I decided that my approach would have to be truthful lying, so to speak.

It was late by the time I had finished and printed all four memoranda. After flicking off the difference engine, I began to reread the copies I had printed.

I studied the first memo. Not so polished as I would have liked, but, given the contents, and its accuracy, I doubted that the press would balk too much.

FROM: Ralston McGuiness
TO: WLA
SUBJECT: Psychic Research Budget Reviews
DATE: October 10, 1993

Background
The Budget Review Office has identified more than a dozen concealed university-based psychic research projects, including those which have already been compromised by some form of public disclosure, such as St. Louis . . .

The majority have been funded under Babbage-related research lines within the Defense Ministry budget . . .

This research has identified clear potential for implementing deghosting techniques . . .

Despite public denials, Speaker Hartpence receives regular reports on major projects . . .

Leaders of virtually all major religious orders, but particularly those of the Anglican-Baptists, the Roman Catholic Church, the Spirit of God, the Unified Congregation of the Holy Spirit, and the Latter Day Saints, have taken positions firmly opposing such research . . .

International Considerations
Similar psychic research is ongoing in the Austro-Hungarian Empire, as reported in both international media and by the Spazi . . .

To date, Spazi reports (attached) indicate that agents of Japan, Austro-Hungary, and New France have been definitely identified in conjunction with espionage surrounding Columbian psychic research . . .

Several unsolved murders, including the Vanderbraak State University incident, appear associated with such espionage . . . clear indications that Speaker Hartpence's staff has begun efforts to divert inquiries onto either New French sources or even former government personnel . . .

Recommendations

Since the presidency has no power over the actual composition and disbursement of Defense Ministry funds and since the Speaker has publicly avoided any comment on psychic research, bringing the matter before the national media would probably prove counterproductive at this time. Some media favorable to the Speaker would attribute any exposure of the Speaker's covert psychic research program to pure political motivations.

Likewise, attempting to meet with the Speaker could also prove counterproductive . . .

Recommend that you continue to use budgetary analyses and disclosure in areas where a greater public sympathy and understanding exist, and where the Speaker's policies run counter to that public sympathy, such as the size of naval forces and the need for totally free transoceanic trade . . .

Also recommend that you avoid any discussions or comments about psychic phenomena and research funding. This one is a loser!

I grinned. While it certainly wasn't perfect, it had just the right feel. It even sounded like Ralston, and the twist was, of course, that the disclosure of the memorandum would be totally against its contents, which would reinforce its validity with the press. Even the sensationalist videolink reporters would appreciate that.

The second memo I had composed dealt with the upcoming presidential budget review of the Defense Ministry outlays.

TO: GDvB
FROM: Elrik vanFlaam
Budget Controller
SUBJECT: Psychic Research Budget Reviews
DATE: October 12, 1993

The new Babbage engines being used by the president's budget examiners have greater integrative capabilities than the earlier models. In addition, the president's budget task force on program funding distribution now has the capability to cross-index disbursements by program category and amount, and such analyses are proceeding.

A leak from the black side of the budget has also been integrated, which will reveal psychic research disbursements by region. Plotting these against the institutions receiving funds will clearly outline the scope and magnitude of the program.

In view of the Speaker's avowed disavowal of Defense Ministry research on psychic phenomena, the publication of any such analyses could prove somewhat difficult to reconcile.

The budget controller's memo was almost innocuous, except for the last line. That was the trick—to make each document as innocuous as possible, but to have the composite paint a damning picture. That way, it also gave the reporters a way to claim that they had "discovered" the scandal, rather than having it handed to them.

The third memo, to GH (Gerald Hartpence) from CA (Charles Asquith), apparently just dealt with press office support. Again, the implications were almost totally between the lines.

TO: GH
FROM: CA
SUBJECT: Press Support Allocations
DATE: October 15, 1993

As discussed, we have reassigned another press officer to provide logistical and informational support to the psychic research issue . . .

The new fact sheets showing a comparative decline in all psychic research will be ready shortly, as will a full briefing book . . .

We should be ready to brief you on the initiative to assume credit for the Japanese initiative . . .

"Whither goest thou?" asked Carolynne.

"I'll make these available to the press."

"Is there no pity sitting in the clouds?"

No pity? "The time is past for pity—that is, if I want to keep my head somewhere close to my body."

"With treacherous revolt . . . this shall slay them both . . ."

"Probably. Except . . . is a false document which brings out the truth a forgery or a fraud?"

Carolynne looked at me, and I thought I saw tears in her ghostly eyes, and then she was gone. I wished I could have gone to bed, or held her, or something. But I couldn't do any of those things. Instead, I began to create another false document. Because it was meant to be crude, it didn't take that long. I even printed it up in the cheap-looking Courier style.

WHY DO THE NEW HEATHEN RAGE AGAINST THE SPIRITS?

The corrupt government in our federal city has conspired to destroy the spirits of our fathers and forefathers. A man is nothing without his spirit. The haughtiest and the mightiest shall find that their possessions and their worldly attributes shall be for naught, and that their wealth shall avail them nothing . . .

After reading the diatribe of the "Order of Jeremiah" through, I printed ten copies on draft on my cheapest copy paper, addressed the necessary envelopes, then went up to bed and collapsed.

21

On Thursday morning I awoke alone, as was definitely getting to be even more common, in a cold and silent house, with snowflakes drifting lazily in the darkness outside my window. The snowflakes were sporadic and mostly disappeared even before I started my running.

I paused by the door, glancing down at the white enamel of the kitchen windowsills, polished virtually every day Marie came. Then I took a deep, cold breath before jogging down the drive. Running in the dark wasn't that much fun, and I had to cut my climb to the hillcrest short of the ridge because I needed to drive to Lebanon to meet a train and return well before my eleven o'clock.

I hurried through making breakfast, deciding to shower and shave after I ate. When I sat down to the hot rolled oats and milk and a strong pot of Russian Imperial tea, I thought about wiring Llysette, but, given her moods in the morning—especially at six o'clock—decided to hold that until later.

After cutting an apple into sections, and slowly chewing, I thought about what else I could do to anticipate whatever disaster would hit, but there's a time to act, and a time to respond. Unhappily, the situation still required me to respond mostly—at least until I could find a lever to unbalance vanBecton. So far, he'd kept pushing, and I hadn't responded until now—with my upcoming distribution of the cheap-looking flier from the "Order of Jeremiah" and the letters from Gerald Branston-Hay.

The memos would come later, and vanBecton wouldn't know that they were from me—assuming everything went as planned, which it wouldn't. In any case, that meant he'd have to push farther. I just hoped I could dodge the next push, or that it wasn't fatal.

In the meantime, delivering my hastily created fliers meant getting them to their destinations without a direct link to Vanderbraak Centre. I did know how to do that. Unfortunately, it meant driving to Lebanon, which was why I had dragged myself up so early.

With that cheerful thought, I rinsed the dishes and headed up for the shower. Pausing at the landing window, I watched a few lazy white flakes drift toward the partly covered lawn before shaking myself back into motion.

I took Route Five south through the scattered flakes before I got on the Ragged Mountain Highway west. I passed Alexandria and the biomass power plant just after seven, slowing for only one hauler filled with wood chips.

The rest of the drive to Lebanon was quiet, with only a few haulers and steamers on the road. I was standing trackside at the station a good ten minutes before the express stopped. I'd already posted the first letter from Gerald to Minister Holmbek in the box outside the station. The second would be posted from Styxx on the way back to the university.

The conductor looked for my ticket as I stepped up.

"No ticket. Need to mail these." I held up the letters.

He smiled, a knowing smile that acknowledged I wasn't supposed to do it, but that he'd seen more than a few men or women who needed faster post service on some debit payments. "Make it quick, sir."

I did, smiling at the conductor on the way down the mail car steps, and resting somewhat more easily knowing that the postmark would be from New Amsterdam.

On the drive back to Vanderbraak Centre, I thought a lot, probably too much, but I did drop the second letter from Branston-Hay into the postbox in Styxx. I doubted either would really get to Holmbek, but they might, although that wasn't their main purpose. The copies I'd kept were the useful ones. Then I reflected and went inside, almost right after the Styxx post center opened, and bought an inordinate amount of postage, knowing that I would certainly need it. If I didn't, the money would be immaterial. The clerk shook her head, her white bonnet bobbing as she did.

With the sun up, I saw a handful more steamers on the way back, mostly battered older farm wagons.

As I finally neared the square in Vanderbraak Centre, I did keep an eye out. A little paranoia never hurts, especially when you know they are out to get you, but there wasn't a local watch steamer in sight, not even when I pulled up in front of Samaha's.

Louie Samaha and another white-haired man glanced briefly at me and lowered their voices—another sign promising trouble—as I retrieved my paper. Wonder of wonders: there were actually two papers in mister Derkin's box, the first time I'd ever seen anything there. Perhaps he did exist.

With a nod to Louie, who nodded back as I left the silver dime on the counter, I scanned the front page of the *Post-Courier*, but the dirigible-turbo fight dominated the ink, and even the charge that Governor vanHasten's son had forged his father's signature to a cheque given to a well-known Asten courtesan was but a tiny story below the fold.

Llysette's Reo was not yet in the car park, but again, that was not especially surprising, not since I was relatively early.

Gilda smiled briefly from the main office.

"Good morning, Gilda. How are you on this wonderfully warm and bright morning?"

"Doktor Eschbach, how kind of you to inquire. Your presence brings light into all of our lives . . . just like a good forest fire brings warmth to the creatures of the wood and vale."

"I do so appreciate your kind words."

"I thought you would. Doktor Doniger is most unhappy, and I think it concerns you, since Dean Er Recchus called him out before he could even finish his coffee, and he was mumbling about former government officials."

"How absolutely cheering." I bestowed an exaggerated smile upon her, and she responded in kind. Then I went upstairs, where my breath almost steamed in the cold of the hall that the overhead glow squares did little to relieve, and unlocked my office.

After getting settled behind my desk, I penned a short note to Llysette, wishing her well with her rehearsals and conveying more than mere affection, then slipped it into an envelope.

By then it was still only a quarter before ten, and, not wanting to waste too much time, I reluctantly dug into the Environmental Politics 2B papers. My reluctance was indeed warranted, given the dismal quality of what I read. Why was it so hard for them to understand that, just because a politician claimed he or she was environmentalist, politicians were still politicians? After all, the subsidies for steamers and the fuel taxes weren't enacted for environmental reasons but strategic ones. Speaker Aspinall never met a tree he didn't think needed to be turned into lumber or a coal mine that he didn't love—but he pushed both the subsidies and the taxes through. Why? Because Ferdinand and Maximilian—the father, not the idiot son who was deGaulle's puppet—would have strangled Columbia if we'd ever become too dependent on foreign oil. Now, the taxes are seen as great environmental initiatives. I tried not to lose my breakfast at the soupy rhetoric asserting such nonsense, and instead contented myself with an excess of red ink.

At ten-thirty I trotted down to the Music and Theatre Department, since I knew Llysette was teaching Diction then. After putting the envelope in her box, I turned to Martha

Philips. "Don't tell her it's there. Just let her find it when she will."

"That's mean."

"I hope it's romantic. We need that around here, especially these days."

"These days . . . ? Wasn't that terrible about Dr. Branston-Hay's accident? Such a nice man. And his boys, they are so adorable. And then the fire."

"Fire?"

"Didn't you hear? Last night, the electrical box shorted. It was terrible. They lost everything—all his years of research, and his own Babbage system. At least they escaped."

"At least . . ." I shook my head. "It wasn't in the paper. I didn't know." So much for Branston-Hay's backup disks. VanBecton wasn't leaving much to chance.

"It will be. Poor woman."

"Strange. First Miranda's murder, then this. The watch hasn't been able to do much. You know, after her murder, they even called in the Spazi?"

"They did?"

"There was a big gray Spazi steamer parked right next to the watch office for two days." I shook my head. "Gerald was doing some sort of research for the Ministry of Defense. He didn't like to talk about it. I wouldn't either, I suppose, not with all the other fires and accidents happening at Babbage centers at other schools. Still, the feds won't let on, and probably poor Chief Waetjen will get the blame for not solving the crimes. And another fire." VanBecton liked fires, or this was a way to pin it on Ferdinand.

"Ah, do you think so, Doktor Eschbach?"

I grinned. "Given the federal government, is there any doubt?" I grinned. "I need to go, and please don't tell Doktor duBoise. Let her find it when she picks up her messages."

"I won't." She smiled faintly, as well she might, since her husband was on the town council that had hired Chief Waetjen.

That had been one of the purposes of my visit, that and

reminding Llysette that I was still around. She had been reserved, or was it just preoccupied with her opera production coming up? Or was I withdrawing from her?

I waved briefly to Hector as he was placing snow shelters over the bushes beside the music building, but didn't see Gertrude anywhere. Hector waved back, in his somber but friendly manner, and I marched back to the Natural Resources building, where I repeated the same conversation with Gilda, not because she was connected to anyone in particular, but because she talked to almost everyone about everything. Except with Gilda, I added one more twist.

"I wonder if the Spazi have their fingers on the chief."

"Don't they have their fingers on everyone?"

We both laughed, but Gilda's laugh died as the good Doktor Doniger marched toward his office.

"Gilda. Where is the memorandum from the dean?"

I went upstairs, actually reading through the text assignments—novel concept—and reviewing my notes for my eleven o'clock before I trudged through the snow flurries to Smythe Hall for Natural Resources 1A.

"I beg your pardon for my breathless arrival, and I do know that you are waiting breathlessly." I held up my hand. "Unfortunately, a number of matters have retarded my arrival, including a few recent deaths." I waited. "I assume you have heard about the accident that killed Doktor Branston-Hay? I hope it is not part of the unfortunate pattern of accidents involving professors at university Babbage centers across the country." I shrugged.

"Accidents?" finally came a whisper.

"You should read the press more closely. However, in answer to your question, there have been explosions and fires at a number of Babbage centers across the country. I do not know if students have been killed, but several professors and staff have died. There was even one incident in Munich. Now, enough of noncurricular speculation! What about solid deposition?"

I looked around the room. "Mister MacLean? What is solid deposition?"

I got a blank look, but eventually, someone got the idea. We didn't get into carbon, and I had to spend far too much time explaining why it was highly unlikely that significant quantities of VOCs would ever be present in any form of atmospheric deposition, solid or liquid.

A faint glimmer of sunlight graced my departure from Smythe, but it vanished as I entered the bright redbrick walls of the student activities building.

After wolfing down the bowl of bland chicken noodle soup at the counter in the activities building, I returned to my office through another, heavier snow flurry, and finished grading the Environmental Politics 2B papers. The last papers weren't that much better than the first.

Since I hadn't heard anything from Llysette, I dialed her number at about quarter to two, but there was no answer. I shrugged and gathered together the papers.

The grass wore a thin sheet of white flakes, but the brick walkways were merely damp, and the snow had stopped falling before I left the Natural Resources building. Perhaps three students nodded to me as I crossed the green back to Smythe. I nodded in return, but all three looked away. I must have looked grim. Either that or the word was out that Professor Eschbach was flattening all markers, or whatever the current slang on the korfball court was.

My Environmental Politics 2B class almost cowered in their desks, except for one brave soul—Demetri Panos, a Greek exile. What he was doing in New Bruges, I never understood. He shivered more in a classroom under a coat than even Llysette did outside.

"Professor, you will be generous in considering our faults?"

I had to smile.

"If your faults show effort and some minimal degree of perception, Mr. Panos." I felt safe saying that, since he'd actually gotten a B, a low B but a B, one of the few. Then I began handing back the papers, trying to ignore the winces and the mumbles.

". . . not graduate school . . ."

". . . what does he want . . ."

I did answer the second mumble. "What I want from you is thought. You have brains. You should read the material, make some effort to comprehend it, and then attempt to apply what you have learned to one of the topics. For example, take the second topic, the one dealing with whether real environmental progress has been made, or whether most of the environmental improvements of the past generation occurred for other, less altruistic, reasons. Were the petroleum taxes pushed through by Speaker Aspinall for environmental reasons, or because the Defense Ministry pointed out the need to preserve domestic petroleum supplies with the drawdown of the Oklahoma fields and the difficulties in extracting North Slope oil?"

Half of them still looked blank. I wondered if that blank expression were a regional trait common to New Bruges or a generational expression common to all young of the species.

Somehow we struggled through, and I got back to the main office. Still no message from Llysette, and I wondered if she were out on a short tour with her group. But would she be traveling so near a production?

Or had I done something to offend her? Finally I picked up the handset and dialed.

"Hello."

"Is this the distinguished soprano Llysette duBoise?"

"Johan, do not mock me."

"I wasn't. I was just remarking on the quality of your voice."

A sigh followed. I waited.

"A long day it has been."

"So has mine. Would you like dinner?"

"We are still rehearsing, and still I am beating the notes into their thick Dutch heads."

"Chocolate before rehearsal? Now? At Delft's?"

"I do not . . ." She sighed again. "That would be nice."

"I'll be at your door in a few moments."

And I was. And another wonder of wonders, she actually was ready to leave, carefully knotting a scarf over her hair and ears as I rapped on the studio door.

"Johan . . ." I got a kiss. A brief one, but a kiss. "For the note. Sweet and thoughtful it was."

"Sometimes I try. Other times, I'm afraid I'm trying."

We walked down the hill to the center of town.

"How are you coming with rehearsals?" I shook my head. "From what I've seen, you're really pushing them to do *Heinrich Verrückt.* Didn't everyone think Beethoven was totally insane for writing an opera about Henry VIII? From what you've told me, it has the complexity of the Ninth Symphony and the impossibility of Mozart's Queen of the Night in every role."

"Johan," Llysette said with a laugh, "difficult it is, but not *that* difficult. To baby them I am not here."

Delft's was almost empty, and we got the table by the woodstove again.

"Ah, much better this is than my cold studio." She slipped off the scarf even before sitting.

Victor's son Francois arrived and nodded at Llysette. "Chocolate? Tea? Coffee?"

"Chocolate."

"I'll have chocolate also, and please bring a plate of the butter cookies, Dansk style."

As Francois bowed and departed, Llysette shifted her weight in the chair, as if soaking in the warmth from the stove.

"Johan?"

"Yes."

"Well did you know Professor Branston-Hay?"

"I can't say I knew him exceptionally well. We talked occasionally. We had troubles with the same students."

"A tragedy that was." Llysette pursed her lips. "Some, they say that it was not an accident."

I shrugged. "I have my doubts. According to the papers, a lot of Babbage researchers are dying in one way or another."

"Is that not strange? And Miranda, was she not a friend of Professor Branston-Hay?"

I nodded.

"Your country, I do not understand." Llysette's laugh was almost bitter.

"Sometimes I don't, either. Exactly what part don't you understand?"

"A woman is killed, and nothing happens. A man dies in an accident, and the watch, they question many people, and people talk. No one says the accident could be murder. But they question. The woman, she is forgotten."

Except I hadn't forgotten Miranda, and I didn't think vanBecton had, either.

Francois returned with two pots of chocolate and a heavily laden plate of Danish butter cookies. He filled both cups.

The chocolate tasted good, much better than the bland chicken noodle soup that had substituted for lunch. The cookies were even better, and I ate two in a row before taking another small swallow of the steaming chocolate.

"Did they question you?" I asked.

"But of course. They asked about you."

"Me? How odd? I barely knew either one—I mean, not beyond being members of the same faculty."

"I told the chief watch officer that very same." Llysette shrugged. "Perhaps they think it was a ménage à trois."

"Between a broken-down federal official, a spiritualistic piano teacher, and a difference engine researcher with a soul written in Babbage code? They must be under a lot of pressure." I refilled my cup from my pot and hers from the one on her left.

She laughed for a moment, then added, "Governments make strange things happen. People must . . . make hard choices, *n'est-ce-pas?*"

"Mais oui, mademoiselle. Like insisting on producing *Hein-*

rich Verrückt in New Bruges. Why didn't you just use one of the Perkins adaptations of Vondel?"

"Vondel? Dutch is even more guttural than low German."

"I think it's interesting. Seventeenth-century Dutch plays turned into contemporary operas by a Mormon composer."

Llysette made a face.

"The Dutch think that Vondel was every bit as good as Shakespeare." I took a healthy swallow of chocolate. The second cup was cooler.

"Good plays do not make good operas. Good music and good plays make good opera."

"You have a problem with Perkins?"

"Perkins? No. Good music he writes. The problem, it is with Vondel." Llysette looked at her wrist. "Alas, I must go. A makeup lesson I must do, and then the rehearsals."

I swallowed the last of my chocolate, then left some bills on the table for Francois.

Llysette replaced her scarf before stepping into the wind. A few damp brown leaves swirled by, late-hangers torn from the trees lining the square.

"Makeup lesson?"

"The little dunderheads, sometimes, they have good reasons for missing a lesson."

"Few times, I would guess."

Llysette did not answer, and we proceeded in silence to the door of the Music and Theatre Building. I held it open, and we walked to her empty studio.

"Take care." I bent forward and kissed her cheek.

"You also, Johan." Her lips were cold on my cheek. "The note—I did like it."

I watched for a moment as she took off the scarf and coat, then blew her a kiss before turning away.

As I walked back to my office, I had to frown. Was I getting so preoccupied that Llysette was finding me cold? She still seemed distracted . . . but she had kissed me and thanked me. Was I the distracted one—not that I didn't have more than enough reasons to be distracted—or was something else going on?

I went back to my own office, where I reclaimed my folder before locking up. The main office was empty, although I could see the light shining from under David's closed door. Whatever it was about me that he'd been discussing with the dean apparently was still under wraps. He was probably plotting something. God, I hated campus politics.

The wind continued to gust as I walked to the car park. A watch car was pulled over to the curb on the other side of the street outside the faculty car park. I started the Stanley, then belted in. As my headlamps crossed the dark gray steamer, glinting off the unlit green lenses of the strobes, I could make out Officer Warbeck, clearly watching me. When I got to the bottom of the hill, he had pulled out, following me at a distance. He followed me across the river, but not up Deacon's Lane.

First Llysette, and then the watch.

At least Marie had left me a warm steak pie, and I had eaten most of it when the wireset rang. I swallowed what was in my mouth and picked up the handset.

"Hello?"

"Doktor Eschbach?"

"Yes."

"This is Chief Waetjen. I just had one additional question."

"Oh?"

"Do you recall whether Professor Miller was wearing a long blue scarf the night she was killed?"

I frowned. "I only felt her ghost. So I wouldn't have any way of knowing what she wore. I hadn't seen her since that Friday, I think, and I don't remember what she was wearing then. You might ask one of the women."

"I see. Well, thank you." *Click.*

I looked out into the darkness onto the lawn, barely visible under the stars that had begun to shine in the rapidly clearing skies.

In belated foresight, the situation vanBecton was setting up was clear enough. Johan Eschbach had been under enormous stress, had even received a health-based pension for wounds from a would-be assassin. Now a murder, perhaps one he had committed in his unstable state, would be found to have turned him into a zombie—one of the more severe varieties. And his ghost would never be found. What a pity!

I walked upstairs and looked outside, seeing a few bright and cold stars between the clouds and wondering how long before I got a caller. Then I opened the false drawer in the armoire, taking out a few Austro-Hungarian items—and the two new shiny nuts I had put there just the day before. Of course, the whole thing was ridiculous, since no real agent would carry anything even faintly betraying, but the items were suggestive—a medallion reminiscent of the Emperor's Cross, a fragment of a ticket in German, the sort of thing that could get stuck in a pocket, a pen manufactured only in Vienna, and a square metal gadget which contained a saw and a roll of piano wire, totally anonymous except for the tiny Austrian maker's mark.

As evidence they might be too subtle, but I didn't have much to lose. I put them in my pockets, not that they were any risk to me, since I'd either walk away or be in no shape to do so.

I studied the lawn, but no one was out there, not that I could see. So I walked back downstairs and washed the dishes. Then I went into the study, got the disassociator, and set it in the corner by the door. I got the quilt from the sofa and rolled it up and set it on the chair before the Babbage console, putting a jacket from the closet around it and an old beret on top. I'd never worn it, not since Anna had sent it to me from her trip to New France years earlier, but I doubted any agent knew what I did or didn't wear in my study. In any case, the lights would silhouette the figure, and, from the veranda, it would be hard to distinguish the difference between me and the impromptu dummy from any distance because the Babbage screen assembly would block a head-on view until an intruder was almost at the windows.

I reached forward and turned on the difference engine. After that, I slipped the truncheon from the hidden holder on the table leg into my belt, then turned on the lights, picking up the disassociator.

I didn't have to wait long before a tall figure in a watch uniform glided up the hill and across the veranda. I shook my head. He was relying a lot on his uniform, and I've never had that much respect for cloth and braid and bright buttons.

He fiddled with the door, opened it, and lifted the Colt-Luger.

Crack. crack.

The young Spazi—I was sure the imposter's name wasn't Warbeck, even if I had appreciated his sense of humor—actually fired two shots into the quilt-dummy before he looked around. Metal glinted under his watch helmet. His large Colt-Luger swung toward me.

Crack.

I jumped and pulled the trigger on the disassociator, then dropped it. The room went dark, but I hadn't waited for that, as I had dropped forward and to Warbeck's right. I could feel him ram into the heavy desk, and his hesitation was enough, even if it took me two quick swings with the truncheon. I had to aim for the temple because I didn't know how effective the truncheon would be with Gerald's mesh cap and Warbeck's regular hat over it.

Still, even in the darkness, I could tell I'd hit him too hard, not that it frankly bothered me much. The Colt thudded to the carpet, but did not discharge again. My effort with the truncheon had been quick enough that there would be no ghost, although the disassociator would have taken care of that detail.

I pulled the flash from the desk drawer and played it across him. He was definitely dead.

After placing those few items I had prepared in Warbeck's clothes, I used a handkerchief to replace the Colt in the military holster, then wrapped his cooling fingers around the weapon before dragging the body out the door and onto the veranda. I used the handkerchief to put his hat by him, then waited in the shadows. I've always been good at waiting. It's what separates the real professionals from those who just think they are.

It must have been an hour before the two others slipped up the lawn through the trees. One carried a large body bag. I felt like nodding. Instead, I waited until they found the body.

"Shit. Somebody got him first . . ."

Both lifted their weapons, and that was enough for me. I held down the spring trigger on the disassociator. One collapsed, and the other shrieked. I waited and potted both ghosts with the disassociator, but the second one resisted. The power meter I hadn't paid enough attention to earlier dropped into the red.

I set aside the disassociator, placed the truncheon in the hands of the collapsed zombie, and took Warbeck's truncheon. I also thought about taking the metal hair net, thinking I might be needing it myself. Then I decided it would be more valuable on Warbeck. The other zombie looked at me blankly—still somewhat there probably because the disassociator had run out of power.

"There's been an accident."

"There's been an accident," he repeated.

"Wait here for help."

"I wait here for help." He wasn't quite expressionless in his intonation, but close enough.

I had to hand it to vanBecton. He hadn't even wanted me as a zombie, and he'd set up Warbeck. Poor Warbeck. He'd just thought he was carrying out a removal. If he succeeded, then I was out of the way, and then he would have been killed trying to escape from my murder.

Waetjen's own boys had doubtless been told that Warbeck had gone off the deep end and to bring him back in one piece or many, but not to risk their lives. They'd also been told I was dangerous, and armed, and not to be too gentle there, either. Neither vanBecton nor the chief was in favor of my continued presence, although it would have been hard for me to convince any judge or jury of that.

That was the hell of the position I was in. If I'd waited, I'd have been dead. If I weren't careful, I'd be in jail for murder, because I couldn't prove, and no one outside the intelligence community would understand, that I was being set up.

My knees were weak. As I walked to the study, I was beginning to understand the difference between being an impartial agent and a directly involved victim. I didn't like being the targeted victim, nor what it was doing to my nerves.

In the study, by the light of the flash I dialed the watch number and began screaming. Chief Waetjen got on the line.

"Who is this?" he snapped.

"Johan Eschbach! There's been a terrible fight outside. I think . . . I don't know. Get someone up here."

"There were two men headed there. Have you seen them?"

"There are three men here. One's dead, one's unconscious, and the other's a zombie."

"Oh . . ."

"And, Chief, I think the dead one's an Austro-Hungarian agent."

"You would now, would you?"

"Well," I said carefully, "someone has to be. The way I see it, your men tried to stop him from potting a former government minister when he started shooting at me. I probably owe them a lot. So do you."

After that, I flipped the switch on the difference engine so that it wouldn't come on when the power returned. Then I went to the closet and reset the circuit breakers. I shivered. Had I destroyed Carolynne as well?

A flash of white by the veranda, a glimpse of the recital dress reassured me. With that, I quickly tucked the disassociator back in the closet, and put the quilt, jacket, and beret away. The sirens echoed from across the river as I flicked through the wireset directory until I found the number. I wished I'd cultivated press contacts in New Bruges, but . . .

"*Post-Courier.*"

"News desk, please."

"Vraal, news."

"My name is Johan Eschbach. There's been a murder at my house, and two zombies are walking around the yard. I used to be a government minister under Speaker Michel, but I now teach at Vanderbraak State University in Vanderbraak Centre. The murdered man is an imposter, and the two zombies are local watch officers."

"We don't take crank calls, sir."

"If you look at last year's *Almanac of Columbian Politics*, my name and profile are on page two hundred twenty-nine. If you don't want the story, or if you want it buried, that's your problem."

A long pause followed.

"Who did you say you were?"

"I was, and still am, Johan Anders Eschbach. The Vanderbraak Centre watch chief, Hans Waetjen, is headed to my house at the moment."

"What happened?"

"I heard someone trying to break in. When I went downstairs, someone shot at me, and there were yells and sounds of a struggle. Then I found the body on the veranda and two zombies standing there. One had a bloody truncheon in his hand. The house is off Deacon's Lane across the River Wijk from the main part of Vanderbraak Centre. You might find it worth looking into." While I talked, I found the number for Gelfor Hardin, who edits and prints the *Vanderbraak Weekly Chronicle.*

"I hope this isn't another crank call."

"It is scarcely that, although I must admit that I have little fondness for armed men who shoot at me and bodies appearing behind my house."

"Why did you call the *Courier?*"

"The occupational paranoia of government service stays with one for life, I fear. A good news story is often a deterrent."

"You say that one watch officer tried to break into your house, and he was killed by two others?"

"I don't know that. That is what it looked like."

"Why would someone be after you?"

"I don't know—unless I happen to be a handy scapegoat for something."

"Scapegoat?"

"You might remember the Colonel Nord incident."

"Oh . . . you're *that* Eschbach?"

"How fleeting fame is."

"Can we call you back?"

"Yes." I gave him the number and wired Hardin.

Hardin didn't answer, but another voice, female, did. "*Chronicle* services."

I gave an abbreviated version of the story to the woman, then walked back out on the veranda. By then, Chief Waetjen was standing there with three other officers beside the dead man and the two zombies.

"Who were you wiring?" asked Waetjen.

"The newspapers. I thought they might like the story."

"You know, Doktor, I could end up not appreciating you very much."

"I understand." I bowed slightly. "But you should understand that I don't like finding bodies outside my house, especially bodies in watch uniforms. It's bad for my digestion."

Hans Waetjen wasn't as smart as he thought, because he'd used sirens and brought three watch officers with him. I was grateful for small favors, since those were the only kind I was likely to get.

He bowed politely. "You understand that my digestion also suffers when I find dead officers and officers who are zombies?"

"I can see that we share many of the same concerns, Chief Waetjen."

"Could you tell me what happened?"

I gave him the sanitized version of Warbeck's efforts, concluding with, "I don't know what Officer Warbeck did, but when the shooting stopped, he was on the veranda, and the two others were just like they are now."

"Just like this?" He clearly didn't believe me, and he was certainly correct, but I wasn't about to oblige him.

"I didn't check exactly, but I don't think anything's changed since I called you."

"What about before that?"

"I heard the noise at the door. Then all the lights went out—"

"You didn't mention that."

"Sorry. They did. I reset the breakers after I called you."

"How could you see?"

"I have a flash in my desk." I glanced over my shoulder. "It's on the corner now—right there."

"How convenient."

"No, just practical. I spend most of my time at home in the study or the kitchen. There are flashes in both places. I have a kerosene lamp in the bedroom."

One of the other three watch officers had set up a floodlight and was taking pictures of the scene on the veranda flagstones.

Another siren wailed, and the ambulance glided up the drive and stopped behind the two watch steamers. I watched and waited until the medics carted off the two zombies with a promise to return for the body shortly.

Chief Waetjen finally turned to me. "I could insist you come in with us, Doktor Eschbach."

"You could," I agreed amiably. "But . . ." I looked at the body on the cold stone and thought of the truncheon with one of the zombies' fingerprints all over it. "Arresting me for something someone else clearly did wouldn't look really good. Especially since we both know that Warbeck isn't Warbeck."

"He isn't?" asked one of the officers, who was using some sort of amplified magnifying glass to study the stones around Warbeck's body.

"No." I smiled at Waetjen, who tried not to glower at me.

"You think you're pretty clever, don't you?"

"No. I don't. There are people a lot more clever than either one of us, and I suggest we leave the cleverness to them."

Waetjen paused. Then he turned to the others. "Finish up the standard procedure. Do you have prints, photographs, complete tech search?"

"We're still working on it."

"Don't forget the outside knob on the door there," I suggested. "It should have Warbeck's prints all over it. And there are some bullets and bullet holes somewhere in the study."

Waetjen didn't say a word, just gestured at the watch officer with the print kit.

The wireset bell rang.

"Excuse me, Chief."

I edged the door open by the inside of the frame and went inside to pick up the handset.

"Hello."

"Do you come in, or do we put you in cold storage?" It was Ralston McGuiness's voice. "Think about your friend, too."

"This is somewhat . . . open."

"Christ, all of Columbia will know something's up. Your nominal superior downtown will call you in, and you'll never come out."

"I'll come in. But where?"

"Use the bolthole we discussed." *Click.*

Trouble wasn't quite the word. More like disaster, I thought. And what Ralston had in mind wasn't exactly friendly. Come in or we'll ensure you never go anywhere, and, if you don't understand, we'll take out one Doktor duBoise. That wouldn't happen immediately, because he'd lose leverage, and he'd want me to think about it, but he'd start with her, and then it would be my mother, Anna, Judith, Eric . . .

The wireset rang again.

"Hello."

"This is Garrison vanKleef at the *Post-Courier*. Is this Doktor Eschbach?"

"Yes."

"Do you think this incident has anything to do with the Nord incident?"

"I would hope not. The last time I heard, Colonel Nord was reforesting semitropical swamps outside of Eglin. And I don't have another wife and son to lose."

"Have the watch arrived yet?"

"Chief Waetjen is standing about fifteen feet from me with three others. He does not look terribly pleased."

"How does he look?"

"As always, stocky, gray-haired, and not very pleased."

"Why should we be interested in this?"

"Call it a feeling. You also might try to find out, though, why the dead watch officer was wearing a funny metal mesh skullcap."

"A funny metal mesh skullcap, you say?"

"Under his watch helmet. I thought I once saw one in the Babbage research center. A rather odd coincidence, I thought, especially after the recent accident that killed the Babbage research director at the University."

"So do I, Eschbach." A laugh followed. "You have a body and two zombies there. Any thoughts on why this happened to you?"

"One thing I did learn from all my years in Columbia was that speculations are just that. It's Chief Waetjen's job to get to the bottom of the mess."

"Do you think he will?"

"On or off the record?"

"On, of course."

"I think the chief will devote a great deal of effort to this investigation, and I trust that he will discover why one of his officers apparently went beyond the call of duty."

"You spent too much time in Columbia, Eschbach. Good night."

I walked back outside.

"More press?"

"Of course. Isn't the press a man's safeguard?"

"Sometimes. If the feds don't get there first." Waetjen snorted.

I understood. The government can't force retractions, but it can suggest that stories never be printed—if it knows in advance. The press still likes good stories, and they like to scream about direct censorship. It's a delicate balancing game, and I'd tried to upset the balance.

Neither of the other three watch officers said anything. So I stood and watched while they poked, prodded, and photographed everything. What they didn't do was take my prints, and that obviously bothered me, because it wasn't an oversight.

It was well past midnight when the chief left and I locked up the house. After pulling the study drapes closed, I plugged the disassociator into the standard recharging socket, and it seemed to work, just the way Bruce had designed it. That was one reason I liked Bruce. When he built something, it did what it was designed to do.

"These things are beyond all use, and I do fear them." Carolynne floated in the study doorway.

"I have gotten a similar impression. The question is what I should do about it."

"Do not go forth today . . . not go forth today . . ." Carolynne's voice seemed faint.

"Do not go forth? What about the people who sent the false watch officer?"

"Graves have yawned and yield up their dead; fierce fiery warriors fight upon the clouds."

If she meant that both the ghosts and the powers that be in Columbia were after me, she was right, but having a ghost's confirmation on that wouldn't help me in Columbia City. So I began to stack all the materials I would need on the side of the desk.

"When beggars die, there are no comets seen . . . alas, my lord, your wisdom is consumed in confidence."

"Probably, but I'm no Caesar. And I can't fight enemies in the federal city from here. Not any longer."

"Let me, upon my knee, prevail in this."

"All right." I had to laugh. "I probably should leave tonight, but I'm too tired. Besides, if he detained me right now, Chief Waetjen would look as though he were trying to run on foam. He'll need to go through all the procedures, and that will take a day or two, making sure that I am very visible. Of course, if I disappear, then I will be presumed guilty. But if I don't I'll either be charged or killed while resisting arrest."

Carolynne listened, but she said no more as I gathered together identity documents and copied real and false memoranda and all the supporting materials. I carried the whole mess upstairs.

I packed quickly but carefully, with working clothes on the top of the valise and suits in the hanging bag. The top suit was shiny, hard gray wool, a threadbare and very cheap old suit I had kept around in case I might need it. I had always hoped I wouldn't, but you always plan for the worst.

Then there was the equipment bag—all the gadgets I'd collected over the years and never turned in. All of us who worked those jobs have such bags. You never know when you might need them again. Some I knew—and I thought Bruce might have been one—did keep firearms they had picked up. You didn't keep issue weapons, not since they really tallied those. But how could anyone tell if you used eight or eighteen yards of plastique, or an electronics installer's belt, or tree spikes, or mountain gear?

Mine had a coil of thin plastic, nearly ten yards' worth. I had two radio detonators, plus a handful of contact detonators. There was the truncheon, plus a complete Federal District watch uniform, including the Colt revolver I'd never used. I'd been undercover back in 1986 when the French president in exile pleaded for Columbian support against Ferdinand, and the federals were afraid that the Jackal's group might try an assassination. We'd had a tip that they had a plant in the watch. They'd had two, actually, and I'd turned in one's uniform instead of mine. Larceny, I know, but when dealing with thieves total honesty is suicide.

I looked up, but Carolynne was gone. Even ghosts don't like being ignored or being thought of as part of the furniture. I sighed, although I wasn't quite sure why, before pulling out the next item, a set of blue coveralls, almost identical to every electrical installer's in the country, and very useful for a variety of purposes. I shook the dust off them and packed them in the bag.

After laying everything out, I collapsed into bed, setting the alarm for an hour earlier than normal, wishing I could get more than five hours' sleep.

But I did sleep, even if I dreamed about ghosts, and iron bars, and driving endlessly on unmarked roads through rain and fog.

22

HALF AWAKE ALREADY when the alarm jolted me out of the darkness, I was still exhausted. After putting on the kettle, I showered, shaved, and dressed quickly, then let the Imperial Russian tea steep while I loaded the Stanley.

First, the equipment bag, the disassociator, and the toolbox went in the false back of the Stanley's trunk; then the rest went into the main part, clearly the artifacts of a traveling sales representative, down to the slightly battered sample book and the worn leather order book.

The sky lightened as I sipped tea and ate my way through a too-ripe pear and three slices of Marie's bread slathered with my own blackberry preserves. I actually made them—had ever since I'd returned to Vanderbraak Centre.

Finally I backed the Stanley out of the car barn and headed into town. I went around the square first, just for effect, before stopping in at Samaha's to pick up my paper. Louie didn't look at me when I left my dime on the counter. Neither did Rose, his equally dour wife.

I didn't open the paper until I was back in the Stanley. The story was played straight—too straight.

Last night, a Vanderbraak Centre watch officer was killed, apparently by another officer, as he tried to enter the home of Johan Eschbach, a former Deputy Minister of Environment. Although Eschbach was not hurt, both the officer who was forced to stop the intruder and another attending officer suffered psychic disassociation.

According to unofficial sources, after firing several shots, the intruding officer suffered a fatal skull fracture, apparently inflicted by a watch truncheon.

Eschbach reported that the intruder wore a strange metal cap, a fact confirmed by the Vanderbraak Watch Chief, Hans Waetjen. Neither Waetjen nor Eschbach would speculate on the reason for the apparent attack or the cause of the psychic disassociation of the other two officers.

Chief Waetjen indicated that a complete investigation is ongoing.

I folded the paper and restarted the Stanley. After I pulled away from Samaha's, I waved to Constable Gerhardt through the wind, and headed northward on Route Five, just until past the woolen mill. There I took the covered-bridge turnoff onto the back road that eventually reconnected to Route Five south of Vanderbraak Centre. In the dimness of the woods beyond the Reformed Church's summer retreat, I twisted the knob under the dashboard to get the thermals on. The thermosensitive paint faded from red to maroon to dark gray.

At that point I changed from coat and cravat into comfortable flannels and put the wallet with Vic Nuustrom's license in it in my pocket. The coat and cravat went into the garment bag in the trunk, along with my real identification.

I took Route Five south almost to Borkum, where the Wijk flowed into the Nieumaas, before taking Route Four west. Wider and smoother than the Ragged Mountain Highway that ran from south of Vanderbraak Centre to Lebanon, Route Four skirted the base of the Grunbergs and entered New Ostend just south and east of Hudson Falls.

Just before I left New Bruges, I ran into a series of snow flurries, but they passed about the time I left Riisville and the girls' seminary there. All the buildings at the seminary were white-painted clapboards, a southern affectation hardly at home in New Bruges.

It was late morning, almost noon, before I crossed into New Ostend and Route Four became the Heisser Parkway. And that was despite some periods where I had the Stanley really moving on the open stretches. One positive sign was that none of the highway watch in New Bruges had stopped me. I had to admit that I began to breathe easier when I saw the sign that said WELCOME TO NEW OSTEND.

By midafternoon I got to the outskirts of New Amsterdam, coming down the new Hudson River Bluffs parkway, two lanes in each direction all the way, with mulched gardens in the median. I even had the now-maroon Stanley close to its red line a few times, but even with the new parkways, driving was definitely not so fast as traveling by train.

I stopped near Nyack to eat and to top off the tanks. I avoided the Royal Dutch stop on principle and pulled into the Standard Oil station. First came the water and kerosene, then the food.

"Both?" asked the attendant, a girl not much older than Waltar would have been.

"Both. Filtered water?"

"It's the only kind we have. Single or double A on the kerosene, sir?"

"Double, please." The double was nearly twenty cents a gallon higher, but the purity more than paid for the price in cleaner burners and, in my case, the ability to redline the Stanley if necessary. Eastern water wasn't usually a problem, but some of the mineralized water in the west played hob with steam turbines, coated the vanes and literally tore them apart.

The flaxen-haired, red-cheeked teenager wore her jacket open over a blue flannel shirt, despite the chill, and whistled something that sounded like the Fiddler's March, well enough that any Brit would have been apoplectic.

Standard Oil or not, the station had a well-mulched flower garden in the shape of an oval that matched the sign. Did the flower patterns spell out "Standard Oil" in the summer? I asked as she racked the kerosene nozzle.

"No, sir. Grosspapa tried, but the blues didn't really work out, and people complained. So I plant whatever suits me now that he can't do the gardening anymore." She smiled. "That came to twenty-five fifty, sir."

I nodded and handed her a twenty and a ten. With the latest round of energy taxes, fuels were running over three dollars a gallon. "Thank you."

"Thank you, sir. Please stop and see us again." She handed me my change in silver.

I drove a quarter-mile down the side road to the Irving Tavern, where I parked and locked the Stanley outside the restaurant. Lace curtains, freshly laundered, graced the windows. On the way into the dark-paneled dining room, where the dark wooden tables still shimmered, their wood set off by glistening white cloths, I picked up a copy of the *New Amsterdam Post.*

"One, sir?"

"Please."

The hostess's white cap could have come from two centuries earlier. She escorted me to a small side table. "We have everything on the menu except for the pork dumplings, and the special is a dark kielbasa with sauerkraut. Would you like coffee or chocolate?"

"Chocolate."

After pouring me a cup, she set the pot in the center of the table and waited as I studied the menu, glancing over the stuffed cabbage while trying to repress a shudder at the list of heavy entrees. If I ate half of what was listed, the Stanley would be carrying double—if I made it out the door.

"I'll have the Dutch almond noodles with the cheeses."

"They're good today." She nodded and departed.

While I waited, I leafed through the *Post* and found the RPI wire story, which I read twice, stopping at the key paragraph.

Although the Vanderbraak Centre watch officer killed in the scuffle outside former minister Eschbach's house has been determined not to be Perkin Warbeck, his true identity remains unknown. Sources who have requested not to be named have indicated that items found on the dead man link him to the Austro-Hungarian Empire.

In Columbia, President Armstrong called for an investigation of the Spazi, asking how the nation's security service could allow a former official to be almost assaulted or murdered.

Speaker Hartpence responded by calling a meeting with top officials of the Sedition Prevention and Security Service.

Ambassador Schikelgruber responded by denying that the dead man had any connection to the Austro-Hungarian Empire.

Public perception—that was the key. It didn't matter what really happened in politics, but what people believed happened. Still, vanBecton would be out to nail my hide, preferably somewhere very dark and unpleasant, that is, if Ralston didn't get me—and Llysette—first. I had to act quickly, but not too stupidly. It's wonderful to be so well liked and wanted. The last paragraph had someone's twist.

Former minister Eschbach, no stranger to controversy from his links to the Colonel Nord incident and the man at the center of the strange occurrences at the university, was not available for comment.

That was disturbing, because I clearly was available when the paper had been put to bed—or had vanBecton and company blocked my wireset? I wouldn't have known. I hadn't tried to call anyone after my comments to the Asten and Vanderbraak papers.

"Here are your noodles," offered the smiling hostess, who apparently doubled as waitress. "And your bread."

Along with the noodles and bread came four thick slabs of cheese—white cheddar, yellow cheddar, Gouda, and a double Gloucester—and cauliflower smothered in processed cheese.

"Thank you."

I forced myself to eat most of the noodles, but I couldn't finish the cheeses or the bread.

"Would you like any dessert? More chocolate?"

"No, thank you."

The heavy lunch came to three-fifty, and I left a dollar tip before I lumbered out to the Stanley.

There really wasn't that much I could do except keep driving, not until I got to the Federal District. Once I left New Ostend and entered New Jersey on the Teaneck Parkway, I had to slow down because the parkway was so rough in spots. That was probably because Speaker Colmer had choked off most road payments to New Jersey more than a decade before, when the incidence of ghosts along newer highways rose as the number of Corsican "family" members precipitously dropped.

Governor Biaggi had protested, but the Speaker refused even to meet with him, politely declining on the grounds that federal grants could not be dictated by local political concerns. That was right after Colmer had met with Governor Espy, the youngest governor ever from the state, and increased the road payments to Mississippi.

It might have been coincidence, but Biaggi dropped his protests and the Spazi dropped their investigation of Governor Biaggi's brother's contracting business.

Around ten that night, my eyes burning, I finally gave up, after winding down past Philadelphia and skirting Baltimore. It had been a long day, after too many days and worries with too little sleep. I wasn't likely to sleep any longer in the future, either, not after I reached my immediate destination.

In a town named Elioak, which I'd never heard of, about forty miles north of Columbia City, I found a motor hotel, not quite seedy, the kind that Vic, my transitional identity, could have afforded. I took a room and walked across the street to the chrome-plated diner meant to be a replica of the Western Zephyr. It wasn't a very good replica. One waitress lounged behind the green-tiled counter, a gray rag in her hand, listlessly watching two white-haired men in the corner booth.

"Fiske could stop any shot, even Ohiri's . . . big lug broke Rissjen's wrists . . ."

"Still remember Summerall . . . got around anybody . . . big reason big Ben never got that hundredth shutout."

"Ben was overrated. Take what's-his-name—the blond guy with the bad legs, played for the New Ostend Yanks for a year. Even he got one in the nets . . ."

I slumped into the worn green leather of a booth for two, on the side where I could watch the door, and glanced at the dark-speckled menu as I waited for the woman to slouch from behind the counter.

"What will you be having, sir?"

"Number four, heavy on the gravy, and make sure it's hot. Black tea." I set the menu back in the holder with a thump.

"Number four, hauler style." A minute later she returned and set down the chipped white mug of tea. "Don't see no rig," she offered.

"No rig. Woolen mill rig, up north. Just on the way to visit my sister. She lives outside pretty city."

"You going to make that tonight?"

"No reason. Don't get along with her man. He's on the road tomorrow. Dumb bastard." I shrugged. "She's happy. I don't mess, but I don't put up with that crap."

"Takes all kinds."

I nodded and sipped the tea—bitter with a coffee aftertaste, just the way most haulers liked it, even in England. I could drink it without wincing, and that was about all I could manage, but the taste made it easy to look sullenly at the smears on the table's varnish.

The fried steak was far better than the tea, and the mashed potatoes didn't even have lumps. The gravy was almost boiling, but the beans looked—and tasted—like soggy green paperboard. I doused them in the gravy and left a clean plate.

"Don't know how you haulers eat them beans. Tried 'em. Taste like green pasteboard to me." The sad-eyed waitress with the incipient jowls shook her head slowly. "You want any dessert?"

"What's good?"

"Banana cream pie. Best thing Al makes."

"One slice and more tea."

"Haulers . . . guts like iron tubs."

Since it had been a long day since my heavy noodle lunch and a light and early breakfast, my stomach hadn't been all that discerning. Then again, maybe lunch had put it in shock. The pie was good, certainly far better than the beans or the tea, and actually had a taste vaguely resembling bananas.

I did manage to lock the room door before dropping almost straight into a too soft bed that felt more like a hammock than a bed. But Vic wouldn't have minded, and I was too tired to care.

23

THE ALBERT PICK House had seen better days, probably back when it had been the Columbian flag hotel of the Statler chain, but it was still clean, and my room was three floors up, high enough to be off the street, low enough for some forms of emergency exit, not that I really wanted that. The videolink set was small. I supposed it worked, but I hadn't bothered to check. Somehow even I wasn't desperate enough to sit and watch video.

With its fake Virginia plates, the steamer was safe enough in the hotel lot. They were actually copies of real plates, but since the originals were still in place on another Stanley, it wasn't likely that anyone would care. I also had Maryland plates and a set from New Ostend racked inside the false trunk, all three sets made up in earlier, even more paranoid days after Elspeth's death and right after I'd purchased the Stanley.

My timing had been lousy, since there was no practical way to do what I needed to on a weekend. So all I could do was scout and plan and ensure that everything would go like clockwork on Monday. It wouldn't, of course, but planning helped reduce the uncertainty—and the worry.

Wearing the nondescript tan trench coat over my cheap, hard gray wool suit, a brush mustache, and a battered gray fedora, I left my closetlike room and walked down the hall. I noted the black plate across the lock of the room two doors down and wondered how long the hotel had been forced to seal it. After all, they couldn't very well rent a haunted room to paying guests.

I entered the elevator, nodding at a young man with lipstick on his cheek and a cravat not quite cinched up to his collar. He hadn't shaved, but he looked happy as he left the elevator in the lobby. I hefted the battered sample case that contained the documents I needed as well as several other items, and strolled across the not-quite-threadbare imitation Persian carpet.

The Bread and Chocolate pastry shop across the street provided two heavy nut rolls and bitter tea. I sipped and chewed until I finished all three and my stomach stopped growling.

Then I slowly walked up Fifteenth Street, turning northwest on New Bruges and pausing for a moment in Ericson Circle. The gray of my clothes fit right in with the sky and my mood. I had plenty of time, and there was no reason to hurry. I could have driven, but you don't get the same feel for things when you're insulated inside a steamer.

The pigeons looked at me from under every gray-painted lamppost, but they were city pigeons and didn't move unless you almost stepped on them. Before long I reached Dupont Circle. The fountain in the circle had been drained and contained only dampened leaves, leaves that would have been removed had the fountain been in the square in Vanderbraak Centre or even in New Amsterdam or Asten, cities that they were. More pigeons skittered around the base of the fountain, and two old men leaned over a stone chess table like weathered statues.

A block up on New Bruges Avenue, holiday-sized flags were flying from both the Chung Kuo embassy and the embassy of Imperial Japan, across the avenue from each other just as they were across the Sea of Japan from each other.

According to my research, vanBecton lived in the upper Bruges area, uphill and behind the embassies. It was a long walk from downtown, but I needed the exercise, and the feel, and sitting around a hotel room would have driven me crazier. So I kept walking, keeping my eyes out for what I needed.

One thing I wanted to find was the local power substation. In Columbia City they're generally disguised as houses, and most passersby don't give them a second thought. You can tell by the power lines, though. On a dead-end half-street off Tracy Place, I found the substation that probably served vanBecton's house before I located the house itself.

At first glance, the substation didn't look much different from a normal, boxy, white-brick attempt at Dutch colonial, but there was a sloppiness in the off-white trim paint, a hopelessness in the way the lace curtains in the false windows were so precisely placed, and an un-lived-in air that permeated everything from the evenly placed azaleas to the cobwebs linking the porch pillars to the white bricks.

To me, those were more apparent than the faint humming or the power lines that spread from the brick-walled backyard.

I paused, resting my left leg on the low stone wall that contained the raised lawn, and balanced my battered case on my leg while I opened it and pretended to check the papers inside. I was actually studying the substation, making a few written notes and a lot more mental ones.

There were definite advantages to working in more affluent areas, and I intended to make use of every one of them. With my notes taken, I walked along the hilly, tree-lined streets.

Some houses had perfectly raked lawns and white-painted trim that gleamed, betraying the more northern origin of their owners. On others, especially those with pillars, the white paint almost seemed designed to peel, giving an aura of the lost South, the time that had begun to fade with Speaker Calhoun's machinations. Senator Lincoln only applied the last nails to the coffin, nails that had led to his murder by Booth, the Anglophilic actor. And yet, despite the fall of slavery and its lifestyle, vampirelike, the essence of the English south still seemed to drift through the Federal District, especially in fog, twilight, and rain.

On a cold hard fall day, more like winter, those houses seemed as out of place as a painted old courtesan at dawn.

I kept walking until I found Thorton Place, and vanBecton's house. It was about as I had imagined it—an elegant, impeccably manicured, false Georgian town house with real marble pillars and slate walks and steps.

I didn't appear to look at his house, instead sketching his neighbor's side garden on a plain piece of paper while I continued studying the false Georgian. There were sensors mounted inconspicuously in various places. I really wasn't interested in the sensors but in the positions of the wireset and power lines. The large maple with the overhanging limbs offered some intriguing possibilities.

After I finished the sketch and some brief notes, I made my way back down Newfoundland, the other cross artery leading back to Dupont Circle, and a memorial of sorts. The debate over that state's admission had nearly led to war with both England and France, and only the advance of the Austrians on Rome had held off what could have been a catastrophe. Quebec still made threatening sounds about Newfoundland, sounds guaranteed mostly to extract trade concessions from Columbia.

Many of the houses on Newfoundland Avenue date from the fifties, with glass bricks and angular constructions that seem to lean toward the sidewalks. Nothing is so dated as past modernism. The demolition crew working on an old "modern" mansion confirmed that, as did my sneezes at the dust. Two empty steam haulers waited to be loaded with debris, and I had to cross the street to the eastern side to get back down to Dupont Circle.

When I finished sneezing, I stopped by Von Kappel and Sons, Stationers, where I browsed through the rag and parchment specialty items, finally selecting a heavy off-cream paper with a marbled bluish-green border. I also bought two dozen large envelopes, the ten-by-thirteen-inch kind with accordion pleats that can hold nearly a hundred pages of documents. The bill for the fifty sheets of classy marbled paper, two dozen matching envelopes, and the bigger document envelopes totaled $49.37.

The clerk didn't quite sniff at my half-open trench coat and cheap wool suit, but he said as little as possible. "Your change, sir."

"Thank you." I put the bag under my arm and made my way across the circle.

Babbage-Copy was at the corner of Nineteenth and N, and they had machines and printers you could rent by the hour.

The balding young clerk put his thumb in his economics textbook and flipped a switch on his console. "Ten dollars. That's for two hours. Copies are five cents a page on the impact printer." He handed me a metal disk. "Put that in the control panel and bring it back here when you're done. Take machine number six."

He was back taking notes on a yellow lined pad even before I sat down. Why, with all the Babbage machines around, didn't he use one for his notes? There was no telling. Some authors still write longhand, although I can't see why. Maybe they're masochists.

Still, I had to set up the week, and that meant starting with a simple one-page introduction—something to tease the reporters. I had some ideas, but it took me several drafts before I had a usable piece.

WHAT IS THE REAL PSYCHIC RESEARCH STORY?

A worldwide wave of fires and bombings has struck Babbage research centers dealing with psychic research. Every major political and religious figure has publicly deplored this violence, yet violence on such a scale is highly unlikely without the resources of some form of organization. Consider these issues:

What organization(s) or government(s) have an interest in preventing psychic research? Why?

Why are militarily related projects the majority of targets?

What has been the goal of such research?

Why has no information on the specific research projects and their results ever been made public?

What role has the Defense Ministry played?

What have the president's budget examiners discovered, and why has that information not been released?

Further specific information will be forthcoming in response to the crisis.

The Spirit Preservation League

That no Spirit Preservation League existed was immaterial. It would, and certainly none of the organized religions were likely to gainsay its purpose.

Then I drafted the Spirit Preservation League announcements that would precede and follow—I hoped—the coming week's actions, assuming that vanBecton and Ralston didn't find me before I found them.

After I got all those completed, I had to hand-feed the marbled stationery to the printer. It jammed a couple of times, but I managed to get the paper feed straightened out, although it ruined several sheets of the impossibly expensive paper. I kept those—no sense in leaving unnecessary traces anywhere. Then I played with the machine to see if I could get a script facsimile, and it wasn't too bad. So I printed the necessary names on the envelopes.

Coming after the cheap and shoddy diatribe of the Order of Jeremiah, I trusted the contrast in tone and the clearly high-quality, expensive stationery would begin to plant the idea that more than a few individuals, crazy and not so crazy, were concerned about the political games being played around the question of psychic research.

After finishing the high-quality printing, I used the copier to make up ten sets of documents in two separate sets. I could only see a need for six, but if I had an opportunity to distribute extras, I wanted those extras handy. All the documents went in the case. No one looks at papers, and they wouldn't look at mine either, unless they knew who I was. In that case, I was probably dead anyway.

During the whole procedure, the clerk never looked my way. He did check the meters, though, when I returned to the turnstile to leave.

"Those extra runs on the printer are a nickel each."

All in all, another fifteen dollars gone, but money well spent, I trusted. With that cheerful thought in mind, and with very tired feet, I took a cab down to the Smithsonian, but I bypassed the Dutch Masters and went instead to the Museum of Industry and Technology. Even when you've seen it all, there's something incredible about it—Holland's first submersible, the first Curtiss aeroplane, the first flash boiler that made the steamer competitive with the Ford petrol car, the Stanley racer that smashed the two-hundred-mile-per-hour mark, the first steam turbine car pioneered by Hughes.

After I marveled at the wonders of technology, I did cross the Mall, looking past the B&P station to the Capitol, white against the gray clouds, to an art gallery, the Harte, which contained mostly modern works. They had a new exhibit, strange sketches by someone named Warhol. I wasn't that impressed.

So I took a trolley back up to the Albert Pick House and collapsed onto the bed for a nap. I didn't wake up until after sunset, when the comparative silence disturbed me. I took another shower and put on a clean shirt and underclothes but the same hard wool suit, and headed to the elevator, where I joined a couple on the lurching descent to the lobby. They both smelled of cheap cigarettes, and I left them behind almost as rudely as my attire would have dictated, quickly checking the full-length mirror before moving past the desk and toward the street. I looked like Peter Hloddn, all right, worn around the edges, not quite haunted.

Trader Vic's was less than a block away, but it was too expensive and too high-class for Hloddn, the traveling ledgerman. Instead, I walked two blocks to a place whose name was lost in the neon swirls meant to spell it out. Inside, the dark wood and dim lights confirmed my initial impression of a tavern, not quite cheap enough for a bar, nor good enough to be a restaurant. I slipped into a side booth for two.

About half the men in the tavern wore working flannel; the rest wore cheap suits or barely matched coats and trousers. The women wore trousers and short jackets, and their square-cut hair made their faces harder than the men's.

At the far end of the narrow room, two singers, one at the piano and the other a woman with a guitar, crooned out a semblance of a melody.

"Drink?" asked the waitress.

"Food?"

She slipped an oblong of cardboard in front of me. From it, I learned that I was in "The Dive." It didn't take long to decide on what to eat.

"How are the chops?"

"Steak pie's better."

"I'll take it and a light draft." I almost asked for Grolsch, but that would have been out of character. The almost-slip bothered me. It wouldn't have happened ten years earlier.

"Morris all right?"

"Fine."

The beer came immediately, and I took a sip, but not much more. I hadn't eaten anything since the morning, one reason I'd probably collapsed. For once I hadn't even felt that hungry. But not eating was stupid in the current situation, and I intended to eat just about everything that came with the steak pie.

Like all of the men in flannel, and some of those in

working suits, I sang the chorus with the singers, careful to slur the edges of the words and swing the heavy glass stein, trying to ignore the incongruity of steins and Old West country songs composed in the last decade or so.

"Favorite rails and dim-lit places,
nine of crowns and spade of aces,
let me drink away the pain,
let me ride that evening train.

"And let those boxcars roll!
Make my point and save my soul . . ."

The pianist was good, but he certainly wasn't any Edo de-Waart, either.

"Here you go." The waitress set the steak pie, wide fried potato strips, and boiled brussel sprouts in front of me.

"Thank you." I began to eat, not caring especially that the singing duo had taken a break. The steak pie was good, the potatoes fair, and the brussels sprouts a decent imitation of sawdust dipped in turpentine. I ate it all and finished the amber beer in the process.

No sooner had I set down the stein than the waitress was there. "You want another Morris?"

"Please."

She was back in instants with another stein. "The whole thing comes to ten."

I handed her ten and a silver dollar.

"Thanks, Sarge."

I nodded and looked at the amber liquid, ignoring the "Sarge." The second Morris had to last for a while. So I sipped it slowly, the only way I could now that my stomach was nearly full.

One of the less square-faced women, probably younger than me but looking older despite the dyed black hair, glanced from an adjoining table.

I smiled sadly and shrugged, implying that I was lonely

but not exactly flush. The green-rimmed eyes studied my cheap dark suit, and she slipped away from the other woman and eased into the other side of the booth. She carried her own stein, half-full.

"Lonely, mister?"

"Peter. Peter Hloddn at your service. Best damned ledgerman on the East Coast—no . . . You can see that's not true." I set down the glass stein just hard enough to shake the dark-varnished oak top a bit. "I sell enough to make ends meet, not enough to support a wife, and that's good because I don't have one, and I couldn't support her when I did."

"Thel. Thel Froehle. You come here often?" She set the half-full stein on the damp wood. All the wood was damp, despite the antique hot-air furnace that rumbled from somewhere beneath the bar.

"No. I can't pay for many overpriced beers. The company doesn't pay for much beyond the room, and I can't always sit and look at the videolink."

"You could go down to the Mall and look at the pictures."

"I could. Sometimes I do, like today, when I'm here on Saturdays." I took a sip of warm beer from the stein, and it tasted more like lacquer the warmer it got. I guess I'm not really Dutch, despite the genes, because I'm not fond of warm beer or beer you have to chew. "How many times can you look at pictures?"

"I like pictures." She shook the thick dark hair that was probably blond beneath the color. Blonds had been out of fashion for almost a decade with the reappearance of the "ghost" look—pale skin set off by dark hair.

"So do I, but I like people better. Pictures don't talk."

"Sometimes it's better when people don't talk."

She had me there, and I tried not to shrug, instead taking a gulp from the stein.

"You drink that fast, and that stuff will kill you."

"Something will. Not going to get out of life alive anyway."

"No." Thel took a small swallow from her stein and licked a touch of foam off her lips with the tip of her tongue. "No reason to bury your face in the suds. You ought to look at what's happening on the trip."

"The old life's-a-journey business. My wife always said we should go first class. She tried, and I went broke, and she left."

"You're cheerful."

"Sorry." Except I wasn't, exactly. My problem was that I saw what was happening, and I didn't like it, no matter how it turned out.

"Cheer up. Things could be worse." She took another swallow from her stein.

I forced a smile in return. I didn't feel like it, since it seemed like every time I started to cheer up, things had gotten worse. "They could be. They have been. Suppose I should be grateful." I sipped the Morris. "You grow up around here?"

"No. New Ostend. Came here with the B and P when they closed the New Amsterdam office."

"Still work for them?"

"Hardly. I work for a legal office down on Fifteenth. It pays the rent."

"Why'd you leave the railroad?"

She gave me a sad smile. "Ghosts. You know how many people died in that accident last year? Half of them seem to haunt the offices."

I had to frown. Ghosts usually stayed near where they died.

"See, when the train crashed through the platform, it was a mess, so they carted some of them upstairs into the offices. Maybe three or four died right there." She shivered. "Don't seem right. Poor souls can't even stay near friends or family."

"Maybe it'd be better if they'd died sudden."

"I don't know." This time her swallow was a healthy one.

"Read something about the government trying to stop

ghosts. Think that would have helped? Would you have stayed there if the office wasn't haunted?"

"Frig the government. Always messing with people. Ought to leave the damned souls alone. Leave us all alone."

"Yeah." I sighed.

"They don't make it easy, do they?" she asked.

I shook my head. They certainly didn't.

She gave me a smile, and stood, her empty stein in her hand. "See you around, Sarge."

Did I really look like an undercover watch officer? Or was that just familiarity? Did it matter, or would it throw off van-Becton's boys?

Since I didn't know, I staggered back to my small, cold room. I would have liked to call Llysette, but that would have been one of the dumbest things I could have done, and I wasn't that stupid or desperate—not yet.

24

WAKING UP WITH a headache in a crummy small hotel room to the sound of air hammers on the street below is not recommended for health, sanity, or a cheerful outlook on life. Then again, why should my outlook have been particularly cheerful?

Ralston McGuiness and Gillaume vanBecton both wanted me out of the way. Hans Waetjen either had orders to frame me for a pair of murders or was being set up so that it was in his interest to do so. My lover had turned cold toward me, or I thought she had, and the family ghost was quoting Shakespeare and old songs at me, or I thought she was. I really couldn't drink, but I'd eaten and drunk too much the night before, or I thought I had. And now I needed to roam through Georgetown to set up a rather improbable scenario that I would have instantly rejected if I'd been my own supervisor back in my Spazi days.

Outside, the sky was cheerfully blue, and the light hammered at my closed eyelids when the air hammers didn't. Construction on Sunday? Why not? After all, this was Columbia, land of free enterprise, and a dollar to whoever provided the best service, Lord's day or not.

Finally I staggered into the bathroom in an attempt to deal with attacks on all internal systems. After that, I tried not to groan while I stood under the hot shower. That was hard because the water temperature jumped from lukewarm to scalding and back again, sort of like my life in recent weeks.

I wore flannel and worn khakis when I left the room. No ledgerman would waste his good suit on an off Sunday.

The Bread and Chocolate across the street was closed, but I found a hole-in-the-wall a block up and around the corner, Brother George's. Brother George's poached eggs were just right, and the toast wasn't burned. I still almost choked because the cigarette smoke was so thick, and I burned my tongue with the chocolate because I was trying not to cough from the smoke.

After breakfast, all of two dollars, which you couldn't beat, even for all the smoke that still clung to me, I took the Georgetown trolley out to Thirty-third and M. I should have worn a jacket, but I hadn't brought anything except the trench coat—a definite oversight on my part, but under stress you don't always think of everything you need. I hoped I hadn't left anything really important behind, but I probably had. I just didn't know what it was.

In Georgetown, I had to scout out Ralston McGuiness's place, and then I had to begin my engineering—heavy engineering.

When I got off the trolley, I shivered for the first two blocks uphill, but walking quickly seemed to help, and by the third I was doing all right, and I had no trouble finding Ralston's place. His name had been in the wireset book, unlike vanBecton's, which had taken some creativity to obtain.

His home was a modest town house off P Street, if a three-story brick town house in rococo dress with a screened half-porch off to the side could be classed as modest. That section hadn't really been fully gentrified, and Ralston took the trolley to and from the Presidential Palace and walked the four blocks each way virtually every day. He'd mentioned that walk in one of his attempts to prove he was just a normal person.

People like Ralston didn't have to worry about security, mostly because no one knew why they would possibly need it. After all, why would a president's special assistant for fiscal review need security protection? And Ralston certainly wouldn't want to advertise that what he was doing was so vital to the presidency that he needed such protection.

The small yard was landscaped carefully, including an ornate boxwood hedge that paralleled the front walk and a dwarf apple tree only fifteen feet from the low front stoop.

I walked past on the other side of the street and went up far enough to see the edge of Dumbarton Oaks before I turned around. It's a private park now, with an art gallery, and the proceeds go to The University—Mister Jefferson's University.

My feet were beginning to hurt, probably because walking on brick and stone sidewalks is harder than running country lanes. I sat down on a trolley bench—serving the upper Georgetown branch that doesn't connect directly with downtown but swings across to New Bruges Avenue and descends to Dupont Circle where you have to transfer. Was what I planned right? Probably not, but what vanBecton and Ralston planned wasn't either, and while two wrongs don't make a right, they might equal survival.

I snorted, feeling cold again, and stood. I began to walk downhill once more with the determined stride of the serious walker, taking in everything I could as I marched by his house. I nodded to the well-dressed couple entering a Rolls-Royce sedan, clearly headed for church, probably the National Cathedral. They actually nodded back, and the white-haired lady offered me a smile.

That wasn't the end of it. I scouted the alleys a bit, just to make sure, before I walked back to the trolley and headed back toward home away from home—the fabulous Albert Pick House.

After I left the trolley on Pennsylvania and Fifteenth, I got a bratwurst from a street cart outside the Presidential Palace, and ate it as I walked down nearly deserted Pennsylvania Avenue. The bratwurst would lead to more indigestion, probably, but I didn't want to collapse the way I had Saturday.

I paused at vanBuren Place, north of the Presidential Palace, when I saw a flicker of white in the shadows. A man in a formal coat ran through the east gate, literally through the wooden bars—it was a good thing they weren't iron—and stopped on the grass. He turned and lifted his hands, as if to surrender, before exploding into fragments of white.

I frowned. The scene recalled something, but what, I couldn't remember. A man surrendering and being gunned down. Now his ghost seemed doomed to relive it, time after time. But who had it been? I shook my head and turned toward the hotel. I had a few more pressing problems than recalling modern or ancient history.

The doorman at the Albert Pick definitely sniffed as I went through, but who was he kidding?

I had the elevator to myself. Once back in my room, I put on the coveralls and the beard. Then I had to wait for the maids to work their way around the corner before I took the service stairs down to the car park. Since there wasn't any attendant on duty on Sundays, I didn't have to worry about how I looked taking the Stanley out—just so long as I didn't look like me.

This time I drove up New Bruges and took California, winding around and crossing the area several times. I wanted to be more familiar with the street patterns before Monday night. I didn't go near vanBecton's place, but straight to the false Dutch colonial that was the power substation. Out came the toolbox with a few items, like plastique from the equipment bag, carefully eased inside. They say you can do anything with plastique except play with sparks, but I still treat things that can blow you apart with respect. It can't hurt.

The locks, both of them, were straightforward, and I was inside in not too much longer than a key would have taken.

Determining the best way to blow a substation isn't as easy

as it sounds, since the walls are thick and I'd have to run an antenna that couldn't be seen to where it could pick up the LF signal from the street. Most probably no one would be by to check the station—detailed inspections don't occur every day—but I couldn't take that chance.

In the end I opted for what you might call hidden overkill, with far more plastique than I needed, because I had to hide it. Then I relocked the door and walked briskly to the Stanley and drove away.

Down on Newfoundland, not too far out, I found a chicken place, Harlan's, which featured a sign caricaturing a southern colonel and food caricaturing fried chicken. I sat at a small plastic-topped table, balancing on a hard stool, and munched through the chicken. What I got was filling, although I wondered how I'd feel later.

I should have taken my time, because I needed to wait until it was dark for the next step, and because I began to feel like combining bratwurst and chicken hadn't been the smartest of gastronomical moves. Instead, I drove out to the zoo, used the public facilities, and looked at penguins. Most people like them, but I feel sorry for them, trapped in their formal wear with nowhere to go and no understanding of what life is all about once they've been removed from their habitat—like a lot of people in the Federal District.

Then I took the Stanley out toward where we had lived, but the firs were taller, and the Gejdensons had added a room and put up a big stone wall around the backyard. I drove by only once, and I didn't slow down. Instead, I turned on the radio to the all-news station.

". . . Mayor Jefferson has requested an increase in federal payments earmarked for crime prevention. The mayor claimed the increases were necessary to combat the growing use of weapons in street crime and in Federal District schools. Speaker Hartpence's office has indicated the Speaker will give the mayor's request full consideration in the next budget."

I shook my head.

". . . at the half, the Redskins are down to Baltimore by two goals. The amazing John Elway scored twice, once from barely past midfield. George stopped more than a dozen shots, but couldn't deny Elway . . ."

Who knew, maybe Elway would replace the legend of Chiri. As the twilight deepened, I turned around and headed toward the Arlington Bridge back into Columbia City.

"Ambassador Schikelgruber will meet with Foreign Minister Gore tomorrow to discuss the issue of placing the second fleet in Portsmouth, England, a step regarded as, quote, 'uniquely hostile,' by the Emperor Ferdinand . . ."

I eased the steamer up California Street and toward vanBecton's house. What I needed to do was simple: just set the plastique in the joint of a tree limb so that it would drop the limb across the power line to the vanBectons'. What I needed was a brace and bit, plastique, a detonator, and no spectators.

The first three were in the trunk. The obstacle to the fourth was a couple parked in an old blue steamer with a huge artificial grille—probably a mideighties DeSoto. Since they were parked practically next to the tree I was targeting, all I could do was drive two blocks away and park . . . and park.

After a while I drove up and down Newfoundland for a time, listening to the all-news radio.

"Elway scored three goals and made the key passes leading to two more as the Redskins lost their fourth straight . . . national korfball team faces the Austro-Hungarian team Monday night in New Amsterdam . . . weather tomorrow, clear and unseasonably cold."

I drove back past the end of the street, but the damned blue DeSoto still sat there. I took another spin out New Bruges Avenue, this time checking out Summer Valley and the new storefronts out that way, still half listening to the radio as I drove.

"To find the additional funds, Mayor Jefferson proposed a reduction in the snow removal budget . . ."

Why not, I reflected. No one in Columbia City could drive on snow anyway.

Then I turned over the back bridge to Georgetown and drove around Ralston's area. I decided to see how I did in the dark. I did fine, and by the time I got back to vanBecton's street, the damned DeSoto was finally gone, and half the upstairs lights in the nearby houses were already off.

After all the driving, setting the plastique was almost anticlimactic. All I did was climb the tree, use the brace and bit, fill the hole and set the detonator, and pat it smooth—and hope that no child found it before the next night.

I was exhausted by the time I climbed the hotel's service stairs and sneaked back into my room. I was also so sweaty that I took a shower. Of course, there were no messages. There seldom were, even at home.

25

BEFORE I LEFT my hotel room Monday morning, I put together the two press packets. The first contained copies of the two letters from "Branston-Hay" to Minister Holmbek and copies of the news stories with my name in them. They were thin—and that was the purpose. It had to appear to the reporters that I was on to something but just couldn't carry it off myself.

The second was the follow-on package from the "Spirit Preservation League," the one I needed to personally send later in the day, after I'd hand-delivered the first classy set of announcements.

After another breakfast of two too many sweet rolls and more bitter tea from Bread and Chocolate, I returned to my room, pasted a goatee in place, and put on a better, tailored suit, covered with my less reputable trench coat when I left the hotel. Two blocks down the street, I took off the coat and folded it over my arm, hailing a cab.

"Where to, sir?"

"Fifteenth Street entrance of the *Post-Dispatch.*"

It took less than an hour for the four quick drops—at the *Post-Dispatch,* the *Evening Star,* the *Monitor,* and the RPI wire service.

Only the *Monitor* reception desk clerk looked at me and asked, "What is it?"

"Purely social, my dear," I answered in my driest and haughtiest accent.

I gave the driver a ten for the entire trip—a five-dollar fare—regretted publicly my lack of dispatch in not dealing with the whole sordid matter earlier, and in general behaved like an overconcerned upper-class ninny.

That done, I put the trench coat back on and walked the two blocks back to the hotel, passing vanBuren Place. The ghost was nowhere to be seen, but two gray-haired men played checkers on one of the stone benches. A young woman, probably a ministry clerk, sat silently sobbing on a corner bench under a juniper. I wanted to console her, but how could I tell a complete stranger things would be all right, especially when I was working to ensure they wouldn't be for some people, just to save my own skin?

I took a deep breath and walked on, reclaiming the Stanley from the hotel lot. I drove out toward Maryland, turning onto Georgia Avenue until I reached the big Woodward and Vandervaal, where I pulled into the public lot. The sky was clouding up, and raindrops sprinkled the windscreen. There was a public wireset in a kiosk behind the hedges, open to the car park but not to Georgia Avenue.

I swallowed and dialed vanBecton's office.

"Minister vanBecton's office."

"This is Doktor Eschbach. Is he in?"

"Ah, well, Doktor . . ."

"Yes or no? If you have time to trace this, so do the people he doesn't want to trace it."

"Just a moment, sir."

The transfer was smooth.

"Where are you, Johan?"

"On my way down to see you, provided I can get there without getting torn up in the process."

"You expect me to believe that?"

"Why not? You know very well who else wants me in out of the cold, so that I can be put coldly away."

"And we're supposed to save you from that folly? Dream on."

"Absolutely. And I have some goodies for you to persuade you to let me do just that. I'll wire you again, and you can let me know."

I hung up, hoping the call would persuade vanBecton to wait just a bit. It also confirmed he was in town. I got back into the Stanley, paid for my brief stint in the car park, and headed back downtown through a misting drizzle. The traffic was heavier than I had recalled, with more horns honking, and even swearing and gestures from neighboring drivers, although not at me. At least, I didn't think so.

A frizzy-blond-haired girl in brown leathers—the country look, I gathered—drove a steam-truck over the median to pass a stalled green Reo. An oncoming hauler sideswiped a boxy old black Williams to avoid her, and she sailed down Georgia with an obscene gesture at the hauler. The rest of us crept by the mess, and I wiped my forehead. Sometimes traffic was worse than the trench-coat-and-wide-brimmed-hat business.

I put the Stanley back in the Pick House's car park and then walked down to the Hay-Adams and found a public wireline booth off the lobby. Like the Albert Pick House, the Hay-Adams had seen better days. Unlike the Pick House, the Adams still retained a touch of class, with the carved woodwork, the polished floors, and the hushed reverence and attentiveness of the staff.

The doorman had even bowed slightly to me, without a trace of condescension to my wrinkled trench coat. Of course, I wasn't wearing a cheap wool suit, either. Even the wireline booth had a wall seat with an upholstered velour cushion—deep green.

With my case in my lap, I put in the dime and dialed one

number, but it just rang. So I tried a second. It rattled with a busy sound. The third got me an answer.

"Railley here."

"Matt, this is the Colonel Nord doktor. Don't mention my name out loud. Do you understand?"

"Yes."

"Are you interested in proof that the Speaker is playing both sides against the middle on the psychic research issue? And that the Defense Ministry is up to its eyeballs in this?"

"Shit, yes."

"Fine. You'll get it. In the meantime, ask yourself this question. Why is it that there have been very few of these Babbage bombings and fires until the Speaker formed his new government? Why does he want to use this issue against President Armstrong? What does he gain?"

"Hold it! What do you know about the Order of Jeremiah?"

"The what?" I lied.

"Order of Jeremiah. I got some trash from them claiming that the 'corrupt federal government' is attacking the spirits of their ancestors."

"What else is new?" I asked. "Every organized religion around has protested the government's psychic research efforts. They haven't gotten very far, though. The research seems to be going on." I paused, then added, "I've got to go. Watch for a package."

I hung up.

Then I called two more numbers, including Murtaugh at the *Evening Star,* with essentially the same message. Murtaugh didn't ask me about the Order of Jeremiah, and he'd probably dismissed it without reading it. Either that or he was playing it close to the waistcoat.

Neither asked me about the Spirit Preservation League, but given the volume of Monday offerings they received, I doubted that either had seen the envelopes, classy as they were. I would have liked to space things more, but time was something I just didn't have.

My briefcase felt heavier and heavier as I walked back to the hotel in the light rain that the radio hadn't forecast.

The entire situation was insane. To get out of the mess I was in, I was essentially going to have to give both the Speaker and the President what they wanted—except without my hide flayed over the package for wrapping paper. I didn't like either Speaker Hartpence or President Armstrong, but that wasn't the question. The question was who could do more damage, and the answer to that was clear enough.

Ahead in the shadows of the alley off L, people dodged toward the street, apparently leaving an open space. As I approached, I saw why. The ghost of a child, probably not more than five, screamed for his mother, his hands stretched up toward the iron fire ladder above. My guts twisted, and my eyes burned. I watched tears stream down the face of a heavyset, well-dressed black woman. She just stood and looked, and I wondered if the child had been hers and what had happened.

Finally I walked on, thinking about the child ghost. He was certainly a disruption, probably unwanted by everyone except his mother. Probably all the major powers had some way of getting rid of unwanted ghosts, yet no one was implementing the technology on a wide scale. Why not?

First there was the religious angle. Ferdinand didn't want to offend the Roman Catholic Church or the Lutherans, or take on the Apostolic Eastern Catholic Church. Speaker Hartpence certainly didn't want to take on everyone from the Mormons to the Roman Catholics, and Emperor Akihito wouldn't want to disrupt the ancestor worship that was still prevalent; nor would the warlords and the emperor of Chung Kuo.

Second was the practical angle. Ghosts kept wars smaller and less expensive. The ghost angle probably was one of the things that had restricted the deployment of nuclear weapons.

Third was the fact that the present situation allowed for hidden and selective use of ghosting-related technologies, and a more obvious use of those technologies would not have been exactly well received, particularly in more open societies like Columbia or Great Britain.

In short, nobody wanted the genie out of the box, and that meant nobody was quite sure what was in anyone else's box.

Then there was the personal angle. Ghosts were perhaps the last contact with loved ones. Did any government really want to be perceived as severing that contact? What would the press say if the government wanted to take that child's ghost from his mother?

I stopped by the car park and locked my case in the trunk, after first removing the press packages and the goatee. The doorman at the Albert Pick didn't quite sniff at me and my buttoned-up trench coat as I carried my damp self back into the hotel and to my room. First I turned on the video to the all-news station. The talking heads discussed everything from the upcoming negotiations over Japanese nuclear submersible technology to the federal watch subsidy for Columbia City. There wasn't a word about ghosts or me. Although that wasn't conclusive, it helped settle my stomach, until I thought about what else I had to do. While I listened, I changed into the blue coveralls that could be a uniform for anything and fixed a short beard in place. As two impeccably groomed men exchanged views on the continuing landing-rights controversy between turbojets and dirigibles in every major air park in the country, I clicked off the set and listened at the hallway door.

When it appeared relatively silent, I slipped out carrying the press packages. I took the service stairs down to the lobby, where I just walked out to the street. This time the doorman didn't sniff at me; he merely ignored me.

The first stop was the *Post-Dispatch.* I walked in off Fifteenth Street with my stack of messages and a log sheet bound to the top.

"Envelope for Railley," I announced.

"We'll take it here," answered the bored desk clerk.

I offered the log sheet, which had two bogus entries above a group of empty lines. "Signature here, please."

She signed, and I handed over the envelope, marked CONFIDENTIAL. At least she didn't rip it open while I was standing there.

Then I took a trolley down and along Pennsylvania to the *Star* building, where I repeated the process.

By the time I finished with the press and the four wire services, I was soaked, even though the rain wasn't that heavy, and tired. Still, I took the service stairs back up to my room.

I dried off and changed back into my hard wool suit, except now I wore the special vest that was actually made of thin sheets of plastique covered with a thin coat of vinyl that could be peeled off. Neither odor detectors nor metal detectors will show anything besides a vest. It's hot, hell to wear in the summer, but in late fall, heat wasn't a problem. The plastic timer went into the compartment behind the big belt buckle. Then I reclaimed my trench coat and put the rest of my clothes in the garment bag. I descended officially—without beard—to the lobby, where I checked out, using cash and getting a frown from the clerk. After stowing the garment bag in the Stanley, I had a ham and rye sandwich at Brother George's, with more bitter tea, before getting the Stanley from the car park. In its dull, almost mottled gray guise, it looked rather like a company car, perhaps a shade too good but not that noticeably expensive.

I drove around the north side of the shabby train station—Union Station hadn't been kept up the way the B&P station had been—and parked about four blocks east of the Capitol. Then I stretched out in the back seat and took a nap. I could have done that at the hotel, except that single men who stay in their hotel rooms during the week are extremely suspect. More important, I wanted Peter Hloddn on the road before all hell broke loose. Even if the watch stopped and woke me, I could claim that, as a traveling ledgerman, I was resting between appointments.

Around four I sat up, not that rested, since I hadn't so

much slept as dozed with a continuing thought to time. I locked the Stanley and took a trolley. The sky was clear again, and a chill wind blew out of the west.

All the Capitol limousines are housed in the top level of the underground New Jersey Avenue garage, and that is linked to the Roosevelt Office Building by a tunnel off the subbasement. Unlike the ministry buildings, the tunnels aren't guarded, just the outside entrances to the buildings and garages. Congressmen and congressladies don't like being stopped going to and from the Capitol building or anywhere else.

So I only had to get into the Capitol, which was easy enough on the last public tour, and then discard the visitor badge and replace it with my own badge, since guards only looked for government badges, not names, once you were inside. If I'd walked in with my own, I would have had to sign in. As a tourist, I'd had to show the Hloddn ID, but no one ever cross-checked. How could they with all the tourists?

I took the east side steps, the ones that have been restored with marble to replace the shoddy sandstone Washington sold to the first Congress, and I waited in line for fifteen minutes after signing in.

"First we'll be seeing the old court chambers. Now, stay with the group . . . The Capitol is very busy when the Congress is in session."

I lagged behind the group, and, once I was relatively alone in Statuary Hall, I bent down to tie my shoes and changed badges. After straightening, I folded my coat over my arm, adopted the diffident, hurried walk of an overburdened staffer, and marched back toward the Garfield Building.

I nodded politely at Congressman Scheuer, who was almost hobbling now but who refused to give up his seniority in the New Ostend delegation. He just looked blankly at me, wondering if he should know me or not, as I walked by.

The Speaker's day limousine was usually retired at five, and the smaller and less obvious evening one took him to the

Speaker's House up at the Naval Observatory, or wherever else he went. Since he did little on Mondays, the odds were that the car would be wiped down and locked by five-thirty.

From the basement of the Garfield Building I took two tunnels until I got to the lower level of the garage, then waited in the corner, occasionally walking from one car to another as various staffers reclaimed their vehicles, until I was sure that limousine maintenance was finished.

Really, the only tricky part was easing myself down the half-wall behind the car. The guard in the front booth by the exit arch couldn't see the rear of the limousine, only the front. I'd figured that out years earlier, even recommended a change to Speaker Michel. That was my last assignment at Spazi headquarters. Michel hadn't paid any attention, not that he paid much attention to anything but the hauling and machine tool industries, and that might have been why he'd lasted one term as Speaker. No Speaker since had paid any attention to the recommendation, either, and that made things easier.

So I crouched behind the dark blue limousine and stripped off my coat and vest. There are two ways to use plastique, and most amateurs don't understand that. Instead, they compensate for their lack of knowledge by using enough to destroy a city block, and sometimes don't even get their target.

If you do it the right way, there's a surprisingly small radius of destruction, but it's rather effective. Then there was what I was doing, which was to create the impression of damage without doing much. After all, my purpose wasn't really to kill anybody—even the Speaker.

Basically it only took a few minutes to turn the vest into a flat sheet of plastique flared around the inside of the rear wheel cover and designed to blow out the wheel and some sheet metal. The gray melded with the undercoat and even covered the timer so that only an expert could tell.

I'd set the timer for about noon on Tuesday, but it wouldn't really matter one way or the other, so long as the plastique actually exploded. Normally the Speaker's limousine was parked right outside "his" door at the Capitol, all day long, guarded, of course, just in case he wanted to go somewhere. It didn't matter to me whether the limousine went anywhere or not. The ostensible point of the explosion was to serve notice on behalf of the Spirit Preservation League that the Speaker was vulnerable if he continued his covert war against ghosts.

The next set of letters to the press would arrive within the day.

After ducking back up to the higher level and wending my way back through one tunnel, I climbed to the main floor of the Garfield Building and exited, lifting my government badge to the bored guard. Nothing ever happens in the Congress; all they ever do is talk. The Speaker really makes the decisions, basically with the help of a few ministers and his personal staff. The guards know most members of Congress have no real power, and it shows.

The guard nodded at me, and I walked out and took a trolley back down Independence.

After walking to the Stanley, I moved it to another side street south of Independence and had an early supper at a Greek bistro I recalled. The memory was better than the food itself, but that's the way it is with memories sometimes. Of course, the waiters were all different, and I certainly looked different.

Then it was time to walk back to the Stanley and get ready. The first piece of business was to get the uniform out of the trunk and change in the back seat. Even if someone saw, what would they see? An off-duty watch officer struggling into his uniform?

The second piece of business was to mail the next set of press announcements at the main post centre. Even if they didn't arrive before the explosion, assuming no one detected the plastique, the postmark would show a degree of planning. If the plastique didn't work, I had more left and would have to cook up something else, probably larger and more deadly, like an explosion somewhere in the Capitol. That I could still manage, although I'd rather not have to try.

Posting the announcements was as simple as driving by the post building next to the shabby Union Station and dropping them in the box. I was becoming ever more glad that I had stocked up on stamps in Styxx before I had left New Bruges. My schedule was getting cramped, to say the least.

After posting the second round of classy announcements, I drove out Newfoundland and parked under a tree about a block from where I could see the approach to vanBecton's house.

It was dark when a limousine pulled up, the driver opened the door, and vanBecton stepped out and walked to the house. The limousine departed, and so did I, driving only a few blocks to the Dutch colonial that wasn't a house but a power substation. There all I had to do was send a signal.

The dull thump, the dust, the puff of smoke, and the house lights going out all around me confirmed that the plastique had done its job, or a reasonable facsimile thereof. But no one went running outside. Cities have so many noises that most people don't notice. Despite the cool evening I was sweating because I had the watch uniform on, except for the hat.

There's always someplace in the city where a big tree overhangs a power line, for all the effort to put the lines underground in conduits. On the hills several blocks north of Dupont Circle, off California Street, where the old money that's gone into government service resides, there are more than a few such trees, like the one I had fixed the night before almost next to vanBecton's house. I triggered the second detonator from a block away, and the tree limb crashed across an already dead power line and a not-so-dead wireline serving the vanBecton residence.

The question was one of speed, as much as anything else. I twisted the thermal switch under the dash, and the Stanley glimmered from dull mottled gray into a lighter, institutional gray. I pulled up in front of the vanBectons' in-city mansion, right where the limousine had been, and donned the watch hat. I left the engine on, walked quickly up the perfect marble-paved steps, and used the knocker, ignoring the bell button.

The door opened a crack.

"I am Officer Wendrew Westen. Are you Herr Gillaume vanBecton?"

Flickering candles backlit the young Federal Protective Officer at the door. "No. Can I help you, Officer?"

I looked doubtful, but answered, "Perhaps. It appears that the power failure . . . There is a large tree . . . Could you at least come and take a look?"

It was his turn to look doubtful. I just waited.

Finally he stepped back and called inside, "There's a problem, something to do with a tree and the power failure."

"Take care of it."

I managed not to grin at vanBecton's less than pleased words.

The young FedPro closed the door behind him and stepped onto the marble under the portico. "What's the problem?"

"It's right at the corner there." I turned and began to walk swiftly in the direction I had pointed.

He hurried after me, and I slipped the blackjack from my belt as I passed the Stanley and stepped around the trimmed yew tree and up to the mass of maple branches.

He never even saw the blackjack coming and went down like a steer in a slaughterhouse. He had a separate key in his belt, which I hoped was the house key, and I extracted the ring and dragged him partly under the tree branch, just to get him out of sight.

With a quick step I jogged back to the house and tried the front door. It wasn't locked. So I opened it and stepped inside. "Hello . . . hello?" I asked in a reasonable facsimile of a lower-toned and less cultured voice.

"What are you doing here?" VanBecton marched toward me. Behind him I could see a plump, silver-haired woman.

"What is the difficulty, William?"

"Officer Wendrew Westen, sir. The FedPro fellow, he tried to move the tree, sir, and he's trapped under it. Thought you'd want to wire for help."

"Wire for help? Isn't the tree what cut off the wireset?"

"Might be, sir," I offered helpfully.

"You idiot, how could I wire for help if the tree is what cut off the wireset?"

I frowned. "Do you want to look, sir?"

"No. I don't want to look. I want you to fix the problem."

Frau vanBecton stepped into the large hall, a space bigger than my study, though not all that much larger than the foyer and staircase had been in my own old Virginia place. She carried a candle lamp.

"Good evening, madame. Terribly sorry." I gave a bow that brought me closer to vanBecton.

VanBecton glowered at me as if I were the problem.

"Perhaps I should run down to the station and get some assistance." I took a step forward and half bowed.

"Dorcas, go check the set again," snapped vanBecton.

"Dear, I just checked it."

"Check it again."

"Yes, dear." She shuffled out of sight.

"Sir. I think you dropped your wallet." I stepped forward and pointed.

VanBecton couldn't help looking down, and I used the blackjack again, right across his temple, almost hard enough to crack his skull and kill him. That was the trouble with political appointees. They still didn't really know the tricks of the trade. All they could do was talk and order people around, and play games with people's lives without ever having paid the price themselves. And there was never any proof; so average citizens would think I was a soulless killer. How could they understand? They didn't want to.

After catching vanBecton and letting him down, I stepped into the parlor next to the briefcase that he had not moved when the power had failed.

"Dear . . . You're not William."

"He told me to wait here. He went upstairs for something."

She looked blank.

"Does the set work?"

"No."

"Are you sure?"

She looked down, and in the dim light I scooped up the case.

"I'm leaving, madame."

After walking into the hall and hoisting vanBecton's limp form, I barely staggered out the steps with him before she started screaming. I ignored the screams and stuffed him and the case in the rear seat of the Stanley and threw myself in front. I guided the steamer out of the small circular drive and away before the neighbors decided to investigate.

The drive out to University and the Woodward and Vandervaal car park was uneventful, as I had hoped. The store was closed on Monday evenings, but the lot was open and vacant. VanBecton was stirring by the time I trained the disassociator on him, but a full jolt to the brain dropped him. When he woke he would be a low-class zombie, and I was effectively a murderer for the fourth time, although the victims all still breathed and talked—if in monosyllables. Until he was ready to walk around, I covered him with the disreputable trench coat and went to work on his briefcase.

Although it took longer, I picked the lock on his case, because I needed the case looking untouched later. I riffled through the papers. Most were useless administrative trivia, not surprisingly since vanBecton would have been far too cautious to put something important on paper, and even if he had, it certainly wouldn't have been in a case he casually carried home.

Surprisingly, there *were* two documents I could use—a set of handwritten notes and the summary budget figures, not those with the line items which could obviously have been very embarrassing but those with the general categories. That would tie very nicely to the material I had already prepared.

The notes were mostly trivial except for one line, the one that read in his clear cursive, *"talks on deghosting—Holmbek and GH."* That just might be enough.

I slipped the cuffs around his wrists, just in case, pulled the lap robe from the holder behind the driver's seat, and threw it across his legs and shoes so that no one could see him. Then I pulled out of the car park and headed out University to the nearest Babbage Copy place.

A dozen copies of the key papers from vanBecton's case would be more than adequate, especially given the relatively selective distribution I would have to use.

There was only one other car behind the copy place, not surprisingly, since students were the big users and most just didn't have it together on Monday nights. That certainly hadn't changed between New Bruges and Maryland.

From the protection of the glassed-in operator's booth, a kinky-haired redhead with bleary eyes peered through her spectacles at the watch uniform. I could see my own faint reflection in the glass of the booth, the goatee and mustache still firmly in place.

I held up the folder. "I need a dozen copies of this."

She looked at the uniform.

"I'm paying. I'm off duty."

"Use machine number three." She handed me a metal counter. "Put that in the control panel and bring it back here when you're done."

I nodded.

She pressed a button, and the turnstile released. I walked into the long room toward the big "3" posted on the wall.

Making the copies and stapling them only took a few minutes. The total came to three dollars. I left her four and went back to the Stanley, still holding its light institutional-gray sheen.

In the lot, I rearranged papers, shuffling some into the

next set of press packets from the Spirit Preservation League and saving some for later efforts.

After checking the still unconscious vanBecton, I drove steadily back toward Georgetown, coming in down New Bruges and cutting across well above the turn in Rock Creek, just to make sure I didn't get anywhere close to the scene of my most immediate crime.

Ralston's neighborhood seemed calm, quiet, and I eased the Stanley under a tree a block away and cracked the window, just listening for a time. Then I drove by, but the place remained calm and quiet, as it should have.

I still didn't like what had to be done—but I liked even less the thought of my own death, and that seemed like the only alternative. Neither the President nor Ralston really wanted me around as an embarrassment. So I had to stop being a potential embarrassment, and that meant making a much bigger mess—and making sure my survival benefited them. Or that my demise would hurt them in ways they couldn't afford to be hurt. It's about the same thing either way.

After a short time, I drove the steamer around the block and parked down the way on the other side of the street, where the shadows partly cloaked the Stanley but from where I could see the house. I had to turn in the seat to watch because I wasn't going to drive past the house again when I left.

Although I would have liked to wait until Ralston headed off for the trolley in the morning, I hoped to be well clear of the capital by then. The one thing I knew was that he wasn't traveling, and that meant he would be home sooner or later, if he weren't already.

I watched for a time, convinced at last that one of the shadows in the house was his. As usual, I hoped to take advantage of human nature—Ralston's, of course. The plan was simple.

First I had to wait until the lower-level lights went out. It was almost midnight when that happened, but vanBecton never stirred, just kept breathing. I still had him trussed, just in case.

When the lights went out, I got out the goodies—the file folder, the disassociator, and the kerosene and wadded paper. Using the cover of the shrubbery, especially the ornate boxwood hedge that ran parallel to the front walk, I edged up to the front door and set the disassociator beside the low front stoop, where it would be concealed by the three steps between door and walk. The file folder with both real and phony papers went next to it.

Then I retreated and, with the watch uniform and thin rubber gloves still on, I took the jug of kerosene and crept up through the azaleas to the corner of the empty screened porch. In the darkness I poured it over the railings and the wood, careful to leave a puddle under the bottom of the railing. Then I wadded up the paper and lit it off, retreating quickly and setting the jug under the neighbor's bushes.

As the flames slowly flicked stronger, I waited between the oak tree and the sidewalk in the shadows. When the fire was going, I ran up to the front door and hammered the knocker. Lights went on upstairs, but nothing happened. I pounded again.

"Who is it?"

"What the devil . . ."

Muffled steps announced someone's arrival at the door, and the glow squares cast a faint light across my goateed and uniform-capped face. The door opened. Ralston stood there. I didn't grin.

"Sir! There's a fire on the porch!"

A frown crossed his face, but the glow squares hadn't reached full power and the orange flames from the porch also had caught his eye. He edged forward, his eyes flickering toward the fire.

I caught his temple with the sap, then broke his fall but let him sprawl across the three steps right onto the front walk. It took only a second to lift the disassociator. My stomach turned, but Ralston had threatened everyone I had left—and meant it. After quickly setting it down by the boxwood well into the shadows away from the door, I dashed back to the steps and yelled through the doorway. "Wire the medics! Get the fire department!"

A youth scrambled down the stairs into the foyer.

"Your father saw the fire and fell. He's hurt. You'd better wire the medics and the fire department."

His eyes flicked to his right, where he could see the orange and red glow through the French doors of the front parlor, and dashed for the wireset.

I ran out front and looked for a hose, and actually found one. After several minutes I was playing water on the blaze, keeping it from spreading too quickly, while a gray-haired woman wept over Ralston and the young man tried to spray water from a second hose which wouldn't quite reach.

When the sirens approached, I motioned to the boy. "Take this one."

He didn't argue, tight as his expression was, and he took the hose.

"Might I use the wireset, madame?" I asked Ralston's wife.

"Go ahead. It's inside the parlor." She didn't even look up, for which I was glad.

I dialed the emergency number for the Georgetown watch. "There's a suspicious fire and an injury at thirty-two thirty-three P Street. Thirty-two thirty-three P Street."

Then I dialed the number for the *Post* and gave a similar message.

"This is the watch. There's a suspicious fire and an injury at thirty-two thirty-three P Street. The injured man is a special assistant to President Armstrong, and there are papers strewn all over the steps."

"What? Who are you?"

I hung up and walked out the front door. The sirens were still several blocks away. Ralston's wife cradled her husband, not looking at me for more than a moment. Their son struggled with the hose, not quite able to keep the blaze in check.

When they looked at each other, I stepped into the shadows, recovered the disassociator, and slipped along the hedge and back down the street to the Stanley.

VanBecton was beginning to stir. After untying him, I left him sprawled on the sidewalk, his case in hand, and guided the Stanley away from the curb, a block later passing both a fire truck and an ambulance careening toward Ralston's.

Then I drove the long way out of the city, circling back to New Bruges and then out to River Road, and eventually onto the Calhoun Parkway with its wrought-iron glow lamps that never shed quite enough light on the pavement.

From where the parkway ended near Damascus and Route Fourteen began, I eased up the Stanley's speed, heading northwest through Maryland toward Pennsylvania, aiming to angle back slowly toward New Amsterdam, continually searching for news broadcasts on the radio.

At one point, beyond Frederick, I pulled off onto a side road and changed out of the watch uniform and into the now wrinkled cheap wool suit, looking over my shoulder all the time. I didn't even see any ghosts, but I felt that I ought to be carrying them in my head, with all the mayhem I'd been creating.

Back on the road, I kept changing radio stations and listening, but mostly I got rehashes of how the Colts had mangled the Redskins.

"Some day Elway had . . . made the Redskins' fullbacks look like stone statues. Jack, they just haven't been the same . . ."

The good news was that what I had done didn't seem to have made the radio news, at least not yet.

After almost weaving off the road twice in ten miles, I finally stopped in a whistlestop called Gettysburg, and took a room at the Sunnyrest Courts, awakening a bearded man who wanted cash in advance.

"You sales types come in at all hours, leave, and don't pay." He put a big fist on the counter and glared.

I was so punchy I wanted to ask if he happened to be a farmer in disguise with a beautiful daughter, but even to me that didn't seem smart. Instead I asked, "How much?"

"Twenty. Checkout is before ten in the morning."

I handed him the bill, and he handed me the key to number eleven.

He watched from the door while I drove the Stanley down to the end. There were only eleven units, and it was the last. As I opened the trunk he slammed his door.

I locked the Stanley, picked up the garment bag, and fumbled open the door to the room. The carpet was bright green, and the spread on the bed was a sicker pale green, and I didn't care.

I bolted the room and struggled out of most of my clothes. I didn't remember much after that, but just before I feel asleep I thought—almost in wonder—about how much easier it used to be.

26

A POUNDING HEADACHE, punctuated by screeching tires, awakened me from dreams I didn't quite recall—except that ghosts were chasing me, spouting Shakespeare and bearing guns that fired real bullets that burned when they went through me. Given that I was sweating and shivering simultaneously, I was certain I didn't want to recall those dreams in any more precise terms. The thin pink blanket and the thinner sick green spread didn't provide much warmth, not when my breath was steaming.

I stumbled over to the wall heater, shivering even more and wondering why it didn't work. Nothing works when it's not turned on. So I punched the button. The wheezing groan as it labored into action, beginning with a jet of even colder air that froze the hair on the back of my forearm, drove me back under the thin covers to regroup. They weren't much help, and I trundled into the small bathroom, the kind where the mortar between the tiles is that gray that is neither clean nor dark enough to convince you it's mildew. The hot water was hot, at least. Of course, I forgot that I was still wearing both goatee and mustache and ruined both, at least temporarily.

Some mornings are like that.

I peeled off both goatee and mustache and set them on the edge of the sink that crowded the shower. Still in the shower, with my shivering finally stopped, I shaved, only cutting myself once.

After drying myself thoroughly, I dressed. Then I remembered to put the soaked mustache and goatee in a waxed paper bag meant for other sanitary uses and slipped it into my garment bag. There wasn't much sense in creating any more of a trail than necessary.

With not much more than a bed, a nightstand, and a lamp, Sunnyrest Courts didn't boast the luxury of videolink. So I had no way to check to see how the Spazi was publicly reacting to the previous day's events, but I doubted that there would be much on the air or in print yet.

The bearded character was looking out the window when I drove off, and he came running into the car space, waving his arms. I just let him, since I had left the key in the lock, and I really didn't want to explain why I was clean-shaven. Besides, he wouldn't get anywhere tracing a gray Stanley with false Virginia plates, and twenty for freezing half a night in a large closet was more than the actual charges. I was confident he'd keep the change.

As I drove down the short main street, I could see there wasn't much choice in the way of places to eat in Gettysburg. I finally stopped at a chain outfit called Mom's Pantry. I'd always avoided chains and places with "Mom" in the name, but I didn't have many options. It was that or the Greasy Spoon. Talk about a scythe or a millstone!

I spent a dime on the local rag, since copies of the *Columbia Post-Dispatch* or the *Evening Star* hadn't arrived. It did contain the story about John Elway and the incredible number of goals he'd inflicted on the hapless Redskins, but nothing about ghosts or violence in the Federal District. Somehow that said something about the whole country.

A heavyset woman with a faint mustache handed me a tattered pasteboard menu and pointed to a booth. "There."

I didn't ask if she were Mom—I didn't want to know.

The waiter took his time getting to my booth, and he was young and unshaven. "Coffee?"

"Tea or chocolate."

"They're extra."

"Chocolate, then. I'll have scrambled eggs and flat sausage, with the potato pancake."

He took the menu and started to pour the coffee.

"Chocolate," I reminded him.

"You get the coffee anyway."

I shrugged and left it.

The sausage and toast were fine, but all I got was grape jelly, and the eggs were like rubber. The chocolate was barely lukewarm and tasted like the instant powder hadn't dissolved. The potato pancake had a vague resemblance to potato—it tasted mostly like soil.

"Is there any other jelly?"

"No, sir. All we have is grape."

I didn't leave a tip. But I didn't feel small about that. How can you leave a tip at Mom's?

When I finally got on the road north, reflecting that the Greasy Spoon would have been a better choice, I turned the radio back on.

"Yesterday the Eagles got a present from Baltimore when John Elway dismembered the Redskins . . ."

I twisted the dial.

". . . when the national korfball team meets the Austro-Hungarian team . . ."

I turned the dial again and got the driving beat of what appeared to be five bass guitars and a bandsaw. So I made another effort.

"At the briefing, Minister Holmbek indicated that the goal is to combine Japanese nuclear technology with the best features of Columbian submersible technology . . ."

With nothing about current political developments, I kept driving through the morning. I managed to find the

Mid-Penn Turnpike and headed east toward New Amsterdam.

It was nearly noon when I stopped to fill the tanks in Unity Springs, just west of New Amsterdam. The place didn't have the papers yet, so I was still in the dark. I found the local post centre and mailed the last set of Spirit Preservation League announcements, designed mainly to suggest that the invisible spirits would be watching the Speaker and his government. I was sure that copies would get to both the Speaker and Minister Holmbek, one way or another.

About a half hour after I crossed the Henry Hudson Bridge, on the north side of New Amsterdam, the radio finally offered some relevant news.

"The psychic research issue exploded again today with the bombing of Speaker Hartpence's limousine, just moments after the Speaker had left the car at the Presidential Palace. Although no one was hurt, statements received by the press claim the bombing was the act of the so-called Spirit Preservation League."

That was it. Was it enough? I didn't know and kept driving.

Again, just to vary matters, I came up the river route, following the Blauwasser north as it wound through the hills of Nieubremmen, the state that almost wasn't until the New Ostend delegation had threatened to annex it.

I finally decided I had to find a place to stop in Windsor, north of Haartsford. I was still too tired to push it, and I needed a good dinner and a decent night's sleep. The road was having a tendency not to stay in place, or at least not where my eyes said it was.

That tendency stopped when I stepped out of the Stanley and was hit with the cold. It might have been early November, but it felt like winter—midwinter. Belatedly I noticed that every one else on the streets, even in their cars, was wearing heavy coats. I hurried into the road hotel office, which was far warmer than outside.

"Little cold out there. See you're from Virginia. Should have brought a coat."

"It wasn't that cold when I left. So I packed it."

"Better unpack it, friend. They're talking snow or sleet for tomorrow."

"Just what I need."

"You want to pay now or later?"

"Now's fine."

"Be twenty-five. Make any wire calls, be extra. Pay them before you leave."

"I don't have anyone to wire." I laughed.

"Must be nice."

"Just lonely."

We both laughed for a moment.

The Royal Court was a step up—a short one—from the Sunnyrest, but it did have videolink and a wireset in the rooms, not that I had anyone to wire or anyone that I dared notify. The spread on the double bed was thick and white, and the curtains were lace, clean lace.

Across the street was a small restaurant called Jim's Place. That sounded more honest than Mom's Pantry. I had a steak with French fried potatoes—*pommes frites,* I guess Llysette would have called them—and the steak was actually medium rare, rather than charred or raw. There were white linens on the table, but not white lace in the windows.

The tea was like the Russian Imperial blend in my own kitchen, but you can't have everything. Most important, no one paid any attention to me, except for my waiter, and his youthful enthusiasm was clearly aimed at a tip. I didn't disappoint him, but that might have been because I felt I was probably disappointing everyone at that point.

After my early dinner, I walked down the street to Arrow Pharmacy—they're everywhere in the northeast—and picked up a copy of the local paper, the *Courant* or some such.

The psychic story was on page one, below the fold, but still on page one. I skimmed through it.

PSYCHIC RESEARCH EXPLODES

COLUMBIA CITY (RPI)—An unprecedented bombing of Speaker Hartpence's limousine just moments after he stepped out at the Presidential Palace has put the spotlight directly on the psychic research issue. Speaker Hartpence and his staff were unhurt, and only the rear left corner of the limousine was damaged.

Initial puzzlement turned to anger and then concern when the "Spirit Preservation League" claimed credit in a series of announcements postmarked well before the blast.

"This issue clearly needs the Speaker's attention," affirmed Anglican-Baptist Archbishop Clelland, in a speech from the National Cathedral just hours after the bombing . . .

"We're not dealing with simple terrorists here," announced watch specialist Herrick Reid. "The paper used in these announcements is extraordinarily expensive, and the language is cultured and rational. Equally important, these people are professionals. Two sets of announcements were postmarked before the explosion. The explosion itself was also carefully designed to minimize damage." According to Reid and other specialists, the Spirit Preservation League has delivered a strong message—that it has the money, expertise, and ability to kill the Speaker with impunity if he continues his "covert" war on ghosts.

Acting Deputy Spazi Minister Jerome questioned whether the blast was really a League effort, citing threats by another group, the Order of Jeremiah . . .

In a related development, Deputy Spazi Minister Gillaume vanBecton remains in a complete zombie state after his kidnapping from his posh upper Bruges home in the federal city. He was found wandering in Georgetown, not far from where presidential aide Ralston McGuiness suffered brain damage from a concussion incurred in fighting a fire at his home. Reportedly, papers found in his case and near McGuiness's home support the contentions of both extremist groups that the Speaker has committed significant federal resources to his war against ghosts. Neither the Speaker nor President Armstrong had any comments about the alleged documents . . .

It was all there, all right. I decided to keep reading. The story on the bottom of page two didn't help my digestion. It was also a wire story, but more personally inclined.

A prominent member of Congress released copies of letters protesting the direction and termination of a secret Defense Ministry research project in New Bruges on ghost elimination technology . . .

The letters' writer, a professor in charge of research, died in an accident days after posting the second letter . . . The letters also indicated possible illegal contract practices . . .

Minister Holmbek had no comment on the charges, which were made by Congresslady Alexander last night . . .

Was it Railley or Murtaugh who knew the congresslady? I had to hand it to whichever one it was. By giving her the letters, the reporter had broken the story without breaking his cover, and no one asked a member of Congress for her sources. But I bet the story had played a lot larger under a byline in either the *Post-Dispatch* or the *Evening Star*.

I leafed through the rest of the paper, and paused on the editorial page. I'd definitely tapped something. The editorial was short, and at the bottom, but it was there.

LEAVE THE GHOSTS BE

For months, this paper and others have been filled with stories hinting that the government has been pursuing technology to destroy ghosts. Now, more proof, and violence, have appeared. Most ghosts are the remnants of poor individuals who died before their time, and apparently the Speaker has decreed that their lingering lifespans should be cut even shorter. Enough is enough. There is no reason to spend federal money on technology to eradicate psychic beings who are all that remain of those once and often still loved. In this time of international tension, there are far better purposes for the money, nor should any government spend funds to exterminate the helpless who cannot harm anyone. Leave the ghosts be!

As I folded the paper and walked quickly back to the Royal Court, trying to keep warm wearing just a suit coat, for some reason I wondered what Herr Professor David Doniger was doing. Then again, what did it matter? For all that had happened, I'd been gone less than a week. I sighed. It seemed longer than that.

I also still had one basic problem. How would I convince Hans Waetjen not to arrest me for murder? Even though I hadn't had a thing, directly anyway, to do with Miranda's and Gerald's murders, the watch clearly didn't have any other suspects. My absence wasn't exactly wonderful, but I hadn't had much choice. Sitting tight would have clearly sealed my fate.

Of course, one of the real murderers might well go unpunished by the watch. The other, I was certain, had to have been the infamous "Perkin Warbeck," and no one could say he'd gone unpunished.

Still . . . one murderer on the loose wasn't the most heartening thought, for a lot of reasons, most of which I really didn't want to think about. So I didn't. I went to bed instead.

27

THE NEXT MORNING the weather in Windsor was worse, with a cold rain falling that froze on everything but salted roads. After a quick breakfast of French toast at Jim's Place, with chocolate, I had to warm up the Stanley for almost half an hour to melt off the ice. That was one drawback to thermal paint—you don't want to scrape or chip anything.

Then I headed north, in four-wheel drive. The three-and-a-half-hour drive to Lebanon took almost five, including the blocked bridge at Waaling, with the windshield being pelted with sleet, rain, and occasional snow.

Once I turned east on the Ragged Mountain Highway out of Lebanon, the snow got steadier, except for intermittent ice flakes.

The Stanley had a good heater, and I didn't freeze. The big drawback was that the paint looked like a rainbow of black, gray, purple, and red. So I had to reset the thermals and let it revert to its base red. The big matters might have gone all right, but the little details were hell.

By the time I got to Vanderbraak Centre, the ice had stopped, and only big flakes of snow were falling. The back roads were slippery, and I had to take the Route Five alternate, which I always hated, but I wasn't exactly ready to drive my red Stanley past the watch station and announce, "Your number-one suspect has returned!" Not yet, anyway. I had a few more items to try to square away.

Obviously I didn't go up Deacon's Lane, but took the back road and walked through the lower woods. I left footprints in the three inches of snow, and my dress boots and feet were soaked, and once again I was shivering. More snowfall would take care of my prints, and warmer clothes and boots would remedy the cold—assuming I could get into the house.

The place was dark, sitting on the hillside, without a single print in the light snow. I walked closer, using the car barn as a shield. Surprisingly, no one was at the house, and I saw no signs that anyone had been there recently. Then again, there wasn't any reason for anyone to be. I was certain that vanBecton and Ralston, and their successors, thought they already had all of Gerald Branston-Hay's gadgets, and Waetjen probably hadn't been told about any of them. Plus, the locals had seen me depart, and had watched the house for several days. But how long do you watch an empty house? Besides, gossip would show when I got back.

So I walked back through the woods and drove the Stanley up Deacon's Lane and into the car barn.

Then I went into the kitchen and dug out some old cheese; the bread had molded. After about three bites, I put on the kettle, then went upstairs and stripped off the damned cheap suit and stepped into a hot shower.

I felt almost human after I dressed, and I laced on my heavy insulated boots this time. I took the last box of biscuits from the cellar and treated myself to chocolate.

As the early twilight and the clouds dimmed the natural light, a white figure drifted into the kitchen, halting in the doorway.

"Good evening, Carolynne," I said formally.

She curtsied, but did not speak.

"Are you all right?" I asked.

"How quickly everything dies . . . we see, in this fickle world, change, faster than the waves at the shore."

"And yet, sometimes, nothing changes." She seemed sad, but I really didn't know quite what to say. The silence stretched out, and I asked again, "Are you sure you are all right?"

"One believed in being faithful . . ."

I couldn't figure that one out. So I asked, "Was the watch here?"

"Alas, sad awakenings from dreams . . . give me back your illusions . . . the voice of our despair shall sing . . ."

"I take it all that despair means they were." I forced a wry smile. "It's not over yet, though. I'm going to have to use the difference engine."

"The white moon shines in the forest; from every branch comes forth a voice . . . but the day of farewells will come."

"I know you're a ghost, but using songs as riddles is hard on me. I'm tired. Can't you say what you mean?"

"Ne point passer!"

She was gone, even if I didn't know exactly what she had meant or why she had said "Never to change!" in French. She was a full, real ghost, as close to being a real person as possible, and yet she never could be real. Did she know that? Did I know that?

"Carolynne . . . I'm sorry."

She reappeared. "Let me sleep a while, while you rest . . ." With that, she was gone.

"I'm sorry, Carolynne, and I will talk to you later."

I hoped she heard me. I did cover the windows in the study with both blinds and curtains, and, for good measure, I hung blankets behind them. With the snowfall continuing, I doubted that anyone would see any faint glimmer of light, and the snow might cover the Stanley's tracks as well.

After gulping down the rest of the chocolate, I got to work, making up a complete package on what had happened, naming names and places—the whole business—and providing complete specifications for all the gadgets except the replication projector. That one was mine, and I intended to keep it that way, if I could.

I did have to unload some things from the Stanley, and that left prints in the snow, but if anyone came that close, they'd probably find other signs I'd returned.

Halfway through my efforts, the wireset chimed. I wondered whether to answer it, but finally picked up the handset. "Yes?"

"Johan, where have you been? Your aunt and I have been trying to reach you for almost a week."

"I haven't been at the house much."

"No, dear, you certainly haven't been. It's too late now, but Anna's nephew—Arlan's son, you remember Wilhelm, don't you?—well, he was killed in a steamer crash in Erie, and I wondered if you would be able to come to the funeral and the wake—"

"Mother, where are you?"

"We are in Erie. Where else would we be? That's where the funéral was. I suppose you're still working."

"Of course." I glanced at the difference engine screen.

"Well, do try to take care of yourself. Anna sends her best, and come see us again before too long. I must go, and do try to take care of yourself, dear."

The handset beeped and went dead. I just looked at it before I set it down.

It was nearly midnight before I finished the three complete sets of documents. Almost as soon as I flicked off the machine, Carolynne reappeared and watched me assemble the packages.

"What have you done, you, who now weeps endlessly?" She seemed to be sitting on the sofa, just like any normal young lady.

"Creating life insurance."

"Down here—*ici-bas*—all men weep for their friendships or their loves . . ."

"Weeping, yes. Blackmail is more like it. I set it up so that this material will be made public if I die. Then the people who know that, and who would suffer if this became known to the press, have a certain desire to preserve my life."

"Down here, all lilacs die; all songs of the birds are short."

"Probably, but I don't have any better ideas."

We sat in the dark for a while, a ghost well over a century old and a man who had done far too much he was not proud of.

"Alas, sad awakening from dreams! Is that all there is? Is that all there is?"

"All what is?"

"Say, what have you done, you, with your youth?"

"I don't know. It's gone, and that is the way it feels." Sometimes—and I thought of Elspeth, and Llysette—it was a blind struggle to preserve someone else's life. Sometimes no one else even saw the struggle.

After a time, I stood. "I have to go for a while."

"Return with your radiance, oh mysterious night."

"I'm scarcely mysterious, but I do plan to return."

"How quickly everything dies, the rose undiscloses . . ." As her words faded away so did Carolynne, and a heaviness dropped around me.

I put on my coat alone and in the darkness, and carried two of the three folders out to the Stanley. The last went into the hidden cabinet in the study for the time being.

I eased the Stanley down the drive with the lights off, and didn't turn them on until I was well down the lane, skidding slightly even in four-wheel drive. Probably I could have stayed at home, but someone might have seen me and just waited until I went to sleep.

The roads were brutal, and I was in four-wheel drive all the way. The good news was that it was highly unlikely that anyone would bother to follow me.

I still thought about Carolynne's last words: "How quickly everything dies . . ." Were they just in my head, my own subconscious? Was I coming undone psychically? Why had I been put in a situation where murder was the only way to survive? Whatever the reason, the sadness behind the words hammered at me.

What could I do about them? Was this all there was? I knew that was a song, one I had heard, but I knew I didn't know where the other words came from, true as they rang. I tried to concentrate on driving, half realizing that I couldn't keep up the insane pace and irregular schedule. I wasn't a thirty-year-old operative, and hadn't been for all too many years.

After pulling into the public parking in the Zuider train station—one of the places where no one was likely to remark upon a car arriving at odd hours—I slept as well as I could until the sun rose. Except it didn't. The snow had stopped, but the sky was cold gray. I found Suzanne's Diner and had a breakfast larger than my stomach really needed, looking over a copy of the *Asten Post-Courier.*

There were only a few stories about the ghost mess, mostly rehashes of what had been in the *Courant* the night before. There was an editorial more along the Dutch lines of why bother with ghosts, very pragmatic and talking about dollars and the need not to waste them—none of that silly stuff about ghosts being loved or being people. Somehow the editorial bothered me.

I waited until close to nine before I drove over to LBI.

Bruce was actually there when I arrived with my package for him.

"Good morning."

"So, the prodigal returns. And you do look like a prodigal."

"Hardly. He had it better. You want to be in the insurance business?"

"Nope."

"How about the reinsurance business?"

"Do I get a share of the profits?"

"You really don't want a share."

"You know, Johan, did anyone tell you that you look like hell this morning?"

"Did anyone tell you that hell probably feels better?"

"You didn't need to tell me that."

"I know." I held up the package. "This is yours."

"I don't want it, whatever it is." He gave a wry smile and a head shake.

"This is an offer you can't refuse."

"One of those again. I knew you'd do this to me, Johan." He sighed. I felt sorry for him. Still, if he didn't help, I'd be feeling even sorrier for myself. So I waited.

"What do you want?" he finally asked.

"Not much. I just want you to post the envelopes in this big folder if I die anytime in the next four years."

"You know, I really don't like the reinsurance business, either."

"I know. It's hell."

"But . . . I'll do it." He took the folder. "I presume you have another one?"

"Yes. That gets posted to my other reinsurance agent."

"Lucky guy."

"He thinks so, too."

Bruce looked toward the parking lot, empty except for our cars. "You'd better get on with your reinsurance before someone ups the premiums."

"You're all heart."

"I know."

I waved and walked back to the steamer and the other folder, glad I had my good boots and heavy coat. The boiler wasn't even cold when I flipped the switch, despite the freezing temperatures outside.

I found the post centre and sent the second envelope off to Eric and Judith's oldest son, a very junior lawyer with a firm in Atlanta. But he was my godchild and a good kid, a young man, really. To make it perfectly legal, I also enclosed a small check for a retainer, to seal, if you will, the attorney-client privilege. I chose him for one other reason. Young Alfred couldn't have built the devices from the specifications if his life depended on it. He probably wouldn't have understood what they meant without a great deal of study, although I seriously doubted that he would open the sealed inner envelope. He took that sort of thing very seriously. I did post it to his home address in Buckhead, though, so some clerk didn't open the whole thing by mistake.

Two probably weren't enough, but I also really didn't want what was in the packages getting out. The whole mess needed to simmer down, not heat up, and that was what I was working for—that and my own self-preservation. Of course, I still had to deal with Miranda's murder, but one thing at a time. I couldn't resolve the murder if I were in a watch cell.

I was tired, but there was no going home yet, not until I made my calls. The first was from the outside wireset behind Herman's Bar and Grill, and it went to Haarlan Oakes, Ralston's former assistant. They put me right through.

"Johan, where are you?"

"In New Bruges. I've been trying to stay out of the limelight. I read that Ralston had an accident."

"Yes. It was rather remarkable, and embarrassing. There were some papers . . . they got to the press. And then there was the coincidence with vanBecton becoming a zombie. It was all rather astounding."

"I imagine that the president would prefer that things were forgotten quickly."

"He has expressed some concern along those lines."

"I would think so. I'm a little concerned myself. With the accidents that happened to those two . . . well, I visited several, shall we say, insurance agents, in the interests of life insurance, you understand?"

"Did you get a good deal?" His voice was hard.

"Oh, it wasn't that kind of insurance. I like living quietly in New Bruges. As I kept telling people, I'd prefer that things remain very quiet. I never did like the commotion. As a matter of fact, I suspect that things will remain quite quiet, quite forgotten, you understand, at least unless someone has to probate, if you will, my estate. Pardon the pun."

"Oh . . . *that* kind of insurance." There was a pause. "I think the president would be very supportive—at least this time."

"I would hope so, and I would hope he and the Speaker could reach an agreement. I am going to call Asquith next, and discuss insurance with him."

"I didn't know you knew Asquith."

"I met him years ago, but I'm sure he'll recall me."

"I suspect so. Well, I'm due to brief the president shortly, and I'll convey to him your sentiments. Under the circumstances, I'm quite sure that he will be pleased."

"I would hope so. After all, I've always been a supporter."

"At least you didn't say admirer." Haarlan actually laughed.

"No, I didn't. But he'll understand."

"So he will. Good luck, Johan. We look forward to seeing you at one of the next presidential dinners."

I took a deep breath, stamped my feet to warm them, and hurried to the Stanley, driving across Zuider to the public wireset outside Narnes, the department store. I probably could have stayed behind Herman's, but then, who knew? Besides, the drive gave me a chance to warm up.

Asquith was Speaker Hartpence's number-two political aide, and I actually *had* met him. He was the one who had requested my resignation.

Again, the operators connected us immediately.

"Johan, I can't say I exactly expected this."

"Nothing surprises you, Charles. I have been making an effort to avoid too much media exposure. But I did read that vanBecton, the number-two Spazi, had suffered some strange form of amnesia."

"I think the entire world knows that, Johan. They also know that the Speaker has been engaging in covert warfare against psychic phenomena—rather elegant wording. It is so elegant that it is almost professorial."

"It could be. After all, the late Professor Branston-Hay

was not only inventive, but elegant. Still, I imagine that the Speaker would prefer that things returned to normal rather more quickly than not . . ."

"He has said very little."

"I would think so. Public utterances can be rather damaging when the press has a few facts to work with."

"Why did you call, Johan?"

"Call it mutual concern. I know the Speaker must be concerned. I'm a little concerned myself. With the accidents that happened to vanBecton and Ralston McGuiness, and all the uproar, well, I visited several, shall we say, insurance agents . . . in the interests of life insurance, you understand?"

"I'm afraid I do. Are the odds good?"

"You'd have to provide the quotes. As you may know, since my retirement, my choice was to live a quiet life. Minister vanBecton, shall we say, wanted to encourage a more active lifestyle. I didn't have much choice, but it just wasn't suitable. I'd prefer to resume a far less ambitious lifestyle, I really would."

"I think the Speaker would appreciate that. Of course, we have no idea what Minister vanBecton's legacy might provide for you, but Minister Jerome will certainly share and respect your wishes for continuing such a quiet lifestyle—teaching and writing public commentaries, is it?"

"Exactly. I would prefer to stay away from technical publications, unless, of course, my estate has to be probated in the near future."

"We understand. You will have to resolve the legacies of Minister vanBecton yourself, though, since some of those were never . . . published. His later efforts were . . . rather independent. And please try to deal with those quietly. That would please the Speaker no end. Like you, he would prefer a subdued result. Pardon my pun."

I hated getting puns back from others, but I wasn't about to complain. "I appreciate your concerns and thoughtfulness. I will certainly try for a quiet and calm return to normal life." I paused, but not enough for him to cut me off. "By the way, I do know of one of Minister vanBecton's, ah, legacies. He seemed to have had a number of conversations with a fellow by the name of Hans Waetjen. Hans is the watch chief in Vanderbraak Centre, and he hired some . . . unusual . . . officers. You might encourage him to return to the fold, so to speak."

"I think something could be managed there. We would all appreciate a certain return to tranquility in New Bruges."

"Thank you, Charles. I will do my best to ensure the same."

"I would appreciate that, Johan. Good day."

I found a quiet bed and breakfast, the Twin Pines, and went to sleep almost as soon as I locked the door and got my boots off.

28

THURSDAY MORNING—IT was hard to believe that so much had happened in a week—I slept in at the Twin Pines, if sleeping in means waking at eight o'clock instead of six. I still felt like I'd been dragged behind a road hauler for a week.

I drove the five blocks to Suzanne's Diner. Most mornings that would have been a warm-up walk, but the sidewalks were icy, and my head ached. I picked up a copy of the *Lakes News*, dreading what I might find, and struggled into a small booth.

"Tea, please," I told the waitress.

"You don't look so good. You want some bayers?"

"That would be nice, thank you."

"Not a problem. Wish everything was that easy." She set two of the white tablets on the table. "Anything to eat?"

"How's the French toast?"

"Not bad if you like rubber. You ought to try the Belgian waffle with blueberries. It's pretty good, and you can get it with sausage for only four bits more." She poured the tea into the big brown mug.

"I'll take it." I handed her the greasy menu and dumped three teaspoons of raw sugar into the tea before I sipped any. It was still bitter, but I took the bayers with the second swallow.

Sitting in the small booth, I watched scattered snowflakes drift outside the streaked window as cars glided past on Union Street. I nursed the tea and my headache until the Belgian waffle came. I didn't have the energy to look at the slim paper.

"Here you go." She set down the plate and a pitcher of syrup with matching thumps. A smaller plate followed with four slices of flat sausage.

"Thank you."

"Not a problem." She refilled the mug with tea.

I nodded again and dumped more raw sugar into it. No matter what my mind said, my body was telling me that I was far too old for what I'd been doing. It wasn't the exercise, but the stress, the looking over the shoulder every other minute. Almost everything had worked out. So why was I exhausted?

The Belgian waffle wasn't quite so good as it looked, but far better than rubber eggs, and the sausage slices had just the right hint of pepper and spices.

When I was finished, I let her refill the mug with tea again. Then I took a deep breath and began to read the *Lakes News*.

There was a tiny blip on the national news page—that was all—about the ongoing investigation of the Spirit Preservation League. The story quoted Speaker Hartpence as saying, "Any attempt to shorten the existence of psychic presences will be opposed. That has always been our policy."

I figured he was half right.

There was also a short editorial—predictably Dutch—that suggested the government in the Federal District should spend more time worrying about the waste of taxes than investing in a psychic destruction technology.

The waitress arrived as I folded the paper to look at the editorial again.

"Leave 'em alone. Leave us alone, too. Government's too big as it is."

I agreed, and I left her a twenty-five-percent tip, both for the bayers and the recommendations, then made my way to the wireset booth in the corner.

I dialed the Vanderbraak Centre watch.

"Watch center."

"This is Johan Eschbach. I'd like to talk with Chief Waetjen."

"I'm sorry, sir. I did not get your name."

"Eschbach. Johan. The fellow whose house you searched. The man you've been chasing for the wrong reason. Could I speak with Chief Waetjen?"

"Yes, sir. Just a moment, sir."

I waited. Were they trying to trace the call? Or was Waetjen on another line?

"Waetjen."

"Johan Eschbach."

"What do you want, Eschbach?"

"I just wanted to know if I headed home whether your people would be inclined to leave me alone."

"You know the answer to that. But let me tell you, Eschbach—"

"I know. I'd better be very helpful, very friendly, and not do anything wrong."

"You understand, I see."

"I understand. I never wanted to do anything in the first place, Chief. Remember that."

"A fellow by the name of Asquith made that point to me. So did another fellow by the name of Jerome."

I could tell Waetjen was angry, not only from the brittle tone but the words. No subtleties. No indirection.

"They can be very persuasive."

"I suspect you were more persuasive. Is that all?"

"That's all, Chief. If I find out anything else that could help you, I'll let you know."

"That would be fine. Good day, Doktor."

Another friend for life. Why did it always seem to end up that way? I'd never even wanted to get involved. All because I'd decided to help Ralston out a year earlier, just let him know what I saw. I'd never even seen that much until Miranda was murdered.

I stepped out of the booth and used the men's room. After that, on the way back through the diner, the waitress smiled. "Thanks, Sarge."

Just because I hadn't shaved that morning and my clothes were wrinkled? Did I really look that tough? Or was she being charitable?

I grinned and left the diner.

Once in the Stanley, I turned back northward. None of the flurrying snow had stuck, and Route Five was clear all the way to Vanderbraak Centre. Deacon's Lane was still icy, though, and I put the Stanley back in four wheel.

Everyone knows everything. By the time I got home around ten, Marie was busy baking, and the house smelled of various good things, including apples and cinnamon.

"Hello, Marie. The wanderer has returned."

"I'm glad everything worked out, Doktor Eschbach. There's an apple pie for later."

"Thank you, Marie. Most things worked out, but I have to tie up a few very loose ends."

"You know, Chief Waetjen sometimes is a little, a little enthusiastic."

"Especially when he's prompted by the Spazi."

"Those people in Columbia City don't know everything." She snorted.

"No, they don't." I certainly hoped they didn't, for a number of reasons.

"You just go off to your study and do whatever you have to. Later I'll fix you a little lunch. You look terrible, Doktor."

"Thank you. Actually, I'm going to take a shower."

Everyone told me I looked terrible. I didn't feel wonderful. Maybe they were right. Maybe a shower would help.

The warm water loosened up a few things, and a shave and the comfort of a big sweater and comfortable trousers helped. I felt recognizably human when I went back down to the study.

I sat down at the desk and put in a call to David, but Gilda answered. "Natural Resources Department."

"Gilda, this is Doktor Eschbach. I've been . . . ill. Is David in?"

"He's over at the dean's office, Doktor Eschbach. When are you likely to be back in?"

"Unless this develops more complications, I should be back on Monday. I would be fine to teach the day after tomorrow, but . . ."

"I don't think Doktor Doniger would want to set a precedent for Saturday classes." She offered a brief laugh.

"I don't think so, either."

"What should I tell your students?"

"Just to make sure they've done their readings. That's all. There weren't any papers or quizzes scheduled." Unfortunately, virtually every class had a paper due in the next two weeks, but I'd deal with that as I could.

"Take care, Doktor Eschbach. I have to go. There's another line ringing."

"Take care. I'll see you soon."

I put down the handset and looked out at the lawn, a blotchwork of snow and brown grass, knowing I was putting off the inevitable. Rather than face it, I finally unloaded all the rest of the equipment and papers from the Stanley and put most of it away, except for the clothes that needed washing or dry cleaning.

Sooner or later I was going to have to deal with the remaining problem. Finally I picked up the handset again.

"Allo."

"Is this the lovely Llysette duBoise, the sweet soprano of New Bruges?"

"Johan." There was a pause. "Where are you?"

"At home. I've been under the weather."

"You have not been home."

"No. I had to take a trip, for reasons of health." More like for reasons of survival. "I'm almost recovered. I was wondering if you'd be interested in dinner tonight."

"Tonight?"

"Why not?"

"Rehearsals, I have—dress rehearsals. Tomorrow we open, and the dunderheads, I do not know . . ."

"I suppose that means no dinner until Sunday night."

"Free I would be Saturday after the performance."

"Then I'll come to the show, and we can do something afterwards."

"Perhaps a quiet evening at your house. Tired you must be."

"I am tired."

"I will see you Saturday. I must go. Another student she arrives."

"Saturday."

For a time, I looked out the window. Marie had taken down the blankets and opened the curtains, again without commenting upon the strangeness of her employer's actions. A few lazy flakes continued to drift out of the sky, but I could tell that the clouds to the west were breaking.

I yawned and realized that I wouldn't be that much good for anything. Perhaps after lunch . . . and perhaps not.

Lunch was good—some sort of dumpling thing with cabbage and sausage and fresh baked bread. Marie had some, but she stood at the counter and watched me, hovering like a brooding hen.

I couldn't eat that much.

"Too tired to eat, Doktor?"

"Too much of too many things," I conceded.

She gave me one of those "what can you expect?" shrugs, followed by a faint smile.

I struggled through a bit more of the dumpling and a half-slice more of bread before I went back to the study, where I alternated between trying to compose final exams and trying to puzzle out the details of Miranda's murder.

Finally, after Marie left and the light outside dimmed, I clicked off the difference engine and looked at nothing.

"Not to notice, while this dream lasts, the passing of

time . . ." Carolynne perched on the corner of the desk in the high-necked dress.

The effect was not quite what she expected because there were a good six inches between her and the desktop, and I had to grin.

"You sound almost surprised."

She gave a little sound, although ghosts didn't really make sounds—I only heard them in my mind, like everyone did, like a sigh. "The large ships, rocked silently by the tide, do not heed the cradles which the hands of the women rock . . . and the inquisitive men must dare the horizons that lure them!"

"You're saying that I'm like all men, off to do great deeds?" I stopped. "I'm sorry. I don't mean to be short with you. I'm still tired, and I'm still worried."

"The large ships, fleeing from the vanishing port, feel their bulk held back by the soul of the faraway cradles. You ask me to be silent, to flee far . . ."

"I know. But it's not quite over."

"Alas, I have in my heart a frightful sadness . . . the woman not even hoped for, the dream pursued in vain . . . cruel one . . ."

I caught the edge in her "voice," not that I could have missed the combination of third-person reference and tone. Jealousy? Concern? "Llysette? I don't know," I repeated. "We're quite a group, aren't we?"

"Not to notice, while the dream lasts, the passage of time, not to choose the world's quarrels, not to grow weary, facing all that grows weary . . ." She glided off the desk and stood in the shadowed space before the bookcase to the right.

I had to swivel the chair to face her. For a time I watched her and thought not only that she had been a beautiful woman and was a beautiful ghost, but that she was wrong. Finally I spoke. "No. I can't make that kind of choice. And neither did you. You had as much choice as any of us. You may not have chosen to fall in love with a married man, but you chose to act on that love. That is a choice. Emotional creatures that we are, we may not choose how we feel, but we do choose what we do."

Another long silence fell between us.

"You ask me to be silent . . . rather ask the stars to fall into the infinite, the night to lose its veils . . ." Her words were somehow choked. "The hand that has touched you shuns my hand forever . . ."

"Whose hand?" But I knew. I had ghosts between me and Llysette, and Llysette between me and Carolynne. Wonderful.

She shook her head and was gone.

"Carolynne?" I called. But she did not reappear, even though I sat in the cold study for almost an hour.

29

Again, I tried to sleep in on Friday morning, but I couldn't. I've never been able to sleep that late. So I dragged myself out, and ran through a misty drizzle that was melting off what remained of the patchy snow. Deacon's Lane itself was clear, with a few icy patches, but the snow on the north side of the stone fence was still boot deep, perhaps because the mist was blowing in from the south.

I only got about two-thirds as far as I had been running, not quite to the top of the hill, perhaps because I was still half looking over my shoulder, feeling that everyone was looking at me—Llysette, the watch, Carolynne, Marie, Asquith, Jerome, David, and scores more.

I knew "Warbeck" was dead. What I didn't know was just how many other little traps vanBecton had set. Probably Waetjen wouldn't go against whatever instructions Jerome and Asquith had given him, but he definitely wasn't in the mood to go out of his way on my behalf. He'd probably look the other way if he could—great comfort!

After a small breakfast—the larder was getting empty again, and I had cheated by eating a slice of Marie's apple pie—I felt good enough to go in to the university and teach class. But showing up would have accomplished nothing since the students had already been told, via Gilda or the grapevine, that I wouldn't be there, and they certainly wouldn't be. Anything to avoid Doktor Eschbach's class!

I did drive down to Samaha's and pick up a week's worth of papers. I left Louie a dollar. He didn't quite look at me, instead just shook his head, as if to ask what the world had come to.

Then I headed to McArdles' for a few supplies, coming out with three bags and probably missing half of what I, or Marie, needed. Constable Gerhardt stayed on the far side of the square as I loaded the Stanley. Coincidence?

I wasn't sure I'd ever believed in that, but I didn't feel like meeting any of the watch—not then, at least.

My sterling housekeeper met me at the doorway as I carried in the bundles. "I was afraid you were trying to go back to work." Marie looked sternly at me.

"No, Marie. I did feel well enough to go get the papers."

"Papers?" She turned a stern eye at the grocery bags.

"We did need a few items."

"Are you sure you should be doing that?"

"Yes, Mother Rijn."

"Doktor Eschbach, someone has to act like an adult. You go off to God knows where. You come back with wet clothes and wet boots—I had to dry those—and you wonder why you're sick. You did not even take a warm coat."

"You're right, Marie. I should be more careful." At that point I knew better than to argue. Instead, I retrieved the papers, and retreated to my study.

I had accomplished something—that was clear from the front page stories in the *Asten Post-Courier*. The Speaker had issued an interim order suspending all federal psychic research contracts and introduced legislation which would simultaneously bar expending federal funds on any research designed to destroy or inhibit psychic phenomena. The proposed bill would also compensate those holding research contracts, provided all documentation and devices developed were turned over to the Spazi for destruction. That destruction would be witnessed and attested to by an impartial committee. The details went on for half a column.

So did the congratulatory comments from most of the world's religious leaders. I was, thankfully, not mentioned anywhere, directly or indirectly. Neither were poor Ralston or Gillaume vanBecton. So quickly are those behind the scenes forgotten when great announcements are made.

I laughed harshly. The Speaker already had the ghost destruction technology locked safely away. President Armstrong already had his psychic replicators and psychic brain trusts. Ferdinand already had what he wanted, and no one was looking in that direction anyway. Now the Speaker could safely get rid of selected unwelcome ghosts while still posing as the great hero of spiritual redemption.

Still, it was better than the wholesale elimination of ghosts and the spectre of mass warfare between nations. That really would have been a horror. So politics triumphed again, and sort of did the right thing.

I folded up the paper, turned on the difference engine, and called up the justice ghost program, trying to see how I could twiddle it into a personage a little more merciful and not quite so stiff-necked.

I'd jiggered perhaps three lines of code when the wireset chimed.

"Yes?"

"Is this Doktor Johan Eschbach? This is Susan Picardilli from International Import Services, PLC, in Columbia City. We'd like to verify your address before we send your project completion cheque."

"What do you need?" Project completion cheque? What project?

"Is it still all right to send this to Post Centre Box Fifty-four, Vanderbraak Centre, New Bruges, code zero-three-two-two-six-two?"

"Yes. That's correct."

"Would you give me your mother's maiden name, please?"

"It is—she's still living—Spier. S-P-I-E-R. Spier."

"Thank you, Doktor Eschbach. The cheque, as agreed, is for ten thousand dollars. If you do not receive this within the week, please contact me directly. My name is Susan. Do you have our number?"

"Yes, thank you."

"Thank you very much, Doktor."

I set down the handset slowly. I was being not only compensated but rewarded and bought off simultaneously by the Spazi—but at whose behest? Asquith's? Minister Jerome's? The Speaker's? At the last, I shook my head. The Speaker, even if he had heard my name in a briefing, probably wouldn't have remembered it. Jerome, I guessed, with Asquith's approval—rewarding their broken tool.

The money just added to my pensiveness. I was still bothered about Carolynne—and Llysette—but Carolynne wouldn't appear while Marie was around, and Llysette . . . well, she was clearly tied up with her classes and production of *Heinrich Verrückt,* probably with another not-quite-under-the-table stipend from the Austro-Hungarian Cultural Foundation. I couldn't blame her for that, not after living the high life as an almost-diva in France before the Fall.

Rationally, I couldn't blame her for a lot, but her recent coolness bothered me. Was it really my doing? I'd sort of fit her in between my disasters, and no one likes to be fitted into the spaces in another person's life. It makes you part of the furniture. Yet we were continually doing it to each other.

Was I projecting too much into Carolynne, hearing what I wanted to hear? Losing my sanity? I thought I heard what she said, but had I? I knew she was real—others saw her. But did they hear what I heard?

I took a deep breath. I needed to talk to Llysette, and merely fighting with myself wouldn't change much. I turned back to the program parameters, adding another expression to the code line.

The wireset chimed as I was fiddling with how to transform another code line in the secondary structure of my mercy and justice ghost.

"Yes?"

"Doktor Eschbach, this is Gilda Gurtler. From the Natural Resources Department—"

"My dear Gilda, how formal we are."

"Doktor Doniger would like to know if—"

"He must be standing at your shoulder."

"—you would be well enough to see him if he stopped by in an hour or so."

"I could manage." I wanted to talk, or listen, to David like I wanted to trade places with poor Bill vanBecton.

"He would appreciate just a few moments very much."

"I would be charmed."

"Thank you, Doktor Eschbach."

"Thank you, Gilda."

I got a click in return. That bothered me. Then I got to thinking. I'd made a number of assumptions, and most of them had been wrong. That bothered me, too. I could certainly have read dear David wrong. He was so boring that no one looked beyond, yet . . . he generally did get his way, as with the course-capping business. And he generally persuaded the dean to go along with his proposals. Even outspoken Gilda changed her personality when he was standing nearby. Why?

I turned off the difference engine, did some quick rearranging of my study, and retrieved the handgun I'd never used in Columbia City. It was all too easy to let down before everything was over, and I had the feeling that things were not yet over—unfortunately—and that I might be in for yet another surprise. Just wonderful.

As usual on Fridays, Marie had already left, to get her own house ready for the weekend. I put on the chocolate, and wandered around waiting, not wanting to be surprised. I didn't have to worry. David's steamer whistled all the way up the drive, and I was waiting at the door as he came in from the drizzle that had turned to an almost steady rain.

He shook his umbrella, folded it, and stepped inside. His beady blue eyes raked over me as I ushered him in.

"You do look a bit peaked still, Johan. It's a good thing you have the weekend to recuperate."

"Would you like some chocolate?"

"I wouldn't wish to impose."

"It's no imposition, David. I was already fixing some." I made a pot while he watched and carried it and two mugs into the study. I even supplied biscuits. But I never turned my back on him.

I took the desk chair, turned at an angle, wishing I'd actually used a shoulder holster.

"Johan, the dean and I were talking . . ."

I just nodded, sipping the too-hot chocolate.

". . . about this whole ghost business. Now, on the surface it really doesn't have much to do with Natural Resources, but you do have a doctorate and the political background."

I nodded again.

"As you know, the university faces some severe financial constraints, especially with the new state budget for higher education." David leaned forward and sipped his chocolate with a faint slurp. "This is good chocolate."

"Thank you." I still watched his eyes. Was he at the house just to talk about ghosts, politics, and natural resources? What linked them together?

"The department has had an increasing number of majors. We're over two hundred now, but the political science department is losing majors. They're down to forty-five, and twenty are seniors. Garth Bach is retiring next spring. He's thinking about taking up his country singing full-time." David shrugged. "We have to think about the future."

"You want to consolidate the departments?"

"Create a larger department of environmental and political studies. In a way, your work with the environmental politics courses makes it a natural idea."

"How do ghosts fit into this?" I asked, trying not to glance toward the desk drawer.

"I suppose they don't, exactly. But when all this . . . disruption occurred"—David made a vague gesture, as if he found the whole business somewhat unpleasant—"and the dean looked into your background, she was rather impressed with your political credentials. Of course, those . . . distinctive . . . credentials would be even more impressive in a department in which politics—I mean the study of politics—played a larger role." David smiled.

I returned the smile. "More chocolate?"

"No, thank you."

In short, David was about to use me as the wedge to expand his academic empire. "I'd be interested in the dean's reaction."

"She was most interested. She spoke about perhaps approaching the trustees for an endowed chair of environmental politics." David smiled even more broadly. "She also hoped that you would be most happy with Professor duBoise, and wondered if, perhaps, the arrangement might be made more . . . permanent, at some suitable time, of course."

I tried not to choke. Wonderful, just frigging wonderful. I was being offered an endowed chair and a choice of courses to design and teach, provided Llysette and I got married.

"I do appreciate your sharing this with me. You've obviously thought it out carefully, and so has the dean. You'll have to pardon me, but I'm still not quite up to speed . . ."

"Quite all right. I shouldn't have come, probably, but I did want to share this with you before—"

"I understand, and I certainly won't break any confidences." How could I? I couldn't exactly propose to Llysette on the grounds that I'd get a better position. In fact, how could I propose at all if it would ever come out? Talk about setting up academic blackmail on top of everything else!

It was better that the Colt wasn't that handy. I wanted to shoot him, but that wouldn't have helped matters at all.

"And I would also appreciate your not talking about Garth's retirement. We're setting up quite a ceremony, and we would like it to be a total surprise."

I set down the mug and stood. "I do appreciate the thoughtfulness, David. I'm sorry if I haven't been as enthusiastic as I probably will be, but . . ." I offered a wry smile and a shrug. "It's been a hard week." That much was true.

"I do understand, Johan. With your illness, and all the political goings-on that must have impinged upon your life . . ." He stood also, the perfect gentleman.

I did manage to keep a smile until his steamer whistled back down the drive, but I had trouble relaxing my jaw when I went back into the study and stared at the blank screen of the difference engine.

"That bastard! That unholy . . ."

I paced in front of the bookcases, then stared out into the rain. Not only was he out to surprise poor Garth into public retirement, but he was flat-assed blackmailing me to rearrange my private life.

"And it grieves me, its wretchedness will be blinded." Carolynne's voice was soft.

"That is an understatement. Did you hear?"

"Though deceitful is the sinful world . . . these times are turbulent. They cause distress to heart and mind." Her voice turned bleak.

I understood. She understood that if I asked Llysette to marry me, David could always hint that she owed the marriage to him, or that I didn't love her enough to ask without that. Sometimes it was clear Carolynne had seen all too much—or was it my projection of what I thought she had seen? I rubbed my forehead.

"The last flower, the last love, are both beautiful, yet deadly."

"I'm learning."

Carolynne vanished, and I went back to fiddling with the

justice ghost since I felt like I was finding precious little justice or mercy in the real world. Even when I tried to console myself with the $10,000 "consulting" cheque from International Import Services, PLC, it didn't help, at least not enough to keep the metallic taste of silver from my mouth. As an agent, you could shift some of the blame to those who gave the orders—some, but not all. But I'd acted on my own, against orders, and a lot of people were either dead or zombies, and it wasn't over. I shuddered.

30

Saturday wasn't any better for sleeping in, either, but I did manage to do a complete run over the top of the hill and to the end of the ridge. After I got back, I even finished most of the exercises, despite a wind that promised freezing temperatures later, underscored by the clear winter blue of the sky.

The snow by the stone fences remained, now topped with an icy crust that would preserve it for the rest of the winter as more and more snow piled onto it over the weeks and months ahead.

Later, following a more leisurely than normal breakfast of apple pie and Imperial Russian tea, I showered, dressed in a warm green flannel shirt and wool trousers, and went to work on drafting my final exams, trying not to think about Llysette and the evening ahead.

Sometime in late morning, after two exams, with two to go, I shook my head, turned off the difference engine, and grabbed my winter parka. The reliable Stanley started without a hitch, even though I hadn't plugged in the heater.

I did use four-wheel drive on Deacon's Lane, just in case, but didn't see or sense any black ice. My first stop was Samaha's.

Louie wasn't behind the counter at Samaha's when I picked up the paper; his wife Rose stood there instead. She actually smiled.

"Good morning, Doktor Eschbach."

"Good morning." I smiled back.

"You be having a good day, now."

"I hope to." Although I hoped to have a good day, or a good evening, David and the dean notwithstanding, my stomach was still tight. I just folded the paper without looking at it and walked across the square to the post centre. The sky was still clear blue, and cold, but the lack of wind made the day seem warmer than it really was.

Unfortunately, on the steps up to the post centre I almost ran into the dean herself, wearing a heavy black coat and matching scarf and gloves. Her scarf bore an oversized golden cello pin. I stepped back.

"Doktor Eschbach, I am glad to see you up and around. David had told me of your illness, and I certainly wouldn't want one of our rising stars laid low, if you know what I mean. I do hope that we'll be seeing some special announcements before too long." She smiled and batted her eyelashes. "We all will be so pleased."

"I am sure that matters will be resolved in the most satisfactory way possible, Dean Er Recchus, and I do appreciate your interest." Like a loaded gun at my temple I appreciated it, but I bowed and smiled again.

She inclined her head, with an even broader smile, and continued down the steps to her steamer.

My postbox contained three circulars, the NBEI bill, and a reminder that I needed a dental examination. The way things were going I needed a lot more than my teeth examined. I scooped up the envelopes and cards and walked slowly back to the Stanley.

I drove around the square on the way back and waved to Constable Gerhardt, who smiled and returned the wave, looking as clueless as ever.

Back home, I put the steamer in the barn, and even remembered to plug in the heater, since I would be heading back out to watch Llysette's directorial efforts that evening.

By midafternoon, with breaks for lunch and this and that—developing exams was always a lengthy and painful process—I ran off the last exam on the printer, the Environmental Politics 2B exam, and took a deep breath. I flipped off the difference engine and reread each of them a last time. I'd proof them once more in a couple of days, but the more times you read them, the more likely you are to catch stupid mistakes. Professors make stupid mistakes. That I was continuing to learn.

"Do you know, I would quietly slip from the loud circle?"

I looked up at the ghost floating by my elbow. "I didn't know you were interested in environmental politics or tests."

"I saw you pale and fearing. That was in dream, and your soul rang." Carolynne's words were soft, faint.

"I'm sorry. You told me, but . . . I'm sorry. You deserve better."

Was she paler than usual? I walked behind the couch and pressed the boss on the mirror. Had the watch tampered with the lodestone when they had searched the house? I swung out the mirror, but the lodestone appeared unchanged.

"Only a brief time, and I will be free."

"Free?" I shook my head. "I'm not about to stop the lodestone. That would be murder of sorts, and you—no one deserves that. You've suffered enough." I eased the mirror back into position.

"How we push away the person who loves us! No grief will soften us cold ones. What we love is taken away." For a moment she almost looked real in the high-necked recital dress, and I thought I could see colors. First she seemed pale, then more real. Was I losing it? How much was in my mind?

I swallowed hard. "Is it always that way? Do all ghosts feel as you do? I never thought about it, but you could as well ask if all people feel as I do. Thoughtless of me."

"I live by day, full of faith."

Faith, for a ghost? "And by night?" I asked as I turned on

the hall light and walked toward the kitchen, since I needed something to eat before I got dressed for the evening.

"And every night I die in holy fire."

I pulled out the butcher's knife and started to slice some ham off the joint to go with the cheddar. Carolynne drifted toward the door, then slipped out of sight. I looked at the knife. I couldn't very well avoid knives, but I could understand her revulsion at the blade.

After I cleaned up the dishes and retrieved a bottle of wine from the cellar for later, I went up to the bedroom to dress. First I tried the light gray suit, but that didn't seem quite right. So I settled on the dark gray pinstripe, the one I'd worn the day I'd resigned as Minister of Environment. The suit seemed looser. Had I lost weight, or was I just in better shape?

"How I loved you even as a child," offered Carolynne, in words that felt more sung than spoken as she appeared in the doorway.

"You are a shameless ghost."

"Ways will I elect that seldom any tread."

"Sorry."

"Never will love be satisfied. The heart will become more thirsty and hungry."

"Are you talking about me, or you?"

"Will she change what she enjoyed?"

"She? Llysette? Are you talking about Llysette?"

"Your splendor is dying on yonder hill." She winked out, probably going back to her lodestone for a recharge, or meal, or whatever.

I shivered at the warning, for it was clearly a warning. Why was I doing this? Was it a last attempt to do what was right? Was that the reason I'd kept persisting with the ghost caricature of justice and mercy? After everything, could I do less than try to set things right?

My stomach tightened more, and my heart raced. Was I having a heart attack? No . . . just an anxiety attack. I took a deep breath.

Before I left the house, I quickly pulled one of the disassociators out of the closet and tucked it in the foot well of the difference engine stand, in case I needed it for demonstration purposes later.

When I got to the university, I parked the Stanley at the end of the row that held Llysette's Reo, and took just about the last space in the faculty car park, although a number of the cars did not have faculty tags. After locking the steamer, I walked down and across to the main entrance. Under the heavy overcoat I was actually too warm, and I wiped my forehead before I walked up the stone steps into the building, unbuttoning the overcoat as I did. I did keep an eye out, just in case I ran into one of vanBecton's "legacies." Then again, if they were good, I probably wouldn't see them until it was far too late. And, who knew, I wondered if that might have been better. I tried to keep upbeat and shook my head, pushing away my fears.

I was earlier than usual, maybe twenty-five minutes before the curtain; except, even in Dutch New Bruges, the curtain never rose on schedule. Only a scattering of people crossed the foyer toward the ramps. There wasn't a wait at the box office, and I showed my faculty card and paid my two dollars.

"It's supposed to be good, Doktor Eschbach."

"I hope so."

After climbing the ramps to the main door of the theatre, I took the program from the usher, a woman student I'd never seen, and glanced at the title page:

HEINRICH VERRÜCKT

OR

THE TRAGEDY OF HENRY VIII

BY

LUDWIG VON BEETHOVEN

AN OPERA IN THREE ACTS

I paused at the back of the theatre, two-thirds of the former gymnasium. The renovation had been thorough enough to put in inclined seating, a full stage, and some acoustical renovation, including dull-looking hangings, but Llysette had still complained that the sound reverberation was uneven and that she had to watch for dead spots on the stage.

I settled into a seat halfway back on the left side, right off the aisle, and wiped my forehead again. I was definitely not in top shape, however much I had played at Spazi agent in the weeks preceding. It was a miracle I hadn't gotten killed.

While I waited, I read through the program. I didn't really know any of the cast, except by name. By the time the lights went down, Llysette's players had almost a full house, even if two-thirds of the audience consisted of friends just wanting to claim they'd seen the opera.

The first act was all right—still some jitters in the cast even though Friday had been opening night—but they all settled down in the second act. The student who played Henry was good; he was a solid baritone, and he had Henry's total arrogance down pat.

At the end of Act III, of course, Henry was imprisoned in the Tower, foaming at the mouth and singing fragments of the same aria that he used to proclaim himself as the supreme head of church and state. Beside him were the ghosts of Anne and Catherine, who continued to plead endlessly in their separate songs. None of the three heard the others, just as they hadn't all along. In the foreground, Mary lifted the cross and sang almost the same words as Henry, thanking God for delivering the crown to her. Yet it wasn't chaotic, but a deeper harmony that was almost eerie.

The curtain fell, and the applause was instantaneous. I applauded with the rest. Especially with a student cast, Llysette had done a magnificent job.

As I clapped, my eyes saw a familiar figure down the aisle—Gertrude, the zombie lady. She wasn't applauding, but sat there wracked with sobs. I stopped applauding before the others, puzzling over her reaction. Gertrude, for whom every day was a good day, sobbing? Gertrude attending an opera? Especially an opera by Beethoven?

What had touched her? In a way I envied her, even as I pitied her. That direct expression of feeling was so foreign to all of us more sophisticated souls.

After the initial crowd dispersed, I made my way backstage, noting that I didn't see Dean Er Recchus; but, then, she would have made her presence known on opening night.

Again I realized that I should have brought Llysette chocolates, but I hoped she understood that I had had a lot on my mind in the past several weeks.

I still had to stand in line as a dozen or so admirers told Llysette what a wonderful job she had done. In a green velvet dress, she was stunning, as usual, and her warm professional smile was firmly in place as she responded to each compliment.

"Congratulations," I finally said, giving her a hug and a kiss on the cheek. "I don't know how you did it, but it was wonderful."

"The sound, how was it?"

"The acoustics? You had them standing in the right places. I could hear it all clearly."

"That is good." She shifted her weight from one foot to another, then returned a wave to one of the students, the girl who had played Anne, I thought.

"Are you about ready to go?"

Llysette pursed her lips and nodded. "I will just follow you. Tomorrow, I must sing for the Anglican-Baptists."

"Again? You don't want me to drive?"

"Better it would be for me to have my own vehicle, I think."

After I helped her into her coat, and after we gathered up all her material, we walked out to the car park. I opened the Reo's door, then set the heavy bag behind the seat, and kissed her before closing the door. Her cheek was already cold from the wind.

"You are always gallant."

"I try."

The Stanley was ready several minutes before the Reo.

Before long Llysette would need to have the burner assembly retuned, I suspected, but I hadn't said anything because she would have pointed out, most logically, that her income was far from astronomical, while steamer repairs were more than astronomical.

Once she waved, I pulled out of the car park—we were the last ones there—and headed down and around the square. We had to wait for a watch steamer to cross the River Wijk bridge, but saw no other cars on the road.

Llysette was out of the Reo by the time I had opened the car barn and pulled the Stanley inside, and her teeth were chattering even after we got inside the house. I hugged her for a moment, then turned on the kitchen lights. After her shivering stopped, I helped her out of the heavy coat and put it in the closet.

"I assume you would like some wine. Or would you like something warm like chocolate or tea?"

"The wine, I think, that would be good."

"Do you want anything to eat?"

Usually she didn't, at least not right after a performance.

"I think not, but you are kind to ask."

I opened the bottle—still Sebastopol—and brought down two glasses. "We can go into the study."

Llysette nodded and followed me.

As I passed the difference engine I flicked it on. I hoped I wouldn't need it, but a demonstration might not hurt. Then I set her glass on the low table in front of us and half-filled each glass. I bent down and let my lips brush her neck. "I missed you."

"You also I missed."

I shook my head. Where could I begin?

Llysette looked somberly at me. "You are serious."

I nodded. "I'd like to talk about our future. It's past time we laid the tarot cards down and set our own futures." I sat next to her. I knew I was rushing things, but if I didn't, I'd lose my nerve, and I was tired of living lies, even partial lies, that were tearing me apart.

"Tarot cards?"

"Fortune-telling cards. People believe them when they really need to plan their own futures."

"An illusion that is. It is one all you of Columbia share, that of choice." Llysette's voice was sardonic.

"We can choose." I didn't want to ask her to marry me, not until I had explained. "Neither one of us is innocent."

She stiffened.

"I have done terrible deeds, and so have you." I frowned. "I don't know whether it's better to bury the past unrevealed or to face it and then bury it."

Llysette put down the wine glass. She had not even taken a single sip. "Too much truth, I doubt it is good."

"In that, we're different, but I don't know that I can be other than what I am. When I play at something else . . . Hell . . ." I took a deep breath. "All my life I've been talking around things, dealing in suggestions and implications, but I want to stop that with you."

"Why is that?"

"Because neither one of us is innocent, and I don't want to be tied up with a woman who wonders about my past, and I don't want you to have to wonder whether something out of your past will separate us." I could see her lips tightening. "Is honesty so bad?" I asked with a forced smile.

"Honesty? Johan, you do not wish to be honest with me. Yourself you wish to be honest with. An excuse am I. Never have you said you love me, except in the bedroom. That is honest?"

I took a deep breath. "I suppose not. But I am trying to change. And I do love you."

"So . . . now it is convenient to admit that?"

I took a deep breath. "I am trying. It's been hard for me. How do you think I feel about loving someone who committed a murder? You killed Miranda. Why, I don't know, but I, fool that I am, shielded you. The timing I gave the watch was wrong, and you knew that. Doesn't that show something? That I care, that I love you?"

"In sex and in murder, you love me?"

"I said I wasn't perfect." I tried to force a soft laugh, but my throat was dry.

Llysette stood and so did I.

"You do not understand, Johan." She half-turned toward the window, to the almost ghostly light of the moon on the lawn outside.

I moved toward the desk, bending and tapping the keys on the difference engine to bring up the program.

"I think I might." In fact, I was afraid I did understand, all too well, but I did not reach for the Colt in the drawer, the more fool I.

"No. No one understands." Llysette turned, and I faced a Colt-Luger, a small one but with a long enough barrel to ensure its accuracy. She had it pointed at me, and the barrel was steady.

"Why?" My voice was surprisingly calm. At least the calm was surprising to me, in finding my lover with a gun designed to drill holes in me.

"Because you remember everything and have learned nothing, Johan. Power must be countered with power."

"So . . . the poor psychic Miranda knew that you were an agent for the Austro-Hungarians . . . the convenient fiction of all that money from the Cultural Foundation."

"The Foundation, it is real."

I was very careful not to move, even though both my own Colt and the disassociator were almost within reach. I still had hopes. Stupid of me.

"You know I could have . . ." I swallowed. If I had turned her in, then the blame would have gone to Ferdinand, and if I hadn't, I would have been framed, and the Speaker would have had a chain of evidence pointing straight to the President's office. Either way, vanBecton would have gotten me, or Llysette, or both of us.

"You do not comprehend, Johan."

"I understand everything—except why you agreed to

serve Ferdinand." I knew that, too, but I wanted to hear her explain it.

"Ferdinand's doctors, they are masters of torture. To the last drop of pain they know what will free the soul and what will leave one tied to a screaming body. This I know. You do not."

Thinking of those thin white lines on the inside of her thighs and under her pale white arms, I shivered. No wonder she would not speak of the scars or let my fingers linger there. And yet I had said nothing when it could have changed things. Why was I always too late?

"I need to show you something," I said gently. "After all, that's what Ferdinand hired you for, and what the New French were blackmailing Miranda to find out."

"Miranda, she was not just a meddler?"

"Her son is being held in New France. He was an importer. She would have done anything, I think, to get him released. Could I sit down?"

The Colt-Luger wavered for a moment, but only for a moment. I slipped in front of the keyboard, keeping my hands very visible.

"How did you know this?" she demanded.

"Her other son told me about the detention. He also told me that she was a witch-psychic."

"She was a witch. That I know. She said that she would tell you, and that you would turn me in. Because you were a Spazi agent still. I wanted to love you, Johan. I love you, and you said nothing. Why did you not tell me?"

"I told no one."

"That, it does not change things."

"I am trying to be honest. I retired from the Spazi years ago."

"An agent, he never retires."

She was right about that, and I was wrong. Lord, how I'd been wrong. "Let me touch the keyboard. Maybe this will help. First I'm going to make a ghost appear—even around you."

Llysette raised her eyebrows, and I noticed the sheen of perspiration across her forehead. Damn vanBecton! What I'd done to him hadn't been near enough. And Ralston—threatening her just to move me around.

"That is supposed to prove what?" The muzzle of the Colt-Luger didn't waver, and she was standing just far enough away that I wouldn't have stood a chance.

"If you are going to shoot me, then you should have something to give to Ferdinand. This is what he wants. The way to make and unmake ghosts. I love you enough to give you that." I lifted my fingers from the keys to the flimsy directional antenna. "Now I need to point this. I won't direct it anywhere near you."

"What are you doing?" she asked, adding in a colder tone, "It does not matter."

"Creating a ghost." I turned the trapezoidal tetrahedonal antenna in the general direction of the couch and the mirror and punched the last key to bring up the Carolynne duplicate. The white figure in the recital gown appeared before the love seat, wavering more than I would have liked, but it was only a rough duplicate, a far too simplified version of the real singer, just a caricature of Carolynne.

Llysette looked at me. "I am waiting, Johan."

"Don't you see?"

"See what? That mist?"

Partial ghost-blindness? Was Llysette sensitive only to the strongest ghosts? She'd said ghosts didn't appear around her, but had that just meant she did not sense them? Was that what the torture in Ferdinand's hands had done? I was in trouble.

"Let me try again." I swallowed and touched the keys to the difference engine and called up the justice-and-mercy ghost caricature, hoping my latest efforts had made it very strong indeed. My knee rested against the disassociator, but I didn't want to think about that, not even then.

The wavering figure of justice appeared next to the faint duplicate of Carolynne, and I could feel that one-dimensional sense of justice—almost a cartoon version of the man with the scales in his hand.

"Justice must be done." The ghost voice was a whisper, but a strong whisper. "Justice must be done."

"Something there is. You make images . . . How will they help?"

I wasn't sure anything would help. Was she programmed to kill me as a form of suicide? Or herself? Neither alternative was going to help us.

The justice figure drifted toward Llysette.

"Justice must be done . . ."

She edged back, as though even she could feel the merciless singleness of that judicial caricature.

"No! Stay away! Johan, I will kill you!"

I ducked and snatched for the disassociator.

"Johan!"

I swung the disassociator toward her and twisted out of the chair, just as a third flash of white appeared behind Llysette.

Crack. I could feel the first small-caliber shell rip through my jacket shoulder. I tried to drop behind the difference engine, but Llysette kept firing the damned Colt.

Crack! Crack!

"Llysette!"

"No! No one's puppet . . . will I . . . be."

Crack!

I pulled the spring trigger on the disassociator and held it, then jerked it sideways. Not another murder. Not another lover dying because of me. My head felt like it was splitting apart, like a crowbar was being jammed into my skull and twisted.

The lights went out, of course, even as the disassociator slewed sideways at the mirror and the huge lodestone behind it.

But even in the dimness I could see the stiffening of

Llysette's face, the faint flash of white as something—something vital?—left.

"Johan. Why have you killed me?"

The dead tone in the voice hammered at me in the darkness, and I looked at the barrel of the Colt.

Crack!

Her hand dropped, and another line of fire went through me, like the blade of a knife. Her Colt dropped on the floor with a muffled thump.

"No . . . no . . ." Llysette's cry was more of a plea than a command. "Please, no . . . NO!!!"

I lost my grip on the disassociator, and I half tripped and half fell into darkness, my hands skidding across the carpet.

That darkness was punctuated with images: Elspeth lying pale between paler sheets and choking up blood; Waltar's closed coffin; two zombie watch officers looking at me; Ralston sprawled across his steps; Gertrude sobbing at the end of the last act of *Heinrich Verrückt;* Llysette's pale face and deader voice.

And the images spun, twirled on the spindle of that single line spoken by the caricature ghost of justice: "Justice must be done. Justice must be done."

I lay there for a long time. A very long time.

"Johan . . . Johan . . ."

In the flickering light of a single candle, Llysette was bent over me, tears dropping across my face and bare shoulder, shivering even as she bound my wound. I did not recall turning over, and I shuddered. My shoulder seared with the movement.

"Johan, do not leave us . . ." Another tear cascaded across my cheek.

Us? My head ached. Why had I done it all? Had I really had to kill Warbeck? Or zombie all those people, especially the watch officers? But they would have killed me, and their guns had been ready. Why hadn't I just told Llysette I loved her? Did I, or had it just been sexual attraction?

A stabbing sensation, almost burning as much as the gunshot wound, throbbed in my skull, behind my eyes. My head burned, ached, and the images flared . . .

. . . standing on a varnished wooden stage, limelights flooding past me, looking out into a square-faced audience, seeing not a single smile . . .

. . . the glint of an oil lamp on cold steel, and the heavy knife slicing through my shoulder, once, then again, and a man wrestling the blade away, trying to rise, watching blood well across a pale nightgown . . .

. . . drifting through an empty house, watching, waiting . . .

. . . a blond boy sitting before the bookshelves, slowly turning pages, his eyes flickering eagerly across the words, my eyes straining to follow . . .

. . . a man winding copper wire, glancing nervously toward the setting sun, fingers deftly working . . .

. . . a woman staring at me, and saying, "Leave the boy alone, or you'll regret it. You understand, ghost hussy?"

. . . drifting through an empty house, watching, waiting, pausing by the covered shelves in the study . . .

. . . a sandy-haired man standing for hours, looking blankly out a window, then burying his head in his hands . . .

. . . listening to the sandy-haired man saying, "I know you're a ghost, but using songs as riddles is hard on me. I'm tired. Can't you say what you mean?" and singing back words he could only hear as cold words, *"Ne point passer!"*—feeling warmth, love, and anger, all at once . . .

The images kept slashing into me, like dreams, half pleasant, half nightmares, and above it all that same statement hammered at me: "Justice must be done. Justice must be done."

Had anything I'd done been just? Yes . . . no . . . yes . . . no . . . both sides of everything whirled in my head, and each side drew blood.

The blackness or the words, or both, hammered me down again.

Sometime later I swallowed, my mouth dry, and opened my eyes. Llysette sat beside me on the floor, her eyes clinched tight, one hand on mine, and I tried to speak, and had no voice, only questions. She looked at me, and more tears fell, but she trembled, and did not speak, only wept and held my hand.

Why had I shut Judith and Eric out? Why had I used poor Carolynne like some experimental animal? And Branston-Hay, had I driven him to his death? And pushed the Spazi into burning his home? Guilt, like a breaker, crashed over me, and I dropped back into darkness.

Was this ghosting? Was I becoming a ghost myself, or a zombie? Why couldn't I move? Was this death?

Llysette was still there when I awoke the second—or was it the third—time, and the candle was still flickering, though so low that wax lay piled on the desk. I was wrapped in blankets.

I wondered why a clean gunshot wound that hadn't shattered bone or an artery—I'd have been dead long since—had floored me. I also wondered why she hadn't shot me dead, or called the Spazi and revealed what she knew.

Instead, she bent down and kissed my forehead, which didn't make any sense, not after she'd pulled the trigger in the first place. But she was trembling, and her face was blotchy, and for the first time she looked far older than her age.

My own vision blurred—with tears, relief. Was I still there? Was there a chance?

"Johan . . ." She shook her head, then closed her eyes for a moment, squeezing my hand gently. "Please, stay with us."

Some of the pieces fit. In the mess, I'd fired the disassociator right into the lodestone behind the mirror, and that had disassociated something from Llysette. I'd seen something. That I knew. But I didn't know what else that might have done or added to my own disassociation. I had suffered some form of psychic disassociation, perhaps extreme guilt.

And I'd gotten some of Carolynne—probably the duplicate version, although I didn't understand how so comparatively few code lines held so much. Or was it only a framework, and were ghosts, even artificial ones, somehow creations of a merciful god merely tied to biologic or logic codes?

But if Llysette hadn't gotten the integrity program, then why was she taking care of me? Why was she so upset? And why was she alive when her face had been so dead and she had cried that I had killed her?

I looked up. The difference engine was off, and there were no ghosts in the darkness.

Llysette's voice trembled. "Loved you, she did." She started to sing, brokenly, "Put out my eyes . . . can see you still . . . slam ear . . . can hear you yet . . . without feet can go to you at will . . ."

Then she just sobbed.

I did manage to struggle into a sitting position and hold my poor singer, even with the burning in my shoulder and my eyes.

"Loved you, she did, poor ghost," she sniffed. "And I also, but not enough." She sniffed again, trying to blot tears that would not stop and streaked mascara and makeup across her face. "Now, two parts, they make a whole . . . and we both love you, and you must not leave us, not when she loved so much."

The words bubbled up on my tongue, but I could only speak them, not sing them. "I grieved . . . so much. I saw you pale and fearing. That was in dream, and your soul rang. All softly my soul sounded with it, and both souls sang themselves: I suffered. Then peace came deep in me . . ."

"And in me," Llysette sang, a lullaby and a love song. "I lay in the silver heaven between dream and day . . ."

She began to cry again, and so did I, for I, too, was whole, out of many parts, as we shared the song I had never known till then, knowing that Carolynne had given us many songs.

31

THINGS DON'T EVER end quite the way you thought.

Llysette and I are getting married. In the Dutch Reformed Church in Vanderbraak Centre. Klaus Esterhoos deserves that much, at least. Eric and Judith will be here. So will my mother and Anna, and, of course, Carolynne will be with both Llysette and me, in a way, and there's no way either one of us can repay her . . . except maybe by trying to do it right this time.

We aren't inviting David or the dean, and we've avoided the trap David set, because I just told Llysette first—like she asked me—and we laughed.

"Such a small man he is. He and the dean, they deserve each other."

"Of course they do."

"Their own happiness, that will be hard for them." But her voice was thoughtful, not hard, and she bent over and kissed me.

"And our happiness?"

"Best we keep it, dear man. The price for all, it was high."

I squeezed her hand, and she squeezed mine. "But they don't know that."

"*Non.* They, they will live where we once did, in a shallow sea."

And they will, in a sea of illusion, where they believe, as I did, that everything I did was for a good cause. People like that always do, and despite my best efforts with Babbage code, there was really no way to create a ghost of justice and mercy. What I had gotten was only a caricature of justice. Then, that's what most people want—caricatures.

We'd thought about moving back to the Federal District of Columbia, with all of Bruce's gadgets, and giving lots and lots of dinner parties, small intimate ones where Llysette sang. Despite Judith's words about honesty, there was still one problem—my "insurance" policies would probably have been invalidated if our profiles got too high.

So . . . if Mahomet can't go to the mountain, the mountain has to come to Mahomet. Even all the way to New Bruges.

Llysette's singing is a key part, of course. She can really bring tears to people's eyes now, especially to mine, and I'm sure that, between the two of us, we can actually raise money for a new performing arts hall.

Bruce and I have refined his gadgets so that we can now project small voices—call them angels. It's not possession, not by a long shot. It just gets their attention. And then Llysette sings. Music—the right music to receptive ears—can do much more than soothe the savage beast. I didn't even have to twist Bruce's arms, not too much, anyway. But I think he really wishes we were moving.

You ask, is it ethical? I can only say that if I survived two ghostly possessions, then they can handle a few voices in concert. Call it an examination of conscience. Are we playing gods? Of course, but people always have, and refused to admit it. For the first time in my life, I'm being honest. So is Llysette.

She sings, and I teach. After all, what else can two academics do in up-country New Bruges?

Our daughter will be named Carolynne, but she won't ever know the details, or the reason, and neither will Speaker Hartpence, nor President Armstrong. But we always will.